AF305292

Ghalen

Ghalen

A Romance in Black

———

Walter Mosley

AMISTAD

An Imprint of HarperCollinsPublishers

HarperCollins books may be purchased for educational, business, or sales promotional use. For information, please email the Special Markets Department at SPsales@harpercollins.com.

hc.com

FIRST EDITION

Designed by Yvonne Chan

Names: Mosley, Walter author
Title: Ghalen : a romance in black / Walter Mosley.
Description: First edition. | New York, NY : Amistad, 2026. Identifiers: LCCN 2025033272 (print) | LCCN 2025033273 (ebook) | ISBN 9780063451551 hardcover | ISBN 9780063451568 paperback | ISBN 9780063451575 ebook
Subjects: LCGFT: Novels
Classification: LCC PS3563.O88456 G43 2026 (print) | LCC PS3563.O88456
   (ebook) | DDC 813/.54--dc23/eng/20260123
LC record available at https://lccn.loc.gov/2025033272
LC ebook record available at https://lccn.loc.gov/2025033273

Printed in the United States of America

26 27 28 29 30 LBC 5 4 3 2 1

Romance

is the

content

of

love

Ghalen

1.

Jamilah Fenestra and Robert Horton met at a farmer's market street-fair in Santa Monica on a cloudless Tuesday afternoon. Jamilah was there to buy beets and onions to slice up and pickle in apple cider vinegar and raw sugar. Robert was mostly a vegan who still wanted flesh to eat, so, he was looking for lion's mane mushrooms in order to make meatless crabcakes.

Though strangers, Jamilah and Robert had noticed each other because back then, in 1999, there were very few Black people who shopped the beachside farmer's market. They nodded a referential greeting but that was all. After that they went about their shopping at different stalls.

Another thing the two had in common was that they had both been brought up to save money and use it wisely. Because of this and due to the six-block-long size of the market they spent quite a while checking out the merchandise and costs.

While they shopped clouds piled up above them and they were both surprised by an explosion of thunder and the subsequent downpour.

Jamilah always carried a small folding umbrella in her purse. Robert had nothing but a sack made from purple nylon netting.

"You want to share the umbrella?" Jamilah called to Robert

when she saw him running by her with just splayed hands held over his head.

"Yes, please," he said.

Saying these words made him think of his mama from South Carolina who, when she was younger, and well, had taught him always to have manners, even with white people if they expressed hospitality.

Jamilah held the small umbrella up high, and he, quite naturally, took up her five-pound sacks of beets and white onions.

"Beets are very healthy," Robert said to Jamilah as they scurried forward, rubbing shoulders and looking for some kind of protection from the unusually hard, wind-driven rain.

"Not after I slice 'em up and drown 'em in vinegar and sugar."

Robert laughed, making Jamilah think of her father, Night Farr, who, on his third tour of duty in Vietnam, disappeared in a place they called the DMZ.

Daddy Night had a big booming laugh, like thunder, her mother would say.

Thinking of Night and war and the drumrolls of artillery fire her father died under, somehow caused the young woman's heart to "open up, like a ripe fig," she said to her friend Minta Lee, a few weeks later.

"There's a shelter," Robert said.

It was a bus stop that looked good to stand against the rain. By the time they made their way there, three other pedestrians had taken seats on the fiberglass bench. There was room on the edge for one more, and Robert, remembering his manners, offered this opening to Jamilah. She sat, taking the two plastic bags of vegetables, and placing them down at her feet.

Feeling happy and looking at the young man as he gazed up through the transparent roof of the bus stop, she asked, "Is the water getting you? You could take the parasol."

"The what?"

"My umbrella."

"Oh," he said. "No, I don't need it."

Jamilah noticed how neat the young man was. His black leather shoes had been spit-shined and his jeans were pleated from a recent pressing.

"So, you pickle your beets?" he asked after a while of studying the sky.

"My father used to do it when I was a little girl and making them reminds me of him."

"That's two big bags of remindin'," Robert said.

"I don't eat 'em."

"No?"

"Uh-uh. Too sweet. I pickle them in quart bottles and my mother passes 'em around to her friends at her church out in Pasadena."

At that moment the rain stopped, causing Robert and Jamilah to look up at the sky and then at each other. What next? their gaze asked.

"We could go down on Montana Avenue," she said, as if he'd voiced the question. "I know a coffee shop there."

Robert hefted the bags and moved his head in such a way that said, *yes, I'd love to.*

"WHY DIDN'T YOU BUY ANYTHING?" JAMILAH WONDERED aloud along the way.

"I was looking for lion's mane mushrooms and nobody had any," Robert replied. And then he asked, "Does your father like your beets?"

"My dad died in Vietnam."

"Oh."

It had been quite a few years since Jamilah had cried. And she didn't cry, even then, at least there were no tears. What moved her wasn't telling him about her loss but his one-word response that seemed to express so much understanding.

Pointing across Montana Avenue she said, "There it is, the Monkey Spit Café," with only the slightest hint of thickness in her throat.

SITTING IN A WINDOW BOOTH GAZING OUT UPON THE wet, sun-soaked streets, Jamilah and Robert would have looked to any stranger like old friends. They talked about the crazy weather and the beautiful Pacific; about Houston, where her family was from and Charleston, where Robert's mother was born but he had never visited.

"Hi," a young waitress said. "How are you, Jammy?"

"Good, Minta. You?"

The waitress was white, her pale hair dyed dozens of barely discernable pastel colors.

"Me too," Minta replied.

"This is my friend Robert."

"Hi, Robert. Have you been here before?"

"No, ma'am."

"Well, we have coffee and pastries. All the pastries are variations on Monkey Bread. We have sweet fruit breads, muffins, bacon bread and gorgonzola too, and garlic Parmesan. You have any questions?"

"You call this place Monkey Spit because of the breads?"

"No. Monkey Spit coffee is one of the rarest brews in the world. The fruit of the beans is chewed by monkeys in Taiwan and India. After that they spit the bean out."

"Wow."

"Yeah. It sounds nasty but it's really good."

JAMILAH ORDERED MONKEY SPIT COFFEE AND ROBERT had green tea. They split a raspberry monkey bread and talked and talked.

"I've been studying the healing effects of food for a few years now," Robert said when Jamila asked him what he did. "What I want to do is start what I'd call a healing kitchen down around Crenshaw."

"What would a place like that serve?"

"Foods cooked in spices that regulate the blood. A lot of turmeric, ginger, and natural oils. Healthy and fresh with natural sweetness and low salt." He quoted all this remembering, word for word, the notes in his journal.

"That sounds great," the young woman said. "Like really, really basic. What people in the community need."

"That's right. I mean you can't expect to get nowhere if you don't use good fuel."

"Are you going to study the restaurant business at college?" she asked, feeling herself become entwined in this new friend's life.

"I'm workin' at a vegan restaurant on Western. It's called Kundakunda. The man runs the place lets me learn everything. I'm not so good at, at, at school. You know I get antsy just sittin' there. I gotta be doin' somethin', you know?"

When Jamilah grinned at him, Robert tried to smile back but ended up having to look down and away.

THEY ATE AND TALKED, LAUGHED, AND SHARED A FEW simple dreams. At one point Minta, the Monkey Spit waitress, came to sit down with them.

"Are you at UCLA too?" the server asked Robert.

"No. I don't go to school right now."

"That's where Minta and I go," Jamilah said.

"What do you study?" Robert asked Jamilah.

"A comparatively new field called medical genetics."

"Wow," he said. "That sounds like somethin' from the Saturday afternoon Science Fiction Theater."

Minta laughed loudly, and Jamilah grinned.

"I'm trying for a double degree, MD and PhD," Jamilah added softly.

"That sounds really good," Robert said. "One'a my mama's boyfriends used to say that we need to climb outta that black box they got us in, outta the box into the rainbow, the aurora borealis."

Robert and Jamilah stared at each other until he became self-conscious and turned to her friend.

"You gonna be a doctor-scientist too, Miss Lee?"

"Doctor of oil painting," she said with a grin. "I'm workin' for a PhD in art."

"So, do painters and doctors study anything the same?" he asked, trying to put their worlds together with them sitting there.

"The one thing that doctors and painters both study is anatomy," Minta said.

"But we didn't meet there," Jamilah added. "When I was an undergraduate, and pretty broke, I looked around for a student job. The best paying one was as a life model for art classes."

"I liked her ass," Minta confided.

Hearing this made Robert look down at the Formica tabletop.

The young women smiled at each other over his discomfort.

"I only did it for a year," Jamilah told him. "And the best thing about it was that me and Minta became friends."

"Minta," someone said.

He was wearing the male version of the midnight blue and silver uniform of Monkey Spit. Tall, blue eyed, and two or more years younger than either Minta, Robert, or Jammy.

"Yes, Howard?" the waitress replied.

"You know you can't sit down with the customers."

"First," she said, "they're my friends. And second, I was off the clock twenty minutes ago."

The hale young white man did not like her attitude.

He stewed a moment, and then said, "Okay. I'll go get y'all's bill."

"Don't bother," Minta told him. "I paid for them before I went off duty."

Stymied and angry, Howard walked away.

"He's such a cunt."

"Minta!" Jamilah exclaimed.

"What? He is."

AFTER THEY LEFT THE COFFEE SHOP ROBERT TOLD JAMI-lah that he had to catch his bus.

"Where to?" she asked.

"I live down on King, in Baldwin Village."

"Well, um, I have a car. I could take you if you want."

"You not afraid to drive down around there?"

"Do you live there?"

"Yeah."

"Are you afraid?"

"No."

"Then why should I be?"

ROBERT LIVED ON THE FOURTH FLOOR OF A BLOCK-LONG four-story apartment building that had a roughened plaster facade that was dyed turquoise. Jamilah pulled her 1974 Saab to the front entrance and parked.

"You saved me two hours doin' this, um, Jamilah. You know that bus takes its time."

"Are you going to invite me in?" she asked.

"You gotta go to the toilet?"

"No."

"Um, sure."

"I don't wanna get all entwined or anything, Robert. I just want to see your house and talk a little more."

THEY MADE OUT ON THE LIVING ROOM COUCH IN ROBERT'S immaculately clean and ordered apartment. She was pressing her thigh down on the straining erection under his daily ironed jeans. He was kissing her neck and trying to remember how to breathe evenly. His hard pounding heart couldn't find an even beat, but he didn't care.

"I don't want to do it today," she whispered. "I want to wait, and I want to know that you can wait too."

"Okay," Robert panted.

"You don't mind?"

"Does it feel like I mind?"

"A little."

"But I'll wait. I will."

She sat up by pressing a hand on his denim-covered erection, then took it away.

"I don't usually do things like this," she said.

"I wish I did it a little bit more but . . ."

"But what?"

"My mother, she had to, to go away."

"She died?"

"No."

"She's sick?"

"Not really."

"What then?"

"My mom was all over the place, you know what I mean?"

"Not really."

"She couldn't keep a job, and even when she did, she always had some boyfriend or girlfriend that, that ended up spendin' the money on stupid stuff. The only thing good about her boy-friends and girlfriends was that they didn't stay long. And, and you see when it was just me and Mama, I had to take care of her. And so, I couldn't do nuthin' that might get in the way'a that."

"You couldn't have friends or girlfriends?"

"I couldn't even watch the TV shows I wanted to see. I had to watch out for her."

"So, when I said I wanted you to wait," Jamilah reasoned, "you knew how to do that because that's what you've always done."

Robert's nod and smile reminded her of a child's bobbing grin.

"Where's your mother now?"

"The crazy house. She shot this one boyfriend'a hers, but the judge said that she was nono compa, uh. menta . . ."

"Non Compos Mentis?"

"Yeah, yeah. When I asked what it meant they said that they couldn't try her because like she didn't make sense."

Jamilah studied Robert then. Her mother would have told her to pick up her purse and walk right outta there. But her father, who died when she was three; her father, she believed would ask her first, to gauge his heart.

"Do you ever see her?" Jamilah asked.

"The second Wednesday of every month. That is, if she's in the mood to see me. Sometimes she's just too mad and then some-times too sad."

"I'm so sorry, Robert. It all sounds really hard, but . . . what you went through made you into a man."

"Just getting older did that." The passion he'd felt with her had been a little like being drunk. But her request to wait was sobering him.

"I don't think so. It sounds like you are sometimes willing to give up what you need for others. That's what it is to be a real man or woman."

"I'd like to see you tomorrow if you want," he replied.

"That would be wonderful."

2.

Over the next few weeks there wasn't a day when Robert and Jamilah didn't at least talk.

They took long walks along the many southern beaches and in Griffith and at Will Rogers parks. One time they went out with Minta Lee and Howard Garrison, the manager of Monkey Spit Café who Minta had called such a terrible name.

Robert was a proficient vegan cook and so made their meals at least half the afternoons of the week.

One day, when they were lazing at Jamilah's apartment in Westwood Village, she suggested that they go to the county art museum down on Wilshire. There were seven shows in the various galleries of the multilevel museum. Jamilah loved art. She worried that her paramour (that was the word she used when explaining their relationship) Robert would get antsy. But he didn't complain or say he wanted to leave. At first, he didn't understand much of anything they saw, but whenever he'd wonder he'd just ask, "What's this one about?"

He was talking about a video monitor that showed a dapper, middle-aged Black man dancing while looking at his reflection in a mirror.

"He looks like he's having such a good time," Robert said. "But how come they're showin' it?"

"Sometimes art doesn't have a recipe," Jamilah explained, not knowing what the piece meant.

"Oh. Huh."

IN ONE LARGE ROOM THERE WAS A PAINTING OF GNARLED trees in front of a row of low-slung buildings. There was something about the branches and leaves that brought Robert in close.

"Stay behind the line," a Black woman in a guard's uniform said sharply.

Taking a step back, Robert turned to look at her. He wanted to yell at her, to call her something that would make her feel ashamed like he did.

The museum guard was short and round. She saw the anger in Robert's eyes and approached him.

"We should go," Jamilah whispered at her paramour's shoulder.

"I think you need to move along," the guard said when she reached them.

"I haven't finished looking at this painting," he said.

"I don't like your attitude," was her answer.

"I don't care about that. You told me to stay behind the line and I am, and I will. But I, I will finish lookin'."

Their eyes were locked. The word *bitch* echoed in Robert's mind's ear but he did not say it.

After maybe a minute the guard came to a decision and walked away.

Forgetting her in that instant, Robert turned back to the largish painting, trying to understand what it was saying. That's how it felt, that the painting was talking to him, trying to explain something hitherto unknown. This knowledge was in and around the branches and leaves of the composition. It had a sound and a physical rhythm, though Robert would not have used those words to explain his feeling.

"I'm going down to the Japanese exhibit," Jamilah said.

"Um," he rejoined, not turning to look at her. "You mind if I stay here and look at this a few minutes more?"

JAMILAH WANDERED OFF TO LOOK AT ALL THE WORKS on exhibit. There were shows about places and some people, like the young women morphine addicts of nineteenth-century Paris. She studied the little paragraphs that curators had used to explain what and why and of what materials the works were composed of.

She saw, read about, and considered each piece. This was what she had always done in school and life in general. She'd been an A student, a competitive runner, a lay counselor to her good friends. *Very lovely, without the distraction of prettiness*, her mother would say of her.

For close to two hours Jamilah, who was used to spending time alone, went through the galleries. When she'd seen everything the museum had to offer, she began to wonder where Robert might be. She imagined that he was wandering around the museum looking for her.

The medical student retraced her route ending up back at the gallery that had the Van Gogh painting he liked so much. To her surprise, he was standing in the same spot gazing at the trees.

The museum guard was there too.

"Hey there," Jamilah said, hooking his left arm with her right.

"Hey."

"Did you go anywhere else?"

"No."

"You just stayed here and looked at this one painting?"

"Yeah. You know, I couldn't understand the other ones we looked at because they didn't say anything to me. You know what I mean?"

"Uh-huh," Jamilah hummed. She heard something, felt something in these words and his tone that she'd not known before.

"But with this one it was just like it was tellin' me somethin' but like in Spanish or Chinese, you know?"

"Did you figure it out?"

"Yeah. I finally realized that it was a painting of something you couldn't see—the wind. The wind bendin' the branches and slappin' the leaves all over. You could even see it in the clouds and the sky above that. I mean, it was crazy seein' one thing but knowin' that there was somethin' more'n that."

Jamilah stopped to look deeper, wondering to herself why she had never approached a painting in that way.

"You want to come back to my place, Robert?"

"I think I need to go home and think about this."

"You can't think at my place?"

"I mostly think about the people I'm with when me and them get together," he said. "Either that or I get quiet. My mother'd always get mad when I wouldn't talk."

"It wouldn't bother me," Jamilah vowed.

"But I," Robert said. "But I think I need to go home. I could come back tomorrow."

"Okay. I'll drive you."

"No, um, I think I just need to be alone for a li'l while."

When they moved to exit the gallery, the short round guard came up to them.

"I'm sorry," she said to Robert. "I didn't realize how serious you were about that painting."

Robert looked at her for a long moment and then held out a hand.

ON THE BUS HEADING BACK DOWN TO THE JUNGLE, THE name often given to Baldwin Village, Robert sat alone, next to a window, in a seat just behind the rear exit. The wafting winds of the trees filled his mind and gladdened his heart.

"Hi," a young woman said as she took the seat next to him.

She was young and Black and smelled of roses.

"Roses," he said.

"Yeah," she agreed. "Rose attar, from Morocco."

"So, it's the real flower?" he asked.

"Yeah. They call it the essence. My name's Aura."

"Robert," he said offering his hand.

"Nice to meet you, Robert." She was lighter colored than either Robert or Jamilah. Her eyes were brown with just a little green underneath.

"You too, Aura."

"Are you a pharmacist?"

"No, uh-uh. How come you ask?"

"You just look so neat. That shirt look like it just come out the drawer."

"And that made you think about a pharmacist?"

"I don't know. I guess. Mr. Larken down at the drugstore always looks neat like you."

"I'm a cook at Kundakunda on Western."

"I seen that place before. Vegetarian, right?"

"Vegan."

"What's the difference?"

They talked until reaching Aura's stop on Buckingham Road.

"If I come by at your restaurant, would you make me sumpin' nice?" she said before stepping down into the exit well.

"Sure would. I work in the mornings Monday through Thursday."

When the bus pulled away from the stop Robert realized that the scent of roses was still all around him. The aroma wound itself into the memory of the windblown trees that had taken up residence in his mind.

WHEN HE GOT TO HIS APARTMENT DOOR, HE COULD hear the phone ringing. By the time he was inside, the answering machine had just engaged.

"Robert," Jamilah said through the machine's speaker. "Are you there? I was just, um, calling to see that you got home all right . . ."

"Hello!" he called into the receiver as he plucked it up off its cradle. "Jamilah!"

"Oh," she said. "Hi. I thought you were still out."

"No. I just came in. You know the buses take a long time."

"I could have driven you."

"Those trees was in my head. I needed to be with 'em a little longer. If they would'a let me I'd've stayed there all night."

"Really?"

"Yeah. I might go back to see it again."

"Oh, uh-huh, I thought you were mad or somethin'."

"Mad about what?"

"That I left you to walk around. That I'm still making you wait."

"I was lookin' at those trees," he explained. "And, and, and I thought, you know, maybe you, you just wanted to be friends."

"No." The tone of Jamilah's voice was plaintive. "It's not like that."

"Oh. Okay. I wasn't mad anyway."

"I wanted to ask you something."

"Yeah?"

"Would you like to come with me to my mother's house to-morrow?"

"Sure. Where she live at?"

"Pasadena."

"Oh, yeah, that's right."

3.

R obert's alarm clock was set to play Beethoven's Fifth Symphony. He didn't like harsh alarm bells, rock, pop, or hip-hop that early in the morning. There was an alarm that was just chimes and another one that played real birds singing. But these were too soft, and sometimes he would just turn over and continue sleeping.

And so, it was Beethoven that he used to wake up at 3:30 a.m. every day.

And every day he'd take a shower, brush his teeth, do three sets of twenty-five push-ups and sit-ups, and iron his work clothes; sometimes he ironed them twice. After all that he made oatmeal with honey and toasted almonds.

While eating he practiced saying hello and good morning, asking how the person he was talking to felt. Then he'd read one of his nature books for half an hour before taking the same amount of time dressing and then teasing out his inch-thick, perfectly even fro.

His morning preparations left him just enough time to get to work.

THE FIRST THING HE DID IN THE LONG KITCHEN OF KUN-dakunda was set up a huge kettle on the dozen-burner stove.

Charles Martin, the owner and head chef, would arrive just when the water started to boil. From there he'd tell Robert the same thing each morning.

"You make the tofu scramble, dice the potatoes, and put them in the oven to bake. After that cut up the fruit and prepare the tempeh," Mr. Martin, a middle-aged, big-bellied, and brawny white man from Brussels, would say.

Robert didn't mind being told the same thing. That way he knew exactly what was expected, and if something changed, he'd have something new to learn.

After the *morning brief*, as Chef called it, the two cooks would work on preparations until the first customer arrived. After that Chef Charles would plate the meals and put them on the serving shelf.

ROBERT COULDN'T REMEMBER WHO HAD TOLD HIM ABOUT good health and food. He was somewhere in a room, maybe a classroom, and somebody was talking about something else but then mentioned that even a restaurant could be like a doctor's office, and it wouldn't cost nearly as much.

Chef trusted Robert to do what was needed. And so, the young cook could work alone, concentrating on the jobs before him.

At six forty-five Maria Vasquez, the waitress and hostess, would arrive. She was a little older than Robert, twenty-five, and from Guatemala. The color of rose gold, Robert thought that she was very pretty but remembered not to say that.

"Hi, Robert," Maria said.

"Hi, Maria. How's your mom?"

"She's good. And how are you? You still seeing that doctor?"

"Jamilah's good but she's not a doctor yet."

"When I was growing up, they always wanted the girls to marry doctors or lawyers. I guess the boys could do it too."

Robert had not thought about marriage. His father never married his mom. As a matter of fact, his mother wasn't even sure of who his father was. It was between two guys named William and one named Talib.

THE MORNING PROGRESSED AS USUAL. EVERYTHING WAS going according to schedule. Robert liked schedules.

"Robert," Maria called from the other side of the kitchen's swinging doors.

It was 11:07 by the digital clock on the wall.

"Yeah, Maria?"

"You got a visitor." The tone of her voice was different from usual. It was like her words were saying something else.

Robert washed his hands with green soap, rinsed them, and then used a shammy towel to dry them off. He walked through the saloon-like doors into the long corridor of the restaurant. To his left there was a long counter where solos and couples would sit. To the right were eight double pairs of tables that sat four.

There were only a few people there, finishing their breakfasts, because the restaurant stopped taking orders at ten thirty. Most of the morning meals they sold were takeout and those that wanted to sit for breakfast were, on the whole, working people who ate fast and then left for their jobs.

At the far end of the counter was the rose-scented Aura.

Robert smiled and walked down the ramp behind the counter until he reached his new friend.

"Hi, Aura. You came."

"Uh-huh, yeah. I always wanted to come see what it was like here."

"You like it?"

Her answer was a big smile under glittering, olive-tinted eyes.

"I was thinking last night," Robert said, "that you would like a fruit and oat bowl and a lemon waffle."

"I love waffles."

ROBERT MADE AURA'S BREAKFAST HIMSELF, AND HE served her too. Then he went back into the kitchen, where Marquis and Alexander, the two dishwashers, had been working since seven thirty. They performed all the *heavy lifting* for the breakfast shift and bused tables in between.

"That's a fine-lookin' young lady you got out there, Bobby," Alexander, an older, sinewy Black man said. "You could get into some trouble there."

Robert could tell by his tone that this was a compliment that had nothing to do with real trouble.

"I thought you had that college girlfriend, man?" Marquis queried.

Marquis was young, the color of tarnished brass.

"I do," Robert said.

"So, you a player, huh?"

Marquis and Alexander laughed.

Robert laughed with them, but he didn't really understand.

After only a few minutes of talk Alexander and Marquis told Robert to go out and talk to Aura.

"You don't leave no fine woman like that by herself, man," Alexander said. "You might look up and she be gone."

"THAT WAS REALLY GOOD," AURA TOLD ROBERT WHEN HE came out to lean on the counter and talk to her. "I never knew no vegetarian food could taste so good."

"I'm glad you like it. I've been workin' here almost a year and a half now. Chef is teachin' me all he knows."

"Did he make these waffles?"

"No. I did. He's at another place he runs up in Hollywood."

Aura reached out to touch Robert's left elbow perched on the counter.

"Where you live, Robert?" she asked.

"On King, right in Baldwin Village."

"That's The Jungle."

"I guess. I mean, that's what they say."

"You like it?"

"Yeah. I like my neighbors and it's rent control."

Aura let her fingers run up to the back of his hand. Her long nails were a red-violet with yellow dots in the middle of each one. The scent of roses was stronger than the night before.

"You got a girlfriend, Robert?"

"Yes I do," he said. "Jamilah Fenestra."

"That's too bad."

"No, I mean, why you say that?"

Aura brought her hand to his left cheek and said, "You're so cute."

"Hi, Robert."

He and Aura turned to see Jamilah standing there, looking serious.

"Hi, Jamilah," Robert said. He leaned over to kiss her as they usually did but she stayed where she was.

"I'm Aura," Robert's new friend said, introducing herself and holding out a not-so-welcoming hand. "Robert was just tellin' me about you."

"Oh? What'd he say?"

"He said that you were his girlfriend, and I said that he was lucky."

"HOW LONG HAVE YOU KNOWN AURA?" ASKED JAMILAH when they were in her red Saab, headed for Pasadena.

"I met her last night on the bus."

"Last night? And you brought her home?"

"No. She lives on Buckingham Road."

"How you know that?"

"Because she told me and, and that's where she got off the bus."

"What was she doing at your restaurant with her hand on your face?"

"Why you mad?" Robert complained.

For some reason the anger on Jamilah's face released, becoming akin to Robert's question.

"I'm not mad. I'm, I'm, I guess I'm jealous."

"Of me?"

Breaking into a grin she asked, "Why wouldn't I be? Aren't you my boyfriend? That's what that Aura said."

PRISTINE FENESTRA LIVED ON MOLINE STREET, NEAR Herkimer. It was a small blue house with a tiny, neatly trimmed front lawn. When Jamilah and Robert got there, Pristine was standing behind the shadow of the screen, at the front door, waiting.

"Hi, Mom," Jamilah said, taking the lead. "I want you to meet my friend Robert."

"Hello, Mrs. Fenestra," he said as if he'd practiced the words. "You have a very nice house."

Jamilah's mother was shorter than her daughter, maybe fifty years of age, and lighter in hue, though still dark-skinned. She had a generous figure under the modern, bright yellow bouffant-style dress cut from plain cotton. The thing that Robert most noticed about Mrs. Fenestra were her eyes; they paid close attention.

"Oh?" she said to Robert's compliment. "What do you like about it?"

"I like how even the grass is."

"What do you mean, even?"

"Mom, we aren't even inside yet," Jamilah objected.

"I just want to know what the young man thinks."

"The way the grass is cut so neat and how it's all the same green with no weeds or runners," Robert said. "And it looks really good next to the blue paint on your house."

The focus in Pristine's eyes deepened, as if someone had asked an unexpected question that she had no answer to.

"Mom."

"Yes, Jammy?"

"Can we come in?"

"Oh. Oh, yes. Come on."

THE ENTRANCE TO THE HOUSE WAS A SMALL VESTIBULE that had a sitting room off to the right, a dining room on the left, and a hallway straight ahead.

Pristine walked down the central hall toward the door at the end.

"Come on," she said again. "I have the garden set for tea. I was expecting you a little earlier."

She led them to a screened-in back porch that looked out onto a very big old oak tree set behind a small stone pond populated by maybe a dozen goldfish.

The table in the *garden* was set with small sandwiches, a large teapot nestled in a green tea cozy, and a plate of different cheeses.

"Sit, sit," Pristine welcomed. Then to Robert, "The plates are on the table behind you."

Jamilah moved to gather and distribute the dishes, and they settled on padded, wrought iron chairs.

"Jamilah tells me that you're a vegan, Robert," Pristine said. "I hope you don't mind if we have cheese."

"I'm not vegan," Robert said. "It's just that I'm a cook in a vegan place."

"So, you eat meat?"

"Not usually. I want to start a restaurant that serves healthy, healing food, and most meats don't really do those things."

"Are you a doctor?"

"Mother."

"What? He says that he wants to be a healer. Aren't healers doctors?"

"He said that he wants to serve healthy food."

"Healthy and *healing*."

"No," Robert said.

"What?" asked Pristine.

"I'm not a doctor."

"Then what would you know about healing?"

Pristine's stare was almost an angry glare, that's what Robert felt. He knew that look. It was the expression that many of his teachers had in school when he'd give any answer, either right or wrong. He knew that he had to answer, he knew what the answer was, but he wasn't sure of what she would make of it.

Finally, he said, "The same things my mother knew when I'd get a fever or a cut. I mean, just feeling for a fever and giving somebody an aspirin is kinda like healing."

Like a microscope, Pristine's gaze intensified.

"You're a surprising young man," the reluctant host allowed.

Robert looked at her but didn't say anything because he didn't understand.

"When I ask you a question you wait for a while before getting around to the answer," she added.

"I do that," he admitted. "Usually when somebody asks me something it's like there's so many answers. Other people answer faster than me, but I have to take my time."

"Did you have to take special classes in school to learn how to do that?"

Jamilah stood up then, moving the heavy chair away with the

backs of her knees. The iron legs, dragging on stone, cried out loudly.

"Come on, Robert," she said. "We're leaving."

"Don't be silly," Pristine chided. "We haven't eaten."

"And we won't either."

"I just asked him a question."

"Well then, let me give you the answer, fuck you."

4.

The next morning, at three thirty, Robert felt a tickle against his lips. When he opened his eyes, Jamilah was descending for another kiss.

"Good morning," she said and then kissed him again.

Before he could return the greeting, she kissed him twice more.

"Hi," he managed to say.

She kissed him and asked, "How did you learn all that stuff?"

"What stuff?"

Robert was thinking about his sit-ups and push-ups, his toothbrush and Beethoven. But he was at Jamilah's apartment and so his schedule wouldn't work here. Part of the reason he was never all that bothered with not sleeping over was that he felt adrift without his morning preparations for the day.

"The way you kissed me," she said and then paused. "Down there like that and the way you went fast and then slow and even when I tried to move you, you'd wait until, until it was just right."

These were the words she wanted to say. She'd been awake since two thirty going over and over the way Robert made love to her. She thought he would be awkward and clumsy, that she would have to show him what to do. She was sure that the reason he didn't complain about her making him wait so long was because he was shy and maybe couldn't even keep an erection.

But instead, he had done everything she'd secretly wished previous boyfriends had done. He knew when what he did hurt or worried her. He knew when her cries were from pleasure and wanting more. And he went on and on until she had to stop and then he held her just right, so that she could feel his desire but knew that he would wait until she was ready to start again.

"I don't know," he said, answering her question and not.

"Have you had a lot of other girlfriends?"

"Not really girlfriends," he said. "I mean, I've had friends who were girls and, and, and then, and then some girls that wanted me just to kiss them and do that stuff you said."

"Just like hookups?"

"Like there was this girl named Sonata that lived upstairs. She lived with her mother, but her mom worked at night and then if my mother was gettin' high and she was asleep, I'd go upstairs to say hi and maybe watch some TV. And one time Sonata was drinkin' and she asked me if I had ever been with a woman and I said no. That's when she showed me what a girl looked like for real and what to do. And, um, well, after we did that a few times she had her friend Nina come over and they'd take turns watchin' and stuff."

"And you liked that?" Jamilah asked.

"They were really nice," he said. "And sometimes, when I'd get dizzy Sonata would or Nina would just hold me, and we'd listen to music. And if I had to go back down to look in on my mom, they didn't try'n stop me."

"How old were they?"

"They were three years older'n I was. But we had to stop when Sonata got a boyfriend for real. She said that Ritchy would kill me if he found out about how big my dick was."

"It is really big," Jamilah agreed. Then she lay down next to him with a serious look on her face, almost the way her mother looked.

"What?" Robert asked.

"Were you mad at my mom?"

"For what?"

"The way she kept asking you those questions like she was testing you."

"That happens a lot."

"And you don't care?"

"My mama told me that when people do that that it's not about me but them. She said that they, um, that they get nervous around people who are different than them."

"And you're different?"

"Oh, yeah."

"In what way?"

"Like when your mother asked me those questions. She wanted me to say what I thought before I thought about it. And because I didn't, she was kinda mad."

"Why do you think that is?"

"I don't know how to explain why it is, only why it ain't."

"Huh?"

"Well, you see, when you met me, you just talked to me like you do with everybody else. And when I said something you didn't understand, you just asked what I meant. It wasn't for a while before you saw something else."

"When was that?"

"When we went out with Minta and Howard, and he wanted to do arm wrestling with me . . ."

Jamilah remembered that they were sitting at an outside picnic table on Venice beach. Howard had asked Robert if he thought he was strong after Minta said that Robert did push-ups every morning.

"Yeah," Jamilah said. "He wanted to show that he was stronger, and you said that you don't do stuff like that."

Howard was moody when being turned down, and he and Minta left soon after.

"What does being different mean to you?" Jamilah asked.

Robert sat up to think about her question. It seemed to him very, very important that he answer her truthfully because she had been better than nice. She had accepted him for what he was before she even knew what he was. There was kindness to her that he wanted to acknowledge—even though he didn't quite understand her like that.

After at least two minutes he said, "I'm going to see my mother tomorrow, would you like to come with me?"

It was Jamilah's turn to take her time. She gazed deeply into her lover's eyes, very much like her mother, and then she kissed him, and then kissed him again.

DRIVING AT RUSH HOUR WAS SLOW GOING ON WEEKDAY mornings going west in LA. Jamilah's phone sounded when she was in that heavy traffic, driving back to Westwood after having let Robert off at Kundakunda for his breakfast shift. The first time Pristine called, her daughter let it go to voicemail. The second time she waited to answer until the sixth ring.

"Hello."

"Why haven't you called me back?" Pristine asked. Her voice was subdued and angry. "I called you seven times last night."

"What do you want, Mother?"

"I shouldn't've even called you, the way you talked to me."

Jamilah had no answer for this complaint. She almost hung up, and then didn't.

"Don't you have anything to say?" her mother asked.

"Like you told me, I already said it."

Jamilah expected her mother to disconnect but instead she said, "Jammy, he's retarded."

"I think it's you that has the problem."

"What are you talking about? It took him longer to answer a question than it does your gram, and she's eighty-two."

"Did he answer your questions?"

"In that weird way he talks. He hardly looks people in the eye."

"He looks me in the eye."

Jamilah changed lanes twice and then pulled to the curb on Olympic. She was so angry that her hands were trembling.

"You wouldn't understand, Mother."

"Understand what?"

"What it is that's wrong with you."

"Me? Here you're going out with a retard and there's something wrong with me?"

Every time Pristine called Robert that slur Jamilah felt it clench in her chest, her eyes would wince shut, sprouting angry tears. Her breaths came in pants, and for the first time she could remember, she wanted to smash something, anything.

In order to calm herself she went all the way back to childhood, in her mind, imagining a place she'd never been—Antarctica, with its blue-white ice mountains, its deep silence.

After half a minute she said, "I hate you right now, Mom. I hate you. You might as well be some southern cracker calling him a nigger—"

Pristine disconnected the call.

Jamilah sat there, waiting for the anger to dissipate. She didn't want to turn on the radio. Music would have been noise.

After a few minutes there came a knock on her driver's-side window. When she looked, it was a policeman standing there, looking in.

She let down the power window, and said, "Good morning, officer."

"Good morning. Are you okay, ma'am?" He had Asian features, but his accent pegged him as born and bred LA.

"My mother just told me that she doesn't approve of my boyfriend because she thinks he's different. I got so mad that I pulled to the curb to calm down."

"That was probably a good decision," the officer said. His name tag was DARREN something. "You know they talk about cell phones and alcohol causing so many accidents, but I think road rage is right up there too."

For some reason these words soothed Jamilah's fury. Later, she thought that it was because Officer Darren supported her decision-making.

"Are you okay to go now?" the cop asked.

"I think so. Thank you."

"You have a good day."

BEFORE GETTING TO WESTWOOD JAMILAH HAD DECIDED not to go to her molecular organic chemistry class. When she got home, she made a matcha tea that Robert had brought her from Kundakunda.

"This tea is specially made for our chef," he'd told her. "If you ever need to calm down just have some'a this."

After brewing the special blend, she sat on the bed that Robert insisted on making up before they left. She was thinking about how good he was, about how much she had learned from him.

The phone sounded again.

It was her mother again.

"What?" Jamilah said into the receiver.

"There's no reason for you to be so rude."

"There's no reason for you to treat a young Black man like trash."

"There is if he is trash, and on top'a that he's with my daughter."

"Then, then there's nothing to say. I think Robert is wonderful. He's better than any other boyfriend I've ever had . . . In every way."

"So, this thing is really serious?"

"Yes, it is."

"Okay then."

"Just like that? Now you accept it?"

"Jammy, you have always been a passionate child, person. You love strong. I accept what you're saying about this young man because I know that's how you feel. But I'm sure when you think this over, when you see how this will affect any children you have, what it will do to your social life, and his too, you will see that he might be a good person, but not the man that you should be with."

"So, the next time we see you, if there is a next time, you won't ask him all those awful questions? You'll be nice and considerate."

"I will," she said, "because I believe in your ability to understand."

ALONE FOR THE NEXT FEW HOURS JAMILAH THOUGHT about the events of the past two days. She'd never been made love to like that before. She'd had orgasms before but had no idea that there were different levels to that experience. This was the first time she ever missed a class or spent a day without reading or research.

But what if her wanting Robert would hurt him, like her mother said? Minta thought he was a nerd and Howard wanted to fight him.

She tried to imagine what their children would be like. Would they be what her mother thought of as normal? And, if so, would they be embarrassed at the way their father was? She could see in Robert the love he was able to express, but even with that, maybe there could be something better for him. Just because he was so wonderful didn't mean that she should be with him.

The phone sounded. Jamilah didn't want to talk to anyone and so didn't even dig it out of her purse. When another call came in, she treated it the same way. But on the third call she got mad. It was only when she looked that she realized it was Robert.

"Hi, baby," she answered.

"Hey."

He didn't complain about her not answering. He wasn't worried about where she was or if she was angry. He had nothing to say cross about Pristine.

"I'm sorry I didn't answer before."

"That's okay. I just wanted to say that I'm finished with work, and I'd love to come over and make us dinner if you didn't mind."

5.

I'm sorry," Jamilah whispered by candlelight in the late night.

They were lying in her bed, fingers laced together, facing each other, breathing soft and low.

"Sorry about what?" Robert asked.

"Um, well, that I don't do all the things you do. I mean, I want to, but I've never even thought about those things."

"That's all right."

"You don't mind?"

"Uh-uh, no."

"You like being with me?"

"When I was at work yesterday," he said after only the briefest pause. "I was just thinkin' about you. I missed you. I don't usually do that."

"You don't miss me?"

"Not, not you. Usually, I only pay attention to what I'm doing or what I'm about to do. But today I kept thinking about you."

Jamilah kissed his finger, licked it slightly.

"It's not only that I'm sorry about," she said. "I'm sorry for making you wait and, and, and leading you on."

"I don't understand."

"I've never done anything like this.'

"Me neither."

"You haven't?"

"No. I mean, I've been with girls. We did those things. But you treat me different. The first thing you ever did was smile. After that you shared your umbrella and then gave me a ride home. I think about that every night."

"You do?"

"Yes."

EARLY, EARLY THE NEXT MORNING ROBERT TOOK THE BUS to his apartment, did his exercises and ablutions while listening to the Fifth Symphony. He read his nature book and ate oatmeal, thinking that he felt different than he had before. There wasn't enough time to iron his shirt and pants, but he had some clothes hanging in the closet that would be good enough.

He made breakfast and joked around with his work friends. Chef Charles taught him how to prepare avocado toast and red bell pepper sauce. Maria took him aside and told him about condoms.

"You know you have to use them if you don't want to get a woman pregnant," she said, almost, he thought, as a warning.

This conversation struck Robert as odd because he didn't believe that he could be a father and so concluded that he would not be one.

WHILE ROBERT ENJOYED THE SIMPLE TASKS OF HIS DAY, Jamilah fretted. She worried that her mother was right, that she was wrong for Robert, that she'd led him on and now he was in love and his heart would be broken when she finally had to let him go.

Jamilah castigated herself for not being able to tell Robert to go home, for wanting him so badly she could feel it in her womb. Before this the only thing she had ever wanted was to be a doctor and a scientist who could understand being human on a molecular level. She wanted to see life and love and God in one image that she could translate for everyone who came after her.

That was all Jamilah wanted and all of what her mother wanted too.

"Just keep on doing your schoolwork, Jammy," Pristine had said, often. "Do that all the time, every day, and in the end, you will be a great hero for women and Black people and everybody else."

Jamilah had boyfriends, ran marathons, learned languages both dead and alive, but none of that prepared her for Robert. One day she realized that she wanted him more than she wanted to see God.

AT ELEVEN FIFTEEN THAT MORNING JAMILAH GOT INTO her red Saab and drove off toward Kundakunda. The heavy traffic did not bother her. Neither did she fret over her destination.

He was waiting for her outside the closed restaurant, holding a bag containing his alarm clock, his oatmeal, and a change of clothes. He heard the double-tapped toot of the Saab's horn, looked up, and locked eyes with Jamilah through the slightly tinted windshield.

When he jumped in the car she kissed him, using her tongue.

"I missed you," she said.

"Me too."

THE FACILITY WAS NORTH OF POMONA, DOWN A DIRT road, under a mountain that seemed to rise straight up out of the ground, making Jamilah think of being in someone's chest just after they'd been stabbed with a granite dagger.

It was a very modern hub of tall buildings and vast lawns. The institution radiated a feeling of wealth and even stylishness. There was nothing that hinted that it was a home for the mentally impaired.

She parked in visitors' parking and went with her boyfriend to the main building.

"How do you pay for this?" Jamilah wondered aloud.

"My mom was a soldier before she had me," he said. "She was in for two years before I was born, so, she has veteran medical benefits."

"HELLO, MR. HORTON," A TALL, COPPER-SKINNED MAN greeted. He was wearing a white smock, black trousers, and brown leather shoes.

"Good morning, Dr. Singh."

"Who's this with you?" he asked.

Jamilah felt that his tone was indulgent, even diminishing.

"My friend Jamilah. She's studying to be a doctor at UCLA."

Dr. Singh's expression changed, and he asked Jamilah, "Premed?"

"No. Third year med school. It's going slow because I'm also doing molecular biology."

"Oh. Excuse me. You look so young."

"I started at UCLA on my sixteenth birthday," Jamilah said, trying not to express the anger she felt.

"I see. And how do you know Robert?"

"Like he said, we're friends. We met at a farmer's market in Santa Monica."

The doctor took a few moments to digest all this information.

"Has Robert told you about his mother?" he asked.

"She lost control and shot a man. The court decided that she was not compos mentis and they sent her here, I guess."

Another moment and he said, "Come with me."

THEY PASSED THROUGH A LOCKED DOOR ADMITTING them to the ward holding patients who might need to be restrained. The door to Myrtle Horton's room was metal and also locked. Dr. Singh went in first, followed by Robert and then Jamilah.

"Hello, Myrtle," Jamilah heard the doctor say.

"Hello, doctor." Her voice was throaty and a little hoarse.

"You have a visitor," Singh continued, "and he brought a friend."

"Hi, Mom."

"Bobby," the throaty voice said, basking in real pleasure.

Jamilah came around the tall doctor then and saw the embrace between mother and son. When they let go Jamilah could see that Myrtle Horton was of normal height for a woman of her generation, maybe five five. Her skin was dark like her son's and her eyes were bright, somehow suggestive of fire.

When those eyes locked on Jamilah, Myrtle smiled broadly.

"Who is this, Bobby?" she asked.

"Jamilah," Jamilah said. "His girlfriend."

Myrtle ran forward and hugged the young woman. They embraced for a good minute.

When Myrtle moved back Jamilah could see that she was crying.

"I can't tell you how happy I am to meet you," she said. "I worry so much about my boy being all alone out there. You know how hard it is for a young Black man in these streets."

THE FURNISHINGS OF MYRTLE HORTON'S ROOM CONSISTED of a single mattress of wadded cotton set upon a metal-spring frame, a simple pine table, about a yard square, and a battered folding chair probably fabricated from processed bamboo.

Myrtle and her son sat next to each other on the bed, while Jamilah dragged the solitary chair over to face them.

After satisfying himself that Robert, his mother, and the baby face medical student were peacefully talking, Dr. Singh exited, closing and securing the metal door behind.

"You never told me you had no girlfriend," Myrtle said to her son. She was holding the young man's hands in hers, turning now and then to include Jamilah.

"I met her since the last time I was here, Mom."

"That was about five weeks ago," Jamilah added. "We were both shopping at an outdoor farmers market."

Myrtle nodded and so did Robert.

"How you been doing, Mama?"

"Pretty bad. They keep me locked up in here and they don't give me enough to eat."

"Should we complain?" Jamilah asked. "That Dr. Singh seemed a little bit haughty, like he might not listen to grievances."

Myrtle tittered and then said, "No, baby. I need t'be locked up. I'd eat the whole stew right out the pot if they let me, I sure would."

"I'm sure they could find a way to make things better for you," Jamilah responded, sounding both certain and supportive.

Myrtle released her son's hands and turned to face his girl-friend.

"What the fuck do you know?" she did not ask.

It wasn't the words alone, or the tone they were delivered in, but something about the false passivity she maintained; something about the way her head tilted to the right and the way her facial features grew soft while her eyes were riveted on Jamilah.

"Um," the future doctor uttered.

"Huh?" Myrtle added. "What you know about Dr. Singh or me or this place? You evah been there when I just lose it and th'ow some stupid fool down on his ass 'cause I could hear him thinkin' bad words? You evah there when I bite one'a the guards so bad that I could taste his blood in my mouth?"

The volume of her voice had risen. Her eyes filled with hatred.

She moved quickly, rising from the bed, intent upon Jamilah.

She moved quickly but Robert was quicker still. He wrapped both arms around Myrtle, pinning her arms, holding her back, keeping her seated.

"Why you grabbin' me, Bobby?" she both whined and warned. "Let me go!"

"Jammy didn't mean it, Mama. She drove all the way out here because she knew how long it takes me on the bus."

Myrtle struggled against her son's embrace, grunting in a low, bearlike growl. She wanted to yell and bite, but Robert, though he didn't look it, was strong. Slowly, slowly she began to calm down. Jamilah thought it was like she'd been given a Thorazine injection, and the drug was taking effect.

"But . . ." Myrtle said to no one, nowhere.

"She been helpin' me, Mama. For the first time in a long time, I can go out to places I never been."

"You can?"

"She dint mean nuthin."

Myrtle turned her head to look at Jamilah. Her eyes had been mollified by the restraining hug. She smiled, showing two teeth rimmed with gold and one, lower front tooth, gone.

"I ain't blamin' you," Myrtle said to the young coed. "It's just you cain't know how hard it is for women like me in a place like this."

"I'm sorry."

"Don't be sorry, listen. It's hard when yo head is broken and you tryin' to do right, tryin' to accept."

Robert had one arm around his mother's waist and the other hand lightly resting on her hands. He was no longer restraining her physically but leaving his caress to comfort and remind her of what she needed to know.

"The main thing you got to learn," Myrtle said, "is that it's always gonna hurt. If you take drugs, it's goin' to. If you drink wine, it will. If you run away down the street lookin' for that dog you lost when you was nine, or your old friends that's been gone away forever. No matter what you do it's gonna hurt. So, when Bobby aksed me how I been doin' I told him about the pain. He know

that the hurt is on the inside. The crack is in my head. I wanna
eat a whole pig, but they won't let me. I wanna go over to Ward D
and see my boyfriend, Lax, but if I did them things, they would
hurt more than not doin' 'em. You understand?"

"Yes, ma'am," Jamilah said, feeling that she was speaking truth.

"It's like when you a child," Myrtle continued. "You eat till
it hurts. A child grows up into a adult but, but with me it never
stops. If I could I'd eat till my stomach would bust. I'd bite the
flesh right off my boyfriend's bones."

"It's okay, Mama," Robert said. "We here. Dr. Singh got my
number and if you ever need me, I'll be here lickety-split."

When Myrtle grinned at his boyhood phrasing, Robert took his
restraining arms away.

"You'd drive him?" Myrtle asked Jamilah.

"Yes, ma'am. I definitely would . . . No matter what."

"No matter what," Myrtle repeated. "No matter what."

Jamilah nodded.

Robert said, "Mama," and reached into his windbreaker pocket.

"What?" Myrtle asked, still nodding her head to the syncopa-
tion of the syllables of the phrase, *no matter what.*

Robert pulled out a gaudy half-face mask designed to cover
the eyes of a partier. It was made from starling and clipped pea-
cock feathers pasted around eyeholes.

Raising both hands to her face Myrtle gasped, "Oh my god."

Delicately, she took the mask in her hands and then pressed
it against her face. Then she looked into a highly polished metal
mirror that was secured to the wall at the foot of her bed.

"It's so beautiful, Bobby," she whispered. "It's like, it's like
she's alive."

She turned to gaze at her visitors through the eyeholes.

"It's beautiful," Jamilah said.

"I thought you would like it, Mama," Robert added.

"It's really beautiful," Myrtle replied. "Her name is Willow, and she comes from a forest far away. And, if I'm good, sometimes she might let me visit where her people is from."

"DOES IT MAKE YOU SAD?" JAMILAH ASKED AFTER A WHILE of driving.

"What?"

"Seeing your mother like that."

"It's the best it could be for her, there."

"You don't wish that she could be cured?"

For quite a while after that Robert looked out the window staring at freeway traffic and the hills rolling by.

Jamilah thought that his answer was that there was no answer but then he said, "They used to give her drugs to stop her from gettin' mad. When I'd come see her then she'd be sittin' in a room full of people who smelled sad. Sometimes she wouldn't even know me. I'd rather she hit me than not even know me. I'm not sad because my mother is here and I can see her any day, except Sundays, they're closed then."

"You are an exceptional man, Robert," Jamilah said after combing through his explanation in her mind.

"How come you say that?"

"Most of the time most people see what they want to see. They see things that remind them of other things, and they mix it all up together until the world they think is there wouldn't make sense to anybody else. But you see what's in front'a you and accept it, you don't waste time wishing for something else."

They were quiet for the rest of the ride.

That night they didn't sleep at all.

6.

After the visit to his mother, Jamilah and Robert began spending time at her apartment in Westwood. She had never experienced physical and definitely not a spiritual closeness with anyone this powerfully, except once when she was a toddler playing with Night, her father, in a 16 mm film her mother projected every Easter.

"That was your father," Pristine would say.

"You miss him, Mama?"

"No. The best thing he ever gave me was you."

"I miss him."

WHEN CHEF CHARLES AND ROBERT WERE WORKING alone one early morning, the big man in the white hat, as he called himself, asked, "You like this young woman, Mr. Robert?"

After a minute's contemplation the young man put down his eight-gallon kettle and said, haltingly, "She makes me feel brave."

After considering this answer the big-bellied chef replied, "I don't get what you mean."

"It used to be, before I met Jammy, that my life was like a map that showed all the places I had to go and how to get there. I had to follow the red lines from one place to the other one. If I ever just had to walk one block outta the way I'd start to sweat. You know what I mean?"

Chef Charles nodded.

"But when I'm with her and she says 'What's on the street on the other side of the block?' I just think, 'Why don't we go see?'"

The restaurateur smiled under his auburn mustache.

"You are a very lucky young man."

Robert thought he was right. Almost everything was perfect.

THE ONLY BLEMISH CAME ONE DAY WHEN ROBERT LEFT the apartment at 4:00 a.m. to take the bus to work. He was walking down toward Wilshire when someone said, "Stop."

Robert kept on walking. He had learned that when people you don't know try to command you that they usually want something from you. And he didn't want to find out what that something was.

"I said stop!" the man yelled.

Then Robert could hear the pounding of running feet behind him. He turned and saw that two uniformed policemen were headed right for him. He brought both hands to the level of his shoulders and waited, expecting them to stop. But the closer cop tackled him, slamming him down to the sidewalk.

For a moment everything turned red, bright red, and then, when the crimson light subsided, Robert could feel his attacker on top of him, pulling at his arms.

"Stop resisting!" his assailant yelled.

"What you want me to do?" Robert cried out.

"Stop resisting!"

"Resistin' what?"

When the second cop grabbed one of Robert's arms, he realized that they were trying to handcuff him.

When they hauled him to his feet, they wrenched his left shoulder.

"Ow!"

"Okay, son," one of the two said. "Why were you running from us?"

The cops were white men, around Robert's age. They were both tall and seemed agitated.

"I wasn't running."

"You kept goin' when we ordered you to stop," the second accused.

"You didn't say police," Robert argued. "You just said stop. I didn't know."

"Why did you resist?"

"I didn't know what you wanted, man. You was just grabbin' on me tellin' me to stop. I already was stopped."

For some reason this complaint brought the policemen's rage down to simple anger.

"You homeless?" the shorter of the two tall men asked.

"No."

"What are you doing on the street this time of night?" asked the taller.

"Goin' t'get the bus down on Wilshire."

"At four in the morning?"

"My shift at the restaurant starts at five thirty down on Western."

The shorter young man said, "This says that you live down on King. That's in Baldwin Village, right?"

Robert realized that the tackler had somehow gotten his wallet out of his pocket.

"Yeah," he said. "That's where I live at."

"Then what are you doing around here?" Somehow, he infused this question with a threat.

"My girlfriend live here. She goes to UCLA."

"You don't really have a girl here, do you?" Shorty accused.

It was then that Robert realized that he was in trouble. His mother had always said, *When a cop starts to doubt what you tellin' him, you in trouble. If they don't believe you then you goin' to jail.*

Robert knew that his mother's answer to that situation was to run like hell. But his hands were manacled behind his back . . .

"We're gonna have to take you into custody until all this is cleared up."

All what? Robert thought.

A car was driving by. The lights glared brightly, and the car stopped. A door opened and someone got out, but Robert couldn't see too well because the headlights shone in his eyes.

"Glaser, Brown," the man from the car said.

"Sergeant Hollis," the shorter cop hailed.

"What's this?" the man called Hollis asked.

"He was prowling around in the dark and when we said stop police he took off," the taller replied.

Looking Robert up and down the senior officer asked, "And you had to beat on him to put on some cuffs?"

"Pretty much."

"What about you?" the sergeant asked Robert, moving close enough for the prisoner to see.

"I didn't run. I kept walkin' because I didn't know they was police. I was goin' to get the bus to work."

The sergeant was a brown man, Black American. He was the shortest, and probably the heaviest, among them.

"Where you work?" Sergeant Hollis asked.

"Kundakunda restaurant down on Western."

"He says he got a girlfriend 'round here," the shorter patrolman said, an ugly sneer on his face. "But we think he's homeless, lookin' for something to steal."

"Is that right, Patrolman Glaser? This man in pressed jeans and shirt, with polished shoes, is homeless? Uncuff this man."

Looking Robert up and down, while taking off the cuffs, Patrolman Glaser said, softly, "That's what we thought."

"So, now you want me to believe that you were out here thinking?"

The sergeant took a voluminous white handkerchief from his vest. This he handed to Robert. The young man took it, not knowing what he was supposed to do.

"You're bleeding," the sergeant said.

He was. From his right temple. It was a good deal of blood, but Robert knew, from a cut he got on the playground when he was nine, that pressure stopped bleeding.

"You want to arrest this man?" the senior officer asked Glaser, the shorter of the pair.

"Yeah," Glaser said. "Because he resisted."

"Okay, but if he really does have a girlfriend and a job at this Kunda restaurant I'm'a make sure it goes on your record, both your records."

"It's four in the mornin'," Brown, the taller cop complained. "And he resisted."

"So you slammed him in his head so hard that he's gushin' blood?"

He must have, Robert thought. But why didn't he remember getting hit?

"You okay?" the sergeant asked Robert.

"Yeah. I'm okay. I just wanna go to work."

"You don't want 'em to look at that wound up in the emergency room?"

"No. I'll drop by my apartment to wash up before I go in."

ROBERT FELL ASLEEP, MISSING HIS BUS STOP BY FOUR blocks. He must have walked to his apartment but didn't really remember doing so. The next thing he knew, after waking up on the bus, he was standing in his bedroom with a rumpled shirt in his hand. He considered ironing the shirt. He wanted, more than anything in the world, to take out the ironing board from the clothes closet and press out the wrinkles. After that he could rub his cheek on the hot fabric and then put it on, feeling the warmth along his shoulders and chest.

He was remembering remembering the feel of a warm shirt when he realized that his head was on the pillow, shoes still on his feet. He wanted to take off the shoes but decided to wait a bit. He realized that he was lying on his right side and worried that he might bleed on the white pillowcase, but then he remembered the white handkerchief received from Hollis and the pressure that stopped the blood.

IN THE HOURS HE SLEPT HE HEARD THE PHONE. IT WAS more than one ring coming from more than one call. He wanted to answer, but every time he almost got up the phone would stop its jangling, and he would fall back into a deep cradle of sleep.

He loved Jamilah Fenestra, loved her, and even though his mother told him that love was like a broken clock, he wanted to be with her forever, until the cows came home, and the roosters roosted, safe from any weasel or fox.

He loved Jamilah Fenestra more than he needed to worry to make sure that everything would be all right.

IT SOUNDED LIKE GUNFIRE IN THE HALL OUTSIDE HIS apartment; gunfire or maybe the sound of those cops' hard shoes when they were running after him. No. No, it wasn't guns or stomping feet he heard. It was more like hammering. Yes, the banging of a hammer on something hard.

"Robert! Robert!"

The yelling next to the angry sound of banging told Robert that he should be frightened, that maybe he was going to get thrown to the ground again. But when he felt like he might get scared he'd think of the words—*Jamilah Fenestra.*

"ROBERT," SHE CALLED TO HIM. "ROBERT, WAKE UP. Wake up."

It was so nice hearing her voice near enough that he could almost see her, touch her.

"Robert, wake up. I'm not playing with you."

Prying his tired eyes open felt like the hardest thing he'd ever done. He wouldn't have done it for anyone except his mother or Jamilah.

And there she was, holding him by the shoulders, propped up on her lap.

"Hey, baby," he said, parroting his mother's words to him when she'd gotten so high that he feared she might die. "Hey."

"What happened to your head?" she asked.

"The police."

Beyond Jamilah's worried eyes Robert saw Chef Charles, flanked by Marquis and Alexander, the dishwashers who did more than wash dishes.

"You guys keep talking to him," Jamilah said. "I'm going to call for an ambulance."

The head cook took Jamilah's place. His breath reminded Robert of the rich fragrance of simmering vegetables.

"You think I could ever have my own restaurant, Chef?" he asked.

"Of course. But what happened to your head?"

"The police thought I was homeless."

"What police?"

"The ones in Westwood. Hollis gave me a big napkin, but I bled all over it and had to throw it away."

"They beat you?" Marquis asked.

"With the ground," Robert said, nodding. But he had to stop that bobbing motion because it made him feel like he was going to fall off the side of a mountain.

Finally, he did fall. Down, down into a dark cavern of stone. Down into a crevasse that held a deep, fast-flowing river of warm sleep.

"ALL RIGHT, LIFT," A MAN SAID. AND ROBERT FELT LIKE he was floating up above the bed.

He was deposited on another bed that started moving.

"Robert," Jamilah called from what felt like far away.

He opened his eyes and said, "Yeah?"

He was looking up at her, but she was walking, and he seemed to be following, riding on a bed, on his back.

"I called the people I know at the emergency room at UCLA," she told him. "They sent the ambulance."

"But I told Hollis I didn't need the emergency room. I just wanna sleep."

"It's okay, honey," she whispered. "You can rest now."

HE AWOKE IN A HOSPITAL ROOM, ON A HOSPITAL BED, feeling rested but still a little tired. A woman in a nurse's attire was looking down on him, a dark-skinned Black woman in a powder-blue uniform. Maybe forty, the nurse wore glasses with thin gold metal frames and gave Robert the impression of great inner strength.

"How you feelin', Mr. Robert?"

"Okay. What's your name?"

"Oriana," she said with a smile. "Oriana West."

"Hello, Ms. West. Am I okay?"

Another smile and she said, "You look like it to me. That's why I'm here. Your girlfriend wanted to see you, and Doctor Tomor told me to come in and feel your head for fever."

"Do I have fever?"

"Cool as a cucumber."

WHEN NURSE ORIANA WEST LEFT THE ROOM ROBERT took a deep breath and turned his head toward the sun-filled window. He spent a while recalling the days when his mother would take him to a park where he could run and tumble on the thick green lawns as much as he wanted.

"Robert?"

Turning away from the window he saw Jamilah and grinned.

"Hey, baby." He tried to sit up, felt a wave of dizziness, and relaxed back against the pillow.

"Don't," Jamilah said, sitting down on the edge of the bed and laying a hand on his chest. "The doctor says that you need to have bedrest for at least a week."

"I can't do that. I got to go to work. You get fired you don't go to work."

"Chef Charles told me to tell you to rest up as long as it takes. Your job will be waiting for you."

Robert took another deep breath. He wanted to sleep more than anything, anything except waking up and seeing Jamilah.

"How do you feel?" she asked.

He spent a few moments taking inventory of his body and his mind. Finally, he said, "Lucky and tired."

"Lucky to get slammed in the head?" she said, softly smiling.

"Lucky to have you."

7.

After a week of staying in bed at Jamilah's, eating the simple meals that she could make, Robert was ready for something different. So, on the eighth day, Jammy stayed home to help him make a great vegan feast.

"Don't you use recipes?" Jamilah asked through the stinging tears of dicing onions.

"After a while you get to know what you're making so good," he said, "that you can just throw stuff together. You can't do that if you're runnin' a restaurant because people expect food on the menu to be the same every time. It's when you cookin' for yourself that things start to change."

Robert stood away from the simmering pot before him and looked out through the window. There were a pair of blue jays on a telephone wire that ran down the block.

"How you feeling?" she asked.

"Good."

"You're not dizzy anymore?"

"Uh-uh," Robert grunted as he began to prepare the masa corn meal. He didn't tell her about the headaches he had every morning or how he was sometimes confused about where he was.

"That's good," Jamilah said. "I guess you'll be going back to work soon."

"Yeah. I'll be happy about that."

"We should probably go down to the police station and tell them that you live here, and you'll be going down to the bus so early."

"Yeah. Okay." He didn't look forward to being in a police station. His mother had always told him to stay away from the cops. But Jamilah was right about him being out so early in the morning, he had to let them know what he was doing.

CHEF CHARLES WAS THE FIRST GUEST TO ARRIVE. HE brought with him three bottles of organic citrus wine and a bouquet of dark red peonies.

"Wine for the man of the house and flowers for the lady," the stout Brussler said handing his gifts to the hosts.

"Thank you, Charles," Jamilah said, calling him the name he'd asked her to use. "The flowers are beautiful."

Within the next half hour Maria, Marquis, and Alex showed up. Jamilah had rented an extra-long folding table and two additional folding chairs for the dinner party. The seating just barely fit in the living room. But everybody seemed happy with the setup. They drank orange wine and nibbled on vegan sourdough bread bought from a downstairs bakery.

"You know," Marquis said after his second glass of wine, "when Bobby told us that he was datin' a doctor I asked him, I said, 'You mean a dock worker?' And he said no, a medical doctor."

"You didn't believe him?" Jamilah asked.

"That was a hard one," Alexander offered. "'Cause we knew that Robert never lied or even stretched the truth. But you don't expect a kitchen helper to be datin' no doctor, at least not no man helper."

"You think a woman cook could get a doctor to go out with her?" Maria asked, a twist to her lips.

"If she was fine," Marquis said, giving a one-shoulder shrug.

"So," said Chef Charles, "it is the love of money and nothing else for you."

"You ask any Black woman out there what's the most important thing she wanna know about a man," Alexander said, holding up his right hand, as if making an oath. "She will tell you that the first thing a man gotta have is a job. And two seconds after that man say he do, she be wonderin' what kinda job."

"I'm a Black woman," Jamilah declared and grinned.

Putting his swear hand over his heart Alexander bowed his head and said, "And you and Robert the only thing keepin' my hopes up."

"So you can get with a rich woman?" Maria joshed.

"So I could be with a woman because of the content of my character and not the color of my money."

They all laughed, even Robert, though he didn't get the joke.

He got up then and brought out the lettuce cups, which were filled with spicy bulgar and drizzled with a few drops of pure balsamic vinegar.

"Damn!" Marquis swore, "this some good shit here."

Chef Charles nodded his agreement.

After the salad Jamilah served coconut and chickpea soup.

"You made this, Robert?" Chef Charles asked.

"Yes, sir."

"You are an exceptional cook."

For a moment Robert was at a loss for words. Everyone was looking at him.

"If his skin wasn't so dark, I do believe that he'd be blushin'," Marquis blessed.

THE MAIN COURSE CONSISTED OF SPICY BAKED CAULI-flower alongside nondairy cheese pasta and red pepper and habanero tamales. For dessert Robert served strawberries glazed with agave and topped with homemade vegan whipped cream.

They were all happy and a little high from the orange wine. Nobody wanted to leave, so they sat around the rented table and told stories.

The eldest of them, Alexander, told about a time he was standing by the highway hitchhiking in Tennessee when . . .

". . . a crazy man wearin' hairy clothes–"

"Hairy clothes? You mean like fur?" Maria queried.

"I don't know," Alex admitted. "It kinda looked like hairs sproutin' right out from his shirt and the weave of his trousers."

"Like a verevolf?" Chef Charles asked. The wine had deepened his accent.

"Naw, man. Listen and you'll see."

The audience sat back in their chairs.

"This big man, might'a been white, jumped outta the woods next to the road. I couldn't tell if his hair was growin' in on his face or if he was wearin' a hoodie. At first, he was just lookin' around, but then he sniffed and turned in my direction. He looked at me wit' these yellah eyes an' then he growled."

"What you mean growled?" Marquis sounded a little scared.

"You evah hear a bear when he mad?" Alexander answered.

Nodding ever so slightly, Marquis said, "I seen it on nature specials."

"Then you know what I mean. He growled an' moved his head around some, and then he shouted loud like a mothah-fuckah."

"What did you do?" Jamilah was quite frightened.

"Do? I runned faster than Usain Bolt on the best day'a his life. I'as runnin' like a bastard but that hairy man was right on my tail, right on it. I mean he was snortin' and snufflin' and every once in a while, he'd let out a yelp like a dog been kicked. And when he did that, I was so scared that I pissed myself while I was runnin'. I was cryin' too. I mean, that highway was empty as far as I could see an' that monster-man was gettin' closer like, like death in a dyin' man's eyes."

Alexander's skin had become ashen, there was real fear in his mien. Anybody listening to that wild story would have had to believe it because he did.

"What did you do?" Jamilah pleaded.

"Ran as hard as a man can run. Up and down that hilly highway, surrounded by live oaks and dogwood trees, the only witnesses to that creature killin' me and eatin' me."

"He wanted to eat you?" Robert asked, almost as if on cue.

"I was sure that when he sniffed, he smelt my blood," Alexander said, nodding at the floor like a doomed man under the pronouncement of Saint Peter. "He was sent from hell alright. And all I could do was keep runnin'. I could hear myself breathin' but I wouldn't let me get tired. I felt the creature gettin' closer, but I refused to give up.

"And then . . ." Alexander went silent for at least a minute, maybe two.

"What happened, Alex?" Maria demanded.

He turned his eyes to the hostess, reticent to finish his story. But his audience could tell that this was one of those kinds of tales that needed to be told through to the end.

"I was racin' up this incline of the tar road, just feelin' the exhaustion goin' down from my neck into my chest. I knew I couldn't make it much further on, but I couldn't stop neither. And then, on my right, just as I was makin' the crest, I seen her."

"Saw who?" Marquis skreiched.

"It was this little white girl, maybe fi'e year old."

"Vere vas she?" asked Chef Charles.

"Comin' out from the woods, wearin' a li'l pink dress and bright red shoes."

"What did you do?" Maria queried.

The storyteller took in a deep breath and then let it out in a gust.

"I was so scared that I was happy to see her. I knew that if that thing chasin' me saw her, he'd stop and have her for a snack while I got away."

"You just left her?" Robert was indignant.

Alexander said, "For twelve steps," and then he nodded.

"Tvelve?" asked Chef.

"Yeah. A dozen steps and I turnt around. That li'l white girl dint do nuthin' to bring on that creature from hell. I turnt around and what I saw was the hairy man on his knees in front'a that child." Alexander had started crying. "His head was down, and she had placed her tiny white hand on it. They stayed like that a minute or so and then the girl went back into the wood with the hairy man right behind her."

"What happened then?" Marquis wanted to know.

"I put out my thumb and two minutes later a red Volkswagen came by, and a lovely young woman named Lavernia gave me a ride all the way to Memphis. And when we got there, she give me another kinda ride."

"But what about the hairy man and the little white girl?" Robert asked, worriedly.

"If you had seen 'em, Bobby, you would know that she was in no trouble from him. They was just some crazy backwoods mothah-fuckahs dint want nuthin' to do wit' niggahs like me."

CHEF CHARLES HAD BEEN A MERCENARY IN HIS YOUTH. He told them about a slaughter he was involved in in southern Africa.

"I didn't kill no one," the pale, pink-skinned man vowed. "Not vit my hands. But I vas dere, and so I vas guilty. That's ven I left my home and came here, became a vegan, and svore to value life."

"What about you, Robert?" Maria asked after Chef's unsettling story of bloodshed and salvation.

"What?" their host asked.

"What kinda story you got?"

"Nothing like they said," he replied with emphasis. "I just go to work and come back home, do three sets of twenty-five sit-ups and push-ups in the morning."

"You on'y work four days a week," Marquis insinuated. "What you do on your days off?"

"Read nature books, sometimes I go see my mom."

"What about that day the police stopped you?" Jamilah asked. "That was different."

To Robert there was only him and Jamilah right then. If she had asked him to jump on one leg like it was a pogo stick, he would have done it.

SO, ROBERT TOLD HIS TALE OF BEING JUMPED BY THE cops for being in the wrong place at the wrong time.

"They threw me to the ground so hard that I went unconscious and had to stay in the hospital for two days and then lay up in bed for a week more."

"Them cops is mothahfuckahs," Marquis spat.

"Zis is true," Chef agreed. "Fuckers."

"Not all of 'em," Robert argued. "That guy Hollis, that sergeant, he saved me."

"Yeah," Alexander did not agree, "but that's how they get ya too."

"What's that supposed to mean?" Jamilah asked him.

"When all they do is the job they been hired for, and you get all grateful. 'Thank the lord this here great man with a badge done saved me.' That's what you feel. But fuck that shit. He ain't save shit. The next time Bobby on the street, and they see his ass, they gonna come around like stingin' flies, just lookin fo' a way in."

This last little tirade put the kibosh on Robert's dinner.

"It's time for me to get home," Chef Charles said. "Robert, Jamilah, it vas a vonderful dinner. Good food and good company. I thank you so much."

Alexander and Marquis left together.

At the door, Maria said, "It was a really nice time. Thank you, guys." Then she hugged and kissed them both.

Robert closed the door and Jamilah kissed the back of his neck.

"Come sit down with me," she whispered into his ear.

THEY SAT AT THE END OF THE RENTED TABLE. JAMILAH made Robert sit at the head.

"That was really nice," she said. "Chef called you an exceptional cook."

Robert grinned and ducked his head.

"Yeah," he said. "Makes me think that I could still do a restaurant if I want."

"Did you ever doubt that you could?"

"I worry about my cooking and all the things you have to remember to make a restaurant work."

"What things?"

"You know, everything . . . from finding a place to gettin' insurance and hiring people know their business. There's salaries and taxes and dealin' with people, customers that get mad."

"But you'll have people working with you," Jamilah reasoned. "Accountants and assistant managers, me."

"But you'll be bein' a doctor and, and a scientist. You won't have time for no hole-in-the-wall dive. And anyway . . ."

"Anyway what?"

"I mean, you know, we together now but that might not always be."

Robert looked down at the table. Jamilah smiled down on his perfectly coifed head.

"I'm pregnant," she said.

Sitting up, Robert placed both hands, palms down, on the table. His brows knitted and his eyes were open wide.

Jamilah's mouth was smiling but her eyes worried.

"What?" they both said.

"I don't know," Robert said before Jamilah could respond. "I just didn't think that I could, um, make you pregnant. I mean, I guess I thought so but . . ."

"Are you happy?" she asked.

"Are you?" he answered.

"If you want the baby, I am."

"Me?"

"Well, you *are* the father."

"I'm a father?"

"Yes, you are."

Robert sat back in the chair, staring at the stained and crumb-covered white tablecloth.

"I'm a father," he said and then looked up at Jamilah, "with you."

She grinned and reached out to hold his hands.

"I've known about it for almost two weeks," she said. "But I didn't want to tell you while you had that concussion."

"We're gonna have a baby? You and me, a mom and a dad?"

Jamilah took in a deep breath through an open mouth. He and she were sharing a truth together.

"We have to go get married," Robert told Jamilah.

"You think so?"

8.

They got the marriage license and married in the same place, at the county clerk's office of LA County. The County Clerk, Stella Hartman, performed the ceremony on a Friday morning. When the formalities were over, the license became a marriage certificate. Robert liked it that the document represented two things. He somehow believed that this strengthened their connection.

"I love you, Robert," Jamilah said on the ride back to her place.

"Could we get a bigger apartment?" he said.

"Don't you love me?" she asked him, unable to keep the worry out of her voice.

"Forever."

"Forever?" The worry gone, now she giggled. "That's a very long time."

"Yes, but it's true."

"But it's just a feeling," she said, fishing for something though she was not quite clear what that something was.

"You the one told me all the things we feel and hear and see are, um, matter, material."

"Yeah? So?"

"My love is in my brain. It's matter. It matters. And things like that last forever. Forever."

That's when Jamilah started to cry.

"Did I say something wrong?" Robert asked.

"No, honey, no. I mean that was just so lovely, so beautiful. I don't think anybody ever really loved me before. People say they love you. I'm sure they believe it too. But they don't know."

"How could you not know that you're in love?"

"When I was a little girl," she said. "My mama didn't cook very well. She would heat up food from cans and buy meat and chicken that was already cooked. Anyway, I used to always love it when we'd have green peas from the can. And then, one day, my uncle Lucas took me out to this farm in Riverside. We picked sweet green peas from vines and brought them up to the front porch where Lucas and his girlfriend, Paine, and I shelled the peas.

"'When do we put them in the can?' I asked my uncle, and him and Paine laughed. When they cooked those peas and we had 'em with dinner it was just about the best thing I'd ever eaten."

"And that's why you cryin'?" Robert asked.

"Yeah, because Lucas told me that sometimes peas are just soft and gray like those canned peas and sometimes, if we're lucky enough, we get to taste the real thing."

"What do you mean?"

"What I mean, Robert, is that I've had boyfriends out the can my whole life, but now that you're my husband it's the real thing."

All the way back to Jamilah's apartment, Robert was quiet. He sat in the living room, on the coral fabric and finished walnut divan, with his hands clasped and his eyes squinting, as if maybe there was something in the far-off distance that he could not quite make out.

"What's wrong, honey?" Jamilah asked him.

"Nothing wrong," he said. "It's just that I like it when I ask you something and you answer me with a story."

"I learned that from you."

MYRTLE HORTON KISSED ROBERT AND JAMILAH MANY, many times.

"Did you throw the bouquet?" Robert's mother asked Jamilah.

"No, Ms. Horton," Jamilah said. "It was a civil service and there was only me and Bobby. And, oh yeah, Miguel. He's the guard at the county clerk's and he agreed to be our witness."

Myrtle's smile was gone and both Robert and Jamilah worried that she might be having what Dr. Singh called a mental relapse.

"And you're having a baby?" Myrtle said dispelling the newlyweds' worries.

"Yes. Yes." Jamilah's big grin was infectious. "Six more months."

The women taking each other's hands made Robert very happy.

PRISTINE FENESTRA SAT GLAZED AND OPENMOUTHED when Jamilah began telling her all the good news. Jamilah and Robert decided that it would be best for her to come alone to her mother's house.

They were sitting on the back patio.

"You married him?"

"I love him, Mama, I do."

"And you let him get you pregnant."

Smiling, the daughter nodded.

Pristine's brow knitted, her hands grasped the fabric of her terry cloth house robe.

"Congratulations," Jamilah said at last.

"What?"

"That's what you're supposed to say."

"Why?"

"Because I'm going to have a baby and you're my mother."

Pristine shook her head slowly from side to side. She brought four fingers of her right hand to the center of her forehead. She shook her head again and then sneezed.

"God bless you," Jamilah extolled.

"And let him damn you."

The young doctor-to-be understood that this moment was the other shoe that had been ready to drop for all the years of her life. She knew this, always felt that she was on the jagged edge with her mother. Her grades, the friends she chose, clothes she wore, even the television shows she watched and if she gained any more than two pounds. It always felt that Pristine was just about to unleash hell on earth if Jamilah did one thing wrong. But, looking across the table at her mom, she realized that this hell would raze them both. Pristine was shivering, sweat ran down the sides of her face. Her demeanor reminded Jamilah of Rumpelstiltskin, an enraged dwarf about to stomp himself into oblivion.

"I want you out of my house," Pristine said. "Out of my house, out of my life, out of my will, out of everything."

Jamilah heard the words but, surprisingly, she felt no fear, no hurt, no impact at all. She believed her mother's hatred; knew that Pristine would gut her with a fisherman's knife if she could. If she had paid for Jammy's tuition, she'd call UCLA and have her own flesh and blood drummed out of the medical school. Jamilah could see her own corpse in her mother's vengeful eyes. She imagined that Pristine would get down on her knees and pray for Jamilah's baby to be stillborn. She would hope for them to be homeless and childless just so they would come to her, ask her for help, allowing her to slam the door on them.

When Jamilah rose from her chair Pristine looked up at her, tears and sweat streaming down her face.

"Goodbye, Mother."

"And don't you ever come back."

"SHE DIDN'T MEAN IT," ROBERT SAID WHEN JAMILAH GOT home. "She's just mad 'cause she doesn't want you with me. She thinks I'm broken, that our baby will get that from me."

Jamilah walked over, sat down on her husband's lap, kissed him, and said, "She's the broken one. If anything goes wrong, it will be because of her."

"I feel sorry for her," Robert murmured.

"I don't know why she hates you. She hates me too."

"Maybe she thinks so, but that's the same as you said about people who don't know how to love right."

"I don't understand, honey."

"I don't either, not all the way, but I don't think that it's hate she feels, I think she's scared."

"Scared of what?"

"That if she lets you go something really bad will happen, something that would break her heart."

"But then why disown me?"

"Because that way it won't be her fault."

Their faces were close enough that they could feel each other's breaths on their skin.

"Come to bed with me," Jamilah whispered.

"Now?"

"I need it."

"But the baby."

"The baby'll be just fine."

9.

Ghalen Romeo Horton was born on July 13 in the first year of the new millennium. He weighed seven and a half pounds, sported a full head of hair, and had eyes just a little bit larger than one would expect. When he was in Jamilah's arms he'd smile, play with her face for a while, and then doze off. On Robert's lap the infant child played and laughed, basking in the unwavering attention of his father's gaze.

ROMEO FARR WAS JAMILAH'S PATERNAL GRANDFATHER. He made it his business to be the man in her life when his son Night was lost to, what he called, the conflagration of war.

"Grandpa?" Jamilah asked Romeo when she was five and had already skipped to the first grade.

"Yes, Sunshine?"

"Most of the kids in school get their last name from their dads."

"Uh-huh."

"But if that's so, then I should have your last name instead of Mama's father's."

"You are a very smart little girl."

"Yeah, but why is my name Fenestra?"

"You used to say Finisher."

"Yeah, but how come it's not my daddy's name?"

"Because even though they were in love, your mother and father never tied the knot."

"What's the knot?"

"They never got married and so your mother's last name went to you."

"Why didn't they do the knot?"

"I'm not absolutely sure but I think that they were so much in love that they didn't worry about all that nonsense. You wanna go get some ice cream?"

AFTER GHALEN WAS BORN ROBERT WAS SO HAPPY THAT it didn't even bother him too much that he'd get lost now and then. Walking down the street he'd sometimes forget where he was and have to call Jamilah to help him figure it out. She told him that she suspected it was the time his head hit the concrete that caused this confusion, the morning the police attacked him without reason.

"You don't think that it's in my DNA?" he'd say to her whenever she blamed the fall.

"No, baby," she'd assure him. "The only thing Ghalen gets from you is a handsome face and a ready smile."

"But it could be the DNA, right?" Robert would ask with trepidation.

"No," Jamilah would then say in the tone that Robert knew would not lie.

He continued to work at Kundakunda until Chef Charles decided to start a new restaurant in Beverly Hills. He called the restaurant Indus and invited the full staff of Kundakunda to come with him. Jamilah was glad that Chef Charles decided to bring Robert, who, because of his tendency to get lost in places or thought, was unlikely to be able to start a restaurant on his own.

"Anyway," Jamilah told Charles. "We talked about it the other night and he said that he might not want to take the time to start his own business because he needs to be there for Ghalen."

"Is Robert going to be enough for you guys to make it?" Charles asked the young doctor-bride. "I mean, he's a wonderful man but—"

"We're there for each other," she said, cutting off any possibility of a conversation. "I'm always telling him things he can do, and he shows me how to live by the way he conducts his life."

FROM THE AGE OF FIVE GHALEN WOULD GO WITH ROBERT to work at Indus when he wasn't at nursery school or kindergarten. Marquis, whose father was a carpenter, made the boy a little chair-desk that he was supposed to sit in while Robert prepared the vegetables and other ingredients for the night's fare. At his little table Ghalen would draw and practice his letters.

In the kitchen Robert rarely got lost in his mind. He was Chef's number two and exceptionally good at keeping everything in order.

Ghalen would sit in his chair, next to the door of the walk-in cold storage closet and wait until Robert came over to visit him. But, also, while his dad worked, Marquis, Alexander, or Maria would often sneak him away for some fun. There were three new waiters and two more kitchen helpers to handle the extra work. They all played with the young boy too.

After a couple of years Ghalen learned certain jobs that he could do instead of being bored in his chair. If he stood up on one of the grown-ups' chairs, he could wash and rinse the delicate dishes that Chef didn't want cleaned by a machine. He could also sweep up messes on the floor, as long as there was no broken glass.

The boy loved the restaurant, knew what was behind every door, and could work any machine, under his dad's supervision.

In the evening, at around four fifteen, Chef Charlie, as Ghalen called him, would take a walk around the commercial blocks of Beverly Hills. After a while Ghalen would go with him on these half-hour excursions.

One afternoon, on their daily walk, CC, another nickname that Ghalen used, said, "I see you're carrying around a real book with you today."

"I like it."

"What's it called?"

"*Winnie-the-Pooh*."

"Who's that?"

"He's a stuffed bear that lives in the Hundred Acre Wood. And he has a friend named Piglet and, and another friend named Eeyore."

"And you can read that book?"

"Uh-huh."

"I don't believe it."

"I can too. Just ask my mama."

"Why don't we sit down on this bench, and you can read some to me."

They had taken a shortcut through a grassy lane with stores and restaurants on either side. Ghalen strode up to a cast-iron bench that was painted pink. He jumped up on it and Chef Charlie sat down beside him. When they were both seated Ghalen handed his friend the book and said, "You pick out any page you want me to read, and I will."

"Any page?"

"Uh-huh."

Charles chose page thirty-seven and handed it back to the boy who read haltingly but with very few mistakes from the first word to the last. After he was finished, he grinned at the older man.

"You see?" Ghalen said. "I can read the whole book."

"Can you read another page?" the astonished cook asked.

Ghalen smiled while handing the book back.

Chef chose three more pages, and the boy read them all.

"How old are you?" Charles asked him.

"Almost seven."

"Only six and you can read that big book by yourself?"

Ghalen nodded. "When I was little, I would sit on my mother's lap when she'd read to me. After a while I started to see the words she was saying."

"You're a very lucky boy to have a mother who can teach you how to read."

"My dad can read."

"Oh, I know."

"I think we're gonna be late for the kitchen, Chef Charlie."

ONE NIGHT, TWO WEEKS AFTER GHALEN HAD TURNED eight, he came upon his father in the living room of their three-bedroom apartment. Sitting at the little desk next to the window, Robert had been paging through a very large picture book about the animals of Africa. Actually Robert had been reading but now he was looking out on Wilshire Boulevard.

"What you readin', Dad?"

"About a animal called the honey badger. I was readin' about them but then . . ." As he often did, Robert drifted off in the middle of the sentence, thinking about so many things that he was, momentarily, lost.

"Have I ever told you about how I read books?" he asked, coming back to himself.

"I don't think so," Ghalen said. The boy pulled up the deep-brown, leather-bound hassock, which he treated as his seat in that room.

Robert looked into his son's eyes and Ghalen peered back.

They had been like that to each other for as long as Ghalen could remember.

"I read words just like everybody else," Robert said, and then he began to read aloud from the book, "'The honey badger is a animal that lives in Asia, Africa, and what they call the sub, sub, subcontinent of India. It's very strong with thick skin you can't bite through and is very brave in battle.'

"You see, I read the first words and then the next words are how I understand what's said, and then I keep reading until it's like I'm in the place that they're talkin' about."

"Like you're in Africa for real?" Ghalen asked.

Robert nodded. "Trottin' along right next to the long-clawed, always hungry honey badger. It's like we're friends gettin' inta trouble like the time you read to me about Huck Finn and Tom Sawyer. I feel the hot sun and smell the musk of the animals. And, and if I let it go long enough, I stop reading and start making up stuff."

"Sounds like fun."

"It is. But sometimes I get a little confused about what's real and what I made up."

"I wish I could do it," Ghalen said. "Sometimes the teachers at school try to make stories into what they call outlines, and it stops bein' fun."

"I know what you mean, son. It's like you're outside havin' a great time and someone says that you got to come in."

Ghalen folded his long skinny legs into what his mother called half-lotus. He loved moments like this when he and his father just talked about things.

"Where'd Mom go?"

"She's in San Francisco at a molecular biology convention."

Jamilah had gotten her medical degree but, after talking to Robert about the future, she decided to go into research.

"When's she comin' back?"

"Tomorrow."

"Okay. I'm gonna go to bed and read my stories and try to get into them like you do."

WHEN GHALEN WAS THREE, ON THE EVENING THAT JAMI-lah graduated from UCLA school of medicine, Robert made her a carrot cake, bought her a dozen yellow roses, and a bottle of organic plum wine. After the party Ghalen fell asleep on the coral couch and Robert put him in his bed.

When he returned to the living room, he found Jamilah sitting at the little desk and looking out on the boulevard.

"Want some more wine?" her husband offered.

"Come sit with me."

He did as she asked.

For some while they looked at each other, not in the eyes but in whole-body gazes.

"I don't know if I want to be a doctor," she confessed.

"But you're already a doctor."

"Not that. I don't know if I want a practice. I mean, when I was a kid you had a GP, a family doctor who knew you by name and took care of you and everybody else in your family. He would talk to you and help you, tell you everything you needed. And the only time you ever went to see a specialist was when your doctor knew that was best. You know what I mean?"

"So . . . is it different bein' a doctor now?"

"It's very expensive setting up a private practice and people who come to you have insurance that won't pay enough for what it costs to be a GP. So, you have to belong to a medical group. But those groups are owned by corporations that tell you how much time you can spend with each patient."

"Like how long?" Robert asked.

"Fourteen minutes, maybe fifteen."

"But what if it takes twenty-five minutes? Can't you just take the time?"

"Yeah, but you'll have to take it away from somebody else."

"And it costs too much to have your own office?"

"Between assistants, insurance, and equipment it'll cost at least twenty thousand dollars a month."

"A month?"

"It's a lot."

"So, why don't you just be a scientist and donate your time to places don't make you see people so short?"

"You wouldn't mind?"

"Uh-uh. I get paid pretty good and you need to be happy at work."

"But I spent all those years getting my degree."

"But then you could help people like those doctors without limits do."

"For free?"

"Yeah, and then you could work as a scientist. That'd be fun."

"Fun. You think being an adult is fun?"

"I'm havin' a good time. Even though there's things wrong I couldn't be happier."

10.

Ghalen was nine when his father refused to let him be promoted to middle school. His teachers all thought that he was too smart and knew too much to stay among his peers.

"But he's not even with kids his own age right now," Robert said to Jamilah. "They already let him skip third grade."

Ghalen was eavesdropping on them, by hiding in the hallway that led to their bedrooms.

"You don't have to shout, Robert," Jamilah complained.

"I'm sorry. I didn't mean to. It's just that I know it would be bad for him to be in a school with bigger kids right now."

"But he's smarter than his teachers," she pleaded.

"That don't matter."

"How can you say that?"

"He's gonna be smart for the rest of his life. He'll be smarter than a whole lotta people he meets and works with. That's not a problem, it's wonderful. Just because he's smarter than someone, it doesn't mean he should go away. It's just like you and me."

"What's that supposed to mean?"

"When I met you, I thought that you were the smartest person that I ever talked to. You had read a thousand books and studied science and medicine, and you knew what was happening all over the world."

Jamilah smiled. Ghalen could see her loving grin through the crack between the door and the jamb.

"We're smart in different ways," Mrs. Fenestra-Horton murmured. "But those children at his school don't challenge Gayley. I know what that's like."

"For you maybe, but our son isn't like regular kids and he's not like the real smart ones neither. He needs to play and to have friends. When he comes home you can show him how to study deeper things, harder things. But right now, he needs to be a little boy."

"How's that like you and me?"

"When I was a kid, they put me in the retarded class. Our classroom was out in a bungalow, away from everybody else. We never had lunch or recess with the rest of the kids. Even if you went to my school, we would have never met. And you know we would have been best friends even way back then."

Jamilah sat back on the coral-colored and walnut couch. Robert had been sitting on Ghalen's hassock, but now he was standing against the wall, the way he always did when he knew something was true but nobody else understood.

"Oh, I see," Jamilah said after a long spate of silence. "You mean that we're taking him away from, from growing up."

Robert smiled at his wife. For all the years they'd known each other she'd listened so closely to things that were hard for him to explain.

"But," Jamilah added, "what if Gayley doesn't like elementary school anymore?"

"We ask him what he doesn't like and then, if he wants to, we let him get skipped ahead or we find another way."

"I wanna stay in the class with my friends," Ghalen said. He had walked out of the hallway.

"But didn't you say that you read the books and did all the lesson plans after the second week?" Jamilah asked her son.

"Yeah. I did. But I still like bein' there. Bruno is my best friend and Lovely Frain said that we could be boyfriend and girlfriend when we get to the sixth grade."

The boy walked into the little living room and took a seat on the couch next to his mother. Neither of his parents chastised him for listening to them, they were discussing him, and he had every right to know what they were talking about.

"But won't you get bored?" Jamilah asked. "If you've already done the work what else can you learn?"

"Mr. Davis is an art teacher and my fifth-grade teacher too. He's going to put up a big piece of paper around the walls of the whole classroom and we're gonna make a mural of the evolution of the human race. It's gonna be six feet high and over fifty feet long and, and Bruno's gonna show me how to make shadows on a drawing."

"And what are you going to show Bruno?" Robert asked.

"I go over some'a his homework at lunchtime. I just tell him where he got the answers wrong and then he goes to figure out how to get 'em right."

Robert smiled at Jamilah, happy that his son could explain better than he could.

"My boys," Jamilah intoned. "You both do better than I can. It's good to know that even without me you'll both do just fine."

"But we'll always have you, Mama."

"And I will always have you."

TOWARD THE MIDDLE OF *THE YEAR OF THE MURAL*, AS Jamilah called it, Ghalen had gone to spend the week with Bruno and his grandparents at a cabin they had rented on Lake Tahoe. Lovely Frain, Ghalen's future sixth-grade girlfriend, would be there too.

Robert worked late that evening to take the place of the

nighttime sous chef, Willa Tormé. They had a good night, but Robert was happy when he got home.

The living room was darker than usual, just one low-watt, electric light was on in there. This meant that Jamilah was still up but unhappy about something.

"Hello," he called.

"In here."

Even in the dim light Robert could still see that she was wearing a mostly yellow and red silk kimono and emerald slippers, also made from silk. She wasn't reading, listening to music, or watching the late-night news. This told Robert that something was wrong. Maybe, he thought, it had to do with her mother.

"Hi," he hailed. "How are ya, honey?"

"Come sit with me."

Robert sat close to her and took her by both hands.

"What's up?" he asked.

"How was your evening?"

He told her about the dinner shift, a small fire that started in the baking oven, and a drunk diner who had come to eat and flirt with Willa.

"He was so mad," Robert said. "I told him that she'd be back tomorrow but that didn't help. He threw his whisky glass on the floor and stomped out."

"Are you going to ban him from the restaurant?"

"I'll tell Willa and Chef Charles. Maybe they'll talk to him."

Their four hands were bound by twenty fingers.

"You know when I went down to San Diego two weeks ago?" she asked.

"Yeah. You were looking to make plastic genes to add to DNA."

"Synthetic, not plastic."

"Yeah."

"Well, there was this doctor there named Henley. Ford Regent

Henley. And he was sent by our boss to get blood on everybody so that we can start using our bodies as the basis for certain experiments."

"Uh-huh."

"They called me almost a week ago and said that they needed another sample."

"They lost the first one?"

"That's what I thought, but when I went in Dr. Henley told me that my sample said cancer. It's probably in my liver."

Robert wanted to get up and walk out of there. He wanted to run. He wanted to put his hands over his ears. There were a thousand questions he wanted to ask but his throat was too tight to speak.

"I'm going to have an exploratory operation day after tomorrow." When she looked up into his face, she could see the struggle he was going through, the tears cascading down his cheeks.

"Baby, don't cry," she said.

"It's just my eyes," he managed to croak. "My eyes."

Jamilah cupped his cheeks with her hands and used her thumbs to wipe away the tears.

"Don't cry, honey," she said. "I don't hardly even have any symptoms yet. The operation is just to see what's there."

Robert hugged her tightly and she held on to him.

"When you hold me like this, Bobby, I feel like nothing could ever pull me away. When you hold me, I always know that we're together forever."

Robert wanted to say that he would hold her forever then, that he'd never let her go and everything would be fine, but his throat closed up again and all he could do was hold on and press his face against the side of her neck.

After they'd held on to each other for a very long time Jamilah whispered, "When Gayley comes home, we can't cry."

"Okay. Okay," Robert sobbed. "Okay."

"Because it might be nothing and he's too young."

"You're too young. Could they give my liver to you?"

"It's too early to talk about silly things like that."

"It's not silly."

"Yes, it is."

THEY REMAINED IN THAT EMBRACE FOR THE REST OF that night, only letting go for as long as it took to go to the toilet. In bed Robert held her from behind, being mindful about not hugging too hard.

"I know that you're going to be all right," he said softly.

"And how do you know that?"

"Because Ghalen needs you. He's going to be a college president or something like that and he needs you to tell him how to get there."

"He needs a good father like you to show him how to be a good man."

"I only know how to cook."

"You know how to exercise and stay clean, how to iron shirts and be kind. You know what's right and what's wrong and, most of all, you know how to love and how to be loved. If my little Gayley turned out to be just like you there would be nothing else I could ask for."

After Jamilah had said this Robert could tell that she'd fallen asleep because of the heaviness of her breathing.

"WHAT IS BREATHING?" HE REMEMBERED ASKING HIS aunt, who really wasn't his aunt, Martine Espada, who lived across the hall from him and his mother when he was little.

"It's the body reaching out to God, telling him everything about you, like a mother's kiss tells her baby that she loves him."

"So, every person that breathes is kissing God and telling him their secrets?"

"Yes, but not only people. Cats and dogs and even ants and fish breathe in his spirit and then breathe out their love for him."

Remembering Martine and hearing Jamilah's soft, even breaths, Robert wondered about his own son and how important it was to protect him from the fear that wanted to come in from almost everywhere.

And then, even though Robert didn't want to, he imagined if Jamilah died, and he had to make sure that Ghalen had everything he needed to be happy and strong. Again, he wanted to run away, but he couldn't, because he was holding Jamilah, and if he let go, she could die. So he lay there next to her, holding on for life. He didn't sleep at all that night, but it felt okay because holding her and seeing her he knew, for at least that evening, she'd be his and alive.

THE NEXT MORNING, HE GOT UP EARLY AND CALLED Chef Charles to say that Jamilah was sick and that he had to take care of her. He made peach-filled waffles and tofu scramble for Jamilah and then went to wake her.

"Hi," she said when he jostled her shoulder. She was smiling, maybe even happy.

"I made waffles and tofu," he said.

"I'll be right in."

THEY SAT IN THE DINETTE WHERE THE WINDOW WAS shaded by an exceptionally tall palm tree. Robert made strawberry-mango nectar to go with the food.

"What do you want to do today?" he asked his wife.

"Why aren't you at work already?"

"I told Chef Charles that you were sick, and I had to take care of you."

"You didn't tell him about the operation, did you?"

"No."

Jamilah took stock of their situation. She understood that he needed to take care of her, to try to save her as best he could. In a way she saw this as a blessing for both of them. Jamilah had seen many terminal patients in the downtown hospital where she interned. So many were alone and so many others had loved ones who either refused to accept or could not understand what was happening. Often, she'd sit with dying adults and children just to be there. Robert understood this need naturally, and she would have to reciprocate.

"Let's go to Griffith Park in the afternoon," she said. "We could walk around and then go to the observatory after the sun goes down."

"And look at the stars," Robert said, joyously.

He had been taken there by one of his *might be* fathers, William Truman, on his seventh birthday. He ate corn dogs and saw the craters of the moon, met a clown who gave him a balloon, and saw a hawk grab a gray rabbit and carry it off to feed her chicks.

SCALING A GRASS-COVERED HILL IN THE LATE AFTERnoon Robert and Jamilah were hand in hand, breathing hard. They settled at the highest point and shared a pomegranate instead of eating corn dogs.

"It's so beautiful here," Jamilah said, resting her head on her lover's shoulder.

"It's beautiful being here with you."

"I don't want you being afraid for me, Robert. I want you to love me, no matter what happens."

"I do love you."

"Yeah, but, if you get all scared about me being sick or maybe even dying, we'll lose a lot of the time we have together, and that's something you can never get back."

She rose up to look at him. He was staring down into the valley of trees below, with a very serious expression on his face.

"What are you thinking?" she asked.

"Um, that, I mean," he said and then stopped.

Jamilah tapped the end of his nose with one finger and said, "What is it, silly?"

"It feels like, when we're together, that we think like one person working out a problem, like one person, not two."

They decided to go home after that, skipping the Observatory for a night alone together.

11.

After spending a week at the cabin, Ghalen came home on Sunday, around midday. Running up the stairwell to the third floor he burst into the living room and saw his mother and father sitting on the pink fabric and dark wood couch. He knew there was something wrong upon seeing them.

"Am I late?" he asked.

"No," Jamilah said. "Why would you say that?"

She stood up, wavered a bit, and then came over to hug her son.

He noticed that she moved differently, as if maybe she had hurt her leg. And her hug lingered a little bit longer than her usual happy-to-see-you embrace. His father shouldn't have been there at all. He was supposed to be at work. Ghalen planned to ask his mother for a ride out to Indus so that he could help with the afternoon shift.

"What's wrong?" he asked.

Jamilah's face looked like it did when she wanted to say no to something that was really yes. But she didn't speak. Instead, she started to cry. Robert jumped up from the couch and put his arms around Ghalen's mother in the same gentle way that she had held her son.

"I'm sorry," came to Ghalen's lips. "What did I do?"

Before answering, Robert guided Jamilah back to the couch and sat her down by descending with her. Then he looked up at his son and said, "We didn't want to tell you this now, Ghalen, but mom is sick."

YEARS LATER GHALEN, THE MAN, COULD REMEMBER THAT moment. It felt like an article he'd read on an online encyclopedia about the tsunami. The emotion surged within him like the insuppressible tidal wave forcing its way onto the land, tearing down everything that had been before. He felt it in his hands and feet, up through his head and in his eyes. But he did not cry. He would not, because, for the first time he realized that he'd never felt another's pain.

"I understood what it was my mother was feeling and my father too," he said to the counselor at the Sierra Conservation Center, a level 1 California State Prison. "It was pain for a loss that I shared with them. I, I knew that I was responsible for them because I was theirs, their child, their genes, their hope."

AT THE DINETTE TABLE, EATING PEANUT BUTTER AND plum jam on cracked wheat bread, Robert explained that Jamilah had cancer in her liver.

"Can they cut it out?" Ghalen asked.

"Not completely," Jamilah said softly. "It's spread. They want to give me chemotherapy, but I don't know if it's worth it."

"But could it help you?"

"Maybe. But probably not and it would make me so sick."

"But, Mom, maybe it could save your life." Though he would not cry Ghalen couldn't keep the whine of pain out of his voice.

"It's true, honey," Jamilah said. "That's what Dad and me were talking about when you came home. He says that black carrot juice might help. That's what Chef Charles says. And it isn't nearly as hard on the body."

Ghalen had just recently turned ten. Even though he'd been singled out as the smartest kid in his school, he knew that he was dependent on knowledge from his parents, their friends, and sometimes his teachers. He felt trapped in his mind because, while he didn't want his mother to die, he had no idea how to save her.

"It's whatever you want, Mama," he said.

Something changed in his mother's eyes when he said this. She smiled at him and said, "But I will need you to help me make up my mind."

GHALEN HAD COME HOME THAT EARLY AFTERNOON. AT nine that night they were still talking. They'd moved from the dinette to his parents' bedroom, spreading out across their vast California king bed. At first, they talked about chemotherapy and its rate of success, and then naturalistic cures celebrated by vegans around the world and throughout history. But soon the talk became about adventures they'd had over the last decade and before. Ghalen's parents told him about how they met and what they taught each other. Then they talked about Jamilah's mother and her father, who was what they called MIA in Vietnam. Robert had three possible fathers, and Jamilah's mother, Pristine, was estranged from the family for reasons they did not give.

"Do you miss your mother?" Ghalen asked Jamilah. He'd known that Pristine Fenestra didn't like his father, but that hadn't mattered to him until that morning, when he realized that he might lose his own mom.

"I love my mother," Jamilah's said after pondering her son's question. "I love her very much. She cared for me the only way she knew how and when that meant she didn't like Dad, well, I had to make a choice between them."

"And you chose Dad."

"Yes," she said, tousling his longish locks. "And I was pregnant with you."

"We send her a Christmas card every year," Robert said. "But she never writes back."

"Does that make you sad, Mom?"

"Yes. But that doesn't matter, because between you and dad I have more happiness than I ever thought was possible."

SOMEWHERE AROUND MIDNIGHT THEY ALL FELL ASLEEP. A few hours later Robert woke up and carried Ghalen to his bedroom, took off the drowsing boy's shirt and pants, then spread the covers over him.

"How's Mom?" Ghalen remembered asking just before falling back into a doze.

"She's sleeping," Robert said to the already slumbering boy.

THAT NIGHT GHALEN HAD A DREAM THAT HE REMEMbered in detail for the rest of his life. Not only did he fully recall the long reverie but, as time went by, he studied it, looking for answers that would never come.

In his dream Ghalen was walking down a hard dirt road in the middle of a very dark forest, like the wooded area around the cottage that Bruno's mom's mom had rented.

Ghalen walked and walked, looking for someone, a woman. When he'd started the journey, he knew who it was he sought but after so many long hours of looking he'd forgotten her name and even her face. This amnesia saddened him, made him feel that he would never get where he was supposed to be going.

In the forest on either side of the road he saw redbirds,

whitetail foxes, a brown bear, and even a honey-colored cougar. He wanted to go off the road to watch the animals, to look closer for the insects he knew must be there. But there was no time to stop or have fun, no time to climb trees or even sing and shout out into the deep silence of the dense wood.

He had to find the Lady of the Woods—the name he'd given to the woman he had almost completely forgotten. It was getting cold, and Ghalen was thirsty. The sun, somewhere beyond the forest canopy, was going down. That's when the boy came to a crossroads. To the left the path went down into a darkness so profound that it seemed to be more like a cave than woodlands. The road to the right was a steep incline ascending toward whatever light—sun or moon—came from the sky. From this road came a din of wild creatures. Their roars and chirps, howls and barks, frightened the boy, brought to mind the cries of dying animals being chased down by predators or hit by speeding cars.

Straight ahead the forest thinned, giving way to a treeless vista, a great field of golden grain. The sun was setting on that field, making it glow. This fertile countryside made him smile. He imagined emerging from the suffocating woods, being free to search for the Lady. But he knew she wasn't there. He could see everything as far as the great arc of the horizon. It was beautiful but the place he most wanted to go represented the abandonment of his mission.

There was a large stone at the side of the path, just before the crossroads. Ghalen decided that it was placed there for travelers like himself to sit and ponder before making the decision of which way to go.

Night was coming, but it was taking its time.

Sitting there, gazing upon that great lush field, Ghalen considered going down the path to the left, leading, he thought, to some great underground cavern where the Lady might well be lost. It would be like night down there. The rocks would be flinty and sharp, wet, and always cold. It was quite possible that she was down there, suffering, maybe dying. But he might never see her in that darkness. And if he went after her he might die without ever knowing if this was the way she went.

Then he considered scaling the sheer and precarious incline of the path to the right. There was light up there to see, and the Lady might well have gone that way instead of entering the great field where anyone might see her and run her down. The animals wouldn't frighten her because she'd lived among forest creatures for the entirety of her life.

Ghalen thought that this might be a good way to go, but the roars and howls frightened him. And even if she wasn't afraid, if the Lady went that way she could have been eaten and all he would find would be her bones, gnawed upon by hungry beasts.

After considering right and left Ghalen wondered if he shouldn't strike out into the great garden of the plain. She wasn't out there, but he was only small and thirsty and probably would never find her, anyway.

SUNSET WAS SLOW IN COMING BUT IT WOULDN'T BE long before night fell, this is what Ghalen thought. He had to make a decision. He had to choose a path.

That's when he thought about retracing his steps and going back the way he'd come.

"If I go back," he said to himself. "Then I could travel far enough to get to a place before I started this search, a place before the Lady got lost. I could go to where I knew her name and I was home and warm, and the world would be just the same as it was before I forgot."

This idea sounded best to the boy. He turned around to glimpse the path he'd traveled for so long. But it wasn't there. Night had finally fallen and everywhere was dark.

Ghalen was sitting on a stone at the side of a path he could no longer see. He couldn't walk now because there were many rocks and fallen branches in the path, also, slippery mud, and sharp-toothed animals.

Ghalen pulled his coat around his shoulders, deciding to wait until morning. But then, in the darkness he had a fright. What if morning never came? What if the night here at the crossroads lasted for months instead of hours? Had he come all this way to be lost like the woman he'd forgotten?

SOMETHING HEAVY FELL SOMEWHERE IN THE HOUSE. Ghalen woke up but he couldn't keep his eyes open. He turned under the covers and found a comfortable position. He was almost asleep again when something bumped.

"Watch it!" a woman said loudly.

It wasn't his mother.

His mother.

Ghalen thought about his mom. There was something that he should remember. Something that he didn't want to remember. His mom . . . was sick.

Ghalen got up and out of the bed so fast that he tripped and fell to the floor. He banged his knee but didn't worry about that as he jumped into his jeans and put on his STEEL DRIVIN' JOHN HENRY T-shirt.

Barefoot, he ran down the hall and toward the front door of the apartment, where the bumps and strangers' talk came from.

When he got to the living room he saw his father, dressed like he was, in jeans and T-shirt, and three people, two men and one woman, all dressed in white and carrying a stretcher upon which lay his mom.

"Mom!" he shouted, running heedlessly toward her.

Before he could get there, he was scooped up by his father, held in his deceptively strong arms.

"Hold up!" Robert called to the two men carrying the litter.

They stopped and Robert approached Jamilah, bending down so that Ghalen could see her clearly.

Her face was drawn and thin, even more lean than it was the night before. Her eyes seemed to have the same trouble Ghalen's did when he first woke up. But she struggled to keep them open. She smiled. And then reached out to touch, then hold his hand.

"My little soldier," she said. "Don't worry. They just have to take a look at me up at the medical center. Come, come closer."

Robert put him down and Ghalen leaned over to hug his mom.

"Look in your sock drawer," she whispered in his ear. "Look there."

She kissed his cheek and then the cot-bearers were off again, heading down the stairs.

"Is she gonna be okay?" Son asked Father.

"She has to be," Father said to Son.

12.

obert and Ghalen wandered back to their rooms to go through their morning rituals. These were very close to the same. They both did push-ups and sit-ups, made their beds, took showers, and brushed their teeth. Robert listened to classical music while Ghalen preferred to move through silence.

Robert ended his morning routine by ironing his work clothes, even though he was not going to work that morning. Ghalen took the time to go over the syllabus he'd created to know where he was in his homework and studies in life in general.

Both man and boy were calmed by these *morning ablutions*, as Jamilah called them.

They met in the kitchen where Robert prepared breakfast using water Ghalen had set to boil. Then the boy set the table, feeling a little brokenhearted because there were only two settings.

When the breakfast was served and they sat across from each other, Ghalen broke protocol and asked, "Is Mama gonna die, Dad?"

Robert sat up, intending to say, no, of course not. But the words wouldn't come. Tears sprouted from the man's eyes. His lips quivered.

Ghalen got up and hugged his father's head with all his

strength. Robert raised a hand, placing it on his son's shoulder. The man cried like a child while Ghalen held on.

GHALEN WAS WASHING THE BREAKFAST DISHES WHEN the phone rang.

"Hello?" Robert answered hopefully. "Yes, doctor. No. I will. Two o'clock? We'll be there."

He hung up the wall phone, grinned, and said, "He said that she was stable and that we could come to see her at two."

Ghalen heard these words, but they didn't elate him as they had his father. He knew that his mother was dying, that she would pass away soon. They'd never go to New York together as she had promised. Promises, he thought, were the same thing as hope. Hoping that something will happen didn't mean that it would.

"That's great, Dad," he said. "We should get her some flowers."

"Yeah. Jammy likes flowers. Sunflowers are her favorite."

Ghalen studied his father, seeing him as he never had. Before, when his mother was there, Robert would get excited about something and she would say something practical, like, *Westwood Florist usually has them.*

"Who called the ambulance this morning, Dad?"

"She was moaning in her sleep," Robert said to the floor. "When I put my hand on her forehead, feelin' for fever, she woke up and told me that something in her chest hurt. She said to call Dr. Fenton."

"Was it her heart?"

"The paramedics said it wasn't a heart attack. I don't know what it was."

This confession saddened Ghalen's father. The young man knew how much respect his father had for intelligence, that

Robert was feeling that, if he were only smarter, if he knew the answers to these questions, then Jamilah would not die.

"Only God could save her," Ghalen said, though he wasn't sure that he believed in God.

"Yeah," Robert agreed. "That's why we go to church."

THEY LEFT THE APARTMENT AT TWELVE THIRTY, STOPPED at Westwood Florist to have them put together a bouquet of six different kinds of sunflowers, and then made the trek through the UCLA campus to the hospital.

Robert had put on his black suit and white shirt but didn't wear a tie because Jamilah was the only one in the house who knew how to make the knot. Ghalen thought that if Jamilah had seen her husband walking across the campus, she would have said that he was very handsome.

Father and son didn't talk much on the long walk. Robert hefted the bouquet and Ghalen walked beside him, thinking about all the responsibilities he would have to take on. Even though he wouldn't say it, Ghalen knew that his mother was already gone, that it would be up to him to make sure that all the little things were done around the house. He wanted to ask his mom about the bank accounts and checkbooks used to pay their bills. He wanted to ask but knew that he couldn't because just talking about a future without her would make both his parents cry.

THEY ENTERED THE BIG HOSPITAL COMPLEX THROUGH two huge, automatic glass doors. At the front desk they were given directions to Jamilah's room.

On the eighth floor they found the nurses' station. Behind the desk sat a dour-faced woman, somewhere in her forties, who had dark circles under her eyes.

"Yes?" she said.

"Hi," Robert rejoined. "We're here to see Jamilah, um, Jamilah Fenestra-Horton."

Ghalen watched as the woman's hard face turned soft and sorry.

"Oh. Um, let me call Dr. Fenton."

She got on the phone, cupping a hand over the speaker and her mouth so you couldn't hear or see what she was saying.

"The doctor said that he wanted to walk us through what we have to do for Mom," Robert told Ghalen, brimming with confidence in his suit, with his flowers, and them being so close to the love of his life.

Only a minute or two later a tall man with a bristling gray mustache, dressed in a knee-length smock, strode up to them. He held out a hand and Robert shook it.

"We tried to call you, Mr. Horton," the mustachioed man said.

"You did call, Dr. Fenton. You told us to get here by two."

"I called again at ten to one, but nobody answered."

"We were buying flowers and then walking up here."

"I'm so sorry," Dr. Fenton said. He glanced at Ghalen, a helpless look on his face. "Jamilah passed at a few minutes past noon."

"What?" Robert asked, truly not understanding.

"It was a pulmonary embolism."

"What are you saying, doctor?"

"Jamilah died, Robert."

"No she didn't. They said that it wasn't a heart attack."

"No, not a heart attack, a blood clot," Fenton said. "In her lung."

Robert dropped to his knees, scattering the sunflowers across the white linoleum floor. Elbows akimbo, he held his hands out to his sides with palms up and head bowed. Ghalen imagined that his father was praying, but for what he did not know.

Dr. Fenton leaned down to help Robert to his feet, but Ghalen said, "No, doctor. Let him be for a minute." These were the words that his mother used when either Ghalen or his dad needed a moment to collect themselves—which was something else she'd often said.

Fenton straightened up and Ghalen gripped his dad's shoulder.

Robert didn't cry. He didn't utter a word. He just stayed on his knees, seeing nothing, saying nothing. The only thing he felt was the boy's hand, clenching the black fabric of his suit, keeping him from sinking through the floor, into despair.

"I SHOULD HAVE LEARNED HOW TO DRIVE," WERE THE first words Robert spoke on the long walk back home.

Jamilah's body had already been taken away to a part of the hospital that they couldn't enter. The doctor's assistant gave Ghalen all the information that he'd have to share with the undertaker in three days.

"If I, I had a car we could have gotten up there faster and I could have talked to her, maybe saved her," Robert added.

Ghalen took his hand.

"They should have let us see her," the distraught husband argued. "I can't know something unless I see it. I have to see and touch things in order to learn 'em. That's what Miss Rozalia said. Did I ever tell you about Miss Rozalia, Gayley?"

"No, Dad," he lied.

"She ran the special needs bungalow for three years. One day she saw me taking a toy car apart and then put it back together. From then on, she worked with me and got me to talk because it wasn't that I couldn't say things but that I was afraid people would laugh at me. She was the reason I got to go to normal classes in the sixth grade and then in junior high school too."

"Mom's dead," Ghalen said.

"She is?"

"Uh-huh."

"I know she must be, I know it, but I need to see her. It's my condition."

"We're gonna get Mom back," Ghalen vowed. "We have to give her a funeral where everybody can come say goodbye."

"But when?"

"We'll be able to see her body in a few days and have the funeral after that."

"We will?"

"I promise."

GHALEN FOLLOWED HIS FATHER UP THE APARTMENT stairs. Once inside he felt emptiness emanating from every corner and in the dimness of the light. That was the first time he actually tried to cry, but could not. Dry eyes felt like a betrayal, the barren rooms just deserts for not loving his mother enough, where even Robert's posture proved his own fidelity.

"I'll make dinner now," the stooped-over man said.

"Okay."

THE BOY WALKED DOWN THE HALL TO HIS BEDROOM, feeling each step as if it were reverberating under its sole. When he got there, he couldn't imagine what to do. He had a laptop computer, as did every kid on the honor roll, but there was nothing on the whole World Wide Web that called to him. He didn't want to read or watch TV, or to call Bruno or Lovely.

But there was something.

Sitting at the edge of the bed, looking down at his useless hands, he remembered her words, *Look in your sock drawer.*

The sock drawer was on the top, leftmost side of the three-tier, nine-drawer pine chest. Ghalen was hoping for something he could use to help his mother. But there was only a dozen or so balled-up pairs of mostly one-color socks. They looked so sad there, so useless. Ghalen reached down and gathered two hands worth of the balls. He lifted them up, maybe intending to throw them on the floor, when there came a raspy sound that yarn wouldn't make.

There, under the socks, was secreted a lime-green envelope.

The return address was on Wilshire Boulevard, to an E.B. in suite 201. The letter was addressed to Mr. Ghalen Romeo Horton. When he tore open the envelope a business card fell out. This card contained the address and phone number of a Miss Emily Barth J.D., Esq.

To my loving son, Ghalen,

This is Mom, Gayley. I love you, you must always remember that. Writing this letter is the hardest thing I've ever had to do. You're still so young, too young to lose me but I couldn't help it.

I love you and your father does too. You are our heart and soul. And so, I deeply regret what I have to ask of you. Your father is a good man. He will protect you, make meals for you, and teach you by showing you how to live. But he's not good at things that have to do with the outside world. Things like paying new bills or going places he's never been. Sometimes he has to go over and over what it is he will have to do. If he doesn't have the time for that he'll get upset and confused. You're going to have to help him with that stuff. He won't be able to plan for my funeral or for anything else that he's never done. It'll be hard, you two living alone without me, but I'm sure you can do it. You're the smartest person I've ever known.

The first thing you'll have to do is call Emily Barth. Her business card is in the envelope with this letter. She has my will, all my insurance policies, and anything that my job has to offer as far as benefits. Em has agreed to meet with you now and again if you need advice or any other kind of help.

I'm dying, baby, and there's nothing anyone can do about that. I have to accept that, and you do too. There's nothing else to say, nothing that either one of us can do about it. Don't tell dad about what the letter says until after you talk to Miss Barth. I've written to him too. The lawyer has that letter.

I love love love you, honey
Your Mother

When Ghalen finished reading the letter for the fifth time, he realized that tears were coming from his eyes. He rubbed the water from his cheekbones and looked at the moisture on his fingertips, wondering if this was sorrow.

13

Once or twice in his life, before his mother died, Ghalen had lied to his father. He remembered the time he'd taken money from Jamilah's business drawer and told Robert that she said he could. And then, only minutes later, he admitted the lie.

But now he lied continually, rarely giving it a second thought.

He considered this new state of dishonesty while crossing Glendon Avenue, headed for the tall office building where Emily Barth had her suite. He'd called Miss Barth from the phone in the living room while his father was in the backyard watering their tomato garden.

"Martindale, Loomis, and Barth," a man's voice answered.

"May I speak to Miss Barth please?"

"May I say who's calling?"

"Ghalen Romeo Horton, Mrs. Jamilah Horton's son."

Ghalen had already decided that if his father came in that he'd hang up, say he was calling Bruno, but that his best friend was not home.

"Hello?" a pleasant woman's voice asked.

"Miss, Miss Barth?"

"This is she. Is this Ghalen?"

"Yes, ma'am. I found a letter from my mother that told me to call you."

"I've been expecting a call, but I didn't know it would be this soon. You don't live very far away now do you?"

"Five and a half blocks."

"Why don't you come over right now. I have a lot to tell you."

THE LOBBY OF THE OFFICE BUILDING HAD HUGE WINDOWS for walls. These glass walls were tinted green making the hall seem somehow softer than Ghalen expected. The boy walked up to a big counter behind which stood a friendly-looking man who wore a gray-green uniform.

"I'm supposed to go to Miss Emily Barth's office," Ghalen said. "Can you tell me how to get there?"

The security guard wore thick glasses that magnified the size of his eyes. Ghalen thought that he looked something like a fish that had learned to live on land. The idea of a species of fish that resembled humans and breathed air made him grin.

The googly-eyed guard returned the smile and said, "Thirty-second floor to the right. Elevators are behind you."

THE DOUBLE DOORS TO SUITE 3201 WERE MADE OF dark, finely finished wood. A shiny golden plaque, affixed to the right-side door was embossed with the names MARTINDALE, LOOMIS, AND BARTH. Ghalen decided that the plate must have been made from real gold, the hallway leading to the law offices was that sumptuous.

He stood there a moment, searching with his eyes for a doorbell, saw none, and then wondered what to do. He knocked and waited but nobody opened the door or called out "Come in." So, he screwed up his courage, turned the right-hand doorknob, and pushed the door open.

The office was a large space with a thick, turquoise carpet and almost festive coral walls. In the center of the space stood a desk that reminded the boy of the grand piano they had at the Constant Traveler Riverside Church. The grand desk was constructed from dark, dark brown wood.

Behind the desk sat a Black woman, a huge lady who seemed to have been chosen for her size to sit at that enormous piece of furniture. Her skin was a lustrous brown and her hair the color of processed, chipped redwood. The woman's round face broke into a friendly smile.

"Can I help you, young man?" she said.

Ghalen did not answer immediately. He was mesmerized by the size and colors, the smile and friendliness of this woman. She had a big chest, and Ghalen wanted more than anything for her to hug him close.

"Cat got your tongue?" she asked. He heard a Texan twang at the end of her question. This made him like her even more.

"No, Miss Mona," he said.

"You know my name?"

"Your nameplate says Mona Tremont. My name is Ghalen Romeo Horton and I'm here to see Miss Emily Barth. She's a lawyer."

"You here to sell her Cub Scout cookies or sumpin'?"

"No, ma'am. My mother died yesterday, and she left, um, instructions with Miss Barth."

When Mona Tremont's expression turned serious, Ghalen worried that he'd said something wrong.

The receptionist looked to her left and then her right. She stood from her big chair and came around the desk to the boy. Leaning over him, she then lifted Ghalen in her arms, squeezing him.

"You poor thing," she said, holding tight. "You poor baby."

When she hugged him, Ghalen's eyes closed, and he let himself feel comforted. He wanted to stay like that, pressed to Mona's big bosom for days. When she started walking Ghalen felt as if he was on the water, supported and reassured by a lake named Mona.

"Poor thing," she said. And then, "This is Ghalen Romeo Horton."

He opened his eyes to find himself in a personal office. There, behind a white desk, was a white woman much smaller than Mona. The white woman wore wire-rimmed glasses and had hair a lighter red than the receptionist's. Mona's hair stood out from her head and face, where the smaller woman's mane was pulled back so tight that he thought it must hurt.

Mona put him down, but before she could pull her hand away, he grabbed two of her fingers, pressing them gently.

"Mm," Mona grunted. "This handsome young man is here to talk to you about his mama who has passed."

"Hello, Ghalen," the woman he suspected was Emily Barth said. "Come have a seat."

Miss Barth's small white desk was made from something synthetic. In front of the desk there were two lime-colored chairs. Ghalen climbed onto one of them, and the lawyer stood and came around to sit in the other.

He turned to see if Miss Mona had a seat, but she was already gone from the office.

Emily Barth was young like Jamilah, and she wore a gray suit that looked like it was a man's. Ghalen was surprised that she sat before him instead of behind the desk.

"How are you?" Emily Barth asked.

"Fine," Ghalen answered with a nod. He was looking directly at her the way his father had taught him.

"I'm so sorry about your mother. I knew her from our freshman year at UCLA. We didn't have many classes together, but we lived in the same dorm, and she was so smart. She came to see me a few weeks ago when she found out about the cancer."

"Uh-uh," Ghalen denied. "She didn't know she was sick until a few days ago."

Emily studied the boy, like a teacher does when they're trying to see how to approach the lesson she must impart.

"Well," she said. "Your mother knew how sick she was for a while longer than that. She didn't tell you and your dad because she wanted to be sure, and she wanted to be prepared if she left you."

"She died," Ghalen corrected.

"Yes, she did. She didn't want to upset you."

But I am upset, Ghalen thought, *and my father is too*. He decided not to say these things.

"How come her letter had a stamp and your name for a return address?" he asked instead.

"Your mother put my return address on it in case, in case she passed before you got it and the letter got lost somehow. I think that she was planning to talk to you about me, but she left the letter in case something happened before she got around to it."

Jamilah had started writing letters to her son when he was five and she realized that he was learning how to read. She'd slip the envelope, with Ghalen's name on it, under his door, in the morning before he woke up. It was an extra-special connection between them.

"What did my mom want you to do?"

"Your mom had me write up a will and gave me her important papers—life insurance policies, and the agreement between her and her employers in the circumstance of her death. She wanted me to explain to you what will happen with the money she leaves you and your dad. And then, after I talk to you about it, we can talk to your father together. That's what she wanted."

"Okay."

"First, do you know what a will is?"

"It's when somebody dies, and they want to say where their money and property goes afterward."

"And life insurance?"

"That's money they save that goes to the family after they die."

"I'm impressed. Your mother told me how smart you are."

Ghalen didn't know what to say to this compliment. He would have rather not been smart if that meant his mother could be instead.

"If you're going to explain things," he said, "then can I have a pencil and some paper to write them down?"

"I can give you a printout of the details to follow along."

"Yeah, but I might not understand. If I write it down, I'll remember what you said when I'm readin' it."

The redheaded lawyer smiled and nodded. She took out a clear plastic clipboard from her white desk, attached ten or so blank sheets of paper, and then handed these and a yellow number two pencil to her young client.

SHE TALKED AND HE TOOK NOTES FOR OVER AN HOUR. Now and again, he'd see a jet plane either coming down for a landing or taking off, headed for some faraway destination. In the lower altitudes there were birds flying alone and in flocks. Below the birds, there were cars moving on the asphalt arteries. And, above all of this, there was a deep blue sky and white clouds that sometimes turned dark. Ghalen wished that he could live in an apartment with the kind of view Emily Barth had. Then, remembering his mother, he felt guilty but could not have said what about.

"Are you listening to me, Ghalen?" Barth asked.

"Yes." He turned to meet her stern gaze. He was used to teachers questioning him in this manner at Holloway Elementary School and in Sunday school at church.

"What did I say?"

"That it would be better if I told my dad that mom had just mentioned that you were her lawyer and that I took it on myself to see you."

There was now an expression of surprise on the lawyer's face.

"Oh," she said. "Yes, sorry, I thought you were looking out of the window, daydreaming."

"Mama says that people think that because I can listen and look at something else at the same time. She wasn't sure but she thought it was because there might be some kinda dis, dis, dis-connection between the left and right sides of my brain.

"But I'm not gonna lie to my dad about mom. He loves her more than anything, ever. He said that before he met her, he never thought he could have a wife, or a son like me."

Emily Barth's brows knitted, and her chin swung a little to the right, as if she had heard something that she couldn't identify.

"Okay," she said. "Your mom just didn't want him to think that she didn't trust him to take care of these business, um, matters."

"He might feel bad for a little while, but he knows that not anybody could do everything. Like if your toilet broke you couldn't fix it, but you wouldn't get mad at the plumber because he could do it better than you."

"So, what are you going to tell him?"

"I'll say that I went to see you because your mom's lawyer and then I'll tell him what you said to me."

"Did you write it all down?"

He nodded dutifully.

"Everything?" she doubted.

"Pretty much."

"About the bank?"

"We have to go there with you and set up an account to,

um"—he looked down at his notes—"set up an account to receive regular payments."

"And the funeral?"

"We need to send invitations to all the names and addresses of everybody on our Christmas card list."

"You really are an amazing young man," she said. "When your mother told me that you'd understand it all, I found it very hard to believe."

"Can I go now?"

"Do you have any questions?"

"When can we go to see my mom?"

"SO, YOUR MOTHER LEFT YOU THAT LETTER?" ROBERT asked at the dinner table that night.

"Uh-huh." Ghalen was concentrated on the stuffed eggplant meal that his father had brought home from Indus. "I think she was worried that going to see Miss Barth would make you sad."

"She right about that. I am sad," Ghalen's dad said. "I wake up over and over again in the night thinkin' that she should be there next to me. I know she's not gonna be there, but only after I get up and look. And, and, and when I hear things in the house like a bump or maybe even a car outside, I have to call out to her. I have to because if I don't, she might think I'm gone."

"Did you eat at work, Dad?"

"Not really. Why?"

"'Cause you're not eatin' your eggplant."

"I'm not all that hungry. You want mine?"

14.

Two mornings later Emily Barth sent a car to come and take Robert and Ghalen to the funeral home. The driver's name was Ivo Blaney.

"I never heard the name Ivo before," Ghalen said.

"Tis Irish," the driver said with a slight nod and a put-on accent. "My father said that if I couldn'ta been born there at least I should have got one'a it's names. Your name sounds Irish too."

"People have told me that," Ghalen said happily from the backseat. "But my mom just liked it and never really looked it up."

Robert was quiet in the seat next to his son. His eyes, as his mother Myrtle might have said, were peeled, looking straight ahead, expecting, hoping, hungering after the sight of his wife. He wore his freshly ironed black suit, and Ghalen had looked up how to make a square knot for his tie.

"Thank you, honey," Robert had said to his son before they went down to the car. "I know your mama would like it for me to have a tie. She always thought I looked good in one."

THE FLEETING DOVE FUNERAL HOME, IN SANTA MONICA, had a mortuary on the premises. The funeral director, Matrice Benning, guided them through the church-like rooms for the services, then to a back area that was cold and had an insistent bad odor.

"We don't usually have people come to see the body until the funeral itself," Matrice was saying. "But Miss Barth asked us to make an exception in your case, Mr. Horton."

"I need to see her," Robert said. "When she died at the hospital, they moved her before I got there, and they wouldn't let me see her. They wouldn't let me see her."

"That's what Miss Barth told us," Matrice replied. "You need to see her, but do you think this viewing would be good for your son?"

Robert was light-headed and walked with his right hand on Ghalen's shoulder. The boy didn't mind. It made him feel useful.

"I'm okay, Ms. Benning," Ghalen said. "I want to see her too."

SHE WORE NO MAKEUP, AND HER MOUTH AND EYES WERE closed. Her skin was the same dark brown but seemed somehow faded. Other than this she looked like herself, and for a moment the boy smiled, something inside him expecting her to open those eyes, sit up, and say, "Hey, baby."

She was covered by a white sheet up to just below her bare shoulders.

Robert strode right up to the gurney and placed his hand on her right clavicle. Standing there, stiff and erect, he cried like a child.

Seeing his father in this state brought tears to Ghalen's eyes, but he forced them down because he knew that his father needed him to be strong.

Looking around the room for something to help his dad, the boy saw a chair in the corner of the small, square room and pulled the heavy wooden seat to where his father stood.

"Sit down, Dad. You can visit for a while."

The gratitude on Robert's face, when he glanced at his son, moved the boy almost to tears again.

"Thank you, son, thank you," he said as he lowered onto the blocky blond chair, perching at the very edge. From there he worked Jamilah's right hand from under the sheet and held it with both his hands as delicately as one might a newborn.

Ghalen stood next to his father, just above his mother's resting face. He watched Robert gazing at his wife, his expression most like an eye opened wide, intent on taking in everything. The man's gentle and yet intense posture of receiving eclipsed his sorrow for the moment.

For Ghalen his mother was dead. She had passed on and there was no way he could be with her. But he could see that this was not true for his father. Impossibly, love seemed to move both ways between the dead woman and the grieving man. Though he could not have explained it, Ghalen felt that he was in the presence of a miracle; that, for the first time, he could see love and not just feel it.

In this way and in this mood, he watched his father as intently as Robert did his wife.

And so, Robert sat, holding Jamilah's dead hand while Ghalen stood like a sergeant at arms attending this somber function. The boy said nothing, thought nothing, just waited. His father had lost more than he had. He loved his mother, missed her terribly, but her death had piled many more responsibilities on his shoulders, one of which was this silent watch where the boy could not give in to hunger, fatigue, or thirst.

Three times during this vigil the door opened, and Ms. Benning looked in, her mostly expressionless face coming very close to showing annoyance.

AFTER A VERY LONG TIME ROBERT SAID, "THERE'S STILL love for us from her."

"What, Dad?"

"You can't lose love by dyin'," he said. "Once it happens it's always there. She can't say it and we can't hear, but we feel it, we know it."

"We always know that Mama loved us?"

"She still does," Robert corrected. He was staring at her face with enough life for both of them and Ghalen too.

This sentiment disturbed the boy. It wasn't that he didn't understand his father's feelings, but he couldn't find that truth in his own heart. And he couldn't share his doubts because his disbelief might somehow wound his father.

"You think we should be going, Dad?"

"You can go," Robert replied. "I wanna stay here."

"But they have to get back to work and we need to get all the invitations ready to send."

"Can't you do that? I don't wanna leave her here all alone like this. She's cold and it's gonna be dark."

But she's dead, Ghalen thought.

"They have to close up, Dad."

"I'll just sit here and hold her hand, keep her a little warm, at least through the night."

When Ghalen got upset or nervous his mother had taught him to slow down by counting his breaths.

"Don't try to figure out whatever's bothering you," she'd said. "Just breathe in and when you exhale count, one. Then two, then three, until you get up to ten. Then you start over. Before you know it, whatever was botherin' you will be smaller and easier to deal with."

He started breathing while his father settled back into his post.

One, two, three to ten and then again, and then again.

Frustration gave way to revelation. The boy placed his hand on his father's shoulder as he had at the ICU when they found out that Jamilah had died. After many long minutes Robert released the dead woman's hand and stood.

"She wants me to take you home and feed you, boy. I know she does."

"I am a little hungry."

"Okay. Let's go."

Robert moved quickly toward the door, as if knowing that if he hesitated that he might never leave.

IVO WAS WAITING IN THE MORTUARY PARKING LOT. HE was leaning against the hood of the car, smoking a menthol cigarette.

"There ya are," he said to father and son. "I was worried that you might'a fallen in."

Robert wasn't listening and Ghalen was too young to be insulted and so they rode home saying little, drifting silently in their own worlds.

Much later that night Robert and Ghalen were seated at the dinette table assembling and addressing the announcements of the funeral. Robert had better penmanship, so he wrote the addresses while Ghalen stuffed the envelopes, sealed, and put stamps on them.

At one point Robert stopped and said, "You put my mom's address on the list by mistake."

"No," Ghalen said. "Grandma Myrtle would be very upset if we didn't invite her."

"But she never leaves the hospital."

"I called Dr. Singh yesterday. He said she could go if we were going to be with her."

"But there's gonna be so many other people there," Robert argued. "You know how nervous she can get around strangers."

"That's okay, Dad. I'll stay with her."

"But what if she gets anxious?"

"She will want to come and say goodbye."

"WHAT'S ALL THESE PEOPLE HERE FOR?" MYRTLE HORTON, Robert's mother, asked Ghalen a week after the boy had last seen Jamilah. She wore a green and yellow dress with bulbous orange shoes. This outfit she called her Easter suit. The ensemble was topped off by a blue hat with a white veil. Under the veil she wore the feather mask that Robert had given her before Ghalen was even born.

The three were standing out in front of the Fleeting Dove Memorial Chapel, a mauve adobe-like structure that was deceptively large. Father and son had sent out six hundred invitations to the service. Matrice told them that was okay because everybody didn't always come, and the nave could seat four hundred sixty-eight.

"These are all Mama's friends," Ghalen proudly told his paternal grandmother.

"She knows all these people?" Myrtle posed with a sneer. "That's too many."

"They wanna come say goodbye," Ghalen argued mildly.

"Too many. Ain't no way to keep 'em all straight in yo' mind."

The people kept coming. Chef Charlie had closed the restaurant, Indus, for the day so that he and all his employees could come pay their respects to Robert's family. Minta Lee, Jamilah's friend from UCLA, came with her husband, the handsome Howard Garrison, who once was her manager at the Monkey Spit Café.

"I'm so sorry," Minta said to Robert. He put out a hand to shake but she pulled him close and kissed his face. Then she looked into his eyes.

While Howard Garrison shook Robert's hand Minta kissed Ghalen three times.

"That's a very sharp suit, Gayley," she said. "Your mother would be so proud of you."

She hugged the boy. He encircled her neck, giving her a willing, almost desperate, embrace.

"That's enough of that now," Myrtle Horton critiqued.

Alexander Farrell and Marquis Dechene, once dishwashers at Kundakunda, were now waiters at Indus. They took turns hugging Robert, then picked up Ghalen between them.

"You be strong now, boy," Alexander advised.

"Come down and see us any time," Marquis added.

Emily Barth came with her girlfriend, Melissa Brown. Cynthia Reddress, Myrtle's daytime nurse, showed up. The dark-skinned Mississippi native had been befriended by Jamilah, who told her that she could be a doctor too.

Even Aura Cress, who Robert once met on a nighttime bus to Baldwin Village, came. After she'd been to visit Robert at his job, she'd decided that she liked eating vegan. Ever since that day, she came to Kundakunda, and then Indus, at least once every two weeks.

The last congregant to come was a woman in all-black. Her close-fitting dress came down to the ankles, showing off a generous figure. Her wide-brimmed hat had a black veil. She approached the chapel, stopping at the bottom of the four granite steps. Looking up at Robert, she lifted the veil.

"Miss Fenestra," Robert cried. "You came."

He descended the stair, approaching the woman of mourning. She took a step back, as if afraid that Robert might try to embrace her.

"Robert," she said.

"I'm so glad you came. You know Jamilah wouldn't be able to rest if you didn't come say goodbye."

The other grandmother's lean face had been stonelike, but the mention of her daughter softened her gaze.

"What happened?" she asked.

"Cancer in her liver."

"Why didn't you call me?"

"You said never call you again."

"I . . ."

Robert had broken her reserve with his truth. She crumpled into his arms. There she cried.

"Com'on, Grandma Myrtle," Ghalen said. "That's my other grandmother, Pristine Fenestra. You two should get to know each other."

Pristine was crying, her face buried against Robert's chest as Ghalen and Myrtle watched.

"What's wrong with her?" Myrtle asked aloud.

"She's sad about my mother, her daughter," Ghalen advised.

Pristine raised her head and turned to see her grandson up close for the first time.

"You're Jammy's son?" she asked.

"Yes, ma'am, Ghalen Romeo Horton."

"Romeo?"

"He was my mother's uncle."

"He was my brother."

"I know."

Ghalen, who had been holding Myrtle's hand, let go and held the selfsame hand out to Pristine.

"It's a pleasure to meet you, Grandmother," he said.

"At least you have good manners," she said and then covered her mouth, maybe understanding that she should have said something else, or maybe nothing at all.

"We love you," Ghalen replied. "Mama always said that she missed you. This is my other grandmother, Myrtle Horton."

The women looked at each other and nodded.

"It's time for the service," Ghalen told them. "There's seats for us in the front center row."

"WE ARE HERE TODAY TO SAY GOODBYE TO OUR FRIEND and fellow traveler, Jamilah Fenestra-Horton," Felicia Jeong, second minister of the Constant Traveler Riverside Church, said to the room full of mourners. "Jamilah was a friend to everyone she met. She was a doctor and a scientist, a mother and daughter, a woman who believed in women and a wife."

Looking across the large audience as she spoke, Minister Jeong ended her introduction as her gaze fell upon Robert.

"The love Jamilah had included her family, her friends, the people she worked with, and her neighbors. But most strongly Jamilah's love encompassed, and was encompassed by, Robert. In a note she left for the one tasked to give this eulogy, she said that Robert Horton was the man that saved her from a life of boring repetition. She said of him . . .

"'Robert was my ladder and my chair. He raised me up and let me rest. He showed me how to see the world and he gave me the most beautiful child any mother could hope for. He showed me what was right without telling me what to do. He made all our meals and laughed out loud, without any trace of shame. When I would come home, he was happy to see me and when I explained what I did at work or play he listened with such intensity that I was able to understand myself more deeply.

"'When I met him, he told me that he wanted to open a restaurant that served healing foods to the people. I told him that I was studying to be a doctor. We were the same, though many people never understood us. What I learned from Robert was there was no understanding when it came to love, only happiness and sometimes pain.'

"These are the words of a woman who had accepted the challenges that the Infinite places upon each and every one of us," Felicia Jeong deciphered. "Under that weight she found love and was buoyed by it. She wanted all of you, especially Robert and Ghalen, to continue with her in your hearts. She wanted us all to leave this place with happiness, not sorrow. Because what we have here today is the expression of love across the barriers of loss and pain.

"What we have here today is beauty and duty, the promise of our sinews and our souls . . ."

Sitting in the front row of the chapel, holding Myrtle's left hand with his right, Ghalen imagined, for just the flicker of a moment, that his mother was in the room with the mourners, that she was not weighted down by sorrow.

The eulogy went on and on, but Ghalen stayed at that moment, where his mother was actually there, and he knew that she would stay.

15.

A hundred or so of the mourners left the chapel to go to Indus, the vegan restaurant of Chef Charles Martin. There they were served organic wine and appetizers carried around on chromium trays by waitpersons who were hired specifically for that occasion.

The tables were all open because the restaurant was closed to the public. Ghalen's father and grandmother were in a corner at the back of the dining room. She was seated in a chair at the right angle of the two walls while Robert stood off to her left, his back against the wall, as he always did when he felt uncertain and misunderstood. The nurse, Cynthia Reddress, sat next to Myrtle, at times holding her hand. For a time, Ghalen sat on the other side of his paternal grandmother, as he felt was his duty. Three times during the eulogy Ghalen had to shush Myrtle when she wanted to say out loud things like "There's too many people here," and "Why is that Chinese girl talking so much?"

"Miss Jeong is Korean," Ghalen said to his grandmother when she complained about the *Chinese girl*.

Ghalen felt that his duty was to look after his father and his father's mother.

But after a while Emily Barth sat down next to him.

In a subdued voice she said, "You should probably go around and thank people for coming."

Upon hearing this Ghalen knew this was the right thing. He was also there for his mother, who would have written notes to everyone who came, wanted to come but couldn't, and even those whose invitation might have gotten lost in the mail.

The only bad notice Ghalen got at school was about his handwriting. Every teacher he had had deemed his cursive—substandard. So, walking around and thanking people was just about the only way he could accomplish his mother's desire.

"Thank you so much for that wonderful eulogy," he said to Felicia Jeong, who was tall and slight, the color of a newborn fawn. "My mother wanted you, and she was right."

The second minister was speechless for a moment or two after Ghalen thanked her. She was used to seeing the silent son of Jamilah and Robert. He looked and acted like a well-behaved boy who needed time to grow and mature. But this was something wholly different.

"Thank you, Ghalen," she said. "Your mother was an amazing and a generous woman. She always donated her time to our little community."

"She used to say that that was why she wanted to be a doctor," he rejoined. "Helping people made her happy and made the people she helped happy too."

Reverend Jeong was pleasantly surprised and enchanted by the young man. The only thing she could think to do was bow with a slight nod.

The youngster smiled broadly, said, "Excuse me," and walked off to his next obligation.

"THANK YOU, CHEF CHARLIE," HE SAID TO THE MAN who footed the bill and provided the space for the reception. "My mom would have been so happy to see how you did all this."

"And she would have been smiling at you," Mr. Martin said. "She would have been very proud."

Ghalen's smile did not fade, but he was thinking that the phrase *would have been* put a period at the end of his mother's life, an ending that he would have to accept.

AFTER GIVING HIS AND HIS MOTHER'S THANKS TO MAYBE fifteen of those in attendance, Ghalen came upon Pristine Fenestra. She was sitting at a table set next to a window that looked out on a thick patch of blooming birds-of-paradise plants, beyond which ran North Beverly Drive.

Seeing his mother's mother presented a problem for Ghalen. He couldn't say *thank you for coming to your daughter's funeral.* He didn't want to apologize for his mother not telling Pristine that she was dying or for his father marrying his mom, causing Mama Fenestra to disown her. But, most of all, he couldn't say nothing. His mother had told him, less than a month before, that she loved her mother. That love needed to be addressed.

So, Ghalen Romeo Horton pulled up a chair next to Pristine at the table at which she sat alone.

"Hello, Grandmother," he said. "How are you doing?"

The elder Fenestra's brows furrowed but Ghalen couldn't tell if she was angry or confused.

"What do you want?" she asked at last.

"I want to know how you're doing and if I could do anything for you," Ghalen said simply.

The woman's frown deepened.

"Why are you asking me these things?" She seemed truly confused.

"Because this is my mother's funeral party."

"Why isn't your father asking me how I am?"

"Because. Because he loved my mom so much that he can't talk. If he tries, he just starts crying."

Pristine's expression began to change, to shift between emotions.

"Are you like your father?"

"What do you mean?" he asked, even though he thought he knew.

"Does it take you a long time to answer a question?"

"I've answered all of your questions quick enough."

Pristine moved her head back like a kitten who has experienced a fright.

"You're sassy," she concluded.

"I'm trying to talk to you, not say anything wrong or rude. It doesn't take me a long time to answer questions. My dad is like that but it's a mental condition. There's nothing wrong with him either."

"How old are you?"

"Ten. How old are you?"

First there was a flash of anger on Pristine Fenestra's face, then this emotion changed into a questioning gaze. She laced her fingers together and placed her chin upon the weave of knuckle-bones.

"I'm sixty-two years old," Ghalen's grandmother answered. "How are your grades in school?"

"I'm the best student in my class."

"Arrogant, aren't you?"

"No."

"Do you get all A's?"

"I get mostly excellent-plus except in cursive. I'm a sloppy writer."

The hint of a smile flitted across her lips.

"Did you disown my mother because she married my father even though you thought he was what you call retarded?"

"I . . ."

"Because that's not true," Ghalen continued. "To begin with, *retarded* is a word you should never use and, on top of that, my father is a good man, a smart man, smarter than most people when it comes to what's right and what's not right."

Pristine's gaze flinched away, like one does when they've tried to look at the sun, but it was too bright to behold. She turned back to meet her grandson's passive stare, tried to speak but could not. She took a deep breath, sighed on the exhalation, and then finally found the words.

"I'm sorry," she said slowly, deliberately. "I've done wrong by you and your father and, worst of all, to my own daughter. I should have been a part of her life. But I was just so damn mad."

This was a very important moment for Ghalen, he learned something, not about his grandmother and her sorrows, but about how to wait and listen when there was more for a person to say. He looked at the black-clad mother as she went through many emotions that he didn't understand.

"I thought," she said and paused. "I thought that your father had defective genes and that Jammy would pass them on to you."

Ghalen had an opinion about what Pristine was saying but still, he held back any response.

"She told me that I was wrong, but I didn't believe her," Pristine said. "I didn't."

"And now she's dead," Ghalen said simply.

"Yes."

"But I'm here and so is my dad. We could be your family. I know mama would like that."

"You would forgive me?" Pristine asked softly.

"No," Ghalen replied, his tone equally hushed. "No, because there's nothing to forgive you about. Mama was sad because you couldn't be there to enjoy your family. She wasn't mad at you because being with me and my dad was what she wanted."

"She wasn't angry?"

"No. She was just so happy that it felt bad that she couldn't share that with you."

Pristine wept softly, mostly silently. Ghalen understood her sorrow, but he had no name to put on it. After a minute or so he reached out to hold the fingers of her left hand. She pulled the ten-year-old up on her lap and hugged him ferociously.

Ghalen's shoulder hurt a little, but he didn't complain. He somehow knew that hugging Pristine was as close as he would get to holding his mother in a final embrace.

They held each other like that for a few minutes. Finally, Ghalen pressed against her arms like a pupa trying to break through the chrysalis he'd entered as one thing and now it was time to leave whatever he used to be behind.

He climbed down from her knee and said, "I have to go say thank-you to people. Mom would want that."

"Yes, she would."

"So, I'll see you later?"

"Ghalen."

"Yes, Grandmother?"

"I know that your father has many good qualities but, do you think you might do better to come live with me? I mean, he's so sensitive and he leaves you to take care of so much. Maybe he'd do better too."

"It would make my mom so sad if I went away. And Dad would be unhappy too."

Saying this, Ghalen turned quickly and walked away from his grandmother.

ALICA FRAIN AND MR. AND MRS. WILLIS WERE INVITED to the funeral, but they only came to the reception at Indus to say goodbye. Lonnette and Frank Chatsworth were the parents of Bruno, Ghalen's best friend. Alica's daughter, Lovely, had promised Ghalen that she'd be his girlfriend in the sixth grade, next year.

Soon after leaving his grandmother Ghalen saw his friends.

"Bruno!" he called, a big grin on his lips.

Bruno was tall with a large frame and a slow, steady smile.

"Li'l G," he said, using the nickname they'd settled on.

"Hey." Ghalen wanted to hug his friend but knew this wouldn't be appreciated, so they bumped fists and nodded with vigor.

Bruno's skin was a rosy, brown color while Ghalen's color was darker but somehow less brown.

"Hi, Ghalen," Lovely Frain said.

The tall and solid young woman was a mixture of Persian and Black Jamaican stock. Her smile was infectious, her hair fell in ebony ringlets, and her skin was the darkest olive.

"Lovely," Ghalen said, forgetting for the first time why he was there.

"Bruno said you were so sad," she said.

"Yeah, kinda I am. Mom was very brave, but I could see how much it was hurtin' her."

Bruno put a great paw on his friend's shoulder.

"You wanna go out back to Chef Charlie's garden?"

IN THE BACK OF THE RESTAURANT LOT THERE WAS A patch of grass, a row of rosebushes against a redwood fence, and a broad pond filled with bright blue-colored and feathery betta fish. There was a marble bench set at the edge of the pond.

Lovely and Ghalen sat side by side while Bruno got down on his knees to inspect the brightly colored fishes.

"How was the funeral?" Lovely asked.

"It was okay."

"My mom said she didn't want me going because they said you could see the body and she didn't want me to see it."

"Yeah," Ghalen said. "I don't think it was too bad. It's just that people wanted to say goodbye and I guess that's easier if you see the body. You know, it's like sayin' good night to somebody who doesn't answer but they still heard what you said."

"Did it make you sad?" Bruno asked.

"Not that. I mean, I guess if she was dead and I came home and saw her, that would be bad, but I had seen her at the funeral home already and my dad was so sad that I was worried about him."

"My uncle died last year," Bruno opined. "He was really old, though. Not like your mother. She was young."

"Yes she was," Ghalen agreed.

"She was beautiful, your mom," Lovely said. "And she was a really good person. All the kids thought so."

"Did you cry?" Bruno asked, turning away from the fish.

"A little bit, but not no big old hollerin' and yellin' and stuff."

"You goin' back to school Monday?" Bruno asked.

"Yeah, but . . ."

"But what?" Lovely wanted to know.

"I'm not gonna stay there."

"Why? Your daddy movin' somewhere?"

"No. It's just that I got a lot to do now that my mother's gone. My dad needs a lotta help and we got a little money, but one day I'm'a have to make the money myself. So, I'm gonna skip the sixth grade and go to the Jackson School in the Hollywood Hills and graduate as soon as I can."

Lovely stared at Ghalen. At first, she was just looking as if he were saying something, but he wasn't. Then her face began to quiver, and finally, tears started to come from her eyes. Her

breathing made her shoulders jump around and Ghalen moved
to put his arms around her. She returned Ghalen's hug, now crying loud enough to be heard. Ghalen saw Bruno, standing there
behind her, his big hands hanging uselessly at his sides.

"I don't want you to go," Lovely whimpered.

"I don't wanna go either," he said into the thick mane of hair.
"But I gotta."

THAT NIGHT GHALEN LAY AWAKE IN HIS BED, THINKING
about Bruno standing there, helpless while Lovely cried. And
about his grandmother, who was naturally angry but still loved by
his mom. He wondered why it was so hard for him to cry. Didn't
he feel sad about his mother?

No, he thought. *I'm not sad. I'm empty.*

16.

Time sped up for the boy after his mother's funeral. For two years he went to Jackson Middle School, a private institution for gifted students, graduated, and then attended Exeter West, a preparatory high school, for the full three years. Over that time his grandmother sued Robert for custody of Ghalen, her lawyer telling the court that his father was mentally incompetent.

Ghalen was afraid that he'd be taken away from his dad. He wasn't worried about what might happen to him, but that his father wouldn't be able to get by on his own. Every night, with the setting of the sun, a sadness would descend on Robert. It would start with him remembering something that Jamilah would do—straighten up the living room or tell Ghalen to take a shower before dinner.

"Then she would say all this science stuff that I never ever really knew what it meant," Robert would say, "but she would smile so bright that it was like a moon or the sky just before you could see the sun rise in the east."

Robert conjuring up Ghalen's mother like this always started pleasantly enough, but after a while he'd realize how much he missed her, and what Ghalen called *a dark place* would set in. Robert would stand against the wall, descend to his knees, and then "go to that place beyond tears," Ghalen wrote in one of his many journals.

And so, Ghalen had to talk to his father, telling him what Jamilah would expect of him. It was Robert's job, for instance, to make
dinner and then wash the dishes, to ask Ghalen what he did in
school that day and try to understand the boy's explanations in
plain language.

"She'd want you to play one of those mind-sharpening games
with me," Ghalen would say.

Dr. Akshar Singh, Myrtle Horton's doctor, gave Robert certain
games to play that would help him concentrate when he lost focus
and became lost. This problem started for him after the scuffle
with the police caused him to hit his head on the concrete. These
mind-sharpening tools were word games and number games,
sometimes eye-and-hand-coordination exercises.

After an hour or two of talking to his son, Robert would come
out of sorrow, becoming a dad again.

Because of the spells of lack of focus that Robert sometimes
experienced, Ghalen took the bus with him to work every morning and then back home most afternoons. In between Indus,
school, and home, the boy would transfer to take a connection to
wherever he was headed. He didn't mind the bus because, while
riding, he could speed-read the assignments for class and do any
other classwork that didn't need handwriting.

Pristine's lawyers were not aware of how hard Ghalen had to
work to keep his father moving forward. But they had records
from Robert's elementary school and some from junior high and
high school too. School counselors wrote about Robert, saying
things like The Spectrum and OCD, sprinkled over with sinister
terms like psychotic response and bipolar disorder. Emily Barth
brought actual psychiatrists and all the people Robert worked
with, and the ministers of his church to bear witness for the
sad man's abilities and beneficent intentions toward everyone
he met.

"Of course, Mr. Horton is sad," Emily Barth said to the judge. "He loved his wife, his son's mother. They had a beautiful relationship. But Robert only missed one day of work in the time since she passed. He's there for every event at Ghalen's school. He doesn't drink or smoke. He attends church every Sunday. The litigant, Mr. Horton's mother-in-law, had not seen her daughter since before Ghalen was born. Having only met my client once, she disowned her daughter and left the family to fend for itself. And, in the time since Jamilah's death, Mr. Horton has done an exemplary job of raising and looking after his son."

ON THE LAST DAY OF THE INQUISITION EMILY BARTH said, "Your Honor, I'd like to call on Robert Horton. He says that he wants to respond to the questions about his ability to be a father."

Ghalen shivered in his chair. He worried that his father would be too anxious to answer questions, that he might stand up from the seat next to the judge's desk and go stand against the wall. If he was really nervous, he might even turn his back to the chamber.

"Mr. Horton," Judge Babette Akana said, waving her hand in greeting. "Approach."

Robert stood up from the chair next to his son. He was wearing a medium green suit, a chocolate-colored shirt, and a deep yellow tie. Aura Cress, the woman he'd met on an early, early bus one night more than a dozen years before, went with him to the Suit Store to buy the ensemble.

A week before, Aura was eating at Indus when Robert came out to greet her. She'd become an assistant pharmacist and had been accepted to Cal State Long Beach for a degree in pharmaceutical science. When Robert told her about how nervous he was about talking to the judge, she said that she'd like to help him pick out a suit.

"THESE HERE ARE TOO MANY CLOTHES," HE SAID, WHEN presented with the many racks of sportscoats, trousers, and two-piece suits.

"What colors make you feel the best?" Aura asked, placing a hand on his elbow.

"Green," he said with absolute certainty. "Green is my favorite color. My favorite."

"Good," she encouraged. "Let's pull out some two-piece green suits then."

They sifted through a dozen or more suits until Robert came upon the perfect hue.

He said, "It's the kinda green makes you think'a one'a them big lawns up on Sunset Boulevard on the way out to the beach."

"Okay," Aura said. "You can't wear a suit without a shirt. What color do you think a shirt should be?"

Robert knew how to pick out clothes. He didn't need Aura for that, not exactly. What he needed her for was conversation that would end up with him making a decision.

"Not green," Robert said about the shirt color. "But maybe the opposite."

"What's that?" Aura asked, sincerely.

"Brown. Brown ain't my favorite but, but it's the strongest color."

"Why you say that?"

"Because it's the color of the soil, the dirt, the Earth."

After that, all they needed was a tie.

"If you gonna go talk to the judge you gonna need a little luck, don't you think?" Aura asked.

Robert didn't answer immediately. He studied the lawn-colored suit and the Hershey dress shirt. From his imagination he conjured a rainbow before him, hovering just over the racks.

"Yellow," he said softly.

"You mean like gold?" she asked.

"Uh-uh, no. Yellow like a ripe banana on a breakfast table."

AND SO, BOLSTERED BY A SUIT OF CLOTHES THAT FELT LIKE courage, Robert walked up to the chair set next to the judge, who was the color of dark honey due to her pure Hawaiian heritage.

Ghalen was very proud of the way his father strode so confidently and the way he sat without a trace of indecision.

The judge's hair spread out like a fan from her forehead and the sides of her wide face. From there the style was like a seashell, curving around her head and back.

"So, Mr. Horton, you have heard what your mother-in-law thinks the situation is."

"Yes, um, yes, ma'am."

"What do you make of the allegations presented by Miss Fenestra's lawyer?"

Robert's face crinkled. This was visible from Ghalen's chair, making the boy nervous. They hadn't discussed what Robert thought about what Pristine's lawyers had said, except to argue against whatever that was.

Robert looked out into the small room, and then back at the judge. He considered the Pacific Islander for at least a minute and then brought his left hand up to caress his lucky banana tie.

"I agree with her, looking at it from her point of view," he said at last.

Emily Barth gripped Ghalen's forearm in alarm. The boy had to clench both fists and his jaw to keep from jumping up and saying "No! He doesn't mean that!"

"What does that mean?" the judge asked.

The wait this time was only half as long, but for Ghalen it felt like an hour.

Then Robert said, "My wife told me that she loved her mother, because Ms. Fenestra had always done her best. She wasn't always right, but she didn't know that. It's like with Jamilah bein' a doctor. Her mother told her that that was what she had to be. She said that, um, uh, practicin' would make her rich and popular among people who were important. But Jamilah wasn't interested in that. She did wanna be a doctor, but to help people, to make sure that even if they was poor or disadvantaged that they could still be healthy. That's what I try to do with healthy foods. Ms. Fenestra wasn't wrong, it just wasn't what Jamilah wanted, not exactly."

"And what did you and your wife want for Ghalen?" Judge Akana asked.

"I thought about that all night long. I knew you would ask and that is what's most important. Ms. Fenestra's lawyer keeps talkin' about how smart Gayley is and how much, um, potential he got. But he never talked about health and happiness, about the time he needs to be a child. He goes to a very good school, and he never gets nuthin' but A's. He's healthy and strong and he has some very good friends. Ms. Fenestra's lawyer says that we have got to bear down on the boy bein' smart and usin' that brain'a his. But he already doin' that. What he needs is to lighten up and just have fun like any other child."

The pride and fear in Ghalen's heart turned into respect. At that moment he realized that he never understood his father's genius. He'd experienced it every day of his life but just took his dad's worldview for granted.

"But what about Ghalen's safety?" the judge offered. "Ms. Fenestra says that he's been left on his own too often."

"I don't know about all that. When Gayley and me ain't workin' at a job or at school, we're pretty much together. He got school friends. He takes the bus on his own. You know from his school records that he only been in trouble one time." Robert stopped for a moment, seemingly looking inward. "But I understand your question, judge. I understand it because I'm a father. When Gayley had fever as a baby, I sat up all night long. I bathed him and blew on him and woke his mother if I got worried. When he's five minutes late I ring his phone. If his fo'head is bunched up I ask him what's wrong.

"But that's where the problem is. You see, Ms. Fenestra's uh, uh, lawyers keep talkin' about drugs and gangs and what they call predators. They keep talkin' about worryin' about where the boy might go wrong. But the way I see it, it's my job to be there watchin' and lovin' him; to be there if, if he need it. Between me and his mother, I think he's learned all that. I do. And if I keep suspectin' that he's gonna go down the wrong road, if I keep suspectin' him, I'm worried that I might give him the wrong idea. I agree that I don't want him addicted or killed. It's just that I let him know that I have trust in him and, if he need it, I'll be there."

"But what if somebody," Judge Akana argued, "some older person or peer pressure pushes him to do wrong?"

Robert raised his gaze to look the magistrate in the eye. From his expression Ghalen knew that he was considering this problem with deep, honest concern.

After a long wait, he said, "Do you have a true answer to that? 'Cause I sure don't. I mean I hope that I have taught my son to come to me, or someone else we trust if he got a problem. I want to know what's goin' on in his heart and mind. I want that. If I see sumpin's wrong, I will do my best, like I did when his mother got cancer. I tried to be there, to save her—I did."

It was the judge's turn to sit back and ponder. There was a strong feeling on her face, that's what Ghalen felt. But he had no idea what she was thinking.

"How long was your wife sick?" she asked, unexpectedly.

"Not that long," Robert said softly. "Maybe a week or so. Maybe longer but it was only that long that I knew about it. I did my best, but there wasn't anything I could do. Nuthin' except be there for her and our son."

"You're saying," the magistrate said and then paused. "You're saying that all you want is what is best for Ghalen."

"Yes, ma'am."

"So, in a way," Judge Akana said, "you and Ms. Fenestra are both right?"

"I think so," Robert replied. "It don't make no sense to fight in a courtroom, callin' names, when we should all be workin' together."

AFTER THE FATHER'S STATEMENT THE JUDGE CALLED ON Ghalen.

"I'm sorry you have had to endure this argument," the judge said to the boy. "So, I only have one thing to ask: What is it that you want?"

"To live in my apartment, with my father, until I grow up and go off to school."

THE COURT DISMISSED PRISTINE'S SUIT AND ORDERED her to pay Robert's legal fees.

The Saturday after the judge's ruling Robert told Ghalen to call Ivo and have him drive them out to Pasadena.

WHEN SHE OPENED THE DOOR TO HER SMALL HOME, Pristine was shocked to see Robert and Ghalen standing there.

"Good afternoon, Ms. Fenestra," Robert said while his legal relative searched for language. "Me and Ghalen came over to tell you that even though we had that that that court battle, we wanna bury the hatchet and be family."

"I don't understand," Pristine replied. "What do you want from me?"

"Can we come in?" Ghalen asked.

"Um, uh, I guess."

She led father and son into the sitting room, where each of them had a big stuffed chair.

Once seated, Robert said, "My wife loved you, always talked about your sharp sense'a humor and your good intentions. I know it was outta love that you wanted to take Gayley here to live with you. You wanted to help more than hurt. I know that. And I wanna tell you, we wanna tell you, that you are always welcome at our home and that we will always come when you call."

Ghalen was prouder of his father at that moment than he had ever been. He had all of his words and ideas in order because this was his wife's mother and he was going to do right, in the right words, by his wife.

17.

halen was due to graduate from high school one month before his sixteenth birthday. He was just shy of six feet tall with a good physique due to the hour of exercise that he went through each morning with his dad. He was handsome and manly in expression, if not in his boyish features. This early maturity came from the close relationship with his father. They worked together to make their life worthwhile. Ghalen had applied to UCLA in order to stay close to home because he knew that his father would fall into sadness if he were left alone. This responsibility didn't bother the young man. He loved his father and learned from him every day.

And, after all, his life was great. He was the designated valedictorian of his class and very popular, the star of the soccer team, and he had three girlfriends, off and on, during the senior year. Even though he was younger than most of his class, his height, fair features, and rare inner confidence made the girls want to get to know him better.

But what the girls liked the most was his detachment. He was a good listener, and kisser, but when he was away from a girlfriend, he didn't miss her. Because of this emotional distance, receiving Ghalen's attentions had become the unspoken goal of quite a few of his female classmates.

They dated him, did homework assignments with him, kissed,

and even had sex with him sometimes. He was detached but not distant. If anyone ever wanted to talk or needed advice or money, he was always willing to help. He had a good job as an assistant pastry chef at Indus, and he received a small stipend from monies that Emily Barth managed. Like his father, he lived most of his life in the present. The future for him had its final moment with the death of his mother. He'd expected to know her all the days of his life, and so, when she died, so did any expectation of what was to come.

"YOU KNOW," EMILY BARTH SAID TO ROBERT ONE AFTER-noon when Ghalen was away at Berkeley for a soccer competition, "he doesn't seem to care about anything but the present. He gets along fine with his schoolfriends, but it seems like he could just as well be alone."

Robert winced and said, "That might be because of me. I think he's always wanting to be there in case I get sad. I keep tellin' him that I'm bettah now. But he still wants to ride with me to work and he calls me when I don't call him."

"He's such a good kid," Emily agreed. "Do you know what he's going to study at college?"

"He keeps on talkin' about linguistics and musicality, um, musicology, that's it, musicology."

"Sounds lonely."

"I told him that he should go away to college, but he don't listen."

"He's worried that you'd die or something."

"But I wouldn't," Robert argued.

"*I* know that, but does *he*?"

"I don't wanna kick him out. I don't want him goin' to the East Coast and feelin' like he have to call me every day."

"What if you had a girlfriend?"

"You mean, what if he had a girlfriend? The girls like Ghalen. No problem with that."

"No. What if you had a girlfriend? You, Robert."

A WEEK LATER, TWO WEEKS BEFORE GRADUATION, GHALEN took a bus to Culver City, to visit his friend Lovely Frain. They hadn't spoken for more than two years, and before that, they had talked only on the phone. But she sent him an email saying that she needed his advice.

He was to meet her at a coffee shop on Hayden Avenue. It was a nice place with service at the front of the coffee bar and a garden through the door that led to the backyard.

Ghalen had nothing against eating meat, but he ordered matcha tea and a raisin scone because that was his comfort food from childhood. The barista gave him a number card on a little stand to put on any table he found in the garden.

The outside eating area was like a bonsai maze, that was Ghalen's first impression. A curving, cobblestone path ran its sinuous way through a garden of rosebushes, each one no more than three and a half feet in height. The path passed little inlets where there were maybe twenty stone tables with matching benches. Ghalen walked the whole circuit, did not see his friend, and settled at a far table beneath a stone wall under a lemon tree that was weighted down with the bounty of its fruit.

Something happened when he sat down on the stone bench at the stone table under the sweet lemon tree, something unexpected and profound. When he settled there his life just seemed to stop. He wasn't thinking about calculus or the paper he was writing about the history of the Vietnam War, about his graduation speech, or even if his father was okay at home, alone. His mother, at that moment, became a fond memory, and nothing seemed to matter. He realized that there was a smile on his face and that the early summer air was light and sunny and fair. It was as if he were headed for that stone seat under the sweet lemon for the entirety of his conscious life–that's what Ghalen felt. A feeling that what the ministers on Sunday called divine.

"Ghalen?"

She wore a luminescent golden scarf on her head, a short black skirt, and a tight-fitting red top that only came down to her rib cage. Her shoes were leather, lacquered with silver paint.

"Lovely?"

"Damn," she said. "You grew."

The seventeen-year-old girl captivated him. Her dark olive skin, her figure, filled out and ready for womanhood, even the tilt of her head took the young man's breath.

"Hey," he said, but his eyes said more.

"Stand up," she commanded.

He did as he was told.

"Oh my God. Damn. You look like a rich Black girl's boy band poster. What happened?"

"I just grew up."

"Mmm! You sure did."

"You want me to go order you sumpin'?"

"No, I already did." She held up her little stand with the number 16 printed on the card.

"Well then, let's sit down."

She was beautiful and, with every passing second, became more so in the almost-sixteen-year-old senior's eyes.

"You like?" she asked when it became obvious that he wouldn't or couldn't talk.

"Lovely, you, you're so beautiful."

For a moment her surety faltered, this compliment cutting through her practiced reserve.

"You too, Li'l G. Damn."

For years Ghalen had been shut down from everything except his schoolwork and his father's welfare. When his mother died, he became a sentinel, a sentry protecting his mother's wishes. But now he somehow knew that was all over.

"I . . ." he said. "Um, what did you need to talk about, Love?"

Her smile and lively engaging eyes dimmed. She tried to smile again, failed, and then said, "It's Bruno . . ."

"What about him?"

"Let's have our drinks and I'll take you there."

The waiter brought Lovely's tea and she asked Ghalen about what he'd been doing over the years. He told her about classes and soccer, his father and working at Indus for extra money.

"You been seein' anybody?" she asked when he wondered about what she'd been doing.

He'd been dating a girl named Talulah but said, "Not really. How about you?"

Her answer was a weak smile under sad eyes and then she said, "We should go."

IT WAS A LARGE HOSPITAL, CULVER BENEFICENT, OFF Venice Boulevard.

"He's sick?" Ghalen asked when he realized this was their destination.

"Yes, and no," Lovely replied. "You'll see."

They got to an elevator, and Lovely turned to Ghalen.

"Me and Bruno hooked up last year," she said. "It just happened, I guess."

"Uh-huh," Ghalen replied. He felt a little bereft but realized through this mild pain that Lovely's beauty meant more to him than just some girl and boy.

"He's been in trouble," she said. "You know, his dad was always gettin' high and his mom wasn't all that good a mother. And I started tryin' to take care'a him. And then we got together."

"Okay."

"You left, Ghalen. I couldn't wait for you."

It was as if his life had been put on hold from the moment he saw his mother's dead body. From that milestone onward he'd been sleepwalking, living the life of someone in between here and there. Standing at the elevator's sliding doors he understood that he was supposed to stay in elementary school and be Lovely's boyfriend. But instead, he wasn't a kid or a teen or anything but someone who was supposed to be there for everybody else.

That's what he had been. But that was over.

"What's wrong with Bruno?"

"Come on upstairs and you'll see."

THERE WAS A UNIFORMED HOSPITAL GUARD SITTING OUT in front of Bruno's private room. Lovely walked up to him and said, "I'm Lena Chatsworth, Bruno's sister. This is our brother, Ghalen. We're here to see Bruno."

The security guard looked at her and then at Ghalen. He frowned and then nodded.

BRUNO WAS LAID UP ON A HOSPITAL BED WITH ONE HAND chained to the metal side guard.

When his friends walked in, he sat up and said, "Damn, Li'l G you done growed."

"Hey, Bruno. How you doin'?"

"Aw'ight."

"Good."

Lovely walked up to the side of the bed and kissed Bruno on the lips.

"Hey, baby," she said.

Before she could move away, he looped an arm around her shoulder and pulled her in for another, deeper kiss.

Ghalen thought he saw some reticence on her part.

"What's with the handcuffs, man?" Ghalen asked.

"She didn't tell you?"

"I thought you guys would talk about it," Lovely answered.

With that she wandered over to the far side of the small room, there to sit in a chair bathed in the rays of the noonday sun. Ghalen's gaze followed.

"She fine, huh?" Bruno said proudly.

"Lovely."

Both youngsters put on grown-up grins.

Bruno was both bigger and smaller than his friend remembered. His shoulders were wider, but he'd lost the baby fat of youth. His face was more angular, with the skin roughened and the beginnings of facial hair. The whites of his eyes were more the color of country cream and, even though he was sitting up in the hospital bed, he seemed to be slouching.

"They arrested me," Bruno admitted.

"For what?"

"I had to stab this suckah."

"Who?"

"They call him Dingle. I don't know his real name."

"You guys were fightin'?"

The prisoner's face twisted, expressing the bad taste in his mouth.

"They tried and ambush me," he said, masticating on bitterness.

"What they want?"

"Rock cocaine. I bought some from Billy Meyers."

"Billy from school?"

"Yeah. He started cookin' at high school and, and I was gonna buy from him and sell to these fools out in Inglewood. Only Dingle pulled out this old-time pistol like the cowboys got on TV."

Stunned, Ghalen shook his head, as if the only way he could understand what his friend was saying was to deny it.

"Oh yeah, man," Bruno replied to the wordless repudiation. "They kill niggahs out here all the time, all the time."

"So, so, so he, he robbed you and then you went after him later?"

"Uh-uh. No. Man, I saw red. I pult out this knife and ran right into him, stabbin' like a mothahfuckah."

Unconsciously, Bruno jerked his right arm to simulate his attack.

"That's why I'm in here instead'a jail," Ghalen's onetime best friend concluded.

"He shot you?"

"In my arm muscle." With his chin Bruno indicated the bandage on his upper left arm. "That's what's wrong. I cain't go into the jail with no bum arm. You know you got to p'oteck yo'self in there."

GHALEN STARED AT HIS FRIEND, RECALLING THE PAST AS he did so. He remembered the semester when Bruno realized how strong he was. Every day, for weeks at lunch, he'd challenge one of the other boys to an arm-wrestling contest. He won every time. The only one he hadn't bested was Ghalen, because whenever Bruno challenged his friend, Ghalen would say, "No, Bruno. I wouldn't want to embarrass you."

It made Bruno mad that Ghalen thought he was the best, and so he started calling him a coward.

"Coward! Goddamned yellah bastid!" nine-year-old Bruno would yell.

Ghalen didn't mind. He gloated over getting to Bruno after he'd overcome every other boy in their class. But then one day Lovely came to Ghalen in the library where he was reading *Treasure Island* by Robert Louis Stevenson for the third time. She sat down across from him at the long study table, not saying anything at first. When Ghalen looked up, he was surprised to see his future sixth-grade girlfriend.

"Lovely," he said, always a little self-conscious at saying her name.

"You got to arm wrestle with Bruno."

"Why?"

"Because he's mad at you all the time."

"That's his problem," Ghalen said, parroting one of his mother's favorite sayings.

"It's yours if you wanna stay bein' friends with him."

Ghalen could not imagine losing Bruno, he was the closest thing to a brother he ever had. On top of that, he always listened to Lovely. In Ghalen's mind Bruno was strong, he was smart, and Lovely was true in every sense of the word.

That evening Ghalen told his parents about his quandary.

Robert said that fighting never helped anybody.

"It cost money and time and pain," the elder Horton said. "Fighting is never a answer to a problem."

"But it's not hittin', Dad. It's just like pushin' your arms."

"But he's angry at you and wrestling is a kind of fighting."

"But he might not be my friend no more," Ghalen argued.

"He'll come around," Robert rejoined.

"I don't know," Jamilah said thoughtfully. "When you said that you didn't want to arm wrestle with Bruno because you'd embarrass him you made it so people laughed at the thing he's the most proud of. That's hard for any man to take."

"But fighting is wrong," Robert argued.

Ghalen remembered his mother smiling at his father. She said, "Well, Gayley, you've heard what we have to say, now you have to make up your mind."

That night Ghalen woke up almost every hour, thinking about what he should do. When he did fall asleep, he dreamt about arm wrestling Bruno. They were grunting and struggling when the art teacher, Mr. Davis, ran up to stop them.

"Fighting is wrong," Davis told them in Robert's voice.

THE NEXT MORNING GHALEN TOLD BRUNO THAT HE'D arm wrestle him at the lunch tables at noon.

At the assigned time the boys sat across from each other surrounded by most of their class. Bruno had an angry grin on his face. Ghalen was struck by this smile that was also a grimace; he'd never seen his friend with a grin that carried that kind of feeling.

Bruno put his right elbow up on the table and, sitting across from him, Ghalen followed suit. Standing at the end of the table, Lovely was looking down on them, and when they were in position she said, "Go."

Bruno was naturally strong and played every sport the elementary school had to offer. But Ghalen did push-ups in six different positions, every morning. So at first, to the class's amazement, the contestants were deadlocked. But Bruno was the stronger and, after maybe two minutes, he started to press Ghalen back. When it became clear that the smaller boy would lose, he suddenly looked up over Bruno's left shoulder and cried, "Mr. Davis!"

When his opponent turned his head to see, Ghalen put all his strength into one headlong push.

Bruno's hand slammed down on the table.

THAT AFTERNOON, AT THE BACK EXIT OF THE SCHOOL, where Bruno, Lovely, and Ghalen usually met, Ghalen stood alone. He wasn't thinking about his contest with Bruno. Instead, he was wondering about what his mother must have been thinking while smiling at his father.

"Hey."

Ghalen turned and said, "Hey, Bruno, where's Lovely?"

"I told her not to come."

"Why?"

Without any warning Bruno socked Ghalen on the jaw, knocking the smaller boy down. Lying there, Ghalen thought about his father saying that fighting is wrong. He didn't know about that, but it sure did hurt. He shook his head and then saw Bruno lowering to one knee. He wondered if his friend planned to keep on hitting him, but he wasn't afraid.

Bruno took Ghalen by both arms and lifted him to his feet.

"Now we're even," he said. "Okay?"

"Okay," Ghalen said behind a confused sneer. "But why?"

"You warned me. You told me that you didn't want to embarrass me, and I called you names. So, I should'a lost. But I had to hit you too."

"Why?"

"Because. Because you made e'rybody laugh at me an' if I didn't hit you I would'a stayed mad."

When Ghalen laughed, it hurt in the left hinge of his jaw. Lovely came to join them and they went off to get ice cream and play.

18.

After Lovely and Ghalen left the hospital, they went to a little park a few blocks away. There they settled on a one-piece pine picnic table. Lovely sat up top and Ghalen on the attached bench below.

"It's good you came to see him," she said. "You know he really loves you. He's all the time talkin' about how smart you were at school. He tells everybody that you was so smart that whenever you two were together it'd rub off on him."

Ghalen understood what she was saying, that his visit to their friend would help to keep his hopes up. But he wanted to do more than that.

"Do his parents know what happened?"

"His dad in jail and his mother moved back east, to Baltimore I think."

"So, who he live with?"

"Me."

"At your parents' house?"

"No. I wanted him to, but they said they didn't like the man he was, um, becoming and so I found us a place down Venice."

"How do you live?"

"I got a waitress job at a coffee house and Bruno's tryin'. That's why he got into all this trouble in the first place."

"So he got a lawyer?"

"Public defender, but he haven't seen him yet."

"I got a lawyer."

"Lawyer for what?"

"She takes care of my mother's documents and money and stuff."

"I don't think that would help. He needs somebody that does criminal cases."

"When I asked my lawyer one time, what would I do if me or my dad got in trouble, she said that she knows lawyers like that."

GHALEN TALKED TO EMILY BARTH ON THE PHONE THAT night.

"I remember Bruno," she said. "He was at the funeral in a dark blue suit. Him and that beautiful girl followed you around like they were trying to protect you. He was in a fight over a drug deal?"

"He really needs help."

"It'll cost something."

"Can you put it against whatever there is in my account?"

"Let me ask around. Maybe we can work something out."

THE NEXT MORNING EMILY BARTH CALLED GHALEN, AND he took a bus down to Venice.

Behind a big, ramshackle house, about six blocks from the beach, were a dozen one-room, plywood cabins that were rented out weekly. Bruno and Lovely stayed in Cabin 11. Ghalen knocked on the door and waited. He was very nervous. This was new for the boy. There was rarely anything for him to be nervous about, except if his father had been out alone and was late coming home. Other than that, life was easy with his dad and the people down at Indus. He'd rarely gotten less than an A in any class, but even when his work was poor, he just ignored it.

But waiting at that lime-colored door he found himself trembling.

When the door came open, he held his breath.

Lovely stood there in a tea-colored silk slip, the hem of which didn't even make it half the way to her knees. Her long black hair was tousled. And her eyes were cloudy with sleep.

"Ghalen?"

"I got a lawyer for Bruno. He's going to see him at the hospital today."

"What? Um, come in."

IT WAS TRULY A ONE-ROOM AFFAIR. THE WALLS, CEILING, and floor were untreated, unpainted, raw. There was a small, stained mattress in one corner and a folding table set next to a scratched-up plexiglass window. Under the table was stored a big brown suitcase. There were no shelves, one dresser, and many other things strewn across the floor. Even years later Ghalen remembered details of that disheveled room: shoes and clothes, some books and a *Hustler* magazine, a tennis ball and a smudged yellow bra.

"Sorry it's so messy. Ever since they arrested Bruno, I just haven't had the time to clean."

"How do you cook?"

"There's a hot plate in the suitcase. The landlady, Miss Mimer, says this place is a firetrap and that if anybody cooks in here, she'll kick 'em out. So, we hide it in there. What did you say about a lawyer?"

She pulled a chair out from the table and gestured for Ghalen to sit. After he did, she lowered into the only other seat.

"Yeah. His name is Jesse Nye, and when my lawyer, Emily, talked to him he said he'd go see Bruno this morning."

Lovely cocked her head to the right with a bewildered look on her face. Ghalen felt that she was like someone who spoke only Spanish trying to understand something very important that was spoken in Mandarin.

"What?" she said at last.

He happily repeated the information.

"How much does that cost?"

"It's free for Bruno."

"Free? Nuthin's free."

"This is. Emily, that's my lawyer, she says that Mr. Nye agreed to let the state pay for it, like he was a public defender."

"And why did your lawyer want to help?"

"She remembered Bruno and you from my mom's funeral."

"But nobody cares like that. Not no more. People take what they can get and fuck the rest."

"No." Ghalen shook his head slowly.

"So, he just gonna help somebody he doesn't know?"

"Yeah."

"Why would he do that?"

"Because I asked my lawyer to ask him."

"Why you do that?"

"Because you're my friend."

"I'm not the one in trouble."

"You felt bad. You called me to see him."

Lovely took in a deep breath very slowly. She didn't watch her friend so much as study him. He was wearing brown slacks and shoes made from a dark blue fabric. His short-sleeved shirt was pale blue, and his hair was cut close to the scalp. Ghalen checked off this inventory as Lovely scrutinized him.

Then she stood, moved her chair closer, sat down, and took both of his hands in hers.

They were close enough that the boy could feel her breath. He thought that she could probably feel his.

After a few moments she moved her head, as if she was about to say something, but she didn't utter a word. Ghalen wanted to say that he had only skipped a morning class and that he needed to get to school. But he didn't speak and so knew that he was going to stay.

Lovely sat up straighter and moved her hands so that she was holding his wrists. His fingers stroked the tarnished silver bangle on her left arm. Again, she looked as if she were about to say something but instead, she raised a hand to his face, stroking his cheek gently. Ghalen closed his eyes. He was holding her one hand in both of his, feeling the smoothness of her leg against the back of his hands.

Opening his eyes he raised a hand to her face. Now they were looking into each other's eyes. She brought her hand down to caress his throat while he was outlining her lips with two fingers. They were leaning ever closer, slowly.

In the back of his mind Ghalen was thinking that this all started in that bonsai garden the day before. When he saw Lovely, he knew that he wanted something, something.

Moving toward the edge of her chair, she kissed him first. He lowered his hand to squeeze her shoulder, and she did to his lips with her tongue what he had done with two fingers. The kissing was slow, and the cabin was so quiet that they could both hear the wetness of their lips and tongues.

Ghalen realized that if either one of them said a word, the spell would be broken. In the middle of a kiss, he lifted her up in both arms and carried her the two steps to the mattress on the floor. She didn't complain because she was still kissing him.

Over the next few hours there were few moments when their lips were not together. They undressed each other, excruciatingly slowly. When they weren't kissing lips, they rubbed their mouths and tongues against newly revealed skin.

Ghalen realized that of the few times he'd had sex that he had no idea what it could be like, how much he didn't know.

"WOW," LOVELY SAID. IT WAS THE FIRST WORD EITHER of them had uttered since they touched. "You've done that before."

"Not like this."

"I'm still with Bruno."

"Yeah. I know."

"I mean, I don't do things like this."

Ghalen's logical brain wanted to point out that she just did something like this, but he kept it to himself.

"You are so beautiful," he said.

She turned over on her side and kissed his shoulder.

"I got to go see Big B," she said.

"You want me to go with you?"

"No. I'll just tell him that you dropped by to tell me about the lawyer before you went to school. 'Cause, you know, I think he might smell it on us."

She sat up and lifted her slip from the floor. She was about to put it on when Ghalen stayed her hand.

"I just wanna look at you for one more minute," he said. "I never want to forget this."

Lovely smiled, posed a little and then said, "Okay. I have to go now."

THAT NIGHT GHALEN'S HEAD FELT LIKE IT HAD THE DAY after Bruno knocked him down. It was a stunned, vacant feeling that the young man hadn't experienced since he was laid out on that concrete curb.

"What you thinkin'?" Robert asked him at the dinette table.

"Um, nuthin'."

"What you do in school today?"

"Um, uh, I didn't go to school today, Dad."

"Why not?"

"I don't know. I just wanted to go around and have fun."

"What you do?"

"I went to a park in Culver City and then took a bus down to the beach."

"Aren't they gonna call you truant or somethin'?"

"I don't know."

"You need me to write you a note?'

This offer nudged Ghalen back to who he was before the bonsai garden.

"No, thanks, Dad. I'll just tell 'em that I skipped. I never did anything like that before. How was your day at work?"

"Good. You didn't come to get me, and I made it home all by myself."

"How was everybody?"

"Good. You know me, I like the same normal things every day. Feels comfortable."

Robert was looking closely at his son.

"What, Dad?"

"What, what?"

"Why you lookin' at me?"

"I like how you look."

"No, uh-uh. When you study something, you usually have something to tell."

"Wellllll, I guess you got me there."

"What is it?"

"Do you remember Aura Cress?"

"That woman who you met on the bus that used to make Mom so jealous?"

"Your mother had no reason to feel like that."

"My English professor said that *reason* is just one letter away from *treason*."

That little bit of wordplay shut Robert down for a minute or two. He contemplated Ghalen's meaning, even if, Ghalen thought, he hadn't understood it himself.

"Well anyway," Robert said at last. "I'm gonna have Miss Cress over for dinner Monday night. I mean, I want to, but I need to ask you if you mind."

"Mind what?"

"Her coming here to dinner. This is your mother's home."

"Can I bring somebody?"

"HELLO?" LOVELY ANSWERED ON THE FIRST RING. "GHALEN?"

"Hey."

"I went to the hospital."

"How was Big B?"

"He liked that lawyer, Mr. Nye. Bruno said that he asked questions like he understood what was happenin' in the street."

"So, he gonna work with him?"

"I think so."

Silence spooled out in the seconds after that transfer of information. Ghalen couldn't think of anything to add. On any other phone call, he would have gotten off to write in his red journal about what he'd been doing for the last few weeks. He found that going over the details of the recent past helped him to understand what he had to do next. He had three journals going at any one time. Red was for the details of everyday life: like going to class, meetings with people, dates, and conversations he'd overheard on buses, in classrooms, and anywhere else that had no specific purpose. Blue was for his school and life studies: there he talked about things like chess, chemistry, and knowledge he'd need one day. The black journal was about his inner life: there he memorialized his mother, wrote about the things he'd learned from his father and also the things he needed to do for Robert, and, now and again, he'd write about those folks that were also a part of his life like his grandmothers Pristine and Myrtle, the people at Indus, and, sometimes, Bruno and Lovely, mostly in memory.

"Bruno told me to tell you thanks."

"A'course, I help him. He's my oldest friend."

After a pause she said, "I wanted to thank you too."

"It's me should be thankin' you, Lovely."

"For what? I didn't do nuthin."

Ghalen's mind refused to utter the words he was feeling.

"If you need anything," Ghalen said then. "I mean, I don't know when Bruno's gonna get outta that hospital, but if you need anything I could do."

"The lawyer said that he won't get out for three weeks. But I'm okay. I got my job. But if you need somethin . . . I'll be there."

"There is one thing."

19.

EXCERPT FROM BLACK JOURNAL #9

*It was on a Monday that I went to Culver City to see Lovely
and then Bruno. I already wrote about that. I respect it that
she is his girlfriend and I know what we did was wrong. But
I couldn't help myself. Really. I don't think she could either.
At Sunday school at the Constant Traveler Church, they say
that the devil comes with treasures so bright that they blind a
person to what's good and right. I don't know if I believe in the
Devil but that's what happened to me and Lovely. For the first
time since my mother died, I had something for me. I knew it
was wrong, evil, but I told myself that I'd stay away from her
for both our sakes. That felt good in my heart, and I took a long
bath in the deep tub and when I got out, I felt clean in both my
body and my soul.*

*But then, on Tuesday I called Lovely, and she told me about
the lawyer going to see Bruno and she asked me if there was
anything she could do for me. That night I had talked with
my dad about Aura Cress coming to dinner on Monday night
and I had asked him if I could bring somebody to eat with us.
I was thinking that if I had to see a woman my father would
be dating, then I could bring one of my girlfriends from school.*

I was going to ask Talulah Stillman, because she said that she wanted to see me again.

Talulah's a very pretty girl but she's not Lovely.

When I spoke to Lovely, I said that I'd do anything to help her and Bruno. That's when she asked if there was anything she could do for me. I told her about the dinner with my dad like I used to tell her things in the old days when we were just friends. She said that she wanted to come, that she really liked my dad.

That was okay. It wasn't going to be in a room all by ourselves out behind a house. My dad and Miss Cress were going to be there. It was like me and Lovely were going to be friends again.

But then, on Wednesday night, after I'd gone to bed, Lovely called. She said that it was lonely in her little cabin. I said that as long as Bruno was away, she could go to her parents' house. But she said that being there would be lonely too. And when I tried to think of other solutions, she stopped me and said that most of her life had been lonely, that even when Bruno was there, she never felt good down deep like she did with me. That's when she talked about how sweet I was when she kissed me like she did and touched me like that. She kept talking and I couldn't help myself. She asked if I had an orgasm and I said I did. She giggled and said that she hadn't finished telling me how she felt.

We talked till three in the morning. That's when I fell asleep.

When I got up the next day, I felt fine. I wasn't worried about the night before because we hadn't really done it again. And so, when she called me Thursday night, I had thought of all the things that we had done on Monday, and I was able to make her feel the way I did. I felt a little guilty about that but not like my soul would be damned or anything.

It wasn't until Friday that it got bad along with being good. On Thursday Lovely said that she was going to tell me what we'd do the next time. What she was going to do to me and the things she would make me do. I had never felt my heart beat that hard, not even when I was doing sprints.

I stayed up all night Friday. At first, I was waiting for Lovely to call and then, when she didn't, I called her phone. When she didn't answer I worried that something had happened to her in that out-of-the-way cabin. Then I worried that Bruno had been released from the hospital and I'd never see Lovely again. But then why wouldn't I be happy for them? But what about me? I couldn't go back to the way things were before that coffee garden café.

20.

What time's Lovely gonna get here, Gayley?" Robert asked his son on Monday afternoon.

"I don't think she's comin', Dad."

"Why not?"

"You know. Bruno's in the hospital and she's got this job at a coffee house."

"How she do her homework with all that?"

"She doesn't."

"Then how's she gonna graduate?"

"Lovely dropped outta school, Dad."

They were in the kitchen, Robert making a spicy eggplant casserole and Ghalen prepping the salad. They usually worked well together, father and son, but when Robert heard this about one of Ghalen's school friends he stopped cooking and leaned back, perching against the high kitchen stool.

"Dropped out?"

"Yeah." Ghalen kept dicing a tomato that he'd already scalded, skinned, and de-seeded.

"What for?"

"It's hard to say, Dad. She had a fight with her parents and, and she had to move out."

"But she needs a education."

"I know but . . . I don't know."

Seeing the sadness in his son, Robert said, "Don't worry, boy. With a friend like you she's bound to find the right way."

AURA ARRIVED AT SIX FORTY-FIVE, THE TIME THAT ROBert said they'd be finished in the kitchen. She was wearing a teal pantsuit with a black blouse under the jacket. Her necklace was an ultrathin gold chain with a fair-size gold ball bearing as its pendant. She sat on the wood and vinyl couch, holding a goblet of deep red, organic burgundy. Ghalen sat on the hassock that had been his chair since before he could remember, and Robert stood across from Aura, his back pressed against the wall.

"Where's your friend, Ghalen?" Aura asked.

"She couldn't make it, had to go to work I think."

"Oh, that's too bad, I wanted to meet her."

"I'm sure you will. I mean, you'll prob'ly come for dinner again."

"I hope so. Your father tells me that you're going to be the valedictorian for your graduating class."

"Yeah. I didn't have the highest score, but all my A's were in advanced placement classes. Maybe I'll come for the celebration."

"And you're only fifteen?"

"Almost sixteen."

"Wow," Aura said. "I had to take my equivalency test when I was twenty. You know they kicked me outta high school."

"Why?" Ghalen really wanted to know.

"I was just a bad girl. From smokin' to boys to men. I'd'a been on my way to prison if it wasn't for my mama dyin' and my grandmother comin' up from New Iberia."

"She took care'a you?" Ghalen asked.

"She did. We used to sit together every night talkin' 'bout the old days and learnin' how to be classy."

"She did a good job on ya," Robert said from his piece of wall.

"Come sit down next to me, Robert." Aura held out her right hand, palm up.

Robert took a deep breath and did as she asked.

Aura turned to Ghalen and said, "I was smokin' and drinkin', holdin' my boyfriends' guns—boyfriends that were twice my age. But somehow my grandmother made all'a that seem useless. She'd take me to buy nice clothes and showed me how to dress and even how to walk."

"You didn't know how to walk?" Ghalen asked. He noticed that Robert was still holding on to her hand.

Laughing, Aura said, "Not the way a lady should walk, all even and balanced. You know, with confidence."

"Time to serve dinner," Robert announced. Then he stood up and headed for the kitchen.

WHILE HIS FATHER PLATED THE MEAL GHALEN TOOK OUT the folding table and the fancy oak folding chairs, setting them up in the middle of the living room. Aura helped him with the table-cloth, napkins, and cutlery. Soon they were all seated and served.

"You want to give the blessing, Gayley?"

"Sure, Dad."

The young man bowed his head and held his hands, palms up, before him. Robert did the same and Aura brought her hands together in Christian fashion, just under her chin.

"Oh Lord, provider of food, grains, and all edibles, thanks to you for giving us food today."

"Amen," added Robert.

"I don't think I've ever heard that grace before," Aura commented.

"It's Hindu," Ghalen said. "It's supposed to be said in Sanskrit, but that doesn't make sense if no one understands."

"Thank you for that."

"Let's eat," was Robert's blessing.

Not long after that, the doorbell rang.

Ghalen's vision shifted. He felt a sudden brightness in the room and there was a skip in every other heartbeat.

"I'll get it!"

ON THE FIRST FLOOR OF THE APARTMENT BUILDING, Ghalen pulled the door open.

She was wearing a gray pastel, almost silver dress suit with a hot pink blouse and no jewelry. The skirt of the suit came down to midthigh, and her heels were red. For a moment Ghalen was speechless.

Before he could find the greeting in his throat Lovely laughed and said, "Hi-i."

Ghalen shook his head in reply.

"I didn't think you were coming," he said at last. "I called."

"I tried to stay away, but I really wanted to see you. I really did."

"Come in."

They kissed and then walked up the stairs arm in arm. At the door to the apartment, she preceded him into the living room.

"She came," Ghalen announced enthusiastically.

Robert jumped up and shook the girl's hand and then led her to the empty chair.

"I'll go get your plate from the kitchen," he told her.

"Lovely this is my dad's friend, Aura Cress."

"It's nice to meet you, Miss Cress. Ghalen told me about you."

"He did? What did he say?"

"Just that you met Mr. Horton on a bus and that you were very pretty."

"Is Lovely your given name?"

"In Persian it's Doost Dashtny. My mother's mother used to call me that, and then the translation became my name."

"It certainly is true," Aura complimented.

Lovely bowed in false modesty and then smiled in thanks.

"Ghalen thought you wouldn't be able to make it because of your job," Robert said, bringing Lovely's plate and placing it before her.

"I know. But I kept remembering all those great desserts you used to make. Like that puff pastry strawberry tart."

"I remember the first time I ever had that at Kundakunda," Aura chimed. "I thought I had died and gone to heaven."

The conversation remained light and friendly for quite a while. They ate salad and eggplant; the adults drinking wine while the teenagers had mugs of hot cider.

It wasn't until the carrot cake dessert that Robert said, "Ghalen told me that you guys' friend got arrested."

Ghalen was afraid that this was too much, that Lovely would run out of the apartment and never talk to him again.

The girl gazed down at her glazed slice of cake for a long moment and then looked up, locking her pool black eyes on his father.

"He was stupid, and he got in trouble."

"Where is he now?" Aura asked.

"In like house arrest in the hospital."

"What's he in the hospital for?" asked Robert.

"He got shot."

"Oh my God!" That was Aura. "Who shot him?"

"The people he was goin' to meet. It's not that bad, just in the arm."

"Is he gonna go to jail?"

"No, Miss Cress. Gayley called his lawyer and she put him in touch with this other lawyer. He made a deal with the prosecutor, and Bruno only has to spend three months in this juvenile halfway house. He gonna have to wear an ankle bracelet, but at least that's better than prison."

This was news to Ghalen. He realized that, since Monday night, he hadn't asked her anything about his friend.

"You called Emily?" Robert asked his son.

"Yeah."

"That was really good'a you."

"He's my friend."

Through his mind's eye Ghalen could see himself sitting upon that waiting stone at the crossroads of his long-ago dream. The dinner conversation went on, Ghalen even participating now and then, but in his mind, he was in a wilderness, needing to decide.

After dessert Lovely and Aura demanded to be allowed to rinse off the dishes and put them in the dishwasher, leaving Robert and his son to put the living room in order.

AS MAN AND BOY FOLDED THE DINING TABLE THEY started talking.

"Have you seen Bruno?"

"One time. That was the day I ditched school."

"How is he?"

"His eyes are kinda . . . I don't know, kinda wild."

"Mm," Robert intoned.

"He's still the same, Dad. He's okay." Saying this, Ghalen was looking for what he most often got from his father: a kind of passive hopefulness that everything would be all right.

Instead, Robert said, "No he isn't, son. He's not the same."

"You didn't see him. He smiled the same and said the same things. He looks kinda like a grown man but, the boy's still inside."

"It looks like that. It does. But when the street gets ahold'a you it just, it just twists you up inside till your heart is all strangled up with your gut." Speaking these words Robert clenched the fingers of both hands very close to each other, making a gesture that most resembled the twisting of a dishrag, squeezing out the last drop of water.

Ghalen stared at his father like some peasant listening to the diatribes of Moses the Mad. From man to prophet to God. He wanted to deny the elder man's claims, but for some reason his mind caught on to his words as truth. They were true. They were.

"I have to go," Lovely said from the entrance of the kitchen.

Her words seemed to Ghalen like a pronouncement. She was leaving, almost gone. And with her would go any chance for Robert's son to become the man he wanted to be, living the life he wanted to.

"How are you getting home?" Robert wanted to know. "Me and Aura could give you a ride."

"Sure," Aura piped.

"That's so nice, Mr. Horton, Miss Cress, but you don't have to. I borrowed my sister's car."

"I'll walk you down," Ghalen offered.

PARKED HALFWAY UP THE BLOCK FROM HIS HOUSE THE boy walked his childhood friend to an old, very old powder-blue Ford Falcon.

"Wow. This car's like an antique," he said.

Lovely took him in her arms and kissed him hard. She pulled back and he was about to say something, but she kissed him again. The next few minutes were consumed by Ghalen trying to speak and her beating the words down with a passion that was even greater than on the first day they were together.

That night he wrote in his journal:

EXCERPT FROM BLACK JOURNAL #9

. . . when Lovely kissed me it felt like I was in a place that was new and very important. Nothing bothered me or scared me. It was so familiar that I literally wanted to cry . . .

LOVELY WAS TRYING TO KISS HIM AGAIN BUT HE HELD
her off.

Her look said, *I'll kiss you all night if you let me.*

"When can I see you again?" Ghalen asked.

Her face tensed up and tears flowed freely from her eyes, but
she said nothing.

"It doesn't have to be tomorrow or soon even. I just need to see
you again."

"Gayley." She was the only person, outside of his parents, to
call him that.

"What?"

"Get in the car and we could drive up north."

"North where?"

"Portland or Seattle."

"You mean for good?"

"Yeah. Just me and you."

"But why?"

"I love you. I've been in love with you since I was six. For most
of my life Bruno was gonna be my friend and you would be my
husband."

Ghalen took these words into his chest, that's what if felt like.
Her words were an invocation willing him to become a man.

"I can get some money," she said. "I know where I can get it."

"But why do we have to run away?"

"I don't want to turn you and Bruno against each other. It
would be like back when we were in school, but worse. Much
worse."

He was at the crossroads again.

"I can't do it right now, Love. My father needs me. And, and
even if I could work that out with him, I couldn't just walk away.
Not without a word."

She stopped trying to kiss him, took half a step back.

"I understand," she said. "If I had a home and a father like yours, I'd never leave. But I have to go, and I had to ask."

"So, what are you gonna do now?"

"I don't know."

When Ghalen moved to embrace her, she pushed him off with unexpected vehemence.

"No," she said. "I have to go."

She went around to the driver's side, unlocked the door, and got in—all of this without looking at him.

He watched the car rolling away, the two red lights on behind. He remembered that this was a quote from a blues song by the Rolling Stones that they had taken from a Delta blues singer, Robert Johnson, that, in turn, he had taken from some unknown lyricist.

IN THE HOUSE GHALEN ATTEMPTED AND FAILED TO KEEP the sadness off his face.

"Son."

"Yeah, Dad?"

"I'm gonna, I'm gonna go on home with Aura. She's . . . I mean . . . I'm gonna stay with her tonight."

"Okay."

"You don't mind?"

"Don't forget to do your push-ups in the morning."

21.

Ghalen didn't sleep that night. He sat up reading an old book of science fiction short stories called *Dilvish, the Damned*. It was wrought in the genre of sword and sorcery, about a mighty warrior and his solid-steel black steed. He kept telling himself that he'd just read one more story and then go to bed, but at the back of his mind he was hoping that Lovely would call and give him another chance. He didn't know what he would say but hoped that the outcome would be different.

It wasn't until after midnight that his cell phone sounded.

"Hello?"

"Gayley."

"Oh, yeah, Dad?"

"I'm coming home."

"Why? I thought you were gonna spend the night with Aura?"

"I saw how sad you were. I know you not ready to let me go like that."

"No, Dad, no. I was just messed up because Lovely was talking about how sad Bruno was, how they might go up north to Washington together. I was just missing them."

"Really?"

"You stay there with Aura, Pops. She seems real nice, and you need a lady friend to hang out with sometimes."

"You sure you don't want me there?"

"For what? To watch me sleep?"

THERE WAS A BOOKSHELF IN THE HALL WHERE THE BED-
rooms were. On that shelf was a paperback book penned by the
Roman poet of love, Ovid. Ghalen read the rather dense text, not
for advice but as a sleep aid.

It didn't work.

IN THE MORNING GHALEN SKIPPED HIS EXERCISES,
planning to go get an English muffin bacon-and-egg sandwich at a
fast-food stand near school. He'd just finished dressing when the
doorbell rang.

Running down the stairs, Ghalen tripped, twisting his right
ankle, but that didn't stop him.

He threw the door open, certain that it was Lovely, come back
to give him another chance. But it wasn't her.

Standing there was a dark-skinned Black man, maybe two
inches shorter than the high school senior. Ghalen felt that he
should have a name for this man's face, like maybe he was from
Indus or an old friend of his father. But the boy couldn't name
him. What marked the stranger more than this familiarity were
his garments. His cotton pants were shapeless, loose, and black.
His white shirt was of rough linen, also loose. His shoes were
sandals made from the discarded rubber of old tires. Ghalen was
later to find out that these were known as Ho Chi Minh sandals.
On his head the man wore a cone-shaped sun hat made from
interlaced wide threads of bamboo. The top of the round hat
ended in a point, and the brim came down to the level of the
man's eyebrows.

The whites of the unknown visitor's eyes were like mosaics of
differing tiles made from lighter and darker ivory, with a few thin

red threads woven through to hold the orbs together. The man's hands were strong but gnarled. This told Ghalen that despite his smooth skin, the man was probably older and had been a laborer for most of his life.

He was familiar and yet unknown, foreign and unique, but still reminiscent of someone from the neighborhood. All this was enough to momentarily push Lovely from the heartbroken young man's mind.

"Can I help you?" Ghalen queried.

Instead of answering, the man allowed a slow smile to spread from his mouth to his eyes. His shoulders, that had been somewhat slumped, straightened.

Ghalen was now met by the man's joyful gaze.

"Ghalen?"

"Yes, I'm Ghalen. What's your name?"

"Night. Night Farr. But I'm called Dem."

Days later Ghalen wrote in his black journal, *A literal shiver went through my soul.*

"Night?"

"Do you know me?"

Backing away from the entrance, Ghalen said, "Come on in, grandfather. Come on up."

GHALEN SAT THE OLD MAN ON THE COUCH IN THE LIVING room, offered him water, which he shook his head at and then wine, which he accepted. Then the boy asked if the man needed something to eat.

"No thank you, son, the wine'll keep me."

"I'm so happy to meet you, sir. So happy."

"You believe who I am just 'cause I say it?"

"I've seen a picture of you in uniform just before your second deployment. Mama had it. When I first saw you, I thought I recognized you, but I wasn't sure."

"I should never have gone." Night shook his head, peering downward.

"They said you were dead."

"Yeah. I know they did. I was always out in the jungle killin' brave and innocent men and women and makin' a mess. I had a string'a men's ears as a necklace and a bamboo knife to kill up close. When I went dark what else could they think? 'Ole Night's been swallowed by his name.'"

"But what really did happen?"

The veteran's eyes shifted from one corner to another, up to the ceiling and then back to the apartment door he'd come through. It seemed to Ghalen that he was considering the question as if it was the first time he had ever been asked it.

Finally, he started to talk. "I was out on a reconnaissance mission deep in the DMZ. Me and PFC Miller and a corporal we called Chin. He weren't Chinese, he just had a big chin. We was way out there lookin' for signs of Charlie, what leaves he wiped his ass wit', what holes he slept in. Then, one quiet mornin' either Miller or Chin stepped on a land mine. I don't know which because I had the lead, maybe seven paces ahead. I know the explosion must'a kilt them boys 'cause it knocked me for a loop."

Night seemed to be considering, rehashing these events as if they were pieces in a child's jigsaw puzzle, looking for sense.

"What happened then?" Ghalen asked in a hushed tone.

"I woke up on a floor-bed made from leaves wrapped in a big plastic sheet. Life had been so rough for so long that even this poor situation felt like it might be heaven. I tried to sit up but I wasn't strong enough, before I could fall back a sure hand shored up my weak back and a woman said, 'You thirsty?'

"It was a Vietnamese girl, no more than sixteen. Phu'ò'ng was her name. She gave me water and rice broth for three days. She tended the wounds in my back, and this here left ear that was almost hacked off, she sewed it back on. Every night she washed my body with water from a clear pond."

It was something about the water, Ghalen thought, that interrupted Night's tale.

"Why didn't she kill you?" the boy asked.

"Why would she do that?"

"Because, because you were there killin' her people."

"Oh . . . yeah. You're American. I almost forgot."

"Aren't you?"

"Am I? I was . . . before Nam. I was and then I wasn't. You know, when I was still a American, I believed there was two things: right and wrong. I was on the one side and they was on the other . . ."

"Who were 'they'?"

"Don't mattah. Don't mattah 'cause it's wrong one way or t'other. Ain't no two sides in life. That's baby talk. Ain't no black and white, it's a rainbow, that's what it is. I was a light sea green and Phu'ò'ng was scarlet with a royal blue at the edges.

"She had been a peasant for a thousand years. Her people lived on that land, where she tended me; they lived there for so long that they blended together, one generation after the other one. That's why she could heal me. The healin' was in her hands."

He stopped talking, but this time Ghalen had nothing to ask.

After a while Night sipped at his wine and then wondered, "You got any rice?"

There was always a little rice in the refrigerator. Robert said that it could be added to anything from cereal to soup.

Ghalen served up a dish of this *utility rice* that he'd warmed in the microwave.

"Brown rice," Night said.

"You don't like it?"

"It's okay. I'm not picky."

After eating for a while Night went back to his memories.

"Phu'ò'ng's husband had been killed by a Vietcong for some insult or disagreement. She had two young children and a garden. That was one thing too many. Because'a that I decided to stay and help her until she could be on her own or my debt was paid. We did good together. Raised a pig now and then. The boy and girl grew. It was like bein' married and best friends who bickered now and then." Night stared into the empty bowl, noticed a solitary grain stuck to the side, picked it out and ate it. "One spring evenin' she come in from the garden droopin'. She was hot and I washed her with a stash of alcohol we had. She cooled down enough to smile and kiss me. That was unusual. We didn't kiss all that much. She said that the jackfruit tree had fruit, but she was too weak to get at it and that I should do it. Then she fell asleep and that night the fever came back. and she was dead before morning.

"Got the jackfruit the next day an' buried her with it. Hoa matched up with a boy who lived about a mile away and Trung headed out to Ho Chi Minh City. Boy wanted a modern life. After a while I worked my way back down to Saigon, got a job on a Dutch carrier, jumped ship in Canada, and made it down here, after a while."

"When was that?" Ghalen wondered aloud.

"Eleven years ago. About that."

"How did you know to come to this address?"

"I was livin' at a day hotel in Redondo Beach. I met this young man, Blanton, who said he could find my wife, Pristine, on his phone. I told him he was crazy but damn if he didn't do it. I bought me a secondhand suit and a near-new pair'a shoes."

"What did gramma Pristine say?"

"'Where the hell did you come from?'"

Ghalen grinned because that sounded just like his mother's mother.

"I asked her if I could come in and she said what for. I asked her where Jamilah was, and she said dead. Then she said about Robert Horton, who she called a retard, and you . . . Ghalen Romeo Horton. I went back to Redondo, found Blanton, and gave him twenty of the one hundred dollars your gramma gave me. And here I am, eatin' rice and drinkin' storebought wine.

"I never really felt much about family before that land mine. I mean, my mother left, and Dad worked all day and half the night. He loved me but we really didn't get along. Soon as I could I moved out and married your grandmother, but she was always on me about sumpin'. War sounded fine to me. But after that land mine, and Phu'ò'ng, I got to know what it was like to wake up and feel like you were where you belonged."

"So, you came here because you wanted to be with family again," Ghalen suggested.

"I guess so," he replied, nodding, and looking down at his powerful hands.

It was then that Ghalen thought about Lovely. One way or another she was gone, off to Washington or Oregon or to be with Bruno. He would miss her, but now he had his mother's father, a man that she revered as much as she did Ghalen's father. It seemed perfectly right that Night was there, asking for a family.

"We have a guest room," he said to his ancestor.

"I couldn't put you out like that. I'm just happy you let me in the front door."

"I know that Dad would want me to put you up. He loved your daughter more than anything. He would offer you a room without question."

"Well," Night said, "I could take a little nap. This American wine goes to my head, and it took three buses to get here."

"I'll go make the bed."

NIGHT SNORED AND FARTED IN HIS SLEEP. GHALEN WENT to the living room to sit in half-lotus on his hassock and read over his Red Journal, not from recent experience, but rather from Red Journal #1, his first, from back when he started telling his story, at the beginning of the first grade. He was only five years old, and all the other kids were six. But his age didn't matter much after the second day. He met Bruno on that day, when Miss Wren-Thomas changed his seat because it was next to a window and the glare hurt his eyes.

The lumbering brown boy looked at Ghalen's journal and asked, "What's that?"

"It's my book where I write down everything that I do, so I can remember it."

"You know how to write good?"

"Yeah, I guess."

"Can you help me make a good Q?"

"Sure thing."

LOVELY FRAIN CAME TO THEIR CLASS ON THE TUESDAY of the second week. She sat down next to Ghalen and smiled at him. Even twelve years later, sitting on the hassock with his impossible grandfather asleep in the guest room, Ghalen remembered that smile.

Bruno said that Lovely was a stupid name, but he stopped saying that after Ghalen asked him, did he remember when Billy Meyers called him Bruno the Bear?

At lunch Lovely shared her chocolate chip cookies with the boys, and they became fast friends forever.

Ghalen was surprised that his cursive hand was so good back then. This made him think of his father, whose writing was so beautiful.

"My mother taught me how to read," he said aloud to no one. "But Dad taught me how to write."

A voice answered, "Readin' and writin' is two-thirds of the way there."

Ghalen looked up at his grandfather. He'd doffed the round and pointed bamboo hat revealing salt-and-pepper woolen hair that gathered around a bald spot toward the back—where some of the Jewish kids' fathers wore their yarmulkes.

"Do you know what the last thing is?" Night asked.

"Arithmetic."

Ghalen liked his ancestor's grin.

"Did you kill a lot of people?" the young man asked.

Night walked over to the couch, sat down, and took a deep breath before asking, "What you readin'?"

"My journal from the first grade."

"Like a diary?"

"Uh-huh."

"And you been writin' in it for all these years?"

"Yeah."

"Damn. That's what they call a true remembrance."

"My dad writes down everything that has happened the day before. He does it in the morning when his mind is sharp."

"Yeah," Night said, looking down at his hands again. "I killed a lotta peoples. Stabbed 'em, shot 'em, blew 'em up, and burned 'em down in their bamboo huts when they was asleep. I killed men, women, and children with my bare hands."

Night turned his head away, and the last word had the sound of crying to it.

Ghalen wanted to say that he was sorry, that he didn't mean to make the man cry. But even through that guilt he wanted to know why a man would ever do something like kill so many people. He wanted the answer but knew that hearing this truth wouldn't save any lives.

He wanted to say something to get them on a better subject, but just then there came the sound of footsteps on the outer stairs.

22.

Anybody home?"

That was the phrase that Robert called out whenever he returned. *Anybody home?* He also said this when he'd arrive at Indus for the morning shift. *Anybody home?*

"We're here," Ghalen called. "In the living room."

Robert strode in from the hallway door with a grocery bag huddled under his right arm. He'd gone shopping like he did almost every day to get the freshest vegetables for their meal.

Night stood up from the couch with head half-bowed and hands folded in front.

"Oh," said Robert.

"Dad, this is Night Farr, Mom's father. He didn't die in Vietnam."

As was his way when there was *more to know than he could take in*, Robert became very still, staring at the head-bowed man. They stayed in their positions for half an uncomfortable minute.

Then Night raised his head and said, "I'm sorry to come into your house like this, Mr. Horton. It's just that I rang the bell and Ghalen answered. I had a little meal and got so tired that I needed to lie down. I guess I must'a been more tired than I thought."

Night's grin had no effect on Ghalen's dad.

"You?" Robert spoke. "You . . . are Jamilah's father?"

"I am."

"But you died."

"No. I was wounded and saved by a peasant woman. She saved my life and then took me in."

"Why didn't you come back? Jammy missed you every day."

"I was alive," Night acknowledged. "But it was like I had died. I had died from the war all around me and the only thing that I could believe in was the, the daily chores on that little farm in the middle'a nowhere."

Ghalen watched his father's face as he digested these words. At first his eyes almost closed and then, slowly, he started to nod. He put the brown paper grocery bag on the floor and moved to his father-in-law gathering him into a powerful hug. Night lay his head against Robert's shoulder.

"She would'a been so happy I don't think her feet would'a touched the ground for a week," Robert said. "She would'a cried and cried. This would be one of the happiest days in her whole life. The first was when Gayley was born, the second was when her and me got together, and then you, Mr. Farr, you, her father— alive after all these years."

ROBERT MADE WHITE RICE TO GO WITH COOKED PINTO beans he had in the freezer, a deep-fried head of cauliflower, and a salad that Ghalen threw together. The generations sat around the dinette table, eating and sharing disparate memories of their mother, daughter, and wife.

"YES, SIR," ROBERT WAS SAYING. "WE MET IN THE RAIN, at that farmer's market. It was a downpour, and we pressed together under her umbrella. I don't think there was a day after that when we didn't at least talk on the phone."

"That's so wonderful," the veteran-father opined. "You know, she was only three years old when I left. I saw her once or twice when I was on leave, but I don't even remember it. There was all them explosions in my ears."

Wanting to be a part of that masculine sewing circle, Ghalen said, "I remember Mama readin' to me. She'd move her point finger under each word as she read it. That's the way she taught me how to read."

"What's the best thing you remember about your mom, Ghalen?" Night asked.

"How she always wanted the best for me and how she listened when dad thought something different."

"How about you, Robert?" the elder among them queried.

"How . . ." Robert said and then stopped. He sat there, at the dinette table, looking deep into the space between them. Ghalen thought that his vision was like an electron microscope investigating the molecules of air mixed in with the food matter lifted by scent into the gaseous atmosphere of the kitchen.

"How she respected me," he finally got out. "It, it felt like the first time ever that somebody didn't treat me like a empty bag of rice. She . . . it was like . . . she cherished me."

"There was so much love in her," Night agreed. "Her mama once told me how she taught her how to hold a teacup at her play tea party. You supposed to stick your baby finger out when you drink."

The generations of men were quiet for a while then.

Ghalen felt that he belonged at that table, that this was his family, his future.

"You say you're stayin' at a day hotel?" Robert asked Night.

"Yeah. It ain't bad. They got like a den downstairs. I play chess there with a couple'a the guys. They got a card table too, but the house don't allow gamblin'. If you wanna gamble you got to do it up in your room."

"You like it there?" Robert pressed.

"Like I said, it's okay."

"Ain't much to it, but you could stay in our guest room if you want."

"I wouldn't put you guys out like that. I mean, I'd love to stay here with you. This the first time I felt like family since Nam, but I don't need to cause trouble. But if I did stay, I guess I could get a job and help you all with the rent and the light bill."

"If you don't mind washin' dishes, I could get you a job at the restaurant I cook at."

"Really? You could do that?"

"Oh yeah. Talk about family, the staff and the chef been together more'n twenty years."

WHEN GHALEN CLIMBED INTO BED, HE WAS ASLEEP BE-fore he could make it under the covers. It was as if Sleep was some kind of stealth-soldier that ambushed him before he could mount any defense. He didn't think about school or Lovely, Bruno or guilt, not even his mother . . . It was like when he was at the bonsai garden coffee shop, without a worry in his head.

And then, at 2:08 a.m., he opened his eyes like it was 7:00 and time to go to school. He had an erection and the memory of Lovely's kisses. The kisses felt so real that he sat up and looked around, thinking that she had to be there, somewhere. He was panting, and it wasn't just about sex. There was also a dead mother, a thousand-year war, a friend betrayed, and a woman he would do anything to be with.

The cell phone was in the kangaroo pocket of his sweat jacket, hanging from his desk chair.

Her number was burned into his mind like her name. But it didn't work. The number had been disconnected. She was gone.

She was gone and there was no way to look for her.

Ghalen thought that he'd be up for the rest of the night, but he fell back asleep with no problem. There he slept on a fresh grave of some young woman he didn't know. The headstone was a disc of marble and the name had yet to be inscribed. The soil was soft but there were stones in it. The night air was chilly, and insects crawled up under him for his warmth and blood.

The bugs burrowed and bit, making him itch, and the ground beneath began to slowly give way. He was sinking into the grave of the nameless dead girl, could feel the soil coming up around his head. He knew that this was a dream but couldn't wake up. He knew that none of this was happening but couldn't open his eyes. His mouth was dry, but he couldn't even reach to the night table for the tumbler of water that was always there.

He tried to call out to his father, but his mouth couldn't form words.

"Uh!" he called. "Mmm! Uh!"

He sank deeper. Then he realized that if he could remember the dead girl's name then he could say it and the nightmare would end. But he didn't know the name, and even if he could know it, he couldn't make words, couldn't speak.

Maybe if I could just say her name in my mind, he thought. *Maybe that would be enough.*

ROUGHENED AND VERY STRONG HANDS HELD HIM, NOT ungently.

"You got some isopropyl, Robert?"

"In the medicine cabinet."

"Go get it and bring a couple'a towels too."

The girl in the grave was named Isolde, Ghalen realized. But this information was useless, as he could not speak. He struggled against the hands holding him just to do something, to feel alive.

"Here you go," Robert said urgently.

Someone was removing Ghalen's pants. His shirt ripped as it

was pulled off, over his head. And then there came the cold. First on his head and face, then across the chest and his arms all the way to the fingers. On his back and legs. Ice, slivers so sharp that they felt like razors cutting the skin.

"That's the fuck cold!" Ghalen screamed. "Stop it!"

But the icy embraces continued. Ghalen writhed against it, but the rough hands held him in place. A flash of sunlight from the long-ago window of his bedroom forced him to jam his eyes closed to keep out the pain.

And then Isolde reached up from beneath. "You are mine," she whispered. The pain her words caused was exquisite, inescapable.

"Isolde!" Ghalen cried aloud, but the incantation did not set him free.

"Get the bucket!" Night commanded. "He gonna heave."

Ghalen was hanging over the side of a precipice, bitter liquid burning his nostrils as it flowed from his nose and mouth.

He was free from the grave but now was on some ancient wooden sailing ship, lost on a turbulent sea. Thrown from one side to another and another, he struggled to attain stability.

He stiffened his body to stop movement around him. He would fight until the end, and he would win the contest, like Dilvish in the Changing Land. But then, all at once, the strength left his body. He fell back, expecting to be swarmed over by a frozen ocean, a corpse named Isolde, and the rough-handed, unseen, assailants.

Instead, he felt warm and murmured over by kind voices.

"You okay?"

Ghalen's head lolled back, and his eyes opened long enough to see his grandfather.

"Where's my dad?"

"I'm right here," Robert said as he sat down beside him on the bed.

"It was Isolde in the grave, Dad. She was talkin' to me."

"That was a nightmare."

"She was tryin' to pull me down like gravity."

"You had fever," Robert countered. "You had to vomit. Me an' your grandfather heard you moanin', and he gave you a alcohol bath."

"It was so cold, and I didn't have no clothes on."

"You had a fever. But now it's fine."

That's when Ghalen finally woke up. His father and grandfather were sitting there, looking at him. The dark green, plastic mop bucket was on the floor, its bottom covered with his bile.

The young man felt younger still, younger, beaten up, saved, and exhausted.

"I had a fever?"

"We gonna give you some aspirin now," Robert said. "Some aspirin and a couple glasses of water and you'll be just fine."

"I'm dizzy."

"You stronger than a young male pig," Night said on a laugh. "You had me strainin'."

"I'm sorry, Granddad, I didn't know."

"That's okay. Young man got to be strong in this world. Young Black man got to be even stronger."

EVERYTHING SEEMED REAL IN GHALEN'S MIND AS HE slept through the morning. The bitterness in his nostrils, the relief that the aspirin afforded. He wasn't worried about Lovely or Bruno, about what was happening with his father out in the world. Everything was just fine without him having to make sure of it.

His eyes were closed, and he was mostly asleep.

THE HAND ON HIS FOREHEAD FELT FAMILIAR. IT WAS gentle and so slight that it could have almost passed for a breeze.

It was a woman's hand, or a girl's. He thought that maybe it was Lovely. She could have dropped by and found out that he was sick . . .

Opening his eyes he saw Aura Cress. She wore a caramel-colored shift, just a shade lighter than her skin.

She really was very pretty, that's what Ghalen thought.

"How are you, Ghalen?"

"Fine, I guess. My dad gone to work?"

"With your grandfather," she said, nodding.

"When did you get here?"

"Your father called me, and I said that I could be with you this morning."

"You like my dad?"

"Is that okay?"

"Yeah. I mean it is if you really like him."

"I do. He's kind and smart and good-looking. You can't really ask for much more than that."

"Except," Ghalen said. "Except for somebody to know you real well and then to care about who you are."

"That's very grown-up of you," Aura complimented.

Ghalen took her hand.

"Oh." She jumped a little, not expecting the connection.

"I think it's kinda like this."

"What?"

"Holding hands like this. Not doin' anything or expecting anything. Just bein' with somebody. If you could do that, then bein' together is easy."

Aura took the span of a few breaths to process his words, then she said, "I um, I have to leave soon. Are you hungry?"

"Not yet. But you don't have to worry. I can make something for myself."

23.

Hours later Ghalen was lying on his back in the bed, watching thoughts as they flitted through his mind. He was feeling exhausted by what seemed like an entire lifetime of attempts and failures.

His phone had rung twice since Aura left for school.

Both calls were from his father.

"You okay, son?" he asked on the first call. Robert always called Ghalen son when he was worried about him and worrying if he, Robert, was doing the right thing.

"Yeah, Dad, I'm fine."

"You need me to pick up anything at the market for you?" Robert asked on the second call.

"Some regular chocolate chip ice cream. Not the vegan kind."

WHEN THE PHONE RANG THE THIRD TIME GHALEN WAS ready to tell his father not to worry, that he was a big boy, and the fever hadn't seemed to come back.

"Hello?"

The reply was a mild exhalation, maybe a sigh.

"Who is it?"

"Me, Gayley."

"Lovely?"

"I just wanted to call before I left." The voice was a little hoarse, but it was hers.

"You're goin' up north?"

"Yeah."

"You have a cold?"

She laughed huskily and said, "Been cryin', baby. You know."

"If you're so sad then why you have to go?"

"Bruno's the one goin'. That means either I'm'a leave with him if he does, and without him if he don't."

"But doesn't he have one of those ankle bracelets at that halfway house?"

"I'm supposed to drive to the alley behind there in an hour. He's gonna cut off the monitor, jump the back fence, and we'll head out of town."

She sounded miserable.

Though he wanted, more than anything, to stop her from leaving, Ghalen couldn't think of anything to say.

"I guess I'll be going," Lovely uttered.

"No," Ghalen pleaded.

"I have to go." She waited a bit for him to say something and then said, "If you wanted to see me so bad, then why didn't you come by my place?"

"You didn't call me and, and you turned off your phone."

"You still could'a come."

Ghalen wanted to say that she could decide to stay, but he knew this wasn't true. She'd made a promise to Bruno and either she'd break it with him and go with Ghalen or she'd stick to her word.

"I can't leave, Love."

"I know."

"I want to, but even though you and Bruno would be hiding

from the police, he'd still be with you. If my father called me and said he was sick or sad or heavyhearted, if he said he needed me even if he didn't, I'd come home."

They were quiet for a minute or so, then, "I'm smiling," Lovely said.

"Somethin' funny?"

"I love you, Gayley, and maybe one day, I don't know, maybe."

When she disconnected the call, Ghalen felt something rise from his shoulders and the top of his head. That something was both a weight and a binding. It was the first time in his life that someone he loved freed him from an obligation. He sat there, on the side of his bed, and slowly, very slowly, without any language to describe what was happening, he began to cry. It was a mournful passionate thing, like the remnants of the spirit that had already left his body; a lost, blind feeling that included his mother, was for her. It was something that had been ready to come out since that day she died, the day he had to take care of his father instead of falling apart.

Ghalen cried. He fell from the bed to his knees, fighting to stop his chest from its severe, bereft contractions. It was like the time when he was six and couldn't stop hiccupping. He was scared that he could never stop, that at night a big moth would get sucked down his throat.

Sorrow slowly ebbed in the boy's core. He slumped down to a jumbled-up prone-like position on the floor and, from there, fell into sleep. The floor was hard and there was no pillow, but he didn't shift around at all.

THAT'S HOW NIGHT AND ROBERT FOUND HIM.

The grandfather tried to wake him up by jostling his shoulder and saying, "Get up sleepyhead." But the sleeper's eyes did little more than flutter. That's when Robert lifted him up and wrapped him in the covers.

"That was a bad fever," Night commented as they stood over him.

"Not only that," Robert opined. "He always takes on too much. Jamilah used to call him her little Atlas, holding up the world."

These words made their way into Ghalen's dream. He was holding a gigantic balloon, that was also a globe of the Earth, above his head. Effortlessly, he tossed the globe high in the air, doing five pirouettes before it came down again.

GHALEN DIDN'T WAKE UP UNTIL 1:16 THE NEXT AFTERnoon. His breathing seemed somehow deeper, and he'd never felt more rested. Aura had been there. She'd left a note on the dinette table telling him that she'd made a vegan/German potato salad and left it in the refrigerator.

The boy brewed Irish Breakfast tea while heating the potato salad in the microwave. He served himself the meal along with a vegan baguette and a bowl of blueberries. He'd brought with him Blue Journal #23 and started to write while eating.

Hi, everybody, mothers and fathers, brothers, and sisters, and so many, many friends . . . Well, we finally made it. We have come to that end, which is also the beginning. I'm very proud to have been chosen to be your valedictorian. It's a great honor and I'm certainly not the only one deserving of it. There are so many in our graduating class who are excellent artists and writers and scientists, great friends, and teammates. We did a good job, that's what I believe. We've had our problems, at home and here at school. We had the student strike against racism. We raised ten thousand dollars to help fight for the environment. We argued about what kind of language could be used in a classroom. But even these arguments showed how much we cared about each other and the education we shared.

I was going to start this speech by saying that today was the best day in our lives; the day when we enter the world as adults, responsible and untried. And this is true, partly. Today we are leaving something behind. But that thing is not just this one day. The last twelve years have been the best days. When I sat down to write this speech I had just recovered from a bad fever. I had slept almost the whole day. In my sleep I remembered my first friends in elementary school, my mother who taught me how to read and who died when I was ten, my father who showed me that reading could be deeper than just words. I experienced a whole life in that fevered sleep. And there was more magic in every day than I can remember in a month. We learned how to play complex games and how to compete without getting angry. I mean, we learned how to lose, understanding that losing is just another lesson. And we laughed deep and long almost every day. We cried too.

We had teachers who taught things that will stay with us for the rest of our lives, and, probably more important, they have taught us lessons that we haven't learned, even yet. We've grown in ways that haven't found words. And we have loved ourselves and each other, taught each other and our teachers. We have learned what it is to become a part of the world we live in.

So, what I'm saying is that this momentous day is something like a perfectly preserved chromosome containing our cultural and spiritual potential, all of that potential, on display in the amber of that twelve years. In the coming year, ten years, fifty years, we will be able to call back to these early lessons and retrieve anything we need, for the rest of time.

Ghalen glanced up at the kitchen clock when he started writing. That was 2:03 p.m. It was 3:14 when he put the pencil down, satisfied.

This was his first and last real draft of the speech. Mrs. Cordet, the coordinator of the graduation ceremony, told him that it needed to be longer and that he shouldn't talk about the strike. She reminded him that there would be cousins and grandparents, aunts, and uncles in the audience. She chided his chromosome metaphor, saying that memories weren't stored like that. She worried that he hadn't mentioned the administration or the monies he'd received enabling him to attend that expensive institution. And so, he penned a new speech, doing everything she asked. He turned it in, making the short and stout Mrs. Cordet very proud. But on the day of graduation, he put the new speech aside and took out his Blue Journal #23. From this he read the original address, the one he felt that he was meant to give.

24.

Time sped up again for Ghalen after the commencement.

He worked full-time at Indus, sometimes six days a week, from June 1 until August 31. There he worked as a pastry chef and sometimes as kitchen helper with his grandfather, Marquis, and Alexander. Chef had a new restaurant in Las Vegas and so was only around the Beverly Hills place once or twice a week. But whenever he was there, he'd take a few minutes with Ghalen.

"When do you start UCLA?" he asked the boy in early June.

"I'm not, Chef Charlie."

"No?"

"Uh-uh. I transferred my application to UC Berkeley."

"Why?"

"My dad thinks I should be on my own for a while and he's got Aura and Grandpa Night there with him."

"He's a better cook than I am," Charles Martin confessed.

"He's a better man than I'll ever be," Ghalen said with conviction.

"Why would you say something like that?"

"Because. Because he carries the whole world on his shoulders and never complains. I don't even think he knows how hard he works."

IN LATE JULY CHEF CHARLIE ASKED GHALEN TO TAKE A stroll with him after the midday rush.

They walked around, commenting on how many businesses had come and gone since Ghalen was a child.

"Remember that bench?" the elder asked. They were passing down a wide and tree-lined pedestrian lane with businesses and restaurants on either side.

It was the stone bench they'd sat upon so many years before.

"You read to me from that book," Charles Martin remembered.

"*Winnie-the-Pooh*," Ghalen said softly. "You didn't believe that I could read."

"It was that I didn't understand your father. In those days I thought people with problems like that wouldn't be able to think about anything but simple jobs. And I was sure that his son would be like him."

Ghalen nodded, pondering the vegan's confession. Then he said, "When I was little, you know, four or five, I'd sometimes ask him a question like, how far are the stars? And he'd stare at me, thinking. And then, after a real long time he'd say, you know, boy, I don't know the answer to that, but I bet they do down at the library.'

"And right then we would go to the little library down on Wilshire and look it up. If you looked at it right, just talking was an adventure with my dad."

Chef Charlie put a hand on Ghalen's shoulder. "You still going to Berkeley?" he asked.

"Yeah."

"I'm going to send you a text with the name Natasha Vile, and her phone number."

"Who is she?"

"If you ever need any kind of help, any kind, just call her, tell her my name, and she'll do whatever you need."

ON THURSDAY, SEPTEMBER 1, 2016, INDUS WAS CLOSED for the day. There was going to be a goodbye party for Ghalen that would last from noon to midnight. Food and drink were free and plentiful, and everybody who was a part of the Fenestra-Horton clan, or their extended family, were invited.

Myrtle Horton and Pristine Fenestra were there from two o'clock on. They sat together near the window wall. An attentive male nurse sat one place away, watching them. At one point Night showed up at their table. He tried to say hello to Pristine, but she turned away.

There were kids from Ghalen's graduation and nearly all the staff, past and present, who worked for the restaurant. There was a four-piece, upbeat jazz band too. They played dance numbers. The second biggest surprise Ghalen had that night was seeing Robert and Aura doing complex dance moves to the music. They twirled and bobbed, duck down and threw one another out and away before bumping back together again. They separated, coming back together with a passion, reminding Ghalen of microscopic creatures moving heedlessly and yet with purpose.

DURING A BREAK IN THE MUSIC, GHALEN CAME UP TO his father.

"Where'd you learn how to dance like that, Dad?"

"Aura belongs to this dance club. I been goin' down there with her for a while now."

"You never said anything about that. I thought you guys were goin' out for dinner or somethin'."

"No," Robert said, a big grin on his boyish face. "Aura said that it would be a good surprise for you and everybody else here."

GHALEN WAS ENJOYING THIS LAST HURRAH. HIS SCHOOL friends told him how great his family and friends were. Aura took it upon herself to teach him a series of simple dance moves that made him look good. While he was executing a turn and then coming back to hook his father's girlfriend by the waist, he noticed a thirty-something white man watching them gambol. Of medium height and strong build, the white man was unfamiliar to Ghalen, and he was watching them intently; not angrily, but just with intensity. The boy made a twirling move with Aura, and by the time he turned back, the man was gone.

A little dizzy from all the turns, Ghalen bowed out from another dance and noticed Night standing by the entrance of the posh vegan establishment. The newly minted graduate ambled toward the elevated entryway.

"How you doin', Granddad?"

"I'm okay."

"Why you standin' by the door?"

"Got to stand somewhere."

"Yeah, okay."

He was about to walk away when Night said, "Hold up, boy."

Ghalen turned back, all his senses alert for the wartime wisdom predicted by his grandfather's tone.

"Crowds scare me," Night admitted.

"You?"

"Why not me?"

"I honestly didn't think you were scared'a anything."

"Shit. Back in Nam you could be walkin' down a Saigon street and anybody, anybody from a six-year-old boy to a ninety-year grandmother might be ready to end your life."

"They'd shoot you?"

"Mostly with bombs."

"Well, uh," the younger said. "I can stand here with you for a while. You know, another pair of eyes."

Night grinned and nodded.

"Lotsa people I never seen before around here," he said.

"Some of them are Aura's friends. People she works with and goes to school with and stuff."

"It's the stranger will get ya."

"Or help you out."

A LITTLE HIGH ON ORGANIC ORANGE WINE, AFTER HELP-ing Night feel lass anxious, Ghalen wandered around the restaurant, saying thanks to the people who had come to celebrate him. As he made these maudlin rounds he was suddenly struck by the memory of the wake for his mother, given in the same place. An unexpected sadness rose up in his body and mind. This grief made the child inside him look around for the safest harbor, his father.

ROBERT AND AURA WERE SEATED SIDE BY SIDE IN THE far corner of the dining room. As he approached them Ghalen heard words that didn't sound happy or celebratory, salubrious, or tipsy.

"What the fuck you doin' with this retard?" a man said, his voice heightened with emotion.

"Get outta here, Manny!" Aura commanded.

"I should kick his ass," Manny replied. "I should kill him."

Without thinking, Ghalen walked onto the scene, ready to protect his father, who was sitting behind the table staring incredulously.

When Ghalen got to the corner table it was only Robert and Aura sitting there, with Manny, whoever he was, standing over them. But then, almost magically, Night appeared there too.

"Get your ass up outta that chair, nigger," Manny demanded. "Get up and I'll kick your black ass."

Manny leaned over the table, grabbing at Robert. His reach was thrown off by Aura, who got hold of his arm. Manny's hand ended up grabbing Robert by the hair. He yanked then, pulling Robert's face down to the table.

"HEY!" Night yelled in a voice that reverberated in a way that made it seem to come from some megaphone calling into a valley of echoes.

Manny turned his head in the wartime veteran's direction. Night's Black fist came toward the hapless antagonist's head, hitting him with such force that he was thrown against the nearby wall.

Ghalen was shocked, then amazed by his grandfather's strength and instinct. The attacker, Manny, was on the floor, up against the wall, bleeding from what looked like a deep crack in his face. Myrtle's male nurse ran over and started tending him.

It was Beverly Hills, and so the police were there within minutes. They questioned Chef Charlie, took a few names, including Night Farr's, and then arrested the unconscious Manny Bluitt, of Redondo Beach, before allowing the paramedics to load him into their ambulance.

In his Black Journal Ghalen described this twelve-minute experience as *psychically trans-dimensional* adding that *it was like a place I never was and then I was back, at a party where no one was laughing.*

"COME ON NOW, EVERYONE," CHEF CHARLES SAID IN A master of ceremonies–like voice. "We're not going to let one drunk stop this party. We're here to celebrate a brilliant and wonderful young man. The best student, friend, son, and pastry chef that we know. Ghalen Romeo Horton . . ."

Though few, the words did what they were meant to. The audience cheered and applauded; they stood, forming a circle around the Belgian-born cook. Night pulled Ghalen from a chair next to his father and pushed him toward the ring of attention, occupied by Charles, who wrapped an arm around the embarrassed boy's shoulders.

"Three days ago, we had a meeting about which of us was best to make a toast to our friend. At first, we thought maybe . . ." Charles placed eight of his fingers against his own chest, eyes open wide.

"Noooo," cried the laughing, friendly, mob.

"That's what they said," Charles continued. "So, then we thought maybe Robert should have the honor."

There came the general sound of agreement among the masses, but Charles shook his head.

"He said no. He don't like public speaking, can you believe that?" Ghalen had never known that the chef was such a ham. "It was a tough riddle, a hard choice. Who could toast Gayley? Who knew him that well and was still old enough to hold up a glass of schnapps?"

Manny Bluitt, Robert's attacker, was almost forgotten by this time.

"Whoever it was," Chef Charlie continued. "Man or woman, blood relative or friend, it had to be somebody who had the words to honor our friend, somebody who knew how to bullshit."

Laughter filled the room, and Ghalen's heart settled on that love.

"We called the president, but he said that this was his bingo night. We asked the police, but they were too busy arresting angry drunks. So finally, we decided on Alexander Farrell."

From the outer rim of the partyers came Alexander. He was wearing a stark red suit, shirt, and tie. His Stetson hat was black with a red feather in it, and his shoes were the deep blue of the Atlantic Ocean. In his left hand he held a tumbler filled with amber liquid. The dishwasher-turned-waiter sauntered up to Charles and Ghalen, brimming with arrogance and pride.

He looked around at the crowd, basking in the moment. Holding the seven or eight ounces of whiskey up high he said, "How y'all doin'?"

The cheering was loud and raucous.

"I hear ya. I do. Ghalen Romeo Horton. He is just about the finest human being, man, or woman, African or Chinese, from today, 2016, or the year one. When he was seven, he climbed up on a kitchen chair to help us with the dishes. When he was eleven, he told me and my buddy Marquis that we should be waiters because we knew what was what. That's what he said—'what was what.'"

Alexander opened his eyes wider than seemed possible, and everyone in the room understood what he meant.

"I mean, from the mouths of babes. The very next day we went to Chef Charlie an' told him that we had got direction from God." Alexander sipped his first toast and gestured for the crowd to follow suit. "I mean. Ghalen did his calculus next to the cabbages . . ." Another toast. "He got his school friends from junior high to high school to come work right here. He could make a carrot cake that takes the cake. And ain't a girl or woman in this world safe from his smile." Toast number three. "But that shit, excuse my Belgian, that shit does not describe my friend."

With seven words Alexander turned the set from an honest-to-God standup routine to the pulpit.

"No, it does not. There's a lotta smart people out there. There's a lotta handsome mothers too." The rooster in the man posed, performing a half turn. "But there ain't that many good people, good men. Like they say, a good man is hard to find, and Ghalen Romeo Horton has been a good man since before he could talk."

The applause started softly and then slowly built into a din, a hullabaloo that lasted nearly two minutes.

In that time Alexander ushered Ghalen to the center spot. Ghalen was nervous and happy, afraid to look anyone in the eye for fear that he'd start crying and never be able to stop.

When the cheering subsided Alexander raised his nearly emptied tumbler one more time.

"To the best of us, for the best of us, and for us, because we are here to see it. Ghalen, we salute you."

Another round of loud praise for Ghalen and for what he was able to call out from his friends.

"Speech! Speech!" the crowd demanded. "Let's hear from Ghalen! Speech!"

"You bettah tell'em sumpin', boy," Alexander's whiskey-soaked breath whispered in his ear.

Ghalen raised his arms, calling for silence. This was the first time he'd ever made such a gesture. He almost lost focus wondering where he learned such a thing.

"Thank you, thank you all," he said.

This was enough. The room went mostly silent.

"I, I knew that I'd probably be asked to say something," Ghalen admitted, shrugging and moving his head from side to side. "I knew it, but I didn't write anything down because I don't really know what to say. I mean, I went to school and worked at this great restaurant. I learned how to take tests and still failed a few. So, I guess the only real thing for me to say is that I am grateful for everyone here today. And part of that gratitude is for the people who brought me here, my mom and dad. There's not a person in this room that I didn't meet because of them. They had good friends, great friends, and they made really good choices. I miss my mom. I feel like somehow, she sent my granddad here to stand in for her. And then there's Grandma Myrtle, who will not suffer fools.

"I could mention everybody here, but you aren't just names on a list. You're living breathing parts of me, as I am part of you. Thanks for being here. Thanks for everything."

"WHO WAS THAT MAN?" GHALEN ASKED FROM THE BACK-seat of Aura's electric Nissan Leaf. "The one that grabbed Dad."

For a few moments Aura drove in silence. Robert didn't say anything, and Ghalen had already asked his question.

Three blocks farther on Aura said, "I used to date him at college. It didn't work out."

"So, you broke up with him?" the younger Horton asked.

"Yeah." You could tell by her tone that she'd rather be anywhere else talking about something other than Manny Bluitt. But, at the same time, she couldn't keep from answering Ghalen's question. "He would get so jealous that I couldn't take it. One time I told him that I had a meeting with a male professor in his office and Manny said, that that could be seen as harassment. When I laughed, he told me that he was going to talk to that professor."

"Talk to him about what?" Robert asked.

"About what Manny called his inappropriate behavior. I mean if I had said that man touched me Manny would have done something terrible."

"Maybe I should delay leaving for up north," Ghalen said, tentatively.

"No," Aura assured. "I have a restraining order against him and that was the third time he broke it. I told the police that. They said that that, along with the assault, would put him away for a couple of years."

They parked in front of the only home Ghalen had ever known, the apartment he and his parents lived in until the day Jamilah died, the place that her father, Night, found, five years too late.

The police had returned later in the evening and asked Night to come to the police station for questioning. He didn't seem to mind. He never minded anything, except spaces crowded with strangers.

25.

Ivo Blaney had been at the Indus celebration but left before the fight. He was invited because he and Robert had grown close in the days since Jamilah's death. Often, on Robert's days off, Ivo would drop by and take him on extended drives. Neither Night nor Aura, not even Ghalen, could explain this relationship.

One day, while Robert was getting dressed, Night and Ivo were having wine and Ghalen was sipping spiced carrot juice.

The Vietnam veteran asked, "What do you and Robert talk about on your drives?"

"Sometimes nuthin'," the professional driver admitted. "Sometimes just about things we seen. You know, Robert's a kind of bird-watcher. He don't know none'a their proper names but he knows everything about 'em. That's what reminds me of myself. I know all kindsa stuff I can't explain, I cain't justify. But that don't mean I'm stupid.

"Spendin' a day on the road with Robert recharges my batteries, let's me see a world that I know, or that he does."

NOW AND THEN IVO WOULD OFFER TO DRIVE GHALEN when he needed to get someplace. He even taught him how to drive and, when the boy turned sixteen, Ivo helped him get a license.

That morning, he was going to take Ghalen and Robert to the train station downtown for the boy to board a train going north. The luggage consisted of two trunks and two smaller bags. When Ivo got to their apartment only Ghalen was there at the curb, sitting on the trunks. The evening before, the police had come to ask Night to come down to the Beverly Hills police station because they had a few questions about the events at the party.

"And Dad and Aura went down there this morning to pick him up," Ghalen explained.

"What they have to ask him about?" Ivo asked.

"The guy Granddad hit is in a coma," Ghalen told the driver. "Because'a that, I guess they wanted a little more information in case something has to go to court. I offered to go with them, but Dad said it was just givin' Granddad a ride and I had to get to school for orientation."

"That's right," Ivo said, like it was an echo of something unsaid. "It's your job to get to school and it's your dad's job to take care of the Homefront."

GHALEN AND THE DRIVER FOUND A REDCAP TO SECURE the luggage and then Ivo accompanied Ghalen to the gate.

"I'll drop by your dad's and ask him if he'll need any help," the limo driver promised as the boy climbed onto the train.

GHALEN HAD BEEN LOOKING FORWARD TO THE HOURS-long train ride. He'd never been anywhere on a real train. It sounded like fun, like a ride at adult Disneyland. He dressed for the occasion, wearing a charcoal-colored Nehru-collared jacket, an off-white raw silk tee that Aura had given him, black jeans, and black fabric shoes.

He was sitting by the window of a half-empty car, reading a paperback book called *The Teachings of Don Juan: A Yaqui Way of Knowledge*. This was a book one of his teachers had suggested. He was engrossed in the mystical story of Native American self-discovery when:

"Excuse me," a young woman said.

She wore a bright print dress festooned with abstract forms in all the primary and secondary colors. She was pretty, Ghalen thought, because she was young. Robert often said that youth is, by definition, beautiful. And this lightheartedly dressed woman exuded youth, if not happiness.

"Yes?" the boy said.

"Do you mind if I sit with you?"

"No. Of course not."

He stood up from the window seat and began helping her with the travel bag she pulled.

"Thanks a lot," she said as Ghalen pushed the bag into overhead storage. "This guy's been followin' me all over the train."

"Oh, then maybe you should sit next to the window, and I'll take the aisle."

She smiled gratefully and moved over to the window seat.

"My name's Ghalen, Ghalen Horton," he said, holding out a hand.

"Welda Bachman," she replied, accepting the clasp.

"Your people from Germany?"

"Austria. How'd you know?"

"Your name." He paused a beat and then asked, "Do you know this guy followin' you?"

"No. He just started talkin' to me from across the aisle. Then he waited till the lady I was sitting next to got up and went to the toilet and took her seat. He was talkin' about this sex stuff, and I moved."

"But he followed you?"

"Yeah."

"Some guys are just jerks, I guess."

"Here he comes," Welda warned.

Looking up, Ghalen saw a young man coming through the car-connecting door. He wasn't as intimidating as Welda Bachman's fears portended, but he looked a little mean and maybe even unhinged. His jeans were dirty, and the lime-colored shirt he wore had rhinestone buttons. His shoes were made from yellowy rattlesnake skin, and his tarnished silver-and-turquoise belt buckle probably weighed a pound. The most disturbing thing about him was his eyes. They were so pale that you could hardly call them gray.

Ghostly, Ghalen thought.

Three days before, Night had asked Ghalen if he wanted a gun to bring along to university.

Ghalen laughed and asked, "Why would I want that?"

"For protection. You gonna be alone up there."

"I'm a kid, Grandad. I don't have any money. I don't belong to a gang. Why would I need protection?"

"Because wherever you go you gonna have more than most'a the people around you."

"That doesn't make any sense. I'm just another kid."

He refused the Luger-like pistol Night offered but finally gave in to accepting a knife the man had carried most of his life. It had an eight-inch blade with a hilt shaped like brass knuckles. Ghalen had this knife, but it was buried in one of his trunks.

"Hey, man," the wiry white youth said to Ghalen. "That your girlfriend?"

"She's an old friend from high school."

"She's my girlfriend."

"Are you?" Ghalen asked Welda.

"No."

"Get the fuck up, man," the late-teen cowboy commanded.

Ghalen wondered at the similarity of his father's experience the night before. He wasn't afraid, but he wondered how a fight would go. He was strong and had been on the wrestling team for two semesters. He'd fight if he had to.

"I said, get the fuck up."

The young man put a long-fingered hand on Ghalen's shoulder.

"Why don't you get the fuck out of here, asshole!" Welda shouted.

The hand tightened on Ghalen's shoulder, and he prepared to grab that wrist with both hands. There was a twist that one of his competitors from Dorsey High had taught him—it included bending the wrist back toward the inner forearm, standing straight up, and then falling into the hold with all his weight. Even if the wrist didn't break, it would be seriously sprained.

"Jeffrey!" a man shouted.

There stood a tall man in the frame of the connecting door. He was wearing yellow jeans under black leather chaps that were lined with red tassels. His shirt was a luminescent green under a buff, sheep's-leather vest that was unbuttoned. His so-called white skin was leathery, his complexion reminding Ghalen of indigenous peoples.

"What?" the younger cowboy said, removing the hand from Ghalen's shoulder.

"What you doin'?"

"Nuthin', Obadiah."

"Then why don't you get back to our car and see to your grip?"

"I was talkin' to this guy."

"Talkin' about what?"

"Um, he was tellin' me a joke."

The man named Obadiah stared at Jeffrey until the young man lowered his head, then walked past him and out of the car.

Ghalen found the silence of the confrontation fascinating. It seemed a great show of strength.

"Oh no," Welda uttered.

The man Jeffrey called Obadiah was walking toward them.

"Don't worry," her shield assured. "I don't think he wants trouble."

"I hope Jeff wasn't botherin' you," the man called Obadiah said upon reaching their row.

"Not at all, sir," Ghalen said. "He was just talkin'."

"I thought you were tellin' a joke?"

"More like a riddle. You know, the one about the man who has a fox, a bag of corn, and a goose, when the man comes to a river where there's a boat that can only take two at a time."

Obadiah's smile revealed dusky teeth, three of which were edged in gold.

"That's a old one," he said.

"Best kind," Ghalen opined. Then he held out a hand for the older cowboy to shake.

"My name's Ghalen."

Accepting the gesture, Obadiah sat sideways on the armrest of the aisle seat of the empty row before them.

"Obadiah. Galen's a cowboy name."

"I think it's as old as the Greeks."

"You two goin' to Frisco?"

"I'm going to visit my cousin in Sausalito," Welda said, a little reluctantly.

"Berkeley for me," said Ghalen. "The university. What about you?"

"Mount Diablo," he said. And then realizing that this wasn't enough he added, "State park. There's this ranch a man named Buford has up there where you can practice bronco bustin' and bull ridin'. I take a group'a youngsters up there every fall to get 'em ready for next season's rodeo circuit. You ride?"

"Not me," said Ghalen.

"I do," Welda said. "But not rodeo, I do riding competitions, sometimes."

"You jump?"

"Yeah. Sometimes."

"Well," Obadiah said, rising to his feet, and handing Ghalen an unexpected business card. "You two make a pretty couple."

"THAT WAS WEIRD," WELDA SAID AS THE CONNECTING door slid shut behind the westerner.

"Jeffrey was," Ghalen agreed, "but I kinda liked Obadiah."

"I guess."

"So, you live in LA?"

"I went to school there but I'm from Sausalito."

"Well, I'm at the dorms at UCB."

"What are you going to study there?"

"Sciences and languages, maybe writing. It doesn't really matter that much."

"Why not?"

"I just wanna see what school life is like but there's nothing I'm burning to learn."

"That's probably smart. When I went to Long Beach State I got lost, had to drop out."

They talked all the way to the last stop.

She was surprised that he was only sixteen. She was nineteen but, by her own admission, had led a sheltered life. She said that she wanted to be a veterinarian when she finished her education. He said that all he needed out of an education was knowledge.

"But how do you expect to make a living?" Welda asked.

"I'm a pretty good vegan pastry chef and I know a lotta places that need that because of the restaurant I worked for in Beverly Hills."

"You're vegan?"

"Naw. I like meat and white sugar, eggs, and bacon."

"Then why do you work as a vegan cook?"

"My dad. He's kinda like a food doctor, and I spent a lot of time with him, especially after my mother died."

THEY ARRIVED AT EMERYVILLE STATION. WELDA WAITED with Ghalen while they unloaded his bags.

"That's a lot," she said, seeing his pile of luggage.

"Yeah, I guess. But I can get a taxi out front."

"My boyfriend is coming to get me," she suggested. "Maybe he can give you a ride."

This was the first mention of a boyfriend, not that Ghalen cared. They'd already exchanged phone numbers, and he wasn't interested in any woman but Lovely Frain.

"Well!" a man's voice called.

He was an inch or so shorter than Ghalen, bearded, and white, clad in dark cottons. He didn't like the look of the young Black man and so, when he approached them, he situated himself between Ghalen and Welda.

"How you doin'?" he asked, looking at Ghalen but speaking to her.

"Fine, Brod. This is Ghalen. He helped me when this guy kept hitting on me on the train."

"Hittin' on you?" he said, still gazing at Ghalen, threat in his tone.

"Yeah," the freshman replied. "Some kinda rodeo kid goin' to bust broncos or sumpin'."

"I wasn't talkin' to you."

"Oh? You were lookin' at me, so I thought maybe you were askin'."

"I wasn't."

"Broderick," Welda said sharply. "He kept that guy from messin' with me."

The young men stared at each other.

"I told him that we could give him a ride with all that baggage," Welda insisted.

"No room," he said.

"That's an interesting name, Broderick, I've heard it before but never met anybody named that." Ghalen was beginning to enjoy himself and wondering why.

"So what?"

"Brod, stop being rude. He hasn't done anything to you or me."

"All right," the boyfriend surrendered. "Let's put the stuff in the back."

Ghalen saw then that the young man had a red pickup truck with a white stripe down the side.

"Gimme a hand with these trunks."

"No," Ghalen said. "I'll figure out a taxi."

"I said I'd take you."

"Take your girlfriend home." Ghalen felt as if he were someone else and liking it.

Broderick's eyes said that he was searching for a reply but couldn't land on one.

"Are you sure, Ghalen?" Welda asked, maybe a little relieved.

"Oh yeah. Sure."

26.

Ghalen stood on the tarmac, watching the back-end of the red Ford pickup truck receding toward the exit. When it stopped before turning into traffic, he noticed that one of the brake lights was out. For some reason this little failure made him realize that this was the first time he'd ever been on his own. He wasn't afraid, not even lonely, but there was something solitary about the moment.

That's when he felt a hand on the same shoulder that Jeffrey the cowboy-in-training had grasped. But this touch was lighter.

"Ghalen?" asked the woman who that hand belonged to.

She was almost as tall as the young man, and that was tall, because Ghalen had grown to six one in the past half-year. Her dress was of one piece, shifting between black and a dark velvety purple. It was more like a single sheet of fabric that had been bunched and folded to adorn the pale woman's body, rather than a dress cut from a pattern and sold off the rack.

She wasn't pretty but most definitely beautiful, that's what Ghalen thought. Her face was long, a head rising out of agony, he imagined, into dignity. Probably over forty, but age didn't seem to be a very important part of her being.

"I'm Ghalen," he said, it was almost a question.

"Charles Martin told me that you'd be arriving here."

"Chef Charlie?"

"That's what you call him?" she asked.

"Yeah," Ghalen said, wondering what it would take to make this woman smile.

"I'm Natasha Vile."

"Oh, yeah. Chef Charlie gave me your number."

"He told me that he did, but that he didn't think you would call."

"Why not?"

"He didn't tell me." Her eyes were emeralds laced in black, with slender brows shaped like deep waves. "But that's why he asked me to pick you up. I guess he thought that if we met, you might be more willing to reach out. Shall we put your things into the back of my car?"

NATASHA VILE'S AUTOMOBILE WAS A 1957 CHEVROLET station wagon. It was painted a very bright scarlet red while the interior was upholstered in black leather. She drove up to where the redcaps had left his luggage and stood by the back hatch as he loaded up the wagon.

"Would you like to come to my house for dinner before daring the school cafeteria?" she asked when they were a few blocks from the train station.

HER HOUSE WAS ON OAK RIDGE ROAD IN THE CLARE-mont section of Berkeley. It was basically a manor house that looked old but was well maintained. An at least twelve-foot wrought iron fence surrounded the property and seemed not to be painted. There were two floors with three turrets that made a third. There was no lawn but rather a small forest of pines, redwoods, and oak. Probably thirty trees in all, Ghalen thought.

"This is beautiful," he said when they were parked in front of the mansionesque double doors of the entrance.

"It belonged to my uncle."

"He was rich?"

"I guess so. Nobody else in the family wanted it unless they could sell it, and Uncle Pluto's will wouldn't allow for that."

"The trees are great."

"Come on in. Dinner's waiting."

Ghalen expected that she'd have servants, but Nathasha had cooked and set the cherrywood dining table for the meal all by herself.

"I have a cleaning woman named Esta who comes in three days a week," she said to Ghalen when he commented on the amount of work she'd done. "Cleaning is hard, but everything else is up to personal choice."

She'd made a pork roast with stewed carrots, baked potatoes, and charred broccolini.

"Oh my God," Ghalen said. "I usually only eat vegan, but this is wonderful."

"I have cherry pie for dessert."

"Wow. You did all this for me?"

"Charles told me that you were a big part of his work, his life. He wanted me to look out for you and I said okay because . . . because he's been my friend in the same way."

"What way is that?"

"He said that you and your father, your mother too, I think, had taught him many things, and that none of you ever asked for anything other than what you earned."

"Like we were some kinda servants?" Ghalen asked, pointedly.

"I know it sounds like that," the woman said. "But where he came from, in the old country, people who worked together, on a farm or whatever, had to rely on each other, believe in each other. That's what he was talking about."

"Huh." Ghalen felt odd. He was supposed to be in a dorm at the university, but he wanted to be there, in this Gothic house with this timeless woman. "What kinda books do you read?"

"Mostly architecture and witchcraft."

"You're a witch?"

"I don't think so. I mean, if I were, then probably everybody is but they don't know it. But why do you ask about reading?"

"I guess at school we're always asking about books and things we've learned. But this isn't school."

The woman's inquisitive, motive eyes studied Ghalen from half a dozen different points, that's what he felt. After this silent interaction she inquired, quite objectively, "If I were to ask you what you've learned lately, what would you say?"

"That the universe is expanding at a rate faster than the speed of light," Ghalen said without hesitation.

"It is?"

"That's what the astrophysicists say. I can't prove it, but I don't know if anybody could prove anything."

"What do you mean by that?" his host asked, smiling at last.

"Well," he said, slowly pondering her question. "If somebody asked me about you, I'd say that you were beautiful, very much so. But if they asked me to prove it, all I could do was show them a picture. Once I do that then the fact becomes subjective and therefore outside the concept of objectivity, you know, truth."

The slender woman's smile thinned, but at the same time seemed to become deeper. Ghalen felt that she was peering into him and became surprisingly shy.

"You're only sixteen," she said at last.

"I'm sorry. I didn't mean to, I mean . . ."

"Don't be sorry. You would feel what you're saying whether you said it or not."

"I just never met anybody like you, like this."

"Like what?" Before that moment the lady seemed serious, inquisitive, as if trying to see if Ghalen was somehow a danger. But now her visage lightened, turned friendly.

"You're just different," he admitted. "This house. When I was back at the train station, I got it that I was alone for the first time. And, when I got here, I don't know, it just proved it."

"And that's why you start flirting with a woman more than twice your age?"

"Age doesn't matter to you," Ghalen said with certainty.

The surprise shown on her face seemed a rare moment. It was like a double response: the first being about his assertion and the second the feeling of being taken unawares.

"I'd like for you to stay here tonight," she requested, rather formally.

"With you?" Ghalen felt a gasp in the center of his chest.

"In turret number three," she said. "I stay in two."

"Because you're too tired to drive?"

"No. I want to have breakfast with you in the morning, after this conversation and before you go off to school."

THE TOP FLOOR OF TURRET NUMBER THREE WAS A PERfectly round room with the wall space comprised mostly of windows. The bed was oval shaped, and the furniture was designed to fit in with the curves and arcs. There was no TV or radio, no art on the walls. The oak floor was composed of slender slats that formed an off-center and intricate design that was reminiscent of an exploding star frozen in the middle of its demolition. The hill descending from the house was a kind of gathered darkness formed by woods. Beyond that were the lights of the city, a river flowing up to and then being split by the island of darkness.

Ghalen turned off the lights and sat on the edge of the bed next to a window. The feeling in his chest, that little gasp of fear, stayed with him. He studied the darkness and light, which had a definite form but still seemed to be moving, shifting under the surface. There were stars above that seemed to be part and parcel of the electric night-lights, as if they were glittering molecules risen from a lake.

Ghalen usually read himself to sleep, going over and over the masterpieces presented by his teachers, the treasures he'd discovered online or in the local library. He would have liked to read one of those books that night, but he didn't want to turn on a light. The darkness seemed to hold him, rock him. His breathing was the clearest and deepest that he could remember. There was something about this moment that he never wanted to let go of.

In this obscure void he felt that he was an escapee from a prison, hiding in the shadows. But he wasn't only hiding, he was also running, and he wasn't only running but headed somewhere, somewhere beautiful.

In the middle of this flight from what he did not know, his cell phone sounded. It went through six musical cycles before he connected the call.

"Hello?"

"Ghalen?"

"Aura?"

"Did I wake you up?"

"No, no, I was just looking out the window."

"Of the dormitory?"

"Yeah."

"What's it like?"

"Different. It feels like I left LA a week ago."

"I remember when I started college," she said. "It felt like magic sometimes. The big libraries and people everywhere talking about ideas."

"True that," he replied, using a phrase that he knew but rarely utilized.

"I just wanted to see if you were okay."

"How's Dad?"

"He's asleep. We had to stay for a long time down at the police station."

"Because of Granddad?"

"No. They wanted to question me and Robert."

"About what?"

"Me about my relationship with Manny, and Robert about why Manny attacked him."

"I don't get it. You have that restraining order and Dad never even heard of the guy."

"Yeah, but cops can't ever take your word for anything. They always think you're lying. They have to, I guess."

"So, what happened?"

"They just kept on asking Robert the same questions over and over. He got really impatient and got up to stand against the wall. The police kept telling him to sit down but he wouldn't, and they tried to make him sit."

"Did they hurt him?"

"It didn't get that far. I had called your lawyer, Miss Barth, and she stopped the interrogation."

"Do you need me to come back?"

"I don't think so. They transferred your grandfather to the Westwood station and interrogated him there. There was this Black officer there, Holly, or something, I think . . ."

"Sergeant Hollis?"

"Yeah, that's it. You know him?"

"Before I was born a Sergeant Hollis stopped those cops who made my father hit his head on the concrete." Ghalen had heard the story at least a dozen times from his father and mother.

"You mean way back when he started to get lost sometimes?"

"Uh-huh. What did Hollis do?"

"He told them that he knew Robert and that he was not the kind of man to cause anybody to get in a coma. So, they just let us both go. Emily said that they didn't have anything on either of us, or on your granddad either. She retained a criminal lawyer, and so there wouldn't be anything for you to do anyway. And you know Robert would be unhappy if you left school. I mean, the only reason he hasn't called you was that he fell asleep on the couch as soon as we got home."

"They didn't hurt him?"

"He's so strong they couldn't even make him sit down," she bragged.

"Thanks for callin', Aura. I'll get in touch with Emily in the morning."

"You take care, baby."

"good morning," natasha vile greeted. she was standing at the huge, black, eight-burner gas stove of the kitchen, her back turned to the cherrywood dining table. It was seven thirty the next morning.

She wore a sunflower-yellow dress that showed off her pale knees and bare shoulders.

"Hi, Miss Vile," Ghalen greeted. "That's a pretty dress."

"Thank you. I made whole wheat blueberry waffles. Do you eat bacon?"

"I do here."

She moved from the stove to kiss the young man on his cheek. They sat and started eating.

Everything, the whole world, seemed new to him, even the simplest things. There was an open newspaper, the *San Francisco Chronicle*, laid upon an empty chair, and a small round, orange-glass vase filled with tiny purple flowers that had yellow centers set perfectly off-center and at the side of the table. Next to the vase were four keys on a small, black metal ring. On a cool breeze, birdsong wafted in from an open window.

"Do you get lonely here, Miss Vile?"

"Call me Nat."

"Okay."

She smiled before saying, "Never. I love this house. Do you mind if I call you Mr. Horton?"

"No. Are you an architect, um, Nat?"

"Only in my mind," she paused before adding, "Mr. Horton."

Ghalen's breath caught again.

"What are you thinking?" she asked.

He put down his fork, trying to make sense of the answer to this question. There had never been a more perfect moment in his life. Not even Lovely's hidden cabin had been so . . . wonderful.

"Um," he uttered. "When I got on the train, I felt something shift."

"Shift?"

"Yeah. Like as if I was in a prison but didn't know it was a prison because I was born there. I had my room and my bed, a schedule that hardly ever changed. I had a bedtime, even though nobody ever told me when to go to sleep."

A look of tenderness came over Nat's face.

"Go on," she said.

"But ever since I got on that train it felt like I was open instead of bein' closed down."

"You like that?" she asked so softly that he could barely hear the words.

"Yeah. I do. But it's not like it feels good. The feeling I have is closest to bein' afraid."

"Fear how?"

"Like a mouse out in the open on a most beautiful day, but still under hawk-filled skies."

"Is that a quote from something you read?"

"I don't know, maybe."

"Tea, Mr. Horton?"

"Please."

27.

They talked about his studies at high school and Nat being a painter. She rendered nature scenes in oils and watercolors, usually of plants from the surrounding forests.

"Do you have one of your paintings here?" Ghalen asked.

"No."

"Why not?"

She considered the question and then said, "The same reason a brick layer doesn't keep a garden wall under the dinner table."

Ghalen grinned, and she smiled in reply.

"I'd like you to do me a favor, Mr. Horton."

"What's that, Nat?"

"Have dinner with me every other week when you can."

"Did Chef Charlie want you to do that?"

"No. All he wanted was for me to make myself available if you needed help of some sort. I want to see you for dinner because I like the conversation."

"Okay, but only if I can cook half the time."

Natasha Vile sat straight up in a pert pose, smiling. She picked up the key ring and said, "You can cook whenever you want if you accept these."

He took the ring and asked, "What are they?"

"To my station wagon. You might need to drive somewhere."

"But what about you?"

"Uncle Pluto also left me a warehouse garage in South San Francisco. There are forty vintage cars parked there. Whenever I need money, I sell one."

THEY PARTED AT THE BRIGHT RED WAGON.

"I had a wonderful time," she said, her cheek pressed against his ear.

"Me too." He backed off a few inches and she made to kiss him. He thought she was aiming for his lips but instead she raised her chin and kissed him on what his mother used to call his third eye.

"See you in two weeks."

AFTER THAT BRIEF INTERLUDE GHALEN MADE HIS WAY down to the South Campus Residence Hall called Unit 3. From there he went to the outside registration line for *E-F-G-H*, where he signed up for three classes: Earth and Planetary Science, Ancient Greek and Roman Studies, and basic Reading and Composition. He had to add a work-study section that he was to perform in the fiction department of the main library.

His father called him every day, and Aura Cress reached out at least two days a week. For the first few months Manny Bluitt was still in his coma and the police seemed to show no interest in his father or grandfather. Every time they talked, Ghalen offered to come home, but Robert always told him, "No, son. This is your time."

TALL, LONG-HAIRED, AND HANDSOME FILLION MOORE was his dormitory roommate. Moore was a white kid from Ohio and had received a scholarship in the sciences but wanted to be a bassist in a rock band. They connected over the fact that they both played soccer in high school, but even though they got along perfectly well as roomies they rarely saw each other outside of the dorm. This was fine by Ghalen. He'd been feeling profoundly withdrawn since the love and loss of Lovely and his fever-fueled commencement speech.

He wasn't depressed or even sad. He carried the solitary feeling around with him like an old friend or maybe a book he was in the middle of studying. There were no expectations of him outside of schoolwork, and that work was pretty simple. He read books and wrote and talked about what he'd read. He didn't have the responsibilities of childhood because Robert had Aura and Night to look after him, and then, there were his friends at Indus.

His mother had become a faded image in his mind. Not something forgotten; more like a transparent angel, so large that his memory of her was permanently superimposed on the clouds.

He went to have dinner with Nat every other Tuesday or Wednesday evening. This was what Ghalen thought of as his moment of grace. He was attracted to the older woman, but she'd made it quite clear that this was just friendship. He appreciated pressing against this limitation, as it reminded him a little of the *prison* of his childhood.

HE WAS INVITED TO PARTIES NOW AND THEN BY CLASS friends and sometimes by kids who lived on his floor. One day, Fillion asked him to come along to a wine tasting-party that one of the TAs in Linear Algebra and Differential Equations had invited him to. Ghalen was pretty sure that this invitation was because he had a car, but he didn't mind.

The party was held in a very large house in the Oakland Hills. Ghalen never found out who the owner of the house was nor even Fillion's friend's name. The roommates were separated soon after they were let into the vast home by a young woman who looked a little like a child playing dress-up in a grown woman's emerald-green evening gown.

"So glad to have you," she greeted in a put-on fancy accent. "We've got bathtub gin in the kitchen, cognac on the roof, and organic wine on the patio."

Fillion preferred the roof and so left Ghalen, promising to meet up with him at the end of the night.

The large patio was overflowing with young men and women holding plastic wine flutes and laughing, laughing, laughing. The young freshman waited in a long line for one of the three one-bartender wine bars.

"YOU FROM SF STATE?" A YOUNG WHITE MAN STANDING behind him asked. He had shaggy brown hair and enormous shoulders.

"No," Ghalen said easily. "Berkeley."

"Smart, huh?"

"I don't know. You?"

For some reason the brawler found this response hilarious. He laughed, slapped Ghalen's shoulder, and laughed some more. His name was Bernard Cragg, but everyone called him Bernie, Bernie C, or, for his best friends, Bernice. He was a rugby player, liked the fight of it.

"That's a man thing," Bernie confided, "not no pussy sport. You got to use every muscle in your whole body, and it hurts like fuck."

Ghalen liked the San Franciscan's honesty. His brutality was authentic and yet he didn't seem at all angry.

"Next," a woman said.

Ghalen turned to the diaphragm-high collapsable bar, which reminded him most of a folding ironing board.

She was olive-skinned and slender by nature, plain faced and yet there was an intense and purposeful look in her eyes. Those orbs opened wide, and she made a gesture with her hands that asked, "What can I get you?"

"Do you have an effervescent orange?" Ghalen asked. They served this type of wine at Indus.

This query surprised the young woman.

"Limonde or Vesqua?" she asked.

"Aaron," he said, using the French intonation, "if you have it."

The woman, whose faux-silken shift was festooned with a cloudy blue photograph for its design, was impressed and a little surprised. She looked the handsome Black youth up and down then said, "Come with me."

"WHAT'S YOUR NAME?" GHALEN ASKED AS THEY MADE their way into the house.

"Verochka."

"Truth," he said as they approached an unpainted wooden door.

She stopped and turned to him, "You speak Russian?"

"I know some Latin."

When Ghalen saw how impressed she was, he thought that she was well named.

"Where's this door go?" he asked.

"The wine cellar, of course."

AT THE BOTTOM OF THE STAIRS STOOD A LARGE AND broad, swarthy-colored man with a frown that might have been permanent.

"He's with me, Yacob," Verochka said.

The big man glowered and then stood aside, revealing a small doorway.

Ghalen followed her through, into a surprisingly large room crowded with wine shelving. Verochka closed the door behind them and threw the latch.

"Is this your house?" he asked the young woman.

"What do you think?" she said, impertinently.

"If I knew, I wouldn't have asked."

She kissed him. It was a wet kiss with a lot of tongue. Her plain looks and the locked door excited Ghalen more than the kiss. There was something primal about it all . . .

That part of their evening lasted no more than four minutes.

And then, "Get up!" she said. "Yacob will get suspicious."

The young man was stunned by the immediacy and the surprise of their encounter. He needed a few seconds to catch his breath.

"Get up!" Verochka demanded.

While she searched around the wine shelves, Ghalen watched, wondering about the power of his orgasm. He'd pulled a muscle in his lower abdomen, and his vision was a little off.

"Come on quick," she said, pulling him to his feet and then pushing him toward the door.

AURA HAD TAKEN HIM ASIDE THREE DAYS BEFORE HIS goodbye party.

"When you get there remember never to ride in a drunk's car and never have unprotected sex with girls you don't know. You could get shot, get sick, or pay child support for twenty years, maybe all three."

He'd taken her advice seriously until the moment he stepped into that cellar.

YACOB EYED THEM SUSPICIOUSLY, BUT GHALEN WASN'T worried. It had been only six minutes, what could he have thought they could have done in that time?

Verochka was very businesslike, two bottles of wine in each hand. He followed her up the stairs and back toward the wine tables. On the way up Ghalen had to concentrate not to look back down at Yacob.

The Russian wine steward left two of the four bottles off with her other friends and then pulled Ghalen away by the sleeve of his coal-colored Nehru jacket. When they'd made it to the front yard of the massive home, she turned to him and asked, "Do you have a car?"

"I do."

"Then let's go."

Resisting as much as he could, Ghalen asked, "Is Yacob your boyfriend?"

For the first time, her cold eyes registered fear.

"I work for him," she spat.

THERE WAS A MOTEL ON TELEGRAPH AVENUE, TOWARD downtown Berkeley, called Priss. It was painted a garish combination of violet, orange, and hot pink. Ghalen drove them there following Verochka's direction.

"Do you have money?" she asked in the parking lot.

"Some."

"It is thirty dollars a night."

"Okay."

AS SOON AS THEY WERE IN THE ROOM VEROCHKA WAS kissing him again. They hadn't even closed the door. He had believed that he wouldn't be pulled in by her so quickly again but was wrong. There was something passionate and desperate, intense, and overwhelming in the Russian's caresses.

"Let me close the door," Ghalen said, leaning in that direction. She held on as he dragged her toward the door and closed it. There they fell into a writhing heap, her on top of him, kissing and tearing at his clothes.

"How many times can you come?" she asked, having a tight grip on his erection.

"Feels like all night."

She grinned ferociously and bit his face.

A LITTLE MORE THAN AN HOUR LATER THEY WERE NAKED, lying on the stale mattress of a queen-size bed.

"Now do you love me?" Verochka asked through a contemptuous sneer.

"What's love got to do with it?" he said, wondering if she'd ever heard the song.

The smile she produced was almost innocent.

"Good," she said. "I hate when men lie to me."

"Did Yacob lie to you?"

"No. He told me that he would put me to work and take all my money, that he would fuck me whenever he wanted, any way that he wanted. That was true."

"What would he have done if he came in on us back there?"

"Beat you and then fuck me in my ass for punishment."

"So why did you do it?"

"I want to kill him."

"And him finding us would have helped you do that?"

Verochka laughed and said, "Let's drink some wine."

She had a corkscrew in her red vinyl purse and the bathroom provided two plastic cups. It took them maybe fifteen minutes to empty the first bottle and unstopper the second.

After a while the conversation came back to Yacob.

"I thought maybe the police would come and take him. Then I could get away to Mexico maybe."

"What if he killed me?" Ghalen asked himself as much as her.

She put a hand on his cheek and said, "I would mourn you for forty days and light your candles for seven years."

It was at this moment that Ghalen realized something was missing in his life. Faith in something, maybe belief.

He thought this intelligence must have been evident in his eyes because Verochka asked, "What are you thinking?"

"I was thinkin' about my dad," he said, mostly out of reflex.

"What about him?"

"In many ways he's a brilliant man. He can do things with his mind that most other people can't imagine."

"Like break stone?"

"He can tell you what you can't see."

"Like Superman?"

"No. He can do amazing things, but sometimes he gets lost, confused. I think it's because so much is happening in his head. And so, I've always had to be there to help him."

"But you are not there now. You are here with me."

Hearing this Ghalen looked deeply into her face. The Russian pulled her chin in and started to lean back.

"You are scaring me, Mr. Ghalen."

"I don't mean to. I was just wondering."

"What?"

"What if, um, what if I knew a place where you could go to that Yacob could never find?"

"What kind of place?"

"A commune."

"Like in Old Russia?"

"No. This place is out in the desert and paid for by a group of rich women who love art. It's an art commune."

"I am no artist."

"No. But I bet you could be. And until then you could be a model."

The young woman smiled at this proposition. Ghalen believed that she understood working, that she could only trust what her body could do in trade for her sustenance and freedom.

"This is how you pay me to fuck you?"

"It's just what I do. What I have to do."

"Like for your father?"

"I guess."

"So how do I get to this art commune?"

"Does Yacob know about this motel?"

"No."

"You're sure?"

"I have run away from him before. He has never found me here."

Something about her claim brought up a question in his mind, "Why did you run with me?"

"For the sex."

"Naw. I might look all right but not worth no beatin' from Yacob."

Verochka's smile turned into a grin.

"I don't know," she said on a slight shrug. "I got this feeling about you."

"When?"

"When I kissed you. I could tell that you wanted something."

"You?"

She shrugged again. "Maybe."

Somehow Ghalen knew that this devil-may-care attitude was what he needed, what he was, down deep.

"I'll tell you what, Truth, I'll give you a little money and pay for three days here at the motel. By the end of that time, I'll have all the answers."

28.

At one of their biweekly dinners, Nat had told Ghalen about Blodeuwedd, a women's art commune that she donated to. It was located about thirty miles outside Palm Springs. Fully half of the rooms of this artists' retreat were excavated beneath the desert floor, receiving much of its light, during the day, through a complex system of mirrors.

"There are five above-ground buildings, thirty residents, two cooks, three maintenance workers, and four guards—all women," Nat told young Mr. Horton while serving his favorite—cherry pie.

"And no men?"

"No man has entered Blodeuwedd since the day it was christened," she said.

"What if some man tried to get in?"

"They have three vicious dogs, and all the guards are armed ex-military."

"Wow. That sounds so cool."

"TELL ME ABOUT THIS WOMAN," NAT REQUESTED WHEN Ghalen floated the idea of Verochka's possible escape to the desert.

He told her about Yacob and her desire to get away from him.

"She isn't a legal resident and her life back in Russia sounds pretty bad," Ghalen told his only true friend in the Bay Area.

"Can I trust her?"

"I don't know. I mean, she didn't know about the commune before we went off together. So, I don't think it was any kind of a plan on her part to get there. She looks out for herself, but it sounds like most people there do that."

"You like her?"

"She's real tough."

"And you like that?"

He liked Verochka's bite and how cavalier she'd been about seducing him under Yacob's nose.

He has killed people back home, she'd whispered in their motel bed. *Maybe here too.*

"I like feeling something," Ghalen said, in answer to Natasha's question.

"You don't feel?"

"Most of the time it's like I'm numb. I don't know why."

"Numb is one thing, but it sounds like this Yacob could have killed you."

"Yeah."

"But you don't care?"

"No, I do care. I do a lot. It made me feel like I could survive or, or be alive. I mean, winning doesn't mean a thing if you don't have somethin' to lose. Right?"

They were sitting in the dining room, she, at the head of the table and he at her right side. Natasha took Ghalen's hand, gripping it hard enough that one of her indigo nails dug painfully into his palm.

"I'm afraid for you," she said.

"Don't be."

"Why not?"

"'Cause it won't make any difference."

GHALEN AND VEROCHKA LEFT THE BAY AREA AT AROUND 3:00 a.m. the next Saturday. Just after eleven that morning, they stopped in Palm Springs to get breakfast at a diner called Handy's. She had oatmeal and a light beer while he ordered huevos rancheros. Enjoying the meal and eating heartily, he was feeling free in the arid desert.

Verochka was studying him intently, watching, as if for a sign.

"Where are you taking me?" she asked.

"'To the last gas station on the eastern side of Mecca,'" he quoted. "That's what you told me, right?"

The Russian continued to stare.

"That woman you talked to, the one named Lil, she's gonna meet us there and take you to Blodeuwedd, outside'a Mecca," Ghalen continued, somehow answering her silence.

"Mecca is in the Middle East," she countered.

"And Paris is in France but there's also Paree's in Idaho, Texas, Arkansas, Missouri, and Wisconsin. Damn, they got a China in Maine."

"Why should I trust you?" she asked, cutting through his palaver.

"I trusted you."

"And I could have gotten you killed."

She looked okay, wearing pink jeans and a powder-blue T-shirt. She was thin and plain on the outside and like a wolverine on the inside. They'd spent the night before together at Priss. She was dismissive and haughty then, sexy and a little mean. But today Ghalen could see the nervousness in her eyes and movements.

"I don't know, Verochka. You're the one who talked to them on the phone."

"Why can't you go with me to them?"

"No men allowed."

"I don't trust that."

"Then let's go over to LA. I got people there. I know a restaurant where you could get a job. Lotsa Persians around there. You like Persians?"

"So, we just buy some gas and go all the way to Los Angeles?"

"It's not that far. We're already in Southern California."

He continued eating while she stared at him, completely absorbed but seeing nothing.

"You could marry me," she suggested. "I mean, I wouldn't be much trouble. You could have other girlfriends. I know how to cook and clean, grow a garden and make babies."

"What do you cook?"

"Hamburgers and chicken soup."

They both laughed.

"I'm not ready for all that, V," Ghalen said. "I'm too young and my dad wouldn't sign the papers."

Her eyes were beginning to tear up.

"Let's go to LA," he offered. "I'll be up north but we could see each other sometimes. You could get an apartment, make friends."

This offer affected her. She sat up straight and glowered at something, somewhere.

"No," she said. "I will go. I'm not afraid of women. And if you don't marry me, that will be too bad for you."

THE LAST GAS STATION ON THE ROAD OUT OF MECCA was called Chalk's Gas. It had one pump that looked to be older than Night Farr. Ghalen pulled up and got out to pump the fuel.

"Hey," someone called.

It was a young Black man, maybe a year older than Ghalen. He was well built like Ghalen and wearing sand-colored denim overalls. His skin, though dark, had other colors under the surface—blond-brown, almost orange, and drifts of a darkness that might have been blue.

"I'm s'posed to work the pump," the young man said.

"Fine with me."

Removing the gas cap and working the nozzle in, the attendant said, "Brother, this ride is sumpin' else. Red like a mothahfuckah."

"Got it from a friend of my dad's."

The worker nodded, glanced into the car, and said, "And may I say, the lady is somethin' too."

Ghalen had learned early not to brag on his good fortune so said, "You gotta lotta Black people out here?"

"Yeah. Mostly from Texas by way of LA."

"Is it nice?"

"If you like it hot and boring."

GHALEN MOVED HIS CAR TO THE EDGE OF THE STATION lot and handed Verochka two small cell phones.

"Why two?" she asked.

"One to call Lil," he said. "My friend who told me about the place said that they don't let people have phones for the first six months. So you can give them the one you use to call Lil and then hide the other one. That way, if you feel you need to get out and can't, all you got to do is send me a text and I'll be on my way."

"From Berkeley?"

"I'll stay in Palm Springs tonight. And then go visit my dad and his girlfriend in Los Angeles a couple of days before goin' back up north."

When Verochka folded him into an embrace it was the first time that Ghalen felt her caring for him. He liked it.

"How will you find me?" she asked softly into his hair.

"Phones are connected."

Leaning back and holding on, Verochka stared into his eyes, trying to communicate something that he felt he should understand.

"Why?" she asked.

"Why what?"

"Is it because of the sex?"

"Me helping?"

"Are you rich? Because only rich people give. And they only give to own."

"Yacob tell ya that?"

Shaking her head she said, "It is like my name."

"True?"

She winced, as if he had jabbed her with a pin.

"Excuse me," a woman said.

She was short, five foot or less, and dressed in a scaly green one-piece coverall. Her long black hair was shot through with gray. Ghalen imagined that her blue eyes were, at one time, brighter.

"Lil?" Verochka asked.

The woman's features were blunt but not unappealing. Her smile said yes.

Verochka kissed Ghalen passionately and then let him go.

"I am ready," she said.

"You have luggage?" Lil asked.

"No."

"That's okay, we have all you'll need out there."

Without a smile or word, the Russian fugitive walked away from Ghalen toward her new life.

Lil gave him a friendly nod and turned to walk toward a powder-blue, ancient VW Bug. He watched them climb in and drive off.

THAT NIGHT, AT THE SANDSTONE INN, THE FRESHMAN sat on a lumpy mattress with his first-floor door open, looking out over a fair-size rectangular swimming pool. The sun was down and a half moon reigned over the eastern plain of the Palm Springs desert. Ghalen's feeling was cold and hard but not angry or sad. Bringing Verochka to the desert had exhausted him. He was glad to be alone again, satisfied that he'd done what he could.

It was after two in the morning when his cell phone sounded.

"Hello?"

"Hi."

"Verochka. You okay? You need me to come get you?"

"No. You don't have to worry, my friend."

"They're okay out there?"

"I think I am home."

They talked for fifteen or so minutes. She had her own room, and the food was good. They wanted her to model a few days a week, maybe work in their desert garden.

"They grow fish in a big tank and recycle water."

"Is it hot?"

"Not in our rooms. They are underground and cool. You have done so much for me. Can I do anything for you?"

"Yeah, yeah."

"What is that?"

"For the first couple'a months text me every week or so, so I'll know you're okay."

"That's all?"

"For now."

NIGHT WAS THE ONLY ONE HOME WHEN GHALEN GOT there, late the next morning. He was wearing his Vietnamese farming clothes and playing a game of chess against a tiny computer that was a small board with the pieces on pegs.

The elder looked up and smiled when Ghalen walked into the kitchen.

"You on break?" he asked.

"Naw. I gave a friend a ride down to Mecca and decided to drop by. I didn't know you played chess."

"A guy I know from Ho Chi Min City sent it. He likes gadgets."

"How's it goin'?"

"Pretty good. I lost every game so far."

Ghalen sat across from his grandfather, in the chair where the imaginary opponent would have been seated.

"You look different," Night said.

"Like how?"

"I don't know. Like somethin's goin' on."

"Maybe there is."

"Manny Bluitt died."

"From gettin' hit? They callin' it murder?"

"The way he got hit, I'd call it suicide."

Ghalen smiled despite the seriousness of the situation.

"Are you in some kinda trouble?"

"His sister, estranged sister, is suing me for twenty-two million dollars."

"That's crazy."

"Maybe they think that big number'll scare me into payin' 'em what little I got. Your lawyer told me not to worry. I told her that I stopped worryin' after the time I got snagged by a king cobra in a neighbor's rice paddy. I was laid up for a week."

"Did you almost die?"

"No. But for one whole day my grandmother, Pleasance Moll, sat with me talkin' 'bout all the peoples I never knew about. I was sad to break off that talk."

"Your grandmother's dead, right?"

"Not that day."

"ARE YOU MISSING YOUR CLASSES?" AURA ASKED GHALEN that night at dinner.

"Only one. I told my professor that I had to be gone, that it was a family thing. He gave me a copy of the lectures and the specific sections I had to read."

"So," Robert said, "you drove this girl out to the desert and left her there?"

"Yeah."

"You didn't even see where they were takin' her?"

"Chef Charlie's friend, Natasha Vile, told me about this place and Chef Charlie told me that I could trust her."

"Then she prob'ly all right," Robert said, "but still, I don't like leavin' a woman out in the desert like that."

"She called me and said she was fine."

"You like this girl?" Night asked.

Ghalen considered the question because he understood the questioner so well. Grandfather Night had been with a woman who saved his life and then put him to work. He knew what it was to experience cross-cultural love. But he'd never said that he loved Phu'ò'ng. He didn't need to. After she died the children were still on the farm. Night decided to stay until they'd figured out what to do with their lives. Phu'ò'ng's younger sister, Cam, came to stay and help with the farm.

Ghalen decided that the question was: Could he have lived a life with Verochka, growing gardens and raising fish in the desert? The answer to that question was yes, he'd be able to do that and enjoy it. But that was only part of the answer. Could the Russian be with him? She bit. She was an angry woman with good reason, but could she be good with him? And even if this was something they both wanted, would they fit together like Phu'ò'ng and Night had done?

"You startin' to ack like your daddy," Night said and then chuckled.

"What?"

"You been starin' at that sea saltshaker for three minutes now."

"I like her very much, Granddad. But I think we're very far away right now, and that's all right."

The elder looked at his grandson but did not speak, didn't even nod.

29.

At a few minutes past four the next morning Ghalen was loading his station wagon with a basket filled with vegan delicacies his father had prepared for the journey. When he was finishing up, Robert came down to say goodbye to his son. This was about the time that the elder Horton would leave to go to work in Beverly Hills.

"How long's it to get all the way to Berkeley?" Robert asked, draping an arm over his son's shoulder.

"If I take I-5 it should be about six hours. I'd like to take the coast highway, but I'm thinking that I better get back sooner."

Robert was staring at his son, thinking about something unsaid.

"What is it, Dad?"

"Lovely called."

Ghalen felt a fair-size and jagged stone lodge in the center of his chest. "Oh?"

"It was two days ago. She wanted your number. I told her that Aura had it, but she wasn't home. I got your number, but Aura does too, and I wanted to hold off a little. Maybe you didn't wanna hear from her or sumpin'."

"Tell Aura that if she calls again just give it to her."

"You sure?"

"Yeah. Lovely's my friend."

WITH LOVELY IN MIND GHALEN DECIDED TO TAKE THE Pacific Coast Highway back up north. It was a longer route and traffic was heavier, but it was mostly beautiful, and he wanted the time to think about the Persian-Jamaican Lovely.

Along with Bruno she was his oldest friend, and she was still the only person, outside of family, that could make him feel something. Verochka brought pain and fear, passion, and purpose, but Ghalen saw these things as secondary. Lovely's rich brown skin and almond eyes, her slow laughter and deep concern for just about everybody had been one of the cornerstones of his life.

She was Bruno's girlfriend and Ghalen didn't leave with her because he believed that he would have to take care of his father for the rest of his life. But now that was different. Robert had made himself a new family that loved and cared for him. And this was Ghalen's family too. He hadn't been shut out, just relieved of some responsibility.

A FEW MILES NORTH OF SANTA BARBARA GHALEN SAW A hitchhiker. A very tall, very Black youth defined more by height than bulk. Wearing mostly green garments and carrying a tan rucksack over one shoulder, he stood stoic and resigned.

The freshman slowed down.

"Where you goin'?" Ghalen shouted out of the open passenger's side window.

"San Francisco," he said, telling the freshman, among other things, that he was not from North America.

"Come on. I'm goin' there too, near enough."

As the youth ran toward the car Ghalen could see that he was, indeed, very tall. He opened the door, folding his long body in and placing the rucksack between his ankles.

The man did not smile but said, "Thank you for stopping."

"How long you been out there?"

"I don't have the time, I mean, a watch."

"No phone?"

"It doesn't work right now. But I think I've been out there around two hours."

Pulling from the side of the highway Ghalen asked, "Where in the city are you going?"

"I don't know. Anywhere you stop will be fine."

"Okay. My name's Ghalen."

"I am Deng."

"From Sudan?"

"Yes," he said, a small note of surprise in his tone. "You know Africa?"

"Never been there but I know a few countries and something about them. Deng is a Dinka name, right?"

The rider's eyes opened wide.

"You know this?"

"I got a pretty good memory, and we spent a whole year in high school studying the peoples and geography of the African continent."

"Most people here think that Africa is one country."

"World's a big place. Most people in it don't know much about five miles around the place they live."

"This is true," Deng agreed. "When I lived in Minneapolis I only knew where I slept, where I worked, and then the government office where I had to go every two weeks."

"You comin' from the Midwest?"

"Yes. I wanted to see the ocean and some old friends."

"You hungry?"

Ghalen offered the various selections from the food his father had prepared.

Eating as Ghalen drove, the two were mostly silent, without discomfort.

"This is very good food," Deng complimented. "Not so many chemicals."

"Thanks. You go back to Sudan often?"

"Never." This utterance, Ghalen thought, was as hard and sharp as the last nail in a coffin before being loaded onto its pyre.

"That civil war still goin' on?"

This question brought out the first smile on the Central African's face.

"It's like asking if there's snow in Minnesota in July. The answer is, not right now."

Ghalen noticed a sinuous, thick scar on the side of Deng's long neck, and decided not to comment.

THEY REACHED SAN FRANCISCO IN THE LATE AFTERNOON.

"Is there anyplace I can drop you?" Ghalen offered when they got to Market Street.

"I have a cousin named Peter. Years ago, we were conscripts together."

"Conscripts? Like in the army?"

Deng gave a curt nod.

"How old are you?"

"Seventeen. How old are you?"

"Sixteen. I was just thinking that seventeen is young for the army."

"So is nine."

"Oh, um, do you know Peter's phone number?"

"He works at a restaurant called Lucy's."

"Well, let's park and look it up."

THE CAFÉ WAS ON TURK BOULEVARD NEAR A BRANCH OF the University of San Francisco. Deng called and got his cousin. They talked in their language for a few minutes and then Deng disconnected the call.

"It's not far from here," the Sudanese said.

"Gimme an address and I'll load it in the GPS."

LUCY'S WAS HOUSED IN A SLENDER, FOUR-STORY BRICK building between a storage facility and an African fabric store. It wasn't a very large place, but they had eleven tables, each of which could have seated from two to five customers. Along the walls were a couple of dozen photographs depicting Sudanese people of all ages and genders. They were posing, working, dancing, and laughing. One old woman, lying on a purple rug was, it seemed, dying.

The restaurant was mostly empty but, Ghalen figured, it wasn't yet evening.

"Deng!" a man called out.

He had come through a swinging door at the back of the rectangular room. A short young man with a round hard belly, with skin like ancient, aged bronze. His clothes were loose but somehow proper, rendered in strong colors that were not bright. This man smiled as he approached the long-distance hitchhiker.

"Peter!" Deng rejoined.

The men embraced. Deng bending down and Peter on his toes.

"Come, I want you to meet my friend Ghalen."

Ghalen walked up to the shorter man. Deng's friend held out both hands in greeting, and Ghalen reciprocated. When the four hands clasped, he said, "Pleased to meet you, Peter."

"Call me Nhial, that is my name. Peter was a soldier like Deng."

"Okay, Nhial. I like your café."

"Thank you, thank you. It isn't much but I hope one day for it to be like home."

"It's pretty great right now. I like the photographs, and the furniture is simple and, um, I don't know, the whole thing like invites you in."

"Looks good, doesn't it? You wouldn't know that I'm missing two out of three cooks."

"They sick?"

"Cold."

"They have colds?"

"No. The ICE men came and asked for their papers. They took them to a federal building somewhere and locked them away."

"Will they be all right?" Ghalen asked.

"Oh yes. They didn't have papers in their pockets and so I will have to pay a lawyer and a fine to get them back. Two days, maybe three."

"You need a cook?"

"Not so easy in San Francisco. We don't eat hamburgers and hot dogs."

"I could help."

"You know our food?"

"I might look a little young but I'm a trained cook. Been workin' in a restaurant since I was seven. You have somebody to show me what to do and I'll know it by the end of the night."

Eyes wide, bright teeth smiling Nhial shouted, "Nafisa!"

"Yes, Nhial?" she said before coming through the door to the kitchen.

She was dark-skinned, more so than most. As tall as Ghalen and slender but not thin or fragile. Her face was open but a slight twist to her mouth made it look as if she'd eaten something sour that might have tasted good.

"This is Ghalen," Nhial said.

She looked the teenager up and down; didn't seem unsatisfied.

"Yes?" the good-bad taste in her mouth inquired.

"He's going to be your new kitchen helper," Nhial told her.

"You know Sudanese food?" she doubted.

"Been cookin' since I was seven," Ghalen said. "Been in a professional kitchen since five. You show me the ingredients, and how you need them prepared, and I will back you up."

A look of surprise showed across Nafisa's face. She took a moment to consider this offer.

"I only need vegetables cut, scalded, and sometimes soaked."

"Every one of those things takes a close look."

"You don't mind women's work?"

"I'll wash the dishes too."

"We only have one sink."

"I only have two hands."

Nafisa smiled, said, "Come with me," and turned toward the swinging kitchen door.

GHALEN WORKED HARD FOR NAFISA. HE STEAMED AND chopped, sautéed and boiled, and helped her maneuver huge skillets and cauldrons. He made quite a few mistakes, but the chef never got impatient.

Deng was popular among the patrons of Lucy's. After only a few calls the restaurant filled up with his friends and those who came with them. The great number of patrons meant that there was a lot of cooking to do.

At one point, after his workload eased, Ghalen offered to make a sesame cake to celebrate Deng.

"You bake?" she asked, unable to keep the skepticism out of her voice.

"Since I was about ten."

THE FEAST PETERED OUT BY HALF PAST ELEVEN. THE revelers went home, and Peter took Deng to his place. Nafisa told her boss that she'd stay with Ghalen to straighten up.

"I don't mean to insult you, Mr. Ghalen," she said after they'd put the kitchen in order. "But you work like a woman, both hard and tireless."

"Until the job is done," he said with a smile.

"You will have a drink with me?"

"I will have two."

SEATED AT A SMALL BUTCHER BLOCK TABLE IN THE kitchen, Nafisa poured two-ounce shots from a bottle that's label was rendered in some foreign tongue. She downed her shot while he sipped. She had a few more drinks, and he didn't quite keep up.

They talked about their lives and the city. She liked America. "The music is beautiful even if the people are not equal to it."

MUCH LATER NAFISA ASKED, "WHY DID YOU PICK HIM UP?"

"Deng?"

"Yes. Deng."

"Why wouldn't I pick him up?"

"He's a big Black man, and he never smiles."

"I'm a Black man."

"Yes, but not from Africa. Not from war."

"You right about that, but you said Deng doesn't smile and he did when I asked if the war was over in Sudan."

"You should have run."

"I don't think so."

"You are not afraid of dying?"

"Oh, I am. But I got this grandfather named Night."

"Yes?"

"He asked me one time who I thought killed the most people. I said, murderers. And he laughed. He said the worst killer killed more people in one day than all the murderers together killed in a year."

"He meant the government," Nafisa said with certainty.

"Naw . . ."

"Then who is this great killer?"

"Mosquitos."

Seeing Nafisa laugh Ghalen sobered for a moment. Her humor was deep and unruly, like a river at springtime, he thought, gushing down a mountainside as if it itself were alive.

GHALEN WOKE UP TO SEARING PAIN THROBBING BE-tween both eyes and their brow-bones. He was a little nauseated and tired even though he had slept for many hours. There was a window with a frilly curtain across the way from the couch on which he slept. Sunlight through the flimsy fabric of the curtains hurt his eyes.

"Are you going to vomit?" a woman asked.

"Prob'ly die first."

Her laughter was a balm. Hearing it, Ghalen was able to take a deep breath.

"What was that we were drinkin'?" he asked Nafisa.

"Araqi."

"From Iraq?"

"No. It is made from dates and yeast in Sudan."

"Dates?"

"It can be strong, no?"

"Stronger'n me, that's for sure."

The tall cook brought him a huge pitcher filled with water and ice and a platter with six cut-up pears.

"Eat and drink," she commanded.

Ghalen went to work.

"Hydration and electrolytes," he said.

She smiled.

"Whose apartment is this?"

"I live here," the woman announced, as if a colonizer.

"Really?"

"Yes. Why?"

"You said that you weren't married. At least that's what I remember."

"I am not married."

"I don't know, I mean, I thought that, in your part of the world, single women were looked down upon if they had men in their beds."

"You are on a couch, not in my bed."

"Yeah."

Ghalen lowered his forehead into his left palm, grunted, and then took a deep breath. This procedure took maybe half a minute. When he looked up, he saw Nafisa staring at him contemplatively.

"Drink more and then eat."

"Uh-huh," he said and then obeyed.

"I was kidnapped from my home with my two sisters," she said while he ate.

"That's terrible."

"One of the men who did this tied up my sisters and started to rape me." There wasn't an ounce of shame or defeat in Nafisa's mien. "My sisters started screaming when he ripped off my clothes. But the man didn't know that I was wearing a wristband that my father had given me. It was one slender piece of bamboo that, if you took off the restraining hoop, it would snap to, straightening out into a knife. I took the sharp end and stabbed it into the soft flesh under his jaw. I did this three times. He tried to crawl away on his back, but I put my heel on his throat to keep him still. He begged me not to let him die. He said he had a wife and children, that he didn't mean to hurt me. He called me a bitch and I stuck the bamboo into his eye. He screamed as did my sisters . . . as I did. The last thing he saw was my naked sex and his blood on my knife.

"Now, Mr. Ghalen, why would I worry about a man in my home?"

The hungover guest shook his head and took a bite of pear. He took a long draw of water and laid back down on the couch.

30.

When he awoke again his cell phone showed that it was 1:13. There had been some messages and calls. Usually, he checked all his messages first, just in case his father was lost somewhere. But that afternoon his first destination was the toilet. After that he had to lie down again. He slept another hour and then went to the kitchen and drank three tall glasses of water.

Sitting at the little kitchen table for a while, he concentrated on breathing while waiting for something inside to begin.

IT ALL STARTED WHEN LOVELY INVITED HIM TO COFFEE in Culver City or, or maybe when his mother died, and he and his father walked back home. He tried to put his parents in context to who and where he was at that moment. His soul, if, indeed, he had a soul, felt like an engine that couldn't turn over, like the permanent twilight of the winter in the far north that he read about.

That's when his cell phone sounded.

"Hello?"

"Gayley."

"Hey," he said, feeling a faraway smile on his lips. "Lovely."

"Did Aura call you?"

"When?"

"Earlier today."

"I don't know. I haven't looked."

"Oh. She gave me your new phone number."

"How are you?"

"Fine. You up in Berkeley?"

"San Francisco."

"What you doin' there?"

"I met this guy from Sudan who needed a ride. The place he was goin' to is a restaurant in San Francisco that needed a cook for a couple'a days."

"You sound weird."

"Just woke up."

"Just woke up? It's almost three in the afternoon."

"Yeah."

"Should I call you later?"

"No. I'm fine. How's Bruno?"

"He got arrested again."

"Hm."

"What does that mean?"

Ghalen would have loved to explain how he felt at that moment. It seemed to him perfectly logical that all of life was a simple machine filled with odd-shaped holes and wooden blocks that tumbled, tumbled down until they hit a hole that fit their dimensions, or they fell through to the bottom and from there into a pit of hot coals.

But this didn't make sense, so he said, "It's too bad. I know how hard he was tryin' to get it right."

"He was," Lovely said, anger in her tone.

"I know."

"He needed you. If you had gone with me, he would have stayed in that halfway house and straightened out."

"What can I do now, Love?"

For a while there was silence from her side. Ghalen didn't mind. He was feeling heavy, not tired, or exhausted but like a rusty iron weight, slowly sinking into a bank of soaked mud.

"Can I come up to see you?" she asked.

"I'd rather come down to LA," he said.

"What about school?"

"I think I'm gonna drop out for now."

"Why? Are you failing?"

"No. No. I just don't know why I'm there. It kinda feels like I'm workin' in a factory that lost its contract or somethin'. Know what I mean?"

"Not really. When will you come down?"

"I might have to work in the restaurant tonight. So, day after tomorrow?"

"Okay."

NAFISA'S APARTMENT WAS ON THE TOP FLOOR OF THE building that housed Lucy's. He went down the stairs to the back entrance of the kitchen. There he came upon Nafisa and a twenty-something Black man with a receding hairline and eyes that seemed surprised at everything they lighted upon.

"Back from the dead?" Nafisa greeted.

"Maybe not all the way back."

"This is my number two cook," she said, "Simon. His aunt had his papers and got him out this morning."

"Congratulations," Ghalen said, holding out a hand.

"Naffie says that you are a powerful cook," the balding young man said. "That is her greatest compliment."

"She taught me everything."

"I teach everyone who works for me everything, but do they learn?" Nafisa complained jovially.

DENG AND NHIAL CAME IN THE AFTERNOON. THEY DRANK homemade beer while Ghalen, Simon, and Nafisa worked.

That night was even more of a party than the evening before. The cooks prepared great bowls of rice and other grains along with goat meat and gravies, green salads and flat breads, sheep's offal, and many bottles of Araqi.

Musicians came to play for their dinners. Mostly strings and drums, dancers and dueling singers mouthing polyrhythmic sounds and words. What Ghalen liked the most was a young boy who played a wooden trumpet that sounded like something he'd once heard in a dream.

"You like?" Cook Number Two, Simon asked.

"Yeah," Ghalen replied. "It sounds like a brass trumpet with hair growing between the notes."

Simon laughed and poured date liquor into their small wooden bowls.

"You are a poet?" Simon asked.

The question struck Ghalen. He thought about it and then said, "A poet. Without words."

HE WOKE UP THE NEXT MORNING LYING ON THE FLOOR between a fat man and a girl no older than he. There were maybe a dozen people sleeping, unconscious, or hungover lying in corners or in small, huddled-up bunches under tables and in doorways.

Carefully, Ghalen sat up, trying not to disturb his sleep mates. At one point his movement caused the big man to grunt and roll over; luckily this was not on top of Ghalen. He then moved to climb over the other sleeper, but when he was passing over her, her eyes came open. She smiled and kissed him lightly on the lips.

HIS BAGS WERE IN THE RED STATION WAGON, WHICH was parked in a barnlike garage behind the restaurant building.

He got in behind the wheel, wanting to drive off, but the familiar seat was so comfortable that he relaxed, thinking about the beautiful African girl, and wondering what might have happened if he'd stayed. He thought again about the great wooden machine of tumbling blocks gyrating crazily. The imagined sound was tremendous but not hostile or disagreeable.

"YOU ARE LEAVING?"

He heard the words, certain that they were in a dream. He sighed and smiled.

"Well?" the voice demanded.

Opening his eyes he saw that she was sitting next to him in the passenger's seat. For how long had he slept?

"Yes," he said. "I have to get back home."

"To Berkeley?" Nafisa asked.

"Los Angeles."

She came from another world. That is what Ghalen thought. Her face, her expression, were beautiful, but he could not read them.

"That's too bad," Lucy's chef said with a sad smile.

"Why?"

"I wanted you to meet my niece—Nasrah. She goes to school at San Francisco State, and I think she needs a man."

"I could come back in a year and a half."

"Why not now?"

"I'm not a man yet."

"You have been a man for a very long time, I think. What you need is a woman to help you find the child you have lost."

There was a ring of truth to this claim. Ghalen was astonished that this woman he hardly knew could see something in him that no one, not even he, had seen or said before.

"I think I could go to UC Berkeley for a hundred years and never hear those words," he said.

"You see?" she claimed, as if he had just proved her point.

ON THE LONG RIDE DOWN THE COAST GHALEN THOUGHT about where he was going, and why he was going there. It was a mistake to get together with Lovely, he knew this. But it was also wrong to stay at school. His father didn't need him, and Nasrah might have been wonderful. He knew all the plays and the players and yet felt that his life was preordained, fated, just as surely as the highway laid out before him.

While thinking these things for the dozenth time he glanced up at the rearview mirror and saw the flashing blue and red lights.

"WHY DIDN'T YOU STOP?" WAS THE FIRST THING THAT the CHP officer said.

She was blond and maybe five ten with almost true-white skin that was somewhat weathered. Her nametag read H POLTER. She was standing at his window, and he was very aware that her partner was hovering on the other side.

"I don't understand, officer," Ghalen said.

"You don't understand English?"

"I did stop."

"I've been following you, lights on and siren going, for at least three minutes." She was very angry. Very.

"I'm sorry, ma'am, I didn't hear it. Or, if I did hear something, I didn't realize it was for me."

"Blasting your radio?"

"No. The radio in this car doesn't work."

"Is this your car?"

"Yes, ma'am."

"License and registration."

Natasha Vile had signed the car over to Ghalen on the third time he visited her home.

"I was thinking," she'd said. "The police might stop you, probably will stop you, and ownership is the best way to identify yourself."

"Why didn't you stop?" H Polter asked again.

She'd passed the papers over to her partner, a black-haired woman a few inches shorter and wider than the inquisitor.

"I didn't hear you and then, when I looked in the mirror, I pulled over to the side."

"Where'd you get this car?"

"Bought from a friend of a friend of my father's."

"How much did it cost?"

"I don't know."

"You don't know?" she yelled.

"My father's friend paid her."

Ghalen kept from fear by wondering why H Polter was so angry. It must've had to do with him not stopping quickly enough, he decided. That and maybe other things.

The dark-haired officer was the color of light copper. She returned with the license and whispered something to H Polter.

After a moment of consideration the head patrolwoman asked, "Where are you going?"

"Home."

"Where's that?"

"Los Angeles."

"Where are you coming from?"

"San Francisco."

"What were you doing there?"

"Attending a party."

"Are there any weapons or drugs in your car?"

"No, officer. No."

"You came all the way to San Francisco for a party?"

"I'm a student at UC Berkeley."

"Why didn't you say that in the first place?"

"You asked me where I was coming from and where I was going. So, that's what I told you."

Their sentences were getting longer. Ghalen wondered what that might mean.

Patrolwoman Polter's hand drifted down to rest on the butt of her pistol.

"You must think you're pretty smart," she said.

"I'm just tryin' to get home."

Ghalen didn't know if it was the words or the resigned tone that suddenly de-escalated Officer Polter's wrath.

She took a deep breath through her nostrils and then huffed it out between her lips.

"You need to pay attention when you're driving, Mr. Horton. When we think a car is trying to get away from us, we are allowed to use deadly force."

ALLOWED TO USE DEADLY FORCE. THESE WORDS REVER-berated through Ghalen's thoughts as he drove down the coast of the Pacific Ocean, traveling in a shiny red car that was older than he. The previous night he and Deng had found themselves sitting at a table together while the music played and people danced.

"Do you know where I come from?" the Sudanese asked.

"I know some things about the place, secondhand," Ghalen acceded with a nod. "But nothing about the wars."

Deng's face was almost small there at the top of the tall man's muscled, sculpted, and contradictorily lean shoulders. His expression held equal parts anger and defeat.

"Can you understand how much pain has passed through my hands?" Deng asked, holding long and slender fingers before his eyes.

"No."

The taller, deeply moved ex-child-soldier grabbed the freshman. "Why not? Why not?"

Ghalen knew that Deng was drunk but decided that this was an unimportant detail. The significance lay in the strength of that grip, the pain leaking out of Deng's understanding of himself, a cracked vessel of spite and self-hatred.

"Because nobody can understand what they haven't learned," Ghalen replied without the slightest emotional response.

There was darkness in the whites of the child soldier's eyes. "How can you even know that?"

"Blood."

"What blood?"

"My grandfather. He was blown up, almost killed in Vietnam. When he almost got killed by a land mine, he told me he felt it was justice coming after he'd murdered so many people, so far away from where he was born."

Deng held on to Ghalen's biceps. At its onset, this grip was the first step toward violence, but now he was merely holding on. The African closed his eyes. *To get a better look*, Ghalen believed.

"Do you think anything happens by mistake?" Deng asked.

"I don't know about that, but I'm beginning to believe that we are all helpless."

HE DROVE ON AND ON, THE THOUGHTS IN HIS MIND clashing against each other like waves coming in from the abyss. He was enjoying the drive while having no direction other than places he'd already been. He didn't want to be a student. He didn't want to believe in a place or a people or love. But he wanted love.

He needed, needed to get someplace where he wanted to be.

31.

Robert was standing in front of the apartment building, watering the little strip of lawn between the sidewalk and the street. This wasn't his job, but when the super got sick a few years before, the vegan cook started doing the gardening around the property. It wasn't much work, and he enjoyed maintaining the lives of the grasses, flowering bushes, the two trees, and tomato plants in barrels at the back of the building.

"Hi Dad," Ghalen called, climbing out of the red wagon.

"Oh, Gayley, it's you. I don't ever think I'ma get used to that big red car."

"How you doin', Pop?"

"Fine. What brings you back down here?"

"I, um, I'm thinkin' of taking the rest of the semester off."

Robert stood a little straighter. Ghalen thought that his father would press his back against a wall if there was one nearby, water nozzle forgotten in his hand, gushing onto the sidewalk.

"Like a few days?"

"I don't know. It just doesn't seem to matter. I mean, most'a the kids there are takin' it easy, gettin' high, playing music, stayin' up all night. I mean, it's fun but it doesn't mean anything."

"They're learning," Robert argued.

"I know, but . . ."

"But what?"

"Chef Charlie's friend and I have dinner together every couple of weeks or so. I learn a lot more from her than in any class. And, and, and for the past few days, I was a temporary cook at a Sudanese restaurant in San Francisco. I met all these people from different parts of Africa and learned about foods from Egypt to Sudan in just one night. There was something real there, not a desk and a classroom where everybody was tryin' to be the same. And, you know, I just finished goin' to school for ten years."

"But college can teach you more," Robert pleaded.

"I'm not sure about that. Watch it, Dad, you're gettin' water all over the sidewalk."

Robert twisted the nozzle to cut off the stream. Then gazed at his son's chest.

They stood out there in front of the upscale Westwood apartment building for some minutes before Robert put the hose down and hugged his son.

"BUT YOU'LL DO SO MUCH BETTER IN LIFE IF YOU GET AN education," Aura was saying at the dinner table that night.

"It's not the education," Ghalen said.

"Don't be stupid. Education is how people make better lives for themselves."

"It's not education, it's—"

"Yes, it is," Aura shouted, cutting him off.

"Aura," Night said. "Let the boy talk."

"But he doesn't know what he's talking about."

"And he's not gonna find out if you don't let him tell you what he thinks."

Aura glared at the veteran, looking as if she wanted to spit on him.

"It's not the education," Ghalen said. "It's the certification. It's learning how to get A's and write papers. It's getting a degree that is there to make you seem like everybody else. It's a fancy way of learning how to do what people tell you to do."

"Those are important lessons," Robert said.

"But, Dad, it's just as important to know when not to take orders."

Robert took the time to consider this obvious truth.

"What else can you do?" Aura asked.

"Does this have to do with that girl you took out to the desert?" Night wondered.

"I don't wanna be with her or anything," Ghalen answered. "But, but she's doing something important with her life, right now, today."

"But how's she gonna make money?" Aura chided.

"I don't know how, but I know she will. There's not one doubt in my mind about that."

"So," Robert said and then halted for a second or two. "So, it's about Lovely."

Ghalen felt a sudden shock of fear.

"Her and Bruno," Robert added.

"It's all changed since then," Ghalen said. "I mean, I remembered how much we learned back then, in school, after school. Back then we were doing things. But now, today, it's just like I'm running in place."

"You're going to have a lot of girlfriends in your life," Aura declared.

"It's not about having," the boy replied. "It's about feeling."

"What the hell is that supposed to mean?"

"When I went to meet Lovely and Bruno," he said. "That was the first time in a long time that I could remember that I wasn't there to help somebody or to make things better. All they wanted was my company because I was their friend."

"Do you mean make things better for me," Robert reasoned. "Is that what you mean?"

Once again Robert surprised and stunned his son.

"Yeah," Ghalen replied, nodding. "I was gonna go to UCLA so I could stay here with you, Dad."

Putting up both hands, as if in surrender, Aura said, "We should stop talking about this now."

"I agree," Night agreed.

Ghalen looked into his father's eyes, asking, without words, what he wanted.

"You wanna gimme a ride down to the Santa Monica pier?" Robert replied to Ghalen's stare.

"Sure, Pop, let's go."

IT WAS THE FIRST TIME GHALEN HAD DRIVEN HIS FATHER. But oddly, the experience was familiar for both of them.

"This is a nice car," Robert said, his window down and his hand surfing the breezes.

"I love you, Dad."

"Me too, son."

"I went to Berkeley because you and Miss Barth said I should."

"I know. I wanted you to be free, livin' life for yourself. You been takin' care'a me since before your mother died. I wanted you to have your own life. It's just that I was thinkin' that college'd be a way to do that."

"I know. I thought so too, before I got there. And one day I'd love to go to school, when there's really somethin' for me to learn. But right now, I'd feel better waterin' the lawn, or paintin' houses."

"Your mother used to tell me that you were the smartest person she ever knew."

"She used to tell me the same thing about you."

"Naw, your mom didn't think I was smarter she just liked the way I'd think about things 'cause it's so different from the way she did."

"I just wanna be on my own for a while, Dad. Working, travelin' maybe. On my own."

"Nuthin' wrong with that."

"You wouldn't mind?"

"It's not my life, it's yours."

Ghalen gave Robert a toothy grin.

"Now that's more like it," his father said.

THEY DIDN'T MAKE IT TO THE PIER, JUST DROVE AROUND for a couple of hours, talking about Jamilah, mostly.

"She's never far from my mind," Robert said to his son when they were stopped at a red light on Sepulveda about to cross Pico, going north.

"Does that bother Aura?"

"No. I don't think so anyway. She knows I love her. She knows I'd never be able to be with her if it wasn't for your mother."

"That sounds like a hard love," Ghalen said, realizing the many possible meanings of these words as they were spoken.

After a few minutes, on the way up to Wilshire, Robert replied, "Hard is good. It holds you up, keeps you honest."

FOR A WHILE THEY RODE IN SILENCE, GAZING AROUND them at nighttime West Los Angeles. Ghalen always loved the look of night, holding on to the semidesert air like an invisible claw.

After five or so minutes, Robert said, "That's what I like about you," as if answering something Ghalen had said.

"What's that, Dad?"

"You the other side'a the world as far as I'm concerned."

"Huh?"

"When I was a little kid in the second grade, they taught us in remedial class that the world was round, not like a circle you draw in the sand, but like a bowlin' ball–a perfect circle no mattah which way you go.

"The teacher was named Norris, Mr. Carol Norris. Some'a the kids would laugh at his name, and he would tell'em that they just stupid remedial kids so what they thought didn't matter. But I never laughed. The fact that the world was like a bowlin' ball made me feel a little crazy. I mean, what if you tripped and fell down? Would you just keep on rollin' down the hill? How could you even stop? I was really upset, and so I kept raisin' my hand after the geography lesson was ovah and dead.

"Mr. Norris told me to keep my hand down and stop askin' remedial questions. He was a mean motherfucker."

"Whoa, Dad," Ghalen interjected.

"He was," Robert said with conviction. "I swear. There's only been three people in my life I ever called a motherfucker, and that motherfucker is one. He talked like we was shit. But that was okay by the time I was seven. I didn't care what he said. So, when recess came and the other kids was playin', I went back to the classroom. He was there, smokin' a Kool cigarette like he always did when we were at recess, physical education, or lunch.

"I walked right up to his desk an' said, 'Excuse me, Mr. Norris.'

"'What do you want?' he told me, all short like he could be. 'Sir, I am very sorry but when you said the world was like a bowlin' ball, I almost lost my mind. I got questions and I just need to know.'

"He'idn't like it but he could tell by the way I was talkin' that I wasn't about to stop askin', so, he put the cigarette out in a ashtray he kept in his bottom draw.

"'Okay, dufus,' he said. 'What's on your stupid mind?'"

"He didn't really say that like that, right?" Ghalen doubted.

"Yes, the motherfucker did. But I didn't care. My mother was healthier back then, and she told me that she would come down there with a gun if anybody said any shit to me. I never told her what he said, because I didn't want her goin' to jail over murder, but I felt like I had power ovah him because'a what my mama would'a done if I said so."

"So what did you say to him?" Ghalen asked.

"It took me a li'l bit to put my words together. He got all fidgety and huffin', an' aks me if I had anything to say. So, I said, it's about the world bein' like the Earth globe. Does that mean that there's another Robert Horton on the exact other side of the ball who is just like me?

"You see," Robert said to his son. "I gave up on the rollin'-down-forever thing because I realized that I had already fallen at least a hundred times. So, if I didn't keep on goin' back then, then I probably never would. But I knew that there had to be somethin' magic about the world if it wasn't flat. So, I come up with the idea that it was like a mirror, and on the other side would be all the people on this side.

"Mr. Norris got a funny look on his face when I asked that. I think maybe he was wonderin' if I wasn't smarter than he wanted me to be. He looked at me all suspicious, and I just looked back. And then he said, 'Yes.'"

"Yes?" Ghalen was amazed and angry. "That motherfucker lied to you?"

"He did," Robert acceded. "But you know that wasn't a bad thing, because what he said was, 'Yes. There's another Robert Horton on the other side of the world. He looks just like you, and he sounds like you too, but over there he's a A student with a mother and a father and he's rich as he could be.'

"When I heard that, I was happy, happy to know that there was a world where I could have a better life and my mom would have a husband take care'a her.

"I had forgot all about that until you were born. Then I knew that as much as he was wrong, Mr. Carol Norris was also right. Here I am wantin' to fit in more'n anything and there you are needin' t'find your own way."

"Wow," Ghalen said, as much to himself as his father. "So, you can see what I'm talkin' about, right, Dad? I need to find my own way."

"I know that, son. I know. But what I'm tellin' you is, is that we got a call from Mrs. Cordet after you gave your graduation speech. She was mad as spit that you didn't give the talk you showed her."

"Why didn't you tell me about that?"

"Aura wanted to, but I told her that you were gonna do what you had to do no matter what."

"So, you weren't mad?"

"I heard your speech, honey. I saw all the kids lookin' up at you, listenin' to every word. Mrs. Cordet wanted you to play by her rules. Only thing I hoped was that she could learn sumpin'."

32.

Ghalen stopped his red station wagon in front of their Westwood apartment building.

"You go on, Dad. I wanna drive around for a while."

"Okay, Gayley. You be good now."

Two blocks away he pulled to the curb again and made a call.

"Hello?"

"Lovely."

"Ghalen. Are you home?"

"Uh-huh. Where are you?"

"I moved to cottage seven."

"In Venice?"

"You comin'?"

"I'll be there in twenty minutes."

Ghalen's cell phone read 11:16 as he walked up to the door of the backyard cottage, number seven. Before he could knock the door swung inward. Wearing a teal-colored silk slip, she threw her arms around his neck and kissed both eyes. She continued kissing him around the face while falling back into the one-room cabin.

There were lit candles here and there, a real bed on a box frame, and a metal stand. The floor was neat and clean, but Ghalen didn't realize any of this for at least an hour.

"I don't have any condoms," were his first words.

"That's okay," she assured him.

Their orgasms came at different times, allowing them to enjoy the pleasures they bestowed on each other. The loving didn't stop, just moved around, from one to the other to the other.

At around one in the morning Lovely said, "I got to stop, baby. She's sore."

"You want me to kiss her?"

"I need to rest a little first."

"Okay," he said, reaching out to touch her shoulder.

"You want something to drink?" she offered.

"Water?"

Smiling, she went to a small refrigerator in the far corner.

"Sparkling or flat?" she called.

"Flat."

LYING ABED, SIDE BY SIDE AND NAKED, THEY SEEMED LIKE a statue cut from a single, dark-hued stone, they were that close.

She kissed his cheek, then flicked her tongue in his ear.

"Uh."

"I'm gonna have to break up with Big B."

"Where is he?"

"In jail."

"For leavin' the halfway house?"

"No. He robbed this guy."

"With a gun?"

"Uh-uh. Beat him up and took his money and his car."

"Shit."

"I'd have to break up with him anyway."

"Why?"

"You. After all that time up in Seattle I realized that me and B are friends—that's all."

"Is that why you came back down to LA?"

Shaking her curly head she said, "Uh-uh, B got into a fight with these guys over sumpin'. I don't know. We came back here, and I was tryin' to get him to turn himself in, or at least talk to that lawyer. He said he was gonna, but he was scared about jail."

"That's when he robbed that guy?"

"He mugged a few people."

"Why didn't he just get a job?"

Lovely moved her face very close to his, moving her eyes around, as if taking inventory.

"Because he's not you," she said and then kissed him.

They fell into a languorous embrace, and from there into sleep.

"WHAT TIME IS IT?" HE ASKED SOME WHILE LATER WHEN he felt her moving around.

"About a quarter to four."

"You sound very awake."

"I gotta get ready."

"Ready for what?"

"I have a job cleaning rooms at the Santa Monica Surf Hotel. My shift starts at four-thirty."

"Can you, can you take the day off?"

"Sorry. They'd fire me."

"You know I been in love with you since that first day you sat at our table. I guess it was lucky Miss Sloan put you there."

"Nuh-uh," Lovely said as she used to when they were children. "I saw you guys and that empty seat, and I walked over before she could say anything."

These were the last words Ghalen heard before sleep came back over him. It was the deepest rest that he could remember—when memory came into play. But before memory, the many months before he could really remember anything, there was a dream.

HE WAS AT THE APARTMENT IN WESTWOOD, TALKING TO his parents. Jamilah was saying that she didn't understand what Robert was saying. He complained that she never understood. Ghalen wanted to say something, to stop them from arguing, but there was nothing he could say, nothing that mattered.

The doorbell rang and Verochka was there. Behind her Lovely was coming up the stairs. He closed the door quickly but, just that fast, there came a knocking.

Knocking, knocking—it just wouldn't stop.

FINALLY, HE WOKE UP, REALIZING THAT HE WAS ON THE bed that smelled like Lovely.

He sat up and swung his legs off the side of the mattress. The knocking started up again. It wasn't hard angry knocking or some stranger's tentative rap. Ghalen figured that it must be Lovely. Either she'd finished her job and left her key, or maybe she'd just left the key and had come back for it.

"All right," he called out. "I'm comin'."

He pulled on boxer shorts, just in case it was the landlady, and took the three steps to the door.

The last thing he expected to see was Bruno.

"What the fuck?" his oldest friend said.

Ghalen froze. He wasn't afraid or embarrassed, just wondering how his friend had gotten out of jail.

Bruno's right fist was coming up fast. Ghalen was remembering the last time his friend had to hit him, out of pride.

The blow to the center of his forehead was hard and surprisingly loud. He fell straight back, shoulders and head hitting the floor at the same time. There was an echo in his mind, that, and a cockeyed view of the room from his prone position. He saw Bruno's back as his friend was running away.

He's probably goin' to get the doctor, Ghalen thought. *He didn't expect to hit me that hard.*

And then, for a long time, he laid there on his back looking up, seeing very little.

THE SCENE ABOVE HIM SHIFTED FROM TIME TO TIME. AT one point he saw a half-moon, hovering in a blue-black sky. Then there was a slightly curved white ceiling that might have been the inner roof of a van, with blue and red lights here and there.

A ruddy-faced young white man leaned over him, checking unknown things, touching his forehead and temples.

"What you want for lunch, Charles?" the ruddy-faced man asked. "Roast beef or Pink's?"

Ghalen wondered if this was a dream or if he was simply mishearing the man, whose breath was bad, rancid.

There was a tightness and pain along the skin and skull of his head where Bruno had socked him.

At some point the images turned into mellifluous colors that had tenuous borders, and music/not music that refused to be turned off. This impromptu concert and the dancing colors played and moved around Ghalen's head until it all began to fade and darken into silence.

It was then that the college dropout wondered if he was dying.

Things become quiet and dark when you die, he remembered from somewhere.

And then it was as quiet as a grave.

"GAYLEY," SOMEONE CALLED.

"Hey, slugabed," another man said.

This last word Ghalen had only heard from his grandfather, the man called Night.

"Do you think he hears us?" his father asked.

"I'm sure he does," said Aura, the woman who had moved in to live with and take care of Robert, who had fallen in love with him since before he and Ghalen's mother had married.

Ghalen could see, out of half-closed eyes, the white ceiling above. He tried to shift his vision to include his father and grandfather, and Aura. And even though he could move his line of sight a little, there wasn't enough leeway. Then he tried to speak.

"What was that?" Robert said.

"What?" asked Night.

"I thought I heard something from Gayley," Aura said.

And, suddenly, he could see her face hovering above him, looking for the sound he'd made.

"*Aura*," he willed his voice to say.

"It sounds like he's groaning," Aura reported. "You think he's in pain?"

"I'll go get the doctor," Robert volunteered.

Ghalen passed out then, though he probably didn't realize it. He felt very weak.

"I can't tell you what he's feeling," a man was saying. "I mean, he's been shot in the head. That alone is going to cause pain. But I don't know what he's aware of. He might be hearing every word we say. He might not understand a thing."

Ghalen wondered who this man was talking about. Maybe, he thought, there was another patient in the room who had been shot by somebody, and the doctor, or even a nurse, was explaining to his family how dire the situation was.

"Ghalen," Lovely Frain said.

Lovely. Hearing her voice, not being able to call out, now

realizing that his arms wouldn't move for him to reach out. Lovely. She was a part of him, even though they were apart for so long.

Lovely.

"Did you hear that, doctor?" Night Farr asked. "His girlfriend called him, and he made sounds. I ain't no doctor but I been around enough headshots to know that means somethin'."

"Maybe," a voice, probably a doctor's voice, agreed. "We want him to be aware. But it's going to take a while for the swelling to go down and for any infections to be treated."

"How long?" Robert demanded.

"A week. Maybe two. Your son is lucky just to be alive. We must satisfy ourselves with that for the moment."

A sound like a strong wind started up after this prognosis. Ghalen imagined himself on a late-day beach with a storm blowing in. He felt the cold go through his body and girded himself for what was to come.

THE COLD WAS INTENSE AND THERE WAS VERY LITTLE light. The boy huddled down in his mind, imagining hunched shoulders, while listening for sounds that meant family and friends and love. He was the one who got shot, he was sure of that now. Shot in the head.

His consciousness was almost like being fully aware— sometimes. But, at other times this awareness was fractured.

He'd come awake running down a Tennessee highway, trying to escape a huge, hairy ogre so close behind him that the monster's spit was splashing on the back of his neck. Then nothing. Then he was lying in bed with Natasha Vile while she was making love to a man her age. A Black man.

"Don't go," Nat said to Ghalen. "He's almost finished, and we have a lot to discuss."

Then he was walking down Wilshire Boulevard late at night and he was only three years old. His parents had forgotten him somewhere and he was walking in the nighttime, having to take a shit. He knew that if he couldn't hold it that he'd never find home again.

His past and future were broken reflections in a cracked, partly melted mirror. His mind flowed from image to image passing through long spates of darkness. His mind was a haunted house where the door to the outside kept moving, moving.

"HOW YOU DOIN', SON?" HIS FATHER ASKED.

His first response was to try and say "Fine." But the word wouldn't come.

"I know," Robert Horton agreed. "I know. You make them li'l grunts because your brain tryin' to figger out how to get your mind back into words. Don't worry, you'll get there."

Ghalen felt relief flow throughout his body. The fact that his father believed was enough to quell the deep loneliness.

He sighed there in the darkness between reflections under the sun of his father's words.

"We could try sumpin'," Robert said.

What? Ghalen imagined saying.

"If you can hear me, try an' make a word two times, two times for I hear you."

Ghalen tried but he'd forgotten the word *or*, maybe he'd forgotten the way to make the word a sound. This frustration called up the cold winds, driving Ghalen back into the igloo of his mind. There, he could survive the cold, protected from the biting, howling wind. There, he could imagine what he was and who he was. In that place no one had died, no one would die. The world was stable and staid.

33.

"...You know, Gayley," she was saying.

It took him a while to realize that he was hearing the voice, and then another while to recognize that it was his grandmother Myrtle. She had been talking for some time to him as he reclined in his small frozen igloo. It seemed that he had been there for a very long time, wondering about the buzzing that was going on in his head. He very much enjoyed that whirring pulsating droning sound because it was the closest thing to something physical that he'd known, maybe ever. Maybe not. Maybe he was physical before the accident, before . . .

". . . a lotta people think that when you different that there's somethin' wrong with you," Myrtle was reciting from a long hard life of bitter experience. "If you cain't take their tests or remember how to say and spell their words, then you not as good as them. They don't know, but we do."

Somehow his grandmother's words found a kind of harmony with the vibrations in his head.

How long had he been there? He wanted to ask her, but still the words weren't aligned.

". . . they think the same things about tigers and rats, honeybees, and leaves. They think that the old oak tree is a fool and that monkeys are insane. But they don't know. They don't know that everything under God is free in its soul. Free in its sufferin' and loose in the world no mattah how much they wanna make you a slave."

She went on and on about what people thought was normal and sane. Ghalen felt love for her then. She was healing him and probably knew that she was.

The winds outside his ice hut kicked up again and then, when the storm was over, Myrtle's restorative voice was gone.

"HEY, LI'L G," HE SAID, AND GHALEN OPENED HIS EYES.

"Bruno." His voice felt old and cracked. How long had it been since he'd spoken words?

"Happy birthday."

Ghalen tried hard to remember his birth date but could not.

"Thanks," he said instead. "You bring me some cake?"

Bruno's grin hadn't changed since they were kids. And, and Ghalen remembered that his birthday was on the thirteenth of July—the day before Bastille Day.

"Sorry I shot you, man," Bruno said.

"That's okay."

"It is?"

"I shouldn't'a been there."

Bruno, who was sitting on a chair near the head of Ghalen's hospital bed, turned his head away.

"You not mad?" he asked, turning back to observe his oldest friend.

"I'm not dead."

They both smiled and bobbed their heads.

Ghalen was feeling weak and a little dizzy. There were aches in his arms and back.

There was a buzzing in his head.

"I was still wrong. Draggin' Lovely all ovah the place with the cops after us. Robbin' people ain't done shit to me. An' you know I was fuckin' bitches all ovah. 'Course she wanna find somebody worf a damn."

Ghalen was wondering about the balance of Bruno putting him into a coma and then pulling him out again.

"Cops after you?" Ghalen asked.

The big and young brown man nodded. "For attempted murder of you."

"Not the robberies?"

"Naw. They had me in jail for that shit, but Mr. Nye told'em that they didn't have enough proof when the two dudes I yoked decided not to testify."

"So, what you gonna do?"

"I wanna say I'm sorry to Lovely. You know where she's at?"

"Last place I saw her was where you saw me."

"Anyway, I wanna say I'm sorry and then head down to Houston. I always wanted to be a cowboy."

"You gonna need a big horse."

"You a good man, G."

WHEN GHALEN WOKE UP, SOME WHILE LATER, HE couldn't remember anything else that he and Bruno had said. He wanted to get up and go to the hall to call his friend back again. But he felt weak and a little awkward, and so he'd only scrunched up to almost a seated position when Aura came into the room, a plastic pitcher filled with water in one hand and an empty plastic tumbler in the other. She looked at him, smiled, and said, "You *are* up."

"Yeah. Who told you?"

"The nurse. She said that you asked her for some water."

"I don't remember that."

"The doctor had said that you might lose your short-term

memories for a little while after you came outta the coma." Saying this she poured water for him and placed the glass on the white metal table next to his hospital bed.

Ghalen wanted to say that he didn't forget Bruno but thought better of it, just in case the police were still after him. Then he wondered if maybe Bruno had been a dream like that igloo.

"SO, WHAT DO YOU THINK ABOUT THAT?" AURA ASKED. She was now seated in the chair next to his bed.

"About what?"

"What I just asked you."

"Sorry, Aura, I was thinkin' about Lovely and Bruno."

His father's girlfriend's face turned hard at the mention of those names.

"Was it Bruno shot you?"

"So, I was definitely shot?"

Aura nodded. "You don't remember?"

"I don't remember a lotta things, like how long I've been in this bed."

"Months. And you don't remember who shot you?"

"There was some seedy-lookin' white dude who had come to the door and kept knockin'. When I answered he told me he wanted my money. And then, when I said I didn't have any money, he hit me in the head. I thought it was just his fist. But I guess there must'a been a gun in his hand."

"You sure it wasn't Bruno?"

"Yeah."

"Because you don't have to be afraid," she said in an assuring tone. "We wouldn't let him get at you again."

"I'm not afraid."

Aura was looking hard at him, a question in her eye.

"What?" Ghalen asked.

"You know anything about a li'l green backpack?"

There was something different about his mind, the way he thought. He looked down and, somehow, this allowed him to look inside his memories. There he saw Bruno wearing blue jeans and a brown leather jacket. In his left hand was something green, maybe a backpack.

"No," he said. "What about it?"

"The police keep askin' about it."

"What the police got to do with it?"

"You got shot," she said.

"Oh. Yeah."

"But you don't remember anything?"

"Not about a backpack."

GHALEN FELL ASLEEP WHILE TALKING TO AURA. SHE was very nice and supportive. He felt a smile on his face in the sleep after their talk.

"HOW YOU DOIN', SON?" ROBERT ASKED.

The conversation had already begun, but this was like the first time he was seeing his father. In a way, the first time ever.

"You look good, Dad."

"You just said that."

"You look good twice."

"How about you?"

"Like a four-leaf clover, over and over." Something they used to say when he was a child.

"Aura said that you said it wasn't Bruno shot you."

"Yeah."

Robert gave his son a long, contemplative look. Ghalen knew that he was searching for the lie, for the reason he might lie. It was a familiar, silent interrogation that the young man had experienced since childhood. It was hard, but at the same time he basked in the love that look represented.

Finally, Robert nodded and put his hand on Ghalen's.

"The police wanna come talk to you," Robert said.

"About the shooting?"

"Yeah. The doctor been sayin' that you're recoverin' from a brain injury and that it might be bad for you to get, you know, interrogated. He told 'em too . . . that they might not be able to rely on what you say. You know, the bullet's still in there."

The way Robert looked at his forehead when he said this made Ghalen smile.

"Tell 'em to come on, Pops. I'm okay for maybe fifteen minutes."

". . . SO, YOU WERE SLEEPING, AND MISS FRAIN WAS gone," Detective Chelsea Frisk asked.

She was around Natasha Vile's age, light brown from someplace other than Africa, and without affect. Ghalen liked her.

"Yes, ma'am," he answered. "I'd come over her place a little before midnight."

"And what did you do?"

"Um . . . visited."

Detective Frisk's eyes were hazel and her makeup so faint that it was almost not there.

"But then you were sleeping, and she was gone?"

"Yes. I remember her getting up and dressing somewhere just before four. She said that she was a maid at a hotel."

"Which hotel?"

"I don't know. I don't remember."

"You don't remember where your girlfriend works?"

"No."

The policewoman had the same interrogative stare that Robert did, but Ghalen was unconcerned about her doubt.

"She was gone," Frisk continued, "and then somebody shot you at the front door."

"Yes."

"Who shot you?"

"A guy I'd never met before."

Again, the detective studied him.

"You didn't recognize the assailant?"

"No. He was a skinny white guy with some hair on his chin but not really a beard."

"And he shot you for no reason."

"Is there ever a reason to shoot somebody?"

"Other than self-defense, no. But maybe if you found somebody sleeping in your girlfriend's bed you might think there was."

"You sayin' this guy might'a been Lovely's beau?"

"Don't fuck with me, kid."

"I think that's enough now," a man, Dr. Abraham Melman, who was sitting near the door, said.

"I'm sorry," the detective defended. "It's just that we know that he's lying."

"You can take that knowledge along with you, Detective," the thirty-something MD replied. "But my patient cannot bear up under any bully tactics."

"I have more questions."

"Write them down."

"This is an attempted-murder investigation."

"The victim needs rest. Your own captain has told you that I am the judge of when enough's enough."

Ghalen was asleep before the detective left the room.

"THEY'RE PRESSING CHARGES AGAINST YOU," EMILY Barth said.

"For shooting myself?"

"For the illegal possession and intended distribution of a con-trolled substance."

"Drugs?"

"Cocaine."

"That's what was in the green backpack?"

"Yes," she said, a sad look in her eyes.

She didn't look any older than when he'd met her as a boy. He felt bad about her somber face. This was his trouble, and he didn't want her feeling bad about it.

"But I never even saw a green backpack."

"It was on the ground, at the threshold of the front door, half in and half out of the cabin."

"And they can blame me for that?"

"They can try. Was it Bruno?"

"No, it wasn't. It was that white guy."

"The police detective, Frisk, she said that they suspect Bruno. He has a bad temper and he found you at Lovely's apartment. She told me to tell you that if you were afraid you don't have to be."

"Did you shoot me, Miss Barth?"

"Of course not. What kind of question is that?"

"So, if I told Detective Frisk that it was you, how would you feel about it?"

His mother's friend's face softened, and she said, "I'll get the same man that went to court for Bruno over that assault case, that Jesse Nye, he'll represent you."

"So, I'm definitely gonna stand trial?"

"We have to prepare as if you are. The doctors must give their consent before you go to court but, sooner or later . . ."

BY THE NEXT WEEK GHALEN COULD SIT UP STRAIGHT IN his bed. He wanted to get up and be going somewhere but was too tired to even try. He'd fall asleep in the middle of a conversation or while reading the first sentence of a book. A male nurse came in twice a day to get him up on his feet and, with the help of an aluminum walker, to walk four times up and down the hallway that ran past his room.

On this walk he met a few of his neighbors, who all had serious to catastrophic injuries. He didn't remember their names, not even their injuries, but he felt real kinship along that corridor.

A FEW DAYS AFTER EMILY BARTH TOLD HIM THAT HE WAS going to stand trial for drug trafficking, Ghalen got a visit from Night.

"You awake?" the old man asked.

"I am now."

"How they treatin' ya?"

"Like a pig that they're fattening for the slaughter."

"What you know about slaughterin' pigs?"

"What I read and what you told me."

"What I tell you?"

"That Phu'ò'ng's daughter, Hoa, had secretly named a pig you raised, and that the day you killed it she said she hated you. She never ate from that pork, and she didn't talk to you for weeks."

"You remember all that?"

"I do."

Night looked at Ghalen with stern eyes. He wasn't trying to read him the way Robert or Detective Frisk did. No, Night was gauging the boy's resilience.

"What if I bundled you up in a wheelchair and took you down to a airport I know?" he asked.

"To take a plane where?"

"Back to Vietnam, out in the country somewhere. I know people'd let us work their farms. It's a hard life but it's about ten times more real than you'd ever have here."

Night sat back in the padded metal visitor's chair and waited.

Ghalen leaned back against the two pillows Nurse Renn had placed behind him when Night was on the way up.

"I want to go with you one day, Granddad. I do. But I feel like I gotta do this first. Get on my feet, face these charges, and heal."

34

A week later Ghalen could get up on his feet whenever he wanted. He was still tired, could still hear that buzzing in his head. But these things didn't bother him. He wasn't sad or depressed. He could read for nearly an hour without falling asleep and had lately been going through books about Adolf Hitler and his inner circle. He thought he knew everything about the Nazis from documentaries and class lectures, but there was more, and for some reason, this interested him.

Somewhere in his internet research he came across the name Johann Georg Elser, a blue-collar German who decided from his studies that Hitler was intent on bringing great suffering to the world.

"Gayley?"

"Lovely." She was standing at the door wearing a pumpkin-hued minidress with a semicirclet of freshly cut coral-colored pansies cocked on the left side of her head.

"You busy?"

"Come on in, girl."

She took him by both hands, kissed his lips, and then lowered into the chair meant for visitors, nurses, and sometimes doctors.

"Hi," she said.

"Hey. How you doin'?"

"Good. How about you?"

"Bruno came by."

"He told me."

"You saw him?"

"Talked to him on the phone."

"What he say?"

"That he apologized to you and then he apologized to me."

"You gonna get back together with him?"

"No. You gonna tell the cops he shot you?"

"Who told you that?"

"He did."

"That's stupid."

"Are you gonna tell?"

"What good would that do?"

Lovely smiled and leaned forward.

"He's really sorry," she said. "He knows we can't be together now and that he has to do something about his temper."

"Did he say anything about a green backpack?"

Her smile receded into a contemplative stare. She bit the inside of her right cheek and then said, "What about it?"

"That's my question."

Lovely's smile slowly reemerged. "He'd found out where I lived and ripped off some dude for a few ounces. He was gonna bring it to me and ask me to run with him. But when he shot you, he was so upset that he dropped it right in the doorway."

"Okay."

"You know where it is?"

"Cops got it. They wanna charge me with dealin' unless I give 'em Bruno."

Lovely looked for an answer to some unasked question, a query without words, in Ghalen's eyes. He didn't have anything for her.

"I'm gonna go back east," she said. "You wanna come with?"

"I got things to do here."

She smiled and then nodded. Standing up from the metal chair, she nodded again and then walked out, her gait giving no hint of hesitation.

GHALEN ENTERED THE FRONT DOORS OF THE STANLEY Mosk Courthouse at around ten that Thursday morning. He was accompanied by his longtime attorney Emily Barth, her assistant, Felton Rogers, criminal attorney Jesse Nye, and Natasha Vile of Berkeley, California. They were headed for the offices of Superior Court Judge Ellen O'Brien.

When deciding on Ghalen's *team*, Night and Robert were ruled out because of the veteran's questionable history and Robert's inability to control his emotional responses. Chef Charlie had suggested Natasha because of her friendship with Ghalen, the fact that her father had been a California judge, and because she had, at one time, *read for the bar*.

The prosecution team consisted of only two members: Detective Chelsea Frisk and Prosecutor Henry Barnes. Barnes was a native Angeleno, African American (he refused to accept the racial designation *Black*), a staunch Republican, and a great believer in law and order.

The two teams were ushered immediately into the judge's plush office. The prosecution was seated to the left and the defense on the right.

Ellen O'Brien had striking gray hair that was combed back like a great mane. Maybe sixty, she exhibited the vitality of a freedom fighter the morning after the final battle in a victorious revolution. Her brown eyes were lustrous, and her eggshell-white skin, unaffected by her years.

"I've called this meeting to clear up a few things about the state of this case," she said after greeting, and seating, the attendees. "Before signing off on this sentence I wanted to see the defendant myself and to understand how we got here."

"Your Honor," Jesse Nye said. He was a thin man, not tall and not quite short, who wore a checkered black-and-emerald-green sports jacket, a yellow dress shirt, bright green cuff links, black trousers, and shoes that looked to be made from ivory. "I appreciate your indulgence because I believe that the prosecution has bullied my client into confessing to a crime that he has not and could not have committed."

"Then why accept the plea bargain, counselor?"

"As his attorney I am bound to the client's wishes."

"Mr. Nye would have you believe that there's been some kind of inappropriate pressure applied to Mr. Horton," Henry Barnes said in a baritone that belonged on an amateur stage somewhere. "We have simply presented our case, made the offer of a plea bargain, and he, wisely, accepted."

"But," the judge countered, "at the time of his arrest he was hospitalized, the victim of a crime."

"After having committed a crime."

"Of selling drugs?"

"There were five ounces of cocaine not half a foot from where he lay. It was obvious to the officers investigating the shooting that Mr. Horton had dropped it there. There was also the residue of a gunshot on his hands, suggesting that he had been engaged in a gun battle."

"Your Honor," defense lawyer Nye complained. "Somebody shot my client in the center of his forehead, at close range. There was no weapon found at the scene. Simple logic would indicate that my client raised his hands when he saw the weapon. That would account for the GSR."

"But what about the fact that your client has confessed to trying to buy drugs from his attacker?"

"It is my contention that Ghalen has been subtly pressured to make that confession."

The judge glanced at Natasha. Their eyes locked. Then she turned to the prosecutor.

"You don't feel that a bullet to the brain is punishment enough, Hank?" Judge O'Brien asked Barnes.

"There's a war being waged on drugs and drug dealers, Your Honor."

"And the defendant, if he is indeed guilty, has suffered from that campaign."

"The law requires that he pay for his crime. He has confessed to the possession of the narcotic."

"But not for firing, or even owning, a firearm."

"Criminal lies," the prosecutor proclaimed.

"I object!" Jesse Nye shouted.

The magnificent judge pursed her lips, in some way denying the validity of each lawyer.

"And what are you doing here, Natasha?" O'Brien asked Vile.

"I'm an acquaintance of the defendant, your Honor. I felt that he needed the moral support."

Indicating Natasha, Henry Barnes asked the judge, "You're friends?"

"We know each other," the judge said, gazing directly into the prosecutor's eyes. "I know almost everyone in this room."

"Your Honor," said Jesse Nye. "Our client was the valedictorian of his high school graduating class. He's an A student at UC Berkeley. He has never been arrested for anything, ever in his life, he's never used drugs, and there was nothing of that sort in his system when he was admitted to the hospital. In truth, the police and prosecutor believe that someone other than a drug dealer shot Ghalen. They have set their sights on an old friend of his, a felon named Bruno Chatsworth. They demanded that Ghalen name his friend as the shooter. When he refused, they came up with these ridiculous charges."

"Charges that your client has admitted to," the prosecutor added with vitriol.

"To save his friend from persecution."

"That alone would be perjury if he testified."

"Only if this friend is the one who shot him."

"So, Mr. Barnes," said the judge, who seemed to be amused by the bickering. "You believe that the defendant deserves four years in prison?"

"He deserves much more than that, Your Honor, but we'll take what we can get."

"Mr. Horton," the judge said then.

"Yes, Your Honor," Ghalen answered, feeling very far away from the emotions in the room.

"Is this confession of your own free will?"

"It is."

"Have you in any way been coerced into making this confession?"

"No, Your Honor, I have not."

"Have you or anyone close to you been offered any special dispensation for this confession?"

"Only the four- to six-year sentence."

O'Brien gave the handsome young man a long look. She took a deep breath and then exhaled, shaking her head slightly with a possible hint of exasperation.

"I accept your confession, Mr. Horton, finding you guilty of possessing an illegal substance . . . as a first-time misdemeanor offense."

"What?" bellowed Barnes.

"Silence, Mr. Prosecutor. The court sentences Mr. Ghalen Romeo Horton to one year and one day to be served at the Sierra Conservation Center."

"Your Honor!"

"Yes, Mr. Barnes?"

"This is an outrage."

"I agree with you there, sir. It is an outrage that you bring me a young man, a victim of attempted murder and charge him for not doing your job. You want him convicted. He is now convicted. Now go away.

"And as for you, Mr. Horton."

"Yes, Your Honor?"

"I want you to stay with me for a few minutes after I dismiss the room."

ALONE WITH JUDGE O'BRIEN GHALEN FELT A WEIGHT fall away from him. The preparation for this trial had been a great burden on his father. One morning he woke up to find Robert sitting on a wicker chair at the end of his bed.

"Dad?"

"Gayley," he said with a big smile.

"What are you doing here?"

"I woke up in the middle'a the night and wanted to see you." Ghalen sat up in half-lotus and smiled.

"So, what do I look like?"

"Like the most beautiful young man that ever lived."

"SO," JUDGE O'BRIEN SAID, LEANING BACK IN THE PAD-ded office chair.

"Yes, Your Honor?" Ghalen replied.

"They really wanted to get you, to put you down."

"Yeah."

"That's all you have to say?"

"I can't really blame Detective Frisk and Mr. Barnes. It's their job to keep the streets safe and they thought I was workin' against that."

"They hate you."

Ghalen had no reply to this accusation.

"And what about you?" the judge asked.

"How do you mean, ma'am?"

"Did I make a mistake in my judgment?"

"I don't think so. I think you did me a few good turns and I intend to use them to the best of my ability."

"What turns were those?"

"Well," Ghalen said, the grin rising from somewhere down deep. "The first thing is that you didn't send me somewhere where it would be hard to survive, you know, like Pelican Bay. The second thing is the length of the sentence and, and the misdemeanor— that means a whole lot. But, but it's even more important that you sentenced me for at least a while. I think I can use that time to organize myself."

A buzzer sounded and the judge picked up her phone receiver.

"Yes, Jozz?" She listened for a moment. "Tell him to give me a few more minutes."

She cradled the receiver and asked, "How do you know Nat?"

Smiling again, he said, "She's a friend of the guy my dad works for, Charles Martin."

"Chef?"

"That's him. How do you know her?"

"We were, at one time, very close."

"She's really nice."

In her dark robe the judge seemed to Ghalen like some great bird alighting upon this truth. She took in a shallow breath and said, "Do you understand what you're getting into here?"

"Probably not completely, ma'am. I mean, I haven't had that much experience, but Mr. Barnes wanted to destroy Bruno's life by making me the weapon. That's not right."

"No," the fierce judge said on a smile. "It isn't. And the Sierra

Center *is* the best of the worst. But you're going to have to be careful. There are all kinds of people in there, some of them not so good."

"Yeah. I don't know. I feel like I have to go through this in order to pay for whatever is wrong. When do I go?"

"My secretary will contact you, tell you when and where to turn yourself in to the authorities."

LATE THAT NIGHT CHEF CHARLES THREW A GOODBYE party for Ghalen. Alexander Farrell was there, though he'd retired after Ghalen's goodbye party. Marquis was there with his eleven-year-old daughter, Belphoebe, usually called Bell. The rest of the guests were Maria Vasquez, along with Night, Robert, Aura, Natasha Vile, and Emily Barth.

"How old are you," Chef asked Ghalen when they were seated.

"You always ask me that. Seventeen."

"Seventeen and you have done more in those few years than I have in a lifetime."

"I'm not so sure about that."

Chef counted off the good and the bad on his fingers. "Valedictorian, shot in the head and survived, saving a woman from a trafficker . . . You speak three languages, and I only have two. Being tried for a major felony and coming away with a misdemeanor. You're a better pastry chef than I, and you look like some kinda god that even white people worship. And, and, and oh yeah, you taught yourself to read when you were four or five—just by watching and listening."

"He's just a boy, Charles," Natasha complained.

"If he sat down across from me at a banco table, I'd fold my cards."

35.

rriving at the courthouse at 5:00 a.m., Ghalen
was taken into custody, given a cavity search for
weapons or contraband, hustled into a bus parked
behind the court building, and then handcuffed to the crossbar
of the double seat in front of him. The man he was seated next
to was white, in his forties, a little faded, Ghalen thought, but
still lively in his blue eyes.

"Name's T Martin but they call me Rex, and sometimes T-Rex,"
was how the older convict introduced himself.

"Ghalen."

"What they got you for?"

"Misdemeanor drug buy." Ghalen had been briefed about
some prison terms by a guy named William who Jesse Nye had
introduced him to.

"An' they sent you to SCC? You know somebody?"

"The judge and the prosecutor didn't get along."

"Lucky, huh?"

Ghalen shook his head along with giving a twist of his right
shoulder.

"Is T your given name, Rex?"

"Yeah. That's what my mother named me. There was a fuck of
a lot of us, and I guess she just ran outta names."

"That's kinda cool."

"At least it's original. And, and, and bein' able to add Rex at the end identifies me as a bad motherfucker."

"I could see that."

"Yeah." When T smiled, he showed that he was missing two lower teeth and one upper. "Your first time at SCC?"

"Yeah. You?"

"This stint. Last time I was in they sent me up there. When I was paroled out, I was doin' pretty good, but I was on a short leash, and I had to go see my auntie. She was dyin' an', an' aksed for me. What could I do? I hitched up to see her in Spokane and they busted my parole."

"But they sent you back here?"

With another gap-riddled grin T said, "I knew this office worker—Jolene's her name. I explained my situation and she talked to Warden Philips's number two, Captain Craig. They let it be known that I was a, a what they call a benefit to the institution."

"How long?"

"Two years if I keep clean. Where they got you?"

"Huh?"

"What dormitory?"

"Oh, oh." Ghalen pulled out a yellow card he was given before boarding the bus. It was printed with his name and other information.

"Um, it looks like they got me in Forty-one A."

"Forty-one A. Forty-one A. When I was last up there that was Cleetus place. Cleetus Jarmon."

"Who's that?"

"He's kinda like a shot caller in the dorm. You see, things are pretty loose up at SCC. So, they try and have one shot caller in each dorm to keep the men in order so that they ain't no need for too much official authority."

"Oh. I guess that sounds good."

"It would," T said tentatively, "except for Cleetus hisself."

"What about him?"

"He want young boys like you to give up some ass. Kind of makes a, what do you call it? A spectacle out of it."

"Why don't they stop him?"

"If he was just a regular con, they probably would. But because he's kinda like semiofficial, and he's the one that makes all the deals, they give him a little slack."

"What kinda deals?"

"If you want a special message sent or some kinda contraband, you give the money to the shot caller, and he makes the deal with guard or staff, whatever."

Ghalen started thinking, wondering what he should do. His grandfather had warned him about what happened in prisons. When Ghalen told Night that it would be okay because he was going to a Level One facility, Night said, "Prison is prison. Blood and gut. It ain't gonna be no Disneyland."

"You prob'ly don't have to worry right off," T said, misinterpreting Ghalen's visage as fear. "Cleetus usually only have one bitch at a time, and he always waits for the medical report on a newbie; don't want no hep or booty flu."

Years later Ghalen would remember that conversation. It was very much like talks he'd had on the first day of any school.

ARRIVING AT THE PRISON IN THE LATE AFTERNOON, they were taken to what was called an orientation center, made to disrobe, and then to put on crayon-blue shirts and darker blue trousers. Ghalen liked the colors, they made him think of an infinite sky that reeked of freedom.

There were twenty-seven new inmates. They were ushered into a room with long desks attended by wooden chairs reinforced by green metal piping. The inmates were new, but not necessarily new to the prison system or young. Many were older, what some might call, less dangerous. After the convicts were all seated, a hale man of middle age walked in. The man was Black (or, more accurately, a yellowish-brown color) and wore a blond suit and bright blue, partially reflective sunglasses. If he were in a composition class, where he was supposed to have to explain a character by demeanor, Ghalen would have called the man jaunty.

"Hello," he said in an everyday kind of tone. "My name is Philips, Warden Oscar Philips. It is my job to make your life here as easy as you allow it. Many of you have been incarcerated by the state before. You're used to harsh treatment and bars, lots of bars. Not the good kind either . . ."

A few of the men chuckled.

"But here at SCC we try and make life more livable. We don't want gangs or violence, mistreatment or lies, to govern your every day. We have good work and a dormitory setup, food that won't make you sick, and a staff that works for and expects smooth rolling.

"Don't get me wrong. We have isolation cells, batons, and bad attitudes when need be. We will protect the well-being of the staff and those prisoners who find themselves singled out, for any reason. All that said, I have an open-door policy. You want to talk to me, you can. If I can help you I will, but, whether I can help or not, I will listen.

"While you're here, you will fight forest fires, work in our gardens, learn a job skill or two, prune our woods so that they don't catch fire, and explore your artistic expression. All this, and all you have got to do is take it easy. Don't fight, curse, insult, or demean. Don't fight.

"So, follow the guards as they take you to your dorms . . . Right now, it's a little tight in here, a few more bunks than we would like. But if you do your best, we will try ours to make your stay comfortable. So, go on to your dorms, settle in, have dinner in the caf, and we should get along just fine."

THE BUNKS WERE THREE DEEP IN DORM 41-A. FOR SOME reason Ghalen got the top bunk, which he liked. In the bunk just below him was Sal Hestor, a Black kid from Daly City who was in for simple burglary. He was doing a three-year stint and wouldn't do anything to get in trouble. Peter Yukimura had the bottom bed. He was fifty-one but looked younger. Peter had run a gambling den in South San Francisco and was sent to SCC after his third conviction.

"Sal likes to talk," Ghalen wrote the next day in a letter to Night, Robert, and Aura. "Peter keeps to himself, but he seems like a good guy. You were right about how prison works, Granddad, but I think I got ahold of it."

ON THE THIRD DAY GHALEN SIGNED UP FOR THE GARDEN. It was outside work that allowed some of the tobacco-addicted cons to smoke and others just to feel the country air. The pay was twenty cents an hour, up to eight hours a day.

Prisoner Yukimura told Ghalen about the job and slowly, over the first few weeks, developed a friendship with the young convict.

ONE NIGHT, AFTER THE LIGHTS WENT OUT, GHALEN WAS awakened by voices, grunts, and a few footsteps down the aisles between distant bunks.

"WHAT'S UP?" GHALEN CALLED DOWN TO SAL.

"That's Cleetus."

"The shot caller?"

"Uh-huh. He gather his people for a public fuckin' of his bitch every other week or so. He gotta big dick an' like to show it off."

"An' they watch?"

"I don't."

"Where it happen?"

"In the north corner. That way no outside guard can see it and the sound is muffled like."

GHALEN LAY BACK IN HIS BUNK, LISTENING TO THE muted cheers, leers, and grunts. He figured six minutes had gone by before jumping down and heading for the sounds of orgy.

THERE WERE SEVEN OR EIGHT MEN, ALL OF THEM BAREfoot and none of them fully clad, standing around a kind of banquette in the rec room. There was a skinny young white kid on his knees balanced on a rickety stool, his anus an angry red with Cleetus's big, erect cock leering next to it. Then Cleetus pushed his member nearly all the way in.

"This is what it's like when he takes the shaft," the brawny, naked, extremely well-endowed Cleetus Jarmon explained to his audience. The Cage-41 shot-caller then jammed his massive erection the inch or so extra into the smallish white boy. When the young man screamed, Cleetus hit him in the back of the head with a foot-and-a-half span of hardwood.

"Shut up or I'ma hit you the fuck harder."

The kid bit his lip as the cellblock shot caller continued the assault.

Ghalen watched. He knew that he shouldn't interfere at that moment, just as he knew that he would have to interfere at some other time. This was a new kind of thinking for Ghalen. He wasn't a fearful sort, but usually, when faced with violence, Ghalen's mind would turn to ways of getting away from danger. But right then, seeing the tortured young man he had to hold back from going down there.

The show went on for an excruciating twenty minutes. After that Cleetus and his audience walked away, leaving the white boy on the floor, clutching at his stomach and bleeding from his ass.

"You need anything?" Ghalen asked the tortured kid.

"You could help me back to my bunk. It's three twenty-three."

"what's your name?" ghalen asked when he'd got the young man to his feet and allowed him to drape his arm over his shoulder.

"Nathan but they call me Neep."

"Well, Neep, that was some shit."

"I hate that mother fucker."

"I don't blame ya. They tellin' me that I'm the next one on the list after you."

"It's evil, brother."

They were making their way down the slender corridors of stacked bunks. Now and then a face looked down on them.

"How many?" Ghalen asked.

"How many he did that too?"

"Yeah."

"This here's three twenty-three."

Ghalen helped him sit and then settled into the space next to him.

"I know eight," Neep said. "They ain't all in this block no more but six of 'em sure the fuck is still in the center."

"They mad too?"

"What do you think?"

"Maybe we could get you a transfer and then, well, I'm next up."

"You want that?"

"I want what'll happen when he try."

TWO WEEKS LATER, WHILE GHALEN WAS PRUNING A huge tomato plant at the edge of the garden proper, Cleetus and a couple of the members of his moveable audience came up to him.

"Time to clean out them pipes," Cleetus told Ghalen.

The younger man didn't reply, just stared at him while leaning on his hoe.

"You hear what I say, young meat?"

"You the one need to listen, niggah," Ghalen said, filled with an anger that was new to him.

"Say what?"

"You heard me."

Cleetus gestured something with his head, and one of his moveable audience took a step forward, toward the young man.

Cleetus's minion was taller and fuller than Ghalen. Being a prisoner, he could probably fight. But Ghalen wasn't worried. The hoe he chose that morning had a thick metal staff. And so, when the devotee of the shot caller had taken three steps Ghalen hit the man with the metal pole of his hoe—three times.

The man went down, almost completely out. Ghalen took one step back and hefted the garden tool again. He'd only struck the first attacker with the pole. There was still the blade to watch out for.

A kind of crazy look came into Cleetus's eyes. From reading the expression on the shot caller's face, Ghalen was aware of the possibility of attack. His response to this potential was a broad smile. A smile that said, *Come on, motherfucker, let's see if you make it back to 41-A with your neck leaking blood.*

Ghalen didn't say a word.

Cleetus's second acolyte was helping number one to his feet.

"I'm a fuck your ass till you die from internal bleedin'," Cleetus promised.

"Anytime, brother hood, any time."

AFTER HEARING ABOUT THE VIOLENT STANDOFF BE-tween the seventeen-year-old and the shot caller, there were four cons ready to work with Ghalen. Three of these men had been raped and publicly humiliated by Cleetus. They kept an eye on him while Ghalen went about his daily business as if he hadn't a care in the world.

Eight days passed before Cleetus made his move.

Ghalen was returning to his dorm when three big men moved out from a large mulberry bush and dragged him down. They blindfolded and gagged Ghalen, beat him with a broom handle. Dragging him off, they gave him no chance to yell or in any other way warn anybody.

He struggled mightily against his attackers, but in the end, they dragged him off. Not to the rec room as he expected but outside somewhere where it smelled bad.

Ghalen was forced to his knees. The blindfold came off and he was looking right at Cleetus's nine-inch, one-eyed, engorged cock. It smelled bad, but he would have bitten it if it weren't for the gag held down with electrical tape.

"I'ma fuck you till there ain't no more ass," Cleetus swore.

Ghalen tried to say something, but the gag was too tight.

"Take it off, Indy," Cleetus said to the man that Ghalen had beaten with an iron hoe.

The helper did as he was asked, careful not to get his fingers near the young convict's mouth.

"So, what were you gonna say, bitch?" Cleetus asked inside of a huge smile.

"You let me go, quit bein' a dorm runner, and move to another unit, and I won't hurt you too bad."

Cleetus laughed hard and long on hearing Ghalen's compromise.

"I'm'a kill you, little nigger," the shot caller promised. Then he approached his captive.

"Now!" A shout was heard.

36.

Having taken high school yoga for his exercise elective over four semesters, Ghalen had the odd ability to stand up quite quickly. Just after the first shout from the cedar wood he performed this maneuver, using the dome of his head to strike Big Dick Cleetus on the tip of his chin. By the time Cleetus hit the ground Ghalen's four accomplices had descended upon the scene. Among three of them, they were armed with a baseball bat, an iron skillet, and an axe handle. The fourth member of his strike team was T-Rex, who carried a thick tree branch, tightly wrapped in barbed wire.

The attack was immediate and unstoppable.

Ghalen's plastic tie bond was snipped off and he was handed a short steel pipe by Pelton, an inmate who had been the lookout for his entire family of thieves before being sent to the SCC.

With the pipe Ghalen worked on Cleetus's arms and legs, especially the joints. Each time the shot caller tried to rise and fight back, Ghalen would hit him in the center of his forehead to inhibit any resistance.

The whole procedure took less than sixty seconds.

"Let's go!" Ghalen shouted, and the revenging army disappeared into the surrounding woods, leaving their victims rolling in the outhouse dirt, moaning in pain.

IT WAS CAMP-WIDE NEWS THE NEXT MORNING. FOUR convicts had been brutally attacked in the woods near the workers' outhouse. This broke the most important camp commandment— don't fight. Cleetus Jarmon had received the worst wounds: nine broken bones, a severe concussion, multiple bruises, and the loss of three teeth.

Ghalen was just waking up when his lower bunkmate, Sal Hestor, told him about it.

"Whoever it was, brothah," Sal said, excitedly, "they kicked the shit out them Mofos. Broke Cleet's big dick."

Upon hearing about this damage, the first thing Ghalen thought was that it wasn't him. Ghalen Horton was not the kind of person to cause that kind of injury. He was a good kid. He always worked out problems with people. He never even considered fighting.

But . . . ever since he was shot, he'd experienced short bursts of rage. It might have been caused by somebody looking at him or just pronouncing a word incorrectly. Once he saw a man kissing a woman and had the urge to attack that man, take that woman.

He hadn't acted on these compulsions, never even gave these feelings words. But once he began the attack on Cleetus it was all he could do not to kill him. Even when he just thought about it the desire for the rapist's blood was powerful.

He felt a strong remorse for what he had done, but not who he'd done it to. Cleetus deserved a beating. His demolition was the democratic response of a voiceless minority.

"Ghalen Horton!" a masculine voice called.

"Here!"

"Report to Warden Philips."

"Yes, sir."

THE WARDEN'S OFFICE WAS AN UNATTACHED BUNGALOW that stood across the way from the infirmary. Wearing his SCC blues Ghalen approached the front door with trepidation. Nearly all inmates committed infractions of one kind or another, almost daily: from keeping a pet to secreting food in the dorms. Being late for a class or a job was an infraction.

But having committed a major felony the night before, Ghalen both felt and actually was guilty.

He knocked on the screen door entrance.

"Come on in, hon," Lara Flaxman hailed.

The warden's assistant was in her fifties, bleached blond, dark-skinned, and well proportioned. There weren't many woman at SCC, and so almost any female there was an object of desire.

Ghalen liked Ms. Flaxman. She was always upbeat and empathetic when some prisoner had to endure punishment.

"Warden Philips called for me."

Her smile would have been lovely anywhere, but there, at the seat of authority, it was resplendent.

"Go right on in," she said.

GHALEN PASSED THROUGH AN OPEN DOORWAY INTO THE warden's good-size rustic office. There was cowboy paraphernalia hanging on the walls, and his desk was fabricated from rough hickory wood. Everything was wood. It almost felt like a cabin far out and away from civilization.

Warden Philips was leafing through a smudged, teal-green folder.

"Warden Philips."

He looked up at Ghalen, a grim expression darkening his face.

"Close that door, will ya?"

The young man did so.

"Did you know about this?" the warden asked.

"About what?"

"Cleetus Jarmon."

"I heard that him and some'a his friends got into a fight last night."

"Not that, this," he said, holding up the teal folder. "We found it in his footlocker this morning."

"I don't know what that is, sir."

Philips stared at the young prisoner for a moment longer than was comfortable.

"You haven't seen these?" the warden asked.

"I don't know what you're talking about, sir. It's just a folder to me."

Rising to his feet and coming around the desk the warden said, "Let me see your hands."

Without hesitation, Ghalen held out both hands, palms up.

The warden inspected them and then said, "Turn 'em over."

Ghalen obliged and this time Philips grabbed at his fingers, looking for something in between them.

"No fresh cuts," the warden commented.

"Not today. But, you know, between the shears, thorns, and splinters I get cut up all the time in the garden."

Holding up the folder Philips said, "He's got pictures of himself raping young men."

"Who?"

"Cleetus. He kept a fucking pictoral journal of his rapes. Polaroids. Did you know about that?"

"Not really, sir. There was a rumor that something like that was happening to some of the younger inmates. I never saw it though."

"You never saw it?"

"No, sir."

"You're just the kind of meat this predator was after."

"Guess he didn't get around to me yet."

The warden gauged his prisoner, sneered at the folder again, and then dropped it on his desk.

"We got a problem here, Mr. Horton."

"Gonna be an investigation?"

"A fucking tribunal if we report it."

Ghalen could see the warden's conundrum. They could mess up the whole rating system, even close the SCC down.

"You know Cleetus?"

"Yeah."

"What do you think of him?"

"Freedom to speak, sir?"

"Yes."

"He's a fuckin' piece'a shit."

The dark-lemon-colored warden studied Ghalen then, making the young man feel that he was a suspect, on the verge of trouble.

"I get good reports on you, kid. Got a good education and you get along with the people in your dorm."

"Thank you, sir."

"Tell me something."

"What, um, sir."

"What would you do about Cleetus?"

Without hesitation, maybe even without a thought, Ghalen said, "Put him in isolation, I mean, after he's healed a little. Then burn that folder and blame him for some kind'a bullyin'. Transfer his ass out to a level two or three, where he would have to sink or swim. And if pickin' on people ain't enough, I know for a fact that he got other contraband in his gym locker."

Warden Philips went around the rough-hewn desk to sit on his rickety hickory chair.

"Have a seat, son."

Ghalen had the sudden urge to cry out that it was him and his friends that had attacked Cleetus. But, instead, he lowered onto the visitor's chair, alighting at the edge of the seat. There he gripped his hands together giving the feeling that they were tightly bound.

"I been gettin' good reports on you, Horton. They say you follow the rules and help out when you can. That's, uh, unusual because you're so young. Most of the time we have to watch over kids your age to make sure that they don't get bullied . . ."

Ghalen suddenly imagined that his father's favorite animal, the honey badger, was inside of him, confined in the cage formed by his ribs. It was clawing to get out.

"But there's never been a problem with you. You don't kiss ass but remain polite. You work hard. You're smart."

The number and weight of the compliments brought Ghalen's head down.

"How'd you like to take Cleetus's place as dorm adviser?"

"Me?"

"We'll put you in charge of cabin paperwork. You can start out helping your crew with their homework and legal correspondence."

"That sounds great, sir. I mean, I'd like to try it out."

"What do you think about the friends got beaten on with Jarmon?"

"He's the head. What good is a fist without a head?"

Oscar Philips, warden of SCC, laughed out loud and slapped the desktop with a powerful left hand.

"Take the rest of the day off, Horton. Think about my offer and come back tomorrow morning."

THE BARRACKS OF 41-A WERE ALMOST EMPTY WHEN GHA-len returned. He went to sit on his upper bunk and continue his reading of the paperback novel *The Long Dream* by Richard Wright. He was feeling elated that he had not been found out and punished. He was also feeling guilty about the violence festering in him.

"Horton," someone called out near the front of the building.

"Yeah?"

"You got a visitor."

Who could that be? the young convict wondered. His father would have called or written. Night would never enter prison walls of his own volition. But it had to be someone he knew. His lawyer? Maybe Natasha Vile. That was most likely it. Natasha didn't live that far away, and she didn't work. She wouldn't be afraid of a prison.

Ghalen jumped from the top bunk and made his way toward the visitors' compound.

IT WAS A LOVELY DAY. THE SCC WAS MOSTLY FREE. THERE were very few prisoners either behind bars or remanded to their quarters. There was good work for low pay and the chill in the air was bracing. Regardless of all that, Ghalen knew that if Jamilah had seen him in that condition, it would have shredded her delicate heart. His father would have been more practical. He would have asked about the food and living conditions and if there were fleas or lice in the bedding. Robert would have asked him if he needed anything.

Thinking about his dad always lightened Ghalen's heart. On the walk over to the visitors' center he made up his mind to use *Robert* as a mantra whenever rage threatened to overtake him.

"Hey! Hey, you!" someone called from across the yard that led to the visitors' center.

It was a tall young white man with light brown hair and massive shoulders. He reminded Ghalen a bit of Bruno.

"Yeah?" Ghalen replied as the young man walked up to him.

"You Ghalen Horton?"

"Uh-huh, yeah." Vaguely he wondered if this was a friend of Cleetus, but he'd learned at the death of his mother that there was no need to anticipate a future. It was going to come no matter how much you prepared.

The big man held out a hand to shake Ghalen's.

"You my nigga," he said with feeling. "That mothahfuckah Cleetus got hold of me when I was first here. That was two years ago, and I been waitin' for the minute I could get at him. You beat me to it, but I don't blame ya. You need anything just call on me, Billy B in barracks nineteen."

"Thanks, man," Ghalen said as prison curtesy required. "Thanks."

The story was already out. They were talking about Ghalen's Raiders from that day on. But he knew it wouldn't matter. The warden didn't care about what he did, just that there shouldn't be any more green folders.

THE VISITORS' CENTER HAD A HIGH ROOF WITH WHITE-washed walls and ceiling. The floors were fitted wood slats, and the small tables, with a chair on either side, were painted a light blue. To the left of the door Ghalen came through was the sergeant's desk, occupied by Sergeant Williams, a Black man from Oakland, California.

"Horton," Williams hailed and pointed as Ghalen came through. "North corner."

In the farthest corner sat a young Black woman behind a blue desk. As Ghalen walked toward her, she realized who he was and stood, actually rose from her chair.

She was tall, maybe five ten, and much more Black-skinned than brown. Slender, she had an angular face with high cheekbones and almond-shaped eyes that were as dark as her skin, surrounded with whites brighter than milk. When she walked up to the desk she smiled with beautiful white teeth.

"Mr. Ghalen Romeo Horton?" she asked, holding out a hand.

Taking the hand, he noticed that she had a slight scar on her left cheek.

"Yes," he said. "Who are you?"

"Nasrah," she replied, bowing her head slightly.

"Wanna sit, Nasrah?"

They did as he suggested.

"You have good pronunciation," she said, still grinning.

"How is Deng?"

"He is well. He got a job as a dockworker in San Francisco. He even smiles every once in a while."

"You're Nafisa's niece, the one she wanted me to meet."

"She said that you were very nice, and when Deng went down to Los Angeles, he looked up your people's address and he found out from your grandfather that you were here."

"He went all the way down there without callin'?"

"He's like an old man," Nasrah said, shaking her head and giggling. "Sometimes I think he can remember times before they had telephones or radios. Yes, he came down without calling, but your mother and father let him stay with them. He had a good time, and when he came back, he told my aunt about what happened to you."

Nasrah peered into Ghalen's eyes deeply, with something like empathy.

Ghalen felt a powerful rush of love pass through him. He leaned toward her and she toward him. Not far enough for an actual kiss but just the promise.

She wore a very bright yellow robe with various insignias on it.

"Your mother told Deng that you were convicted of drug trafficking but that you did not do this."

Ghalen struggled to answer the implied question, but his beating heart kept him silent for a few moments.

"Um. Uh. You see I got this friend who was mad at me. When he ran into me, he lost his temper and shot me." Ghalen pointed at the bullet wound where his third eye should have been. "He was a drug dealer, and when he ran away, he dropped some'a his stuff. The police wanted me to turn him in and when I refused, they took me to court over the drugs."

Nasrah smiled at Ghalen. He felt a cheer in her gaze. It came across like the applause for his soccer team when they made a good play on a sunny afternoon on a grass field.

37.

They talked for nearly an hour, even though usual visiting time at SCC, except for with lawyers or lawmen, was limited to thirty minutes. Ghalen figured that the warden was rewarding him with the extra time.

Nasrah was in her third year of study in astrophysics at SF State. She wanted to get a PhD and return home to study the night skies of her homeland and have four or five children.

"God is in the stars," she said with great confidence.

"And we are made from stars," Ghalen replied.

"You do not ask me why I would go to a backward country like Sudan to be a scientist," she said.

"America is backward," was his response to this call. "Our only reasons for science are war and profit. No one pays a researcher to discover the textures of atoms unless rubbing them together produces either fire or gold, maybe both."

That was when Nasrah reached out to touch his hand.

"You understand this?"

Letting his fingers curve around the edge of her palm, he said, "The Greeks thought of art and science as the same. They learned that from the Egyptians, at least that's what Aristotle said."

"How many years of college do you have?"

"About point four."

Her smile soothed his heat and, also, deepened it.

"I only ever met one guy from your school," he said. "His name is Bernard, but his best friends call him Bernice."

"The rugby player!"

"You know him?"

"He is, like my mother says, a nice guy wrapped in a rough package."

Ghalen was realizing from the ragged power of his heartbeat that the violence and rage his head wound had unleashed was better defined as passion. This revelation came about when Nasrah said that Bernard Cragg, the rugby player, was wrapped in coarse cloth.

THE REST OF HIS TIME AT SCC WAS LIKE A KALEIDO-scope attached to a perpetual-motion handle. Sometimes he was an adviser to his barracks-mates, researching laws or symptoms, writing letters home, or untangling the wordings of verdicts passed down years before. He started a soccer team, developed a general plan for inmates to follow that would increase their chances for parole. He helped to settle disputes between those that carried a perpetual war around in the back of their minds—like he did.

He once developed the desire, the craving, to brutally rape Jesop Hendricks.

Jesop was a young guy of indefinite race—small and defenseless. Whenever Ghalen saw him, he felt disgust. He wanted to hurt him, humiliate him, to make him bleed. All this was made worse by young Hendricks's dependence and attachment to 41-A's shot caller.

One night, in his sleep, the rage came upon him. He got out of his bed and went to Jesop's bunk. There he stared down at the sleeping, pathetic, scrawny kid. He was ready to violate him. No one would dare try and stop him.

"Hey, hey, brother man," someone said.

It was T-Rex, his first friend in the world of incarceration. T had transferred to 41-A on Ghalen's recommendation after he'd been promoted.

"What?" Ghalen asked, his voice weak, unfocused.

"Wanna take a walk out back?"

THERE WAS A SMALL PICNIC TABLE BEHIND A STAND OF mulberry bushes a few feet from the fire exit of the building. No patrols ever went there.

T did not ask about how it was going or what was on Ghalen's mind. Instead, he talked about his training as a carpenter and what he planned to do with it when he got out.

"My brother-in-law got a garage he don't use out behind his house in Sacramentah. I raised my little sister, Kris, and she love me so much that, in her eyes, I'm not the same man as I really am. So, Gaston—"

"Who?" Ghalen asked, momentarily shaken from his inner fury.

"My sister's husband is a Frenchie. When she was in the army, they had her posted in Paris, at a military HQ they got. Anyway, Kris and Gaston got married, even though he's thirteen years older than her. They moved to California, and now Gaston has set up a whole workshop for me. And what I plan to do is make some solid furniture an' sell it on what they call consign-ment. I figure if I can do good enough somebody might hire me to work at their place. Either that or maybe I'll make enough to pay myself."

"You can see that?" Ghalen asked. Just asking the question made him feel weak, like if he stood up, he'd fall over.

"You mean, can I see myself doin' all that?"

Ghalen nodded.

"Yeah. I figure that there's always a future till there ain't no more."

"Always a future," Ghalen repeated.

"Yeah. An' no mattah what, you can make a difference to what that future is. It's like that old black-and-white movie they showed last month, *The Picture of Dorian Gray*."

Another turn of the kaleidoscope.

"Wanna go in now, man?" T asked.

THE NEXT MORNING GHALEN ASKED LARA FLAXMAN, Warden Philips's executive assistant, to move Jesop Hendricks from Barracks 41-A.

"What should I give for a reason?" she asked, gently.

"It would just be better."

FOUR DAYS LATER HE WAS VISITED BY NASRAH.

"You seem a little sad," she said after they'd sat for a quarter hour talking about the kind of rice served at SCC.

"I wan, I wanted, I wanted to kill this guy didn't do nuthin' to me. I wanted to kill him so bad that I could taste it."

"Why?"

The answer seemed to get stuck in Ghalen's gullet. It took him a few seconds to say, "He's just a little pussy don't deserve a second chance."

Nasrah took both his hands in hers and then waited for their eyes to connect.

"Wherever you go after they let you out of here, I will be there," she said.

"But what about your school?"

"Are you going to the North Pole?"

"No," he said unable to hide his grin.

"Then I will be with you."

ONE WEEK LATER, WHEN GHALEN WAS TOLD HE HAD A visitor, he was surprised to see that it was a man. A tall and slender and very Black man. This man smiled when Ghalen entered the visitors' barracks, smiled, and climbed to his feet.

"Deng!" Ghalen cried, rushing forward to embrace his friend.

"No body contact!" Sergeant Williams called out.

Letting go and laughing, the young men took their chairs across the table from each other. At first, they just looked at one another, happy for the comradeship.

"What are you doing here?" Ghalen inquired with a big smile and a shake of his head.

"Nasrah told Nafisa that you needed a man to come talk to you. She told me, and I talked to your father . . ."

"My dad?"

"Yes, he told me to tell you that his heart would be broken to see you in here and he doesn't want to embarrass you. He also told the warden that I was your cousin, and he gave me a pass."

"All that?" Ghalen said. "Why?"

"The boy you were going to hurt," Deng said in answer, and more. "What were you going to do to him?"

"Beat the motherfucker, man," Ghalen said, suddenly enraged.

"But what, how were you going to beat him? What were you going to do?"

"Break his jaw with my fist then fuck his ass so hard he wouldn't even know what was hurtin' more."

Ghalen almost choked on his breath. This was exactly what he would have done, but he had never said it aloud. He started shivering.

Deng watched, impassive and cold.

It took a few minutes for Ghalen to calm down again. He was wondering if it was a good thing to see his friend there.

"Vengeance," Deng uttered. "Death."

"Yeah."

"One time, long ago, I saw a boy from a village far out in the woods. He was older than me, fat. He was laughing and running and taking flowers from the bushes. I hated him. I wanted to kill him, but my group colonel had given me a mission. I was supposed to deliver a message to one of our people a few miles away. It was worth my life not to fulfill my mission."

Deng and Ghalen were looking into each other's eyes by this time, the ex-soldier's words taking on the sound of ritual.

"I ran down into the path in front of the fat boy. I told him that he was in my way, and he should leave, get out of my way. The fat boy laughed at me. I was skinny and had worms, my eyes were as yellow as his were white.

"Get out of my way!" I yelled at him. "He laughed at me, and I hated him more. He told me to run away myself or he would crown my head with bumps. I picked up a clod of mud and threw it at him, hit him on the shoulder of his white shirt. Then he ran at me, screaming that he would kill me, and I remember smiling. He saw my smile but was too fat to stop himself before his big belly ran into my bayonet. It had been hidden under my shirt. Now it was buried in his gut. I stabbed him a hundred times. I counted every one. When it was over I was covered in fat boy blood. It was in my hair and between my toes. I tasted it. I loved it. I was still grinning like some dabu'a after a kill."

Deng's breath had gotten deeper. He was staring down at the table between them.

"And, and, and, and then I climbed down from the road to a stream where I washed the blood from me like the Christ wiped away the blood of sin . . ."

"What happened then?" Ghalen asked, meaninglessly.

"I don't remember. I don't know if the fat boy's family found him or if I ever took the message to the man I was supposed to meet. The only thing I know is that, many months later, I was told

to bury three of my friends. They had been killed on a success-
ful mission against our enemy. I, I remember looking down on
the face of Dieter, an eight-year-old corporal who was my friend.
When I looked at his face, I saw the fat boy, and my body went
cold, cold as the dew on a dead man's face. It wasn't till then that I
knew I had to leave. It wasn't until then that I knew I was sharing
my body with a demon."

"That's how it feels when I get angry sometime," Ghalen said.
"But it's not some demon makin' me do shit or wantin' to. I do the
shit. Me."

For many minutes the two men were silent: breath and bad
memories.

"You still see those fat boys?" Ghalen asked.

"Every day. Sometimes more."

"How about that knife?"

"It's out in the parking lot, in my car."

"So . . . there's no getting away from it?"

"I have not killed or raped, not even stolen from or slapped
anyone since the day I threw dirt on Dieter's face. I will never be
forgiven but I won't hurt anyone if I can help it. If I can help it."

WHEN GHALEN WAS BACK IN HIS BARRACKS, SITTING ON
the top bunk, he tried to understand if Deng had really come to
see him or if it was just a dream trying to heal the wound in his
brain. The one thing he knew was that he hadn't killed anyone yet,
and Deng, or the spirit of Deng, had come to let him know that
things could be worse.

He realized that his rages were probably connected to his
head wound, that the bullet in his brain might have thrown off
his ability for self-control. So he went to the library and asked
if he could do a search on the internet about traumatic brain

injuries. After a few hours he found a story about a man named Phineas Gage.

IN 1848 TWENTY-FIVE-YEAR-OLD PHINEAS WAS TAMPING gunpowder into a hole to prepare for some kind of mining explosion. The friction detonated the explosive while he was hammering, and the three-and-a-half-foot steel rod tore in under his cheekbone and through his left front temporal lobe, landing over eighty feet away.

Phineas survived, and it wasn't until sometime later that some of his friends began to notice emotional changes in the young man. Once hardworking and good-natured, Phineas was now perceived as surly, quick to anger, and liberal in his use of foul language. The damage to his brain was extensive, but still it was similar to Ghalen's own injuries. There was some dispute over the extent of Gage's emotional changes, but the great minds at Harvard College now thought that there was some connection between brain injuries and personality shifts.

38.

The day before the day of Ghalen's release from SCC came upon him like a sudden revelation and, also, like a predator in the night. For the last few months of his sentence, he had tried to stay inside whatever day he was living through. The young man had learned to try and do this by reading a book called *The Three Pillars of Zen*, by Philip Kapleau. There was an old hardback version of this book in the *religions* section of the prison library. Ghalen had come across it in an effort to find a way to control his rages. He started the search for Eastern discipline after hearing one of his phys ed instructors, Lon Hoy, suggesting to his class that Zen Buddhist meditation, and the ideas behind that practice, had helped him control his anger.

Ghalen hadn't been able to squelch these feelings, but Kapleau's book seemed to say that it was possible to pass through an emotion without getting trapped by it. He'd read the book seventeen times in three months: an everyday practice that was a constant reminder of what it was to live with rage.

He still felt uncontrollable anger at odd moments. He still wanted, sometimes, to destroy, the way Deng had destroyed the fat boy for being happy.

Going home was his dream, but he told himself that he'd be better dead than causing others to feel pain. Never actually considering suicide, he imagined being dead instead of making dead; of simply stopping on the way to the commission of a sin.

The image in his mind was of him driving down a highway, looking for Deng's fat boy, when, all of a sudden, he pulls to the side of the road, walks out into the wilderness, and then just lies down, willing himself to become one with the forest.

THERE WERE TWELVE CONVICTS SCHEDULED FOR RE-lease around the time that Ghalen was to leave. Warden Philips decided that this novel situation made it worth trying to have a kind of graduation service. So, he called the twelve men to his office and asked them if they'd like a ceremony to celebrate their liberation.

Leaning almost nonchalantly against his hickory desk, the warden waited until the twelve were seated around him.

"You are all very different people," he said, gazing from one to the other. "The oldest is seventy-five while the youngest, Ghalen, has just turned eighteen. But all of you, or almost all, have family and loved ones, friends too. So, in a way, this is like graduation from high school or even college. Freedom is something to be celebrated. It's better than a diploma. If you can hold on to it, it's better than ten million dollars.

"So, what do you think?"

"Can I have my kids come?" asked Press Roberts, a stickup man that had served eight and three-quarter years.

"That's what it's for, Mr. Roberts," the warden replied.

"Yeah," said the white bearded white man, hesitation in his tone. He'd turned forty-three at SCC. "It's just, you see, I got nine kids and not me, nor any'a their mothers, got the money to pay for to get 'em all up here."

"I've considered that," Oscar Philips said. "The prison fund will pay for any family member plus two friends. And anybody close to you has an open invitation if they can make their way up here."

"I ain't got nobody," Cord Ashton Williams said. Black and sixty-nine, Cord had been convicted of the murder of his wife's boyfriend, a man named Del. "My ex died hatin' me, an' her kids say that they prob'ly wadn't mines noways."

"That's okay, CC," drag racer Craig Whortley assured. "We all gonna be there for each other. Sure nuff."

The thirty-nine-year-old sandy-haired street racer had served eleven years for the vehicular homicide of his best friend, Bert Salt. They were racing and crashed. Bert's wife hated Craig and pushed for the maximum sentence.

All the men, except for Tiny Seacrest, said that they'd like a celebration. And even Tiny agreed that he'd come if they promised to serve barbecue.

THE FREEDOM SERVICE, AS IT CAME TO BE CALLED, WAS slated for the next day. Ghalen found himself alone in barracks 41-A, admiring the suit Natasha Vile had sent for him to wear. He'd hung it from the side of his bunk. Dark blue jacket and trousers with a pale blue shirt and black leather shoes. There were blue socks too, but Ghalen had decided to wear the shoes with bare feet because that somehow represented prison for him.

"Hey there, motherfucker."

Ghalen turned to see Storm McDaniels. Big, flushed red, and covered with permanent pimple-like bumps, he was Cleetus Jarmon's best friend at SCC. He hadn't participated in the rapes, but that was only because he wasn't interested in them.

"Storm," Ghalen greeted, something tugging at the back of his mind.

"I waited for this." These words from Storm had the ring of a vow.

"For what?" Ghalen asked, though he thought he knew.

"For the day when you could taste it, bein' released. I waited for this minute, here and now, to show up an' take your life."

"Oh. Hm." Ghalen realized that there was no rage in him right then. All the anger in the room was anchored to the human brickhouse—Storm.

"Huh? You gonna ack like I ain't shit? Ain't nobody here, brother. Ain't nobody gonna save you."

He was standing three paces away. Ghalen suppressed the smile he felt. There was something about seeing anger without participating in it that made him glad. He didn't know if he was going to survive—after all, Storm's biceps were half the size of Ghalen's head—but he wasn't scared. He was learning . . . something.

"You ain't scared'a me, man?" Storm warned.

Ghalen had often wondered how the big, red-faced man had ever gotten sent to SCC. He was a bad man, and everyone knew it. Maybe there was some kind of political connection between prisons that allowed men like this to get a break from the monotony of higher security institutions . . .

Storm took a step toward Ghalen, and without thinking, the young man leapt, headed downward toward the floor it seemed, aiming at the forward-moving kneecap. He hit that knee with his left shoulder. It bent all the way backward, cracked loudly, and failed.

The scream coming from the bad man was piteous and painful. On the floor, he tried to reach for the backward-bending joint, but the agony was too great. Storm began crying, begging, without intelligible words, for the agony to be over.

Ghalen grabbed the con by the back collar of his coarse blue shirt, then dragged the would-be killer through the hall to the front door and out into the crisp mountain air. He hauled the failed avenger down six wooden stairs and dropped him on the concrete while he cried out loud and begged.

Ghalen felt no satisfaction at Storm's suffering. This was simply what was meant to be. The killer had been delivered from his intentions, and the pain was his education.

GHALEN MADE HIS WAY TO THE WARDEN'S OFFICE AND told Lara Flaxman that Storm McDaniels had tripped walking down the stairs of 41-A.

"I'd'a dragged him to the infirmary myself but he's too big and I worried that I might hurt him more."

FROM CAMP CENTER GHALEN MADE HIS WAY UP THE mountain, over the fence that was supposed to hold all prisoners in, and farther, to a small pond that was deceptively deep. This pond was fed by three downflowing streams and, it was said, by an underground river. From there, it seemed to Ghalen that he was, for the first time, aware of the life he was living. He had taken an action that he believed would save two lives. He had broken many rules on the way to that action and would be made to answer for the infractions.

"And it makes perfect sense," he said aloud. "I did wrong, and I did right. I hurt Cleetus and he hurt others. Cleetus hurt others and they hurt him. Then Storm came at me, and I kept him from going bad by breaking his knee. What I did was right, and it was also wrong, and so now I will have to stay incarcerated for following a path that could not be changed."

Ghalen sat there for many hours doing his moral calculations and wondering how he'd found himself, once again, next to his dead mother, caring for his grieving father, feeling as little as possible because that was his duty.

HE DIDN'T MAKE IT BACK TO THE BARRACKS UNTIL AN hour or so before sunset. T-Rex was sitting on the front steps of 41-A. He was smoking a cigarette.

"I told 'em you wouldn't'a run," he said when Ghalen got close.

"They thought I tried to escape?"

"They thought you had escaped."

"Then why aren't the sirens goin'?"

"I guess they wanted you to get away."

"Because'a what happened to McDaniels?"

"After they shot a local into his knee, Storm told the warden that he stumbled and didn't remember nuthin' after that." T smiled. "He might be a bastard but he ain't no pussy."

39.

Ghalen was awake and out of bed, packed, had done his many exercises, wrote in his three journals, and was fully dressed by seven forty-five the next morning. He wore everything Natasha Vile had sent except for the blue socks, which were neatly folded into his one rucksack, a small canvas square that contained everything he owned. He was about to be free, and not free. He was about to go home, but not as who he was, not as who he wanted to be. Instead of happy, he was hopeful. Hopeful that he could live inside himself without becoming Storm, without losing his way. It was then he remembered the story that Alexander Farrell told of being chased down a Tennessee highway by a man who was also a demon. He remembered the dream he inherited from that story, the dream of either hopelessly searching for a woman or abandoning her and living his life.

"Hey, dude!" T-Rex called out.

"Over here," Ghalen rejoined.

"You lookin' good," T said, coming into the area of Ghalen's bunk.

"It fits."

"Like a rubber on a ready man."

They laughed and headed down to the tennis courts—the only place fit for a ceremony of that type.

THE PARTICIPANTS AND PRISON OFFICIALS HAD CHAIRS set up on one of the two courts and the visitors, 103 of them, were arranged in the bleachers. Twelve prison guards were on hand for the unlikely circumstance of trouble breaking out, and a podium was set up with a microphone and speaker for addressing the audience and soon-to-be ex-cons.

The first speaker was Chaplain Rosa Martinez of Los Angeles. Mother Rosa visited SCC every third Sunday and often spoke to prisoners, one on one, over a dedicated line that the warden had instituted. Chaplain Martinez wore a long white dress with a midnight-blue shawl wrapped around her shoulders against the morning chill. She looked to be forty but was probably a decade beyond that.

"I am so happy to see you all here today," the bright bronze-colored woman said. "You have all come so far and still you are at the beginning. I know so many of you. We have talked and laughed and confessed our sins. Now you are going down the mountain and into the world. Now you are surrounded by friends and loved ones, by an institution that, until this very afternoon, imprisoned you. But today you will be going out into freedom, with all its pitfalls and limitations. You have worked hard to get here. And you will have to work even harder to keep from falling back into the pit that spat you out in the first place.

"It will be very difficult, but I have faith. I know all of you. I know the goodness in you and the pain. It will hurt but you have learned to live with pain, to love through pain, you have learned that pain is a teacher as well as a punishment and you have also learned that if you understand that lesson, then you will never fail again."

Mother Rosa looked down for a moment and then up again. "But enough about the challenges you will face. You know them better than I do. You have all the tools you will need. From the looks of this service, you have all the love you need. You have, and only you have, brought yourselves this far. There is no reason to doubt yourselves or your success. You have each other and, more than that, I have given each one of you a graduation card. Therein you will find my three phone numbers. If you ever need to talk to someone, call me. If I am not there, I will most certainly call you back."

The gossamer-clad holy woman made her way from the jury-rigged stage, and for a full minute, it was empty.

Then Warden Philips strode up on the dais. He wore a brown suit that looked a little big on him. He grabbed the podium with both big brown hands and looked all around.

Ghalen thought that often people plan that look, telling the audience, maybe a little dishonestly, that he is including them all. But Philips seemed to be truthful in his expressions. Ghalen imagined that he was holding on to the lectern so as not to lose balance and fall.

"I have only one message for you," he said, sounding like he was being stern with himself. "That is one of thanks. Thank you, Lester Hatter, for leading your squad against fourteen forest fires and saving everything from elk to men. Thank you Basrah Lotimar for counseling those of us who have gotten older and need a little help remembering what day it is. Thank you, Ghalen Romeo Horton . . ."

Before the warden could finish his praise, twenty-nine members of the audience cheered and hooted for the man they had come to celebrate. From Natasha Vile to Bruno Chatsworth, almost everyone who knew Ghalen had made the trek up the mountain.

"Thank you, Ghalen Romeo Horton," the warden repeated, "for letting me volunteer you to give the commencement speech. And thanks to all the family and friends for coming here to show your support when you could have turned your backs. This is a blessing, because, after all, the more of us that are free means the more freedom that exists.

"And now, it is honestly my honor to introduce to you—Mr. Ghalen Horton."

A great many of the assembly, even some of those that had never heard of Ghalen before, rose to their feet, applauded, and cheered.

Ghalen jumped up from his chair and took the long step to mount the dais.

"Wow," he said. "This is great. One time, in high school, I gave a talk like this. When I did it, I thought that I'd never have the chance to do something so great again. Never. But today puts that day in the shade. Because today is resurrection day. Today is the day when we climb up out of the hell of our own making. Today is the day when we say goodbye to our chains. Not only the chains on our bodies, on the doors behind which we sleep, but also, and more importantly, the chains wrapped around our minds."

Ghalen paused and the assembly cheered again.

"Because, you see, the most important lesson we learn here is that the only one who can call us guilty is ourselves. I stole that watermelon. I cut down that innocent man. What reason did I have? There is no reason. Reason doesn't steal. Reason doesn't kill. Reason don't make babies and leave them behind."

At that moment Ghalen saw Deng in the fourth row sitting next to Nasrah and Nafisa.

"Reason doesn't love, the heart does. And once we are in love, and once we are free, there is no going back from there. This service, this observance is a blessing on us, a promise we make to the people who have come here to sanctify the long road both before and behind us. It is up to me and to you that we don't break that trust. Chains mean nothing. Prisons mean nothing. The gas chamber means nothing. All that matters is our ability to do what's right in the face of what's wrong. What's right in the face of what's wrong. That's where we're headed, that is when we will arrive. We have to remember that there are no excuses, that there is no forgiveness. All we have is our own truths. And if I can, and if you can, hold on to that simple prayer, then, no matter how hungry we get, we will be satisfied.

"And if, and when we are satisfied—that is to say, when we are quenched, slaked, and assuaged—that is when we can stop, no matter where we are, no matter where we've been, no matter where we're going, we can stop and give thanks for freedom, for prison, for hunger and bein' fed. That's what I have learned here from you, all of you. These are our lessons, and all we have to do is remember and give thanks."

Ghalen stopped there, in the middle of a preparatory breath. He hadn't written his words; he hadn't submitted them to memory. Everything flowed because it was all he had thought since the day the doctor told him and Robert that Jamilah was dead. She was dead and she was love and without her in the world his pain would have never been able to be so sweet.

He walked away from the dais, and the assembly cheered and cheered.

THE TENNIS COURTS PROFFERED A FEAST AND THE ONCE-in-a-lifetime family of the people of the liberated prisoners laughed and congratulated, hugged and kissed. There was barbecue and corn bread, vegetable medleys, and lemon pie. The speakers played music and some people danced while others spent time with staff and the 103 loved ones who came.

IVO BLANEY, THE DRIVER WHO BROUGHT GHALEN AND his father to the funeral home that prepared Jamilah's body, walked up to Ghalen when he descended the dais and the people were still applauding.

"That was a beautiful speech, ma boy," he said.

"I'm so happy you came, Mr. Blaney."

"I had to, son. It has been such an honor to know you and your dad. We drove up last night and I will take you back in the morning, after we stay at the motor lodge that Chef Martin rented."

"Really? He rented rooms for everybody?"

"Everybody who needed—like me."

THE TWENTY-NINE FRIENDS OF GHALEN, PLUS GHALEN, went to Vladamir's Inn on a nearly deserted beach just south of Petaluma. Chef Charles rented all thirty-seven rooms, even though some would go empty. Those of his staff who were also friends of Ghalen had brought up the meal for that night the evening before. The motor inn's breakfast room had been transformed into a Vegan Hall, and everyone helped with preparation and service.

Both Ghalen's grandmothers had come; Myrtle was accompanied by her institutional nurse, Cynthia Reddress, who volunteered to drive Robert's mother up to the ceremony and back from the event. Lovely was there with her girlfriend Magna Olee, a Polish woman of great height and strength. When Ghalen had asked Lovely if she was gay now, she replied, "I'm just me, Gayley, just me."

The music was mostly '90s fare, and the food was the best most anyone there had ever eaten.

From the moment they got on the small bus that Ivo drove, Ghalen and Nasrah sat side by side, kissing and talking, making up for all the time they had imagined being together.

They held hands when they got off the bus and spoke to the many loved ones and friends. Ghalen introduced his fiancée, because they became engaged on the bus ride, to those who had not yet met her. They stopped to kiss and then embrace, again and again.

They barely left each other's side, but when Bruno came up, gently touching Ghalen on the shoulder, the Freedom Child, as Aura called him, turned to Nasrah, and said, "Me and Bruno gotta go talk."

VLADAMIR'S INN WAS SITUATED ON A CLIFF AND HAD EX-clusive access to a stairway carved into stone that provided 212 steps down to the beach. By moonlight the two young men, who had been friends for one plus a dozen years, picked their way down the Two Centuries Stairway to the beach, which was composed of both stone and sand.

When they got to the beach, they doffed their shoes and sat on two stones that faced each other. Ghalen was missing Nasrah and feeling the ocean chill, but he wasn't antsy or resentful. His friend had his hands held up to both sides of his head, as if he were trapped in an inescapable silence, locked into that position by some invisible pillory.

After a while of this silent communing Ghalen said, "Hey."

This was the key.

"I shot you, man," Bruno said almost as one word. "I shot you."

The three-quarters moon, cut into three sections by two long, almost horizontal, clouds, was both yellowish and blue with no hint of green. Ghalen marveled at the color and light.

"Yeah," he said after the moment of the confession had passed.

"What you mean, yeah? I came so close to takin' your life that I went to a church and just sat there. I cried for you, brother. Deep shit cryin' like my lungs was about to huck up. And then you standin' up there on that stage, talkin' 'bout they ain't no for-giveness, that I got to forgive myself."

"It's okay," Ghalen said. "It's over now. It's over and it was all for the best."

"How you see that? I shot you in the brain, bullet still in there."

"And Lovely told me that you got a job and a wife."

"Like I robbed it from you."

"Naw, man. I got what I need. I learned what I had to."

"That's what Cordelia says."

"That's your wife?"

Nodding, Bruno said, "Only she ain't here 'cause Romeo too young to travel."

"Who?"

"We had a baby and I named him after you."

"How old?"

"'Bout a mont'."

Ghalen stood and wrapped his friend into a bro hug so strong that Bruno was dragged to his feet. They held each other and then backed off. The debt was dissolved, and the friends climbed back up to Vladamir's.

NASRAH KISSED THE BULLET WOUND IN THE MIDDLE OF her lover's forehead.

"Deng says that you had to have a thousand years of luck saved up for you to survive being shot like this," she said.

Ghalen reached for her, but she pushed his hands away. Then she pulled up the padded chair from the plank-desk that sat before the window-wall that looked out over the ocean. The lights were out in their room, but the moon shone in. The window was half-open, allowing the crash of waves to engulf them. Nasrah pulled down the dark blue trousers and the pale blue boxers. He made to touch her again, but again she pushed his hands down.

"You are wanting me," she observed.

"Yes," he replied, almost swallowing the word.

"Now we will see how long."

"Can't you see how long now?"

"Not how long it is, how long you want."

"You know I been in prison."

"Waiting for you, I have been imprisoned too."

Ghalen had no idea how long she had waited, but his intensity only got stronger.

"Why you doin' this?" he said, as if asking for forgiveness.

"Because I want our first time to make me with child, your child."

"You got to hurry then, 'cause, you know, this dick got a mind of its own."

40.

Maintaining his prison time schedule, Ghalen woke up at 4:44 a.m., a minute before he was programed to rise. He made his way to the breakfast room, where he found his father and Chef Martin toasting with Monkey Spit coffee in memory of Robert's first date with Jamilah.

This was a great concession for the Belgian cook. It was a rare thing for him to break the Vegan Code.

"Good morning, Ghalen," Chef Charlie said, rising from his padded folding chair.

"Mornin'."

"How are you?"

"For the first time ever, I feel free. At least as free as a man can be in a body like this, under the weight of the world."

They shook hands and the chef said, "It's difficult to understand how such a good life could be so hard."

Ghalen nodded, and then nodded again.

"That coffee smells good," the young man/ex-con said.

"Help yourself. I'll leave you and your father to talk."

"Okay. But, before you go, I'd like to thank you for all this." Ghalen held his hands up, moving them in widening circles. "I know how much it must'a cost you."

"It is only what I owe."

"To a pastry chef?"

Charles Martin, the mercenary-turned-cook, looked at the young man with deep affection combined with a little confusion.

"Yes," he said, nodding a little and wincing some. "I owe it to you, and even more than that, to your father. It might not seem like it, I might not act like it all the time, but without your father I would never have done so well. Robert pushed me, backed me up, proved to me that I could do more. I have had three restaurants that he made with me. And now there's a financial group behind me. With their money I'll be able to start restaurants in five states. Your father, and some of the others, will be given stock in these places. That is only right."

"I'M SORRY I NEVER CAME UP TO SEE YOU," ROBERT SAID to his son when they were alone in the deep silence of the early morning dining room. "But Mama always told me that if you can't hold back your tears you ain't doin' nobody no favor in jail."

"It's so great to see you, Dad."

"Was it bad?"

"In the end . . . I guess not."

"You didn't hate bein' locked in and treated like a, like a criminal?"

"I don't know. I guess it always seems like you're locked in somewhere. I mean, look at you, locked in your everyday schedule. Look at you, who live your life so, so, so planned out that the one time you stopped eating a slice of bread with dinner, you lost ten pounds in six months."

Robert smiled at the memory, and then he frowned.

"But," he said, "I wanted the life I been livin'. To be married to your mother. To work with Chef Charlie. To have you read to me when my eyes got tired."

"Yeah, Dad, but you loved gettin' up the same time every morning."

"So?"

"Then I was born, and Mama said that I'd wake you up at a different time every night. She said that when I had fever you worried more'n she did, that you were scared and that you had bags under your eyes the size of steamer trunks."

"'Course I was scared. I love you."

"Yeah. And because'a that love you got up when you had to, and you got scared but never ran away. You never ran away, and I didn't either."

Robert Horton gazed at his son as he always had, with a kind of reverence and joy. He reached across the coffee table to hold hands.

They sat like that for as much time as they could, not speaking, not letting go.

"How you boy's doin'?"

"Come join us, Aura," Robert invited, rising to his feet.

"Yeah," Ghalen agreed.

She sat next to her common-law husband, and Ghalen got her coffee.

"What you guys talkin' 'bout?" she asked after the first sip.

"Doors open and doors closed," Ghalen said.

It was as if Robert's de facto wife heard something rustling in a corner somewhere, something that she could not quite identify.

"How are you, Ghalen?" she asked.

"Different, I guess."

"Is it the wound? I mean, sometimes, after you were back from the hospital, I could see some kinda crazy in your eyes."

"I used to lose my temper like that," Robert interjected. "I remember one time when I went to a museum with your mother and a security guard thought I was tryin' to touch a painting. She told me to step back and I all of a sudden hated her. Hated her with all my heart."

"What did you do then?" Ghalen asked.

"Nuthin'. I told her that I was gonna look at that paintin' and I wadn't gonna touch it at all."

Ghalen turned to Aura then. He was about to say that he might have had the same hate Robert had in his heart, but for Ghalen the rage would have made it to his hands.

"Hey, people," Night Farr greeted from the outer door.

"Granddad."

"Look at my boy," the veteran-deserter said. "Like Buster Keaton when that house wall fell on him."

"It missed," the grandson said.

"Always," Night intoned. "What you'all sayin' this early in the mornin'?"

"Breakfast," Chef Charlie announced from the double doors that led to the kitchen.

He and Marquis brought out the tofu scramble, avocado toast, broiled grapefruit halves, pickled tempeh, and green tea.

While they were serving, Bruno, Magna Olee, Lovely, and Natasha Vile came in. The empty room got populated. The once-quiet space then filled with the sounds of words, laughter, and the clinking of silverware on porcelain.

By 7:00 a.m. almost everyone was down at breakfast. They toasted orange juice tributes, told prison jokes, and ate and ate the foods of freedom.

"I once had a friend who had exscaped from jail twenty-seven times," Alexander Farrell proclaimed, getting to his feet, and raising an educative finger.

Alex had retired and met Silla Marcel, a young Black woman from France who had come to the United States to learn about a heritage that people back home didn't understand. She was twenty-nine years old, and Alexander was sixty-nine. They fell in love, and on top of that, she loved his endless fount of stories.

"Twenty-seven?" Marquis Dechene doubted loudly.

"Uh-huh," Alexander said. "His name was Dietrich Hall. Packed hisself into a laundry bag, crawled out through a sewer they were workin' on, stole a guard's uniform an' just walked out the front door, got his sentence declared a mistrial, went to the toilet on the seventeenth floor of the court building and somehow climbed his ass down to the street. Mothahfuckah broke outta jail so many times that the governor had him appointed to a special group that studied how to make prison more secure. Can you believe that?"

"No," Marquis replied, a big smile on his face. "I cannot."

"One time his cellmate died and somehow Dee got in the coffin with the dead man. Ain't no security on a prison hearse, so he just waited till they got to a stop sign on a country road and jumped out the back."

"Why'd he keep gettin' caught?" Ghalen asked.

"That is the right question," Alexander complimented with a toothy grin. "Dee didn't mind prison, not really, but sometimes he got so bored that he started thinkin' up plans to get the hell outta there. Now once he had a perfectly good plan"—the elder hunched his shoulders—"Well, he had to use it, now, didn't he?"

"She's dead!" Myrtle Horton cried as she blundered into the dining hall. "She's dead in her bed!"

Robert jumped up from his chair crying, "Pristine?" Despite all odds, the two grandmothers had become friends and decided to share a room.

"Dead as dead can be. I tried to wake her up. I did. But she just lay there like a lump'a clay."

THE ROOM WAS A SIMPLE FARE. TWO SINGLE BEDS, against opposite walls, and a walnut-stained plywood desk that looked out of a wide window over the Pacific Ocean. Ghalen could see that his grandmother Myrtle Horton had made her bed. He wondered if she always made her bed immediately after getting up or did she make it after realizing her roommate's passage; maybe that was some kind of prayer or modesty.

"She's dead," Aura Cress, the pharmacist, said.

"From what?" Robert demanded.

"I'm not a doctor but her lips look blue, and her skin is pale. Usually that indicates heart attack."

CHEF CHARLIE CALLED THE HOTEL MANAGER AND SHE called 911. The ambulance was there first. The paramedics tried to revive Jamilah's mother but exhibited no real hope for her survival.

A pair of uniformed cops came ten minutes after the paramedics. They wouldn't let the body go, and once they found the reason for the gathering, they detained Ghalen, called for the county coroner and police backup.

Ghalen's room was searched, and he was put in one of the empty rooms under guard.

"YOU CAN'T ARREST A MAN IF YOU AREN'T SURE THERE was a crime," Chef Charles bellowed at Lena Peña, the sergeant in charge of the situation. "There were nearly forty people here."

"We're not arresting him," the senior officer claimed. "We're just detaining him until Dr. Beaman, the coroner, gives us a probable cause of death."

Ghalen heard this argument outside the flimsy door of his room. He'd been handcuffed and made to sit on the bed. It was there where he had possibly the most intense inner conflict of his life. His mother's mother was dead. She was an angry and quirky woman who had given her daughter years of pain. But Jamilah loved her. Her death on the first day of his liberation felt wrong, like meat going bad or the passing of an infant not yet able to speak.

There was also, in his makeshift cell, the fact that he'd committed no crime. He'd been innocent from the moment he entered the SCC. He was the victim but was sent to prison. And, as much as he wanted to feel blameless, to mourn both his mother and grandmother, to start a life with Nasrah; as much as he had allowed himself to believe that he was a free man, Ghalen's heart expected the worst. He could hear it beating, feel it pressing against his chest—wanting out.

Now they were noodling around the idea that he might be a murderer. Here in a town with hardly any Black people, he was suspected because he was a Black man, an ex-con, and maybe, also, because he was a stranger.

He closed his eyes and started counting his inhalations from one to ten and then back again. At first all that registered was the fear of spending the rest of his life away from the people he loved. Then he happened upon his mother's face and the desire to lay against her breast. After a long while of images and then counting, feeling and then nothing, inhalation and then exhalation, Ghalen was in a space that had no up or down, horizon, past, or future. He didn't know where he was exactly, but it felt right.

It felt right, the sounds he could not hear, the life he knew so little of, the stars so far away, they say, and the act of breathing, of living.

"MR. HORTON," A MAN SAID. WAS THIS A MEMORY? WAS it someone outside the door talking to his father? Was it his guard, the armed, uniformed officer sitting across from him on a straight-backed maple chair?

"Mr. Horton."

This time he felt a hand on his shoulder.

"Yes?" he asked without opening his eyes.

"Are you awake?"

It was a silly question, designed to turn his attention away from center and out again.

Ghalen opened his eyes to see a tall white man in a formal-looking police uniform. He was certainly a superior officer, there to make a judgment that he was not qualified to pass.

"I'm awake," Ghalen answered.

The cop's skin was informed by an underlying patina of gray. His eyes were a stronger gray, and the wisp of hair coming down from his official cap was a faded white.

Ghalen couldn't tell how tall the standing man was.

After a good long look the officer asked, "Did you know Pristine Fenestra?"

"Aren't you supposed to be telling me my rights?"

"Only if you think you are in jeopardy. As of right now you're not a suspect."

"No? Then why am I sitting here in chains, with an armed guard?"

"Hestor," the senior official said to the brown patrolman.

"Yes, sir."

"Take off the cuffs."

"What's your name?" Ghalen asked the man in charge.

"Captain Arlo."

"Pristine Fenestra is and was my grandmother, Captain Arlo."

"Do you know how she died?"

"It might have been a heart attack, I guess. I'm not no doctor."

"Had she been diagnosed with heart disease?"

"I have no idea. I've been away and we didn't talk about things like that even when we got together."

"Are you on parole?"

"Come on, man, you already know all that."

The captain pursed his lips, considered, and then said, "You don't have to give me an attitude. I'm here to help."

Ghalen felt a familiar rage. He hoped that this did not show on his face.

"What did the coroner say?" he asked, instead of leaping up and strangling the police captain.

The captain took his time studying the detained ex-con. His nostrils widened and Ghalen wondered if Arlo too wrestled with inner demons. Captain Arlo took a deep breath, but this wasn't an attempt to calm down.

"You are free to go, Mr. Horton. I'll know how to get in touch with you through the felon registry."

"I was convicted of a misdemeanor, sir. But I'll be happy to give you my numbers."

41.

After the police were gone, after the paramedics loaded Pristine into the ambulance and drove away, taking her down to the town morgue. After Aura talked to the coroner about where the body should be transported to, in Santa Monica. After all that, it was time for the rest of the party to depart.

But while all these preparations went on, Nasrah brought Ghalen back to their room and set him down on their bed.

Weeping angrily, she said, "I thought I had lost you. After the police chained you and locked you in that room, they said that I couldn't even talk to you. I told them that we were betrothed, and they grinned, covering their lips, pretending to hide their disgust.

"Deng told me that he had a gun and that he would fight to get you free. I almost said yes. Almost."

Then she began to cry in earnest.

Ghalen held on to her, saying everything he needed to with the strength and tenderness of his embrace.

"Is it always to be like this?" Nasrah whispered after the flow of tears slowed.

"Yes," Ghalen said softly. "Like this. You holding me and me you. We will always be with the ones we love, and we will have children. And they will have us."

"But why did they take you like that?" Nasrah asked.

For long minutes after she posed this question Ghalen considered. At first, he thought that there was no answer, that it was just a kind of insanity that all living creatures suffered. He thought of butterflies in spiderwebs and earthquakes that swallowed entire civilizations. He thought of an errant bullet cutting down a young mother, but then, he realized that those examples were just bad luck, and not fate, not explanations.

Someone knocked on the door.

"Yeah?" Ghalen called out.

"Time to go," Night Farr said.

"Five minutes."

After another minute had passed Ghalen began to speak.

"I love you, Nasrah. I do. So, I don't want to lie, and the answer to your question is so hard to understand. But I think it is that we live in a world where people do not believe in themselves and so they can't believe in each other. It's easier to distrust than to believe. That's America, maybe the whole world, maybe it's all the people that ever lived."

"So, you're saying everyone fears and despises everyone else?"

"In a way, yes, but not everyone all the time."

"I don't understand."

"The colonel who made Deng a killer, who showed no feeling when his child soldiers died. That colonel might have had a son he loved, or a mother. One day he might have awakened and realized that what he did was wrong. Or maybe he could be shot in the head like me and that would open a door to even worse actions."

"You are not evil," Nasrah asserted, pulling away from her lover's embrace.

"I am sometimes. Deng is not evil, but one time he killed a man and ate his heart. I know this because he told me about it. He said that he could never get the taste and the texture completely out of his mouth."

Nasrah took Ghalen by the sides of his face and kissed his scarred forehead once more.

"So, we just let this go?" she asked.

He kissed her forehead, then she took him by the hand and led him out the door.

ROBERT AND AURA, GHALEN AND NASRAH, BRUNO AND Ivo, along with Night Farr were in the big bus headed back down to LA.

"Man, that was a mess about your grandmother," Bruno said to Ghalen as they passed the Highway 5 Exit for Huron.

Before this they had avoided the topic of Pristine's death at Ghalen's release party.

"She was a wonderful woman," Robert said.

"She was," his son agreed. "But you know, at the party by the beach she took me aside and told me that it was your fault, Dad, your fault that I ended up in jail, that because you couldn't control me I went wild and got into all that trouble."

"She did not," Aura decried. "Ghalen, we all know that you're innocent. It was them cops wanted you to bear false witness that trumped up them charges."

"She told me that I should come live with her and go to UCLA, that dad could come live at her house too, as long as everybody followed her rules."

"That bitch," Night Farr said of his ex. "She drove everyone and everything away."

"Yes," Nasrah agreed. "A man must live his own life."

"All that's true," Ghalen allowed. "But I don't see it that way."

"How you see it, son?" Robert asked.

"Control was the only way grandma knew how to show love."

"What's that s'posed to mean?" Ivo asked from behind the steering wheel.

"She came outta the hardness," Ghalen said. "Her people came up in tough times and everyone had a job they had to do if they were gonna survive. Their salaries all went into the same pot. They had chores even after they grew up and moved away. If you didn't follow the rules you'd feel it."

"Yeah," Night agreed. "I remember Pris once told me that her older sister, Monique, was goin' out the do' to go on'a date. Her mama was sewing by lamplight and said, without even lookin' up, that Monique was gonna stay home and help look after the kids. Moan said fuck you and when she turned away Mama th'ew her scissors and stabbed her right in the calf. 'Fuck me, my ass,' that's what big Mama said."

Everyone on the bus either laughed or smiled. They all knew how hard it was coming out of poverty.

Hearing these words Ghalen said, "She was tellin' me she loved me by blaming my trouble on Pops. I know he did his best. I also know that his best was better than hers. But all I was listenin' to was her saying that she loved me and wanted to protect me the only way she knew how. I wasn't gonna do what she said, but I hugged her and told her I loved her, because I did, and Mom did too."

There was silence on the bus for quite a while after that.

"Yeah." Bruno was the one to break the silence. "Yeah. I almost killed outta thinkin' I loved somebody."

"I killed," Night said solemnly. "I killed at least one human being every week—for three years. I loved that. I lived for it. I was proud of it. It made me feel like I was an American. And now it's the worst thing I know, the only thing I'll never forget."

"In my country," Nasrah said, "we lived with anger and violence. We loved each other the way your grandmother did. The more we cared, the harder we had to be."

"Yeah," Robert said in a tone of submission. "My mama shot

her man in his own bed. Kept on shootin' 'im. The mornin' fore she did that, I asked her how she could live with a brute like him, and she said how much she loved that man. I always thought that she was just crazy, but she wasn't. She loved him and he loved her, but they hated each other too. They had to . . . Don't ask me why."

WHEN IVO DROPPED BRUNO OFF AT HIS APARTMENT building on South Sierra Bonita Avenue, Ghalen asked the driver to wait a minute while he ran in with the friend who had almost murdered him.

They went in through the unlocked front door of the redbrick building. The hallway they entered was dark and filled with the laughter of children. From tiny kids to bigger ones, they ran out of one door or another and then into somebody else's apartment with the door ajar. There was music of different types with a dominance of hip-hop and soul singers. The air smelled of cooking and sweat and perfumes.

"Hey Big B," a woman's voice called out sensually.

To the right, from yet another open door, a generously built young Black woman with impossibly long lashes, leaned against that doorjamb looking Ghalen's friend up and down.

"Rita," Bruno said in a clipped but not unfriendly tone. "How's Roderick?"

"He away," she said. "How's Cordy?"

"Waitin' upstairs."

THEY ASCENDED THREE TIERS OF STAIRS, WALKED DOWN another hall, coming to a door that Bruno had the key to. He worked the lock, opened the door a crack, and then called, "I'm here with company."

"Wait a minute!" a woman cried. Bruno held the doorknob a few seconds and then she said, "Okay."

Following his big friend, Ghalen beheld a lovely room that had furniture upholstered with bright, silk-like fabric and equally bright flat bamboo flooring. The woman standing in the middle of the space was tall, zaftig, and Asian, her skin the color of organic cream. She wore a black kimono that clung, and in the crook of her left arm was a baby who was staring at his namesake.

"Ghalen Romeo Horton, I want you to meet Cordelia Park-Chatsworth and Romeo Chatsworth." Ghalen walked up to the smiling woman and held out a hand. She batted the gesture away and hugged him with her free arm.

"Finally," she said. "I didn't think you was evah gonna come outta that jail."

The baby giggled and Ghalen experienced a happiness so strong that it seemed to him like a bright and vast red sky.

"He's beautiful," Ghalen said.

"He told me that he wanted you for a godfather," Cordelia confided.

"If that's okay with his mom and dad."

"Ghalen's gotta go," Bruno told his wife. "He got a bus full'a people downstairs."

"Okay, but you gonna come back for dinner this Friday," she commanded.

"Yes, ma'am."

FROM THERE IVO TOOK THE REST OF HIS PASSENGERS up to the Westwood apartment. They took out their bags and things, bade the driver goodbye, and went in.

Night called a car to take him downtown to his girlfriend's, Gora Bondarenko's, place. They'd met at a private monthly event, held for veterans of all stripes. This event was called a Veterans

Dance Night. She'd been an army nurse in Croatia and liked the way Night moved his body.

AFTER MAKING LOVE A FEW TIMES, NASRAH AND GHALEN lay depleted next to each other in his childhood bedroom, on his adolescent bed. She'd brought three sandalwood-scented candles that flickered on the windowsill.

She kissed his left nipple, making him shy away.

"Tickles," he protested.

"Bring it back here and let me kiss it again."

"Are you, are you gonna bite it?"

"Did you bite me?"

"I don't know if I could take it."

"But you have to."

AT FIRST GHALEN'S SLEEP WAS LIKE BEING IN HEAVEN. He was peaceful and at ease, with the woman he loved. She'd told him that she was pretty sure that she was pregnant already and he was proud, even as he slept. Then that red sky of joy returned, seemingly to help his happiness. But the red turned sour and the background sounds of the children playing in Bruno's halls began to sound like heavy blows on vulnerable flesh. He heard bones cracking and men yelling warnings to stay back, to stay away.

When he climbed out of the bed Nasrah made a sound that seemed to complain that she was losing something. He blundered away from the bed and went out to the hall. From there he went to Night's room, pulled open the bottom dresser drawer, and took out the pistol Night wanted him to take to college. He loaded the .45 six-shooter and then, the gun in his right hand, his finger on the trigger, he walked out to the living room and sat on the hassock that had been his since as long as he could remember.

He had once known that he was going to come to this place, body and soul, but had somehow forgotten about it. Now he was there, not awake and yet not asleep, between two choices—only two. He was going to kill everyone in that apartment, or he was going to kill himself.

This knowledge brought a severe pain that started at the center of his forehead and went all the way through to the back of his head. He stayed sitting, trying to understand how he still loved Robert and Nasrah, Night, and so many others. How could he love and be so angry at the same time?

"Ghalen."

Robert was standing there, back against the wall.

"How long you been there, Dad?"

"Long time."

"I don't know what to do."

"Yes, you do."

"It hurts so bad."

"Then give it to me."

When Ghalen heard these words, he knew that he understood them but could not say what they meant. He wanted to explain his father's request but could not. He wanted to cry but knew that would make his pain bubble over into blood.

Then he sat up and handed the pistol to his dad. The pain stopped; the binary decision was no longer an issue.

"Go to bed, son."

42.

S o, your father took it?" Nasrah asked.

That was the next morning after Ghalen had explained, as well as he could, what happened the night before.

"I, I think so," he said. "I looked in Granddad's drawer and it wasn't there. It seemed so much like a, like a dream. Maybe Grandpa Night took the gun with him. What, what, what should we do?"

They were sitting on the bed. With one hand on her belly, Nasrah grabbed a finger of each of his hands with the other.

"We are a family," she said. "We love each other. We will talk to Night and Robert and Aura too. Once we find out what happened we will come together and work it out."

"But I might have killed you and our baby."

"I don't think so."

"Why not?" he said, his voice rising with concern.

"Because you didn't."

"Only because my dad was there."

"Are you sure it was him?"

"Who else could it be?"

"Might have been a spirit. Might have been the him inside of you."

"That would be crazy."

"Maybe you had to be a little crazy—in order to do what was right. You need to listen to me, Gayley. I love you and I will kill you myself if I really think you are a danger to our children."

"You would do that?"

"Yes."

"What if you make a mistake?"

"I won't."

"What if—"

"No more questions. You are a good man with a powerful heart. I am your woman, the baby inside me is your child. You have to believe that together we are strong enough to do what's right."

GHALEN MADE BREAKFAST FOR THE FAMILY AND DECIDED not to discuss the previous night. They talked and laughed, began to make plans for Pristine Fenestra's funeral.

After washing the dishes Ghalen told Nasrah that he was going for a walk.

HE WENT DOWN WESTWOOD BOULEVARD TO WILSHIRE AND then walked the six miles to Ocean Avenue. From there he made it over to the Santa Monica Pier. At the very end of the amusement park wharf, down half a flight of stairs, was the dilapidated old pier where people had been coming to fish for more than a hundred years.

He sat there on a weathered bench and looked out over the ocean. He was pretty sure that he wouldn't jump in, but he had to put himself there, just to make certain.

There was a stiff breeze making agitated little waves that crashed on the pilings below. Now and then he felt the spray of salty water and heard the cries of seagulls and the croaking of crows.

He hardly knew Nasrah, but that in no way stemmed his

passion for her. He believed that she loved him and that they would have a family. And maybe he could find someone to talk to; some psychotherapist or *roshi*. There were medicines and disciplines, even the Constant Traveler Riverside Church.

He wasn't afraid to die. His mother had faced death with sorrow, not fear. His father lived his life of rituals as if it would never end.

"Hey, boy."

Robert was standing there, maybe five feet away. His white shirt and gray-green trousers were freshly ironed, and his cloth-black shoes were tied with impossibly even knots.

"Is it you, Dad?"

"Of course it's me. Who else could it be?"

"Was that you last night?"

"It was."

"What are you doing here?"

"Lookin' for you, of course."

"How'd you find me?"

"You always come here, boy. Been doin' it since you been takin' the bus on your own."

Robert sat down next to his son on the splintery bench.

They sat there listening to the beach sounds and, also, the intermittent yells of the riders on the pier's roller coaster.

"There's something wrong with me," Ghalen said after a long time.

Robert had no reply.

"I don't know what to do."

"You don't always have to know. Sometimes it's just good enough that you wanna find out."

"I guess," Ghalen said, uncertainly.

"You got shot in the head," Robert said in the commanding tone that he rarely used. "I mean, if you was meant to die that was the time for it. I got hit in the head by a sidewalk. Ever since then, now and then, I get lost. I look around me an' say 'Where the fuck am I?' Ever since Aura and Night moved in wit' me they put their GPS things in my clothes. I'll be standin' on the sidewalk on Hauser Boulevard lookin' down at the gutter. And then Aura calls out and I see her standin' next to her car and I remember everything. It's the same with you."

"How do you see that?"

"You get mad. You wanna do things that you don't wanna do. It's a part'a you but it's that wound that brought it out. We got to work on that."

"How'd you get here, Dad?" Ghalen asked, remembering Nasrah's suggestion that he might be a spirit.

"Aura drove her car because it was the only one big enough for Night and Nasrah, me and you."

"They in the parking lot?"

"Let's go home, son."